THE SAMURAI'S OCTOPUS

A Yoshiwara Mystery

Books by Jonelle Patrick

The Last Tea Bowl Thief

Only in Tokyo Mysteries

Painted Doll

Idolmaker

Fallen Angel

Nightshade

THE SAMURAI'S OCTOPUS

A Yoshiwara Mystery

A novel by
JONELLE PATRICK

Published 2026 by Seventh Street Books®

The Samurai's Octopus. Copyright © 2026 by Jonelle Patrick. All rights reserved. No part of this publication may be reproduced, stored in a retrieval system, or transmitted in any form or by any means, digital, electronic, mechanical, photocopying, recording, or otherwise, or conveyed via the Internet or a website without prior written permission of the publisher, except in the case of brief quotations embodied in critical articles and reviews.

Cover image © Shutterstock / Engr. Shahbaz and Rawpixel.com
Cover design by Jennifer Stinston
Cover design © Start Science Fiction

This is a work of fiction. Characters, organizations, products, locales, and events portrayed in this novel either are products of the author's imagination or are used fictitiously. Any similarities to real persons, living or dead, is coincidental and not intended by the author.

Inquiries should be addressed to
Start Science Fiction
830 Morris Tpke, 4th Floor
Short Hills, NJ 07078

PHONE: 212-431-5455
WWW.SEVENTHSTREETBOOKS.COM

10 9 8 7 6 5 4 3 2 1

978-1-64506-115-1 (paperback)
978-1-64506-129-8 (ebook)

Printed in the United States of America

花魁
Oiran (óy-ron)

The highest-ranking courtesans in the brothels of the Yoshiwara pleasure quarter from the seventeenth to the nineteenth centuries, in Edo, Japan

*An oiran and her child attendants
by Utamaro Kitagawa c. 1790*

CAST OF CHARACTERS

MEN WHO VISIT YOSHIWARA

Takahisa Takeda—head of the Takeda samurai clan
Kiyohisa Takeda—his son
Masatoki Koga—Edo City administrator, member of the samurai ruling class
Doctor Vandermeer—the shōgun's translator and Dutch Learning expert
Ichiro Vandermeer—the translator's elder brother
Goldbelly—nickname of a successful silk merchant; Pearl's patron
Lord Oda—the aristocratic host of the moon-viewing party

HOUSE OF TREASURES

White Pearl ("Pearl")—the House of Treasures' first-rank oiran and their number one courtesan
Little Bird ("Birdie")—Pearl's child attendant
Little Flower ("Flower")—Pearl's other child attendant
Lucky Doll ("Dolly")—Birdie's "Elder Sister," the courtesan who raised her after her mother died

CAST OF CHARACTERS

Auntie—the House of Treasures' manager
Saheiji ("Jester")—a customer detained at the House of Treasures until he pays his debt
Peach—second-rank courtesan
Feather—second-rank courtesan
Butterfly—second-rank courtesan
Mistress Moon—the House of Treasures' assistant manager

HOUSE OF PEONIES

Tiger—a courtesan's orphan; Birdie's friend
Priceless Jewel ("Jewel")—Takahisa Takeda's first oiran; House of Peonies' number one courtesan
Willow—aging House of Cranes courtesan, trained at the House of Peonies

OTHERS

Shinjō ("Madame Truth")—fortuneteller who lives by the moat
Madame Nomura—mistress of the Nomura geisha house

1772

Yoshiwara Pleasure Quarter
Edo, Japan

It's the kind of balmy spring evening that inspires even mediocre poets to greatness, but nobody is gazing at the cherry blossoms. The pink clouds overhead can't compete with the pageantry unfolding on Teahouse Street. Procession after procession of beautiful women in costly robes are parading down Yoshiwara's main boulevard as the sky deepens to dusk, and wealthy men are about to outspend each other with legendary foolishness until dawn.

But for every queen of the night, there are a hundred beauties eager to take her place. And for every lord who can afford the attentions of a first-rank courtesan, there are a thousand solitary men who turn their backs on the glittering display and glance around before joining other furtive figures slinking down the shabby street just inside the Great Gate.

Head down, Takahisa Takeda walks with purpose, aiming his steps toward a wooden building with a tattered lantern hanging out front. He gives a woman's name and a coin to the crone who makes sure men aren't interrupted by the next customer before they're finished.

"She's busy right now." The woman stows the money in her sash. "You can wait over there." She jerks her chin toward the bench by the door where two men are already ignoring each other.

He perches at the far end. Studying the dirt between his feet, he recalls the last time he waited outside this door. His fantasies never include the stink of moat water, but now that he's here, the foul odor both repels him and sharpens his desire.

A man emerges, still adjusting his sash about his hips.

When it's his turn, he mounts the steep stairs and slips without invitation into the woman's room. She greets him with a sum. He agrees, even before his eyes adjust to the dim light from the single smoking candle. She doesn't smile. She never smiles. Her sash is tied loosely in front—why bother with a proper knot? Lowering herself onto the pallet in the corner, her collar gapes, the coarse skin of her neck at odds with the girlish pattern of her kimono. As he sheds his jacket and tobacco pouch, she glances at him and turns away, but not before he sees the look on her face.

His desire shrinks, recoiling from the sting of her distaste. Does he not give her good money to conceal it? How dare she suggest that a woman like her would spurn a man like him if he weren't paying! He grabs a fistful of her robe and yanks her upright. The urge to possess her returns. Now that he has her attention, he means to get his money's worth.

Afterward, he counts out the coins and leaves them in a dish by the door. He owes her no such courtesy, but putting them directly in her hand would be unseemly for a samurai. As she picks herself up from the pallet, he slides her door shut behind him, averting his eyes from the next fool already rising from the bench outside.

The guilty anticipation that sped his steps over the mountains on his annual timber-selling trek to Edo is now spent, and the sooner he leaves her behind, the better. Regrets chase him like a flock of crows as he hurries toward the main boulevard. He has spent money he can't spare. Done things he hadn't intended. That grubby amulet dangling between her breasts, smelling more of sweat than sandalwood. The musk of unwashed hair at the nape of her neck. He shudders. What compels him to disgrace himself with a woman like that? Disgusting. Revolt—

"Sorry!" they both say at once.

The big oaf squints at him.

"Takeda-san?"

Takeda stares, can't quite place him. Boldly striped silk wraps his considerable girth, one plump hand fingering a fox-shaped *netsuke* bead attached to his tobacco pouch. Surely this can't be—

"I thought it was you," the timber broker says with a smirk.

How dare that son-of-a-merchant stand there, unapologetically flaunting the fat percentage he skims from selling lumber for samurai families like the Takedas! Is it not illegal for an abacus-clicker to dress more lavishly than his betters?

Takeda manages a grudging bow. Merchants like this fat toad are supposed to rank beneath the farmers who feed the nation and the artisans who craft the tools to make it run, and farthest of all below the samurai who bought nearly two hundred years of peace with their blood. Merchants grow nothing, make nothing, defend nothing, but somehow, the lowest of the low have become the richest of the rich.

"What brings you to Yoshiwara today, Takeda-san?" The trader's sly smile adds, *don't pretend I didn't catch you on the most disreputable street in the pleasure quarter, ticking off your sins like a string of prayer beads.*

"Why does any man come to the pleasure quarter?" *As if he's not here to indulge his own wiggly little perversions.*

"I'd never have guessed a samurai of such distinguished lineage as yourself would be interested in the modest entertainments of Yoshiwara." *And knowing how little you make off the Takeda timber, I'm surprised you can afford them.* "I'd ask you to join me," the merchant murmurs with false regret, "but I'm afraid I have some urgent business to conduct this evening. Perhaps some other time?"

When crows swim and fish fly. At least he's saved the trouble of refusing. The pittance this jumped-up swine got for the Takeda timber last year was barely enough to keep them in rice and retainers. He can't afford to reciprocate.

"Speaking of business..." The middleman's eye strays to a teahouse across the street. "I'm afraid I must excuse myself, or I'll be late." Sketching a bow, he darts in front of an approaching oiran procession in time to hail a dandy just arriving at the teahouse, ushering him inside with greedy glee.

Takeda had assumed their timber agent was years older than himself, but now he's not so sure. How unpleasant to think that someone observing the man in that gaudy getup talking with a samurai in the stiff "city" kimono he inherited from his father might think him the elder of the two. This morning he'd spied a few more threads of white in his topknot before it was oiled, but inside he still feels like a young man: wiry and tough, a man easy to underestimate, who then bests you in a fight. He'd had plenty of practice at that in his boyhood every time his brothers danced around him, pulling their eyes up on one side and down on the other, crying "Squinty! Squinty!" It wasn't his fault that the pox had spared their smug little faces and branded his alone. He'd made them sorry.

The House of Peonies procession arrives, and he turns to watch, skipping over the lantern-bearer and child attendants to glance at the novices—silly, giggly girls, in their trailing butterfly sleeves—before studying the second-rank courtesans, who are pretending to be demure or haughty, but aren't above casting a nod or a wink at the right man.

Murmurs ripple through the crowd as the oiran they've been waiting for finally appears, dressed in robes that cost more than most of them make in a year. Slow and sinuous, she glides forward like a swan parting the sea of men pressing in from either side, flipping the weighted hem of her kimono with each swaying step to reveal a flash of scandalously red underrobe. Her oval face is powdered the pure white of a spring moon, her eyebrows charcoaled into graceful feathers. And her lips! Her lips are painted as red as the parasol bobbing above her, the pomade's iridescent sheen whispering that she's one of the few courtesans who can afford the tens of thousands of safflower petals that were crushed to make it.

What he wouldn't give to be waiting for this one at a teahouse right now! He shifts his hungry gaze to the hem of her robe, and *there*, a crotch-tightening glimpse of bare foot. He adjusts his kimono, embarrassed by the unwelcome stirring. Turning to follow her receding parasol down the street, his attention is drawn instead to a column of smoke towering over the Great Gate.

Fire.

It's burning somewhere far beyond Yoshiwara's walls, but now that he sees the smoke, he can smell it too. And must have been doing so for some time, because the sky is a strange, pale orange. Could this be the same blaze that was making a vague smudge on the horizon this morning, the one he'd dismissed as being too distant to alter his plans?

He curses under his breath. The wind must have shifted, because now the plume of smoke is pointing in a different direction, and the fire is heading straight toward the inn where he left his servant and traveling pack.

Hastening to the line forming at the Great Gate, he retrieves his swords from the gatekeeper. Lesser men stream past, and his mood sours even more. Now that he knows what kind of lowlifes are wearing the most stylish kimonos, he no longer admires them.

Slapping his longsword into its scabbard, he sheaths the short one, striding past the merchants climbing into their palanquins. Lazy bastards. He deals a savage kick to a rock in his path. Nearly half his life is over, and what has he got to show for it? A wife who'd married him only for his position. Three useless daughters, but only one son who'd managed to survive his first year. And a village full of restless retainers, who must be fed whether they cut timber or not.

Why hadn't the gods blessed his family with luck, instead of cursing them with honor? After their Tokugawa allies had become the rulers of all Japan, his ancestor had been awarded a fiefdom several days' journey northwest of Edo. But while the shōgun's longtime loyalists wallow in the kind of rich, flat bottomland that produces bumper crops of rice every year, minor supporters like the Takeda clan barely eke out a living on rough terrain that's good for growing only one thing. Trees, trees, and more trees. Which cost a lot more to harvest, transport, and sell than rice, and must be converted into rice to pay their retainers. And the rice merchants—curse their money-grubbing souls—take a cut coming and going.

Ashes drift past like black snow. A large flake lands, quivering, on his sleeve. He slaps it off, leaving a streak. The main road that angles toward the inn is just ahead, but he must battle upstream against the river of refugees flowing out of the city in the opposite direction. They're shuffling along with terrified determination, lugging misshapen bundles of randomly packed possessions, children slung on their backs, sacks of rice, a wriggling piglet. Some are bundled in as many layers as they can wear, some are shivering in what they had on when the wall of flames arrived with such speed that all they could do was flee with their lives.

The roar of the fire is louder now, the sky a ripe persimmon. It feels more like evening than afternoon. He coughs, raises the crook of his elbow to cover his mouth, picks up his pace.

He should be getting close. And . . . yes, the inn is still standing, although it looks abandoned, curtains flapping, door standing open. His traveling pack is still in the cupboard where he left it, but there's no sign of his servant. He must have fled when he saw the fire.

He hoists the bundle onto his shoulders with a grunt. If he'd known he'd have to carry it himself, he'd have packed lighter. Bent under its weight, he joins the fleeing townsfolk, batting at the swarming ashes as if they were mosquitos.

Another stream of refugees swells the river of humanity, from a neighborhood where plenty of the lazy so-and-sos can afford servants to save them the trouble of walking. Their lacquered palanquins now rock above those trudging on foot as they climb past the outskirts, the crowd's misery casting more gloom than the pall of smoke.

But Takeda has little sympathy to spare for strangers. How is he going to sell the Takeda timber now? Judging from the three . . . no, four . . . streams of smoke rising along the horizon, the losses will be staggering. Destruction on such a grand scale will lead to reconstruction on a grand scale, but—

The old resentment rises inside him like a bitter tide. The city will need lots of lumber to rebuild, but he already knows who will be getting those contracts. Not the Takeda clan. The capital city is burning to the ground, and his family won't make a single copper *mon* from it. He has tried everything to obtain an introduction to the officials who buy construction supplies on behalf of the shōgun, but you have to belong to the right family or be introduced by the right people to even get an audience. You have to have influence to get influence. You have to be rich to get richer. Lashing out with his walking stick, he punishes a stand of roadside bamboo for this injustice.

Stepping out of line, he clambers up a rocky outcrop to check the fire's progress. Stops at the crest, aghast. Even though he's been breathing smoke for hours, he's unprepared for the spectacular and awful sight of the shōgun's city in flames. Over a quarter of Edo has been reduced to a smoking black hole, and the fire is still widening in a voracious red ring. His eyes dart over a landscape made unfamiliar by destruction, searching for landmarks. There, between drifting curtains of smoke, Edo Castle sits untouched behind its stout stone ramparts and moat. But the barracks surrounding it are gone. The Nihonbashi Bridge, gone. And where Zojōji Temple once stood, only the gate remains. He can't see Yoshiwara at all behind the billowing clouds, but the neighborhood where his middleman did business is nothing but ashes. How will he find him now? Has he made this trip for nothing? If he goes home empty-handed—

Something falls from a bundle bobbing along on the back of a merchant's minion on the road below. The package bounces into the weeds, but the factotum trudges on. Takeda waits, watching. Is no one coming back to claim it? When he's sure, he scrambles down to search the tall grass. He'd never steal a persimmon from a farmer's tree, but the ones on the ground are anybody's lunch.

There it is. He brushes it off. Peeks inside the wrapper. A roll of fine kimono silk! Pleased at the windfall, he forgets his troubles for a moment and stuffs it into his pack. Turns to consider the oncoming horde. Perhaps he can salvage something from this trip after all. Where there's one dropped treasure, there might be more. From above, it looked like the fire has crept dangerously close to the neighborhood where high officials live, but the wind is blowing against it at the moment, so it should be safe to get closer and see what he can find. Striking out against the flow, he keeps a sharp eye on the ground beneath the oncoming feet.

And it pays off. An hour later, he's richer by a splendid tobacco pouch, a painted fan, and an assortment of fine tortoiseshell combs that dropped unnoticed from the hair of wealthy women as they fled.

He ignores his stinging eyes and scratchy throat as he makes his way through the outskirts, pressing on because the pickings are getting richer as the tide of refugees thins. A lady's jeweled hair ornament. A handkerchief knotted around three gold coins.

The two-story houses standing shoulder to shoulder along this street are wider, more finely crafted than the ones farther out. Waterfalls trickle unseen in walled gardens behind firmly locked gates. This is where the *hatamoto* live, those vassals who are despised and envied above all others by provincial samurai like the Takedas. Their great-great-grandfathers had been awarded positions of trust by the first Tokugawa shōgun, and their families continue to occupy every seat of influence, controlling everything from the price of rice to the timber for new barracks.

They'd all fled, of course. Takeda hasn't seen another living soul for some time. Those who live in this neighborhood can afford to save their own skins at the first whiff of smoke, leaving behind all but their most precious possessions to be protected by their perennial good luck and the police who roam the streets, deterring looters. This close to the fire, though, patrolmen are few and far between. He coughs, eyes the sky. A few more blocks, then he'll turn back.

Over the distant crackle of the flames, he hears a shout. His head snaps up. Nobody ahead. One block over?

A woman shrieks. He peers down a gap between two garden walls, but it's nearly dark now, hard to see anything in the flickering light of the advancing flames. The woman's cries grow louder and more desperate. He curses. Poor or not, he's still a samurai, and wears two swords; he can't ignore the obligation that goes with them. Sidling down the narrow cut between the two houses, he loosens his longsword in its scabbard, eyes fixed on the gap at the end. A horse sidesteps past, a man leaps off.

He pauses, flattening himself against the wall. Only samurai are allowed to ride. If the man on horseback is police, he might not have to get mixed up in this after all. More shouting, then some ungentlemanly scuffling as two men grapple past the end of the alley, kicking up a cloud of dust. Does the patrolman need help? Should he show himself? He hesitates, remembering the valuables in his pack. Valuables that weren't his an hour ago.

The unmistakable *shring* of a weapon being drawn. The woman shouts a warning, and his hand tightens on the hilt of his sword, but he hears no second blade leave its scabbard. More grunts, then a building in the distance collapses so loudly, he almost misses the "Hya!" of a rider urging the horse to go, go, go.

Silence, except for the roar of the fire.

He creeps to the end of the alley and pokes his head out. The galloping horse is careening away at full tilt, nearly at the end of the street now, a man and a woman clinging to its back. Her partly unbound hair streams behind as they disappear around the corner.

It's not until he turns to retrace his steps that he sees the body lying face down in the road. He runs to the man's side, shocked to find it dressed in the wide-shouldered vest and matching pleated trouser-skirt of a Tokugawa retainer.

The man who rode away on the horse is not the man who arrived on it. Worse, the dead man is no policeman, he's a man of rank.

Takeda rolls him over, but he's past help, and his eyes are drawn to something made of gold lacquer lying in the bloody dirt. It's an *inrō*, the kind of small, multitiered case men use to carry necessities while wearing a kimono. Avoiding the parts that are sticky with blood, he picks up the box with two fingers, then catches it with his other hand as it begins to slide apart. The cord holding the sections together is broken. He casts about, looking for the large *netsuke* bead that should have kept it from slipping through the wearer's sash. It must be nearby. There, rolled off to the side. An intricately carved octopus, heavy enough to be ivory.

He glances back at the body, resisting an impulse to tidy the skewed topknot and pull down the rucked-up sleeve. He can't risk getting blood on his "good" kimono; he doesn't have another. Should he retrieve the dead man's swords, though? As a samurai himself, he knows how the man's family would treasure such heirlooms. He crouches to pull away the uniform vest to check the family crest on his kimono.

There isn't one. That's odd. He glances at the man's face.

And recoils in horror. Scrambling to his feet, he backs away. He'd better get out of here. Now.

Only demons and foreigners have eyes like the ones staring lifelessly up at the smoke-roiled sky. The wrongness of someone who doesn't belong here dressed like someone who does sets off all kinds of alarms. Even though the victim is less than Japanese, the death of a man in Tokugawa uniform will invite the kind of attention he can't afford. Whoever finds the body can deal with the swords, if the fire doesn't get here first.

But what about the *inrō* and the octopus? He looks down at the objects in his hand. Even dirty and bloodied, their quality is unmistakable. He would never court divine retribution by robbing the dead, but these hadn't belonged to the man lying in the street. Samurai never wear *inrō* with their uniforms.

Another roar as a building collapses, this one much closer. He hastily wraps the pieces in his hand towel and shoves the bundle into his pack. Loping away from the fire, he doesn't slow until it's time to rejoin the refugees and head into the hills.

When the night air is once again cool against his cheeks and the wind whispering through the pines is louder than the roar of the fire, he stops to adjust his pack to a less-sore spot on his shoulders. Refugees have been streaming out of Edo for hours, so it may be a while before he finds an inn with a spare pallet for the night. He resumes his trek. Tomorrow will be soon enough to decide whether to give up and go home or return to Edo and see what can be salvaged of his mission.

Tramp, tramp, tramp, tramp. What had brought those three people to that deserted Edo street? One woman, two men. The woman was being threatened, but by which man? The big shot with the fancy *inrō* or the foreigner in a Tokugawa uniform who'd arrived on horseback?

Takeda steps off the road to pry a pebble from his sandal, wondering why the dead barbarian had been dressed like a samurai. What a shock. Like seeing a monkey in a teahouse. The only foreigners allowed to set foot on Japanese soil are the Dutch traders, but they're only allowed off their island near Nagasaki once a year to deliver their annual tribute to the shōgun. He'd seen their procession from afar—great hairy creatures, so closely related to beasts that their faces are still half covered in fur—but despite the dead man's unnaturally round eyes, he'd been dark-haired, clean-shaven. And he didn't have that telltale beak of a nose. Is that why he'd mistaken him for Japanese, at first?

The bigger mystery is, why had only the rich *hatamoto* drawn his sword? The dead man's was still in its scabbard. Why would a high government official attack a man in a Tokugawa uniform? Had the man who arrived on horseback caught the *hatamoto* committing a crime? Or perhaps it was the woman who'd committed the crime. They'd escaped together, after all. Could the killer have been protecting her? Who was she? His daughter? His wife? His mistress?

So many questions, so few answers. All he really knows is that a foreigner in a Tokugawa uniform is dead, and a *hatamoto* killed him.

He passes another inn. No vacancy. Plods on, shaking his head to clear it. Why is he wasting time puzzling over a crime that doesn't concern him? The answers won't put a single *mon* in his family's pockets; he should turn his thoughts toward something that will. His back aches and there's a fresh blister on his heel. Time to find a place to lay his head for the night. He hates sleeping rough, but if the next inn is as full as the others, he'll give up and make the best of it.

Around the next bend, he spots a dim light shining through the trees. It's a post station, but not a very nice one, judging by the warped gray siding and grass growing between the roof tiles. Nevertheless, he stops to enquire. The rooms are packed with fleeing Edoites, says the fox-faced innkeeper, but he might be able to squeeze in one more. For a price.

Muttering about highway robbery, Takeda hands the scoundrel an unreasonable sum, then curls up in the proffered corner as best he can, arms around his traveling pack. Despite the fleas, the snoring, and the stench of unwashed travelers, he falls asleep as quickly as a stone dropping into a well.

When he awakes the next morning, the sun is well into the sky. He unbends stiffly, climbs to his feet. He's sore from yesterday's exertions and his throat is raw from breathing smoky air, but the hours of rest have cleared his head. He will return to Edo and wait for the fire to be contained, so he can take advantage of any opportunities that might flower in the wake of the disaster.

As he shovels in the bowl of rice and scrap of fish offered as breakfast, something else occurs to him. He may not know why that foreigner was killed, but it might be profitable to discover who did it. The *hatamoto* who dropped that ivory octopus will be even less eager to face an official inquiry than he is. What's more, the killer's name may already be within his grasp.

Draining his cup of weak tea, he shoulders his pack to put some distance between himself and the inn before picking a spot to wade through the knee-deep bracken into the hush of the forest. He digs the *inrō* from his pack.

With a corner of his hand towel, he wipes away the dried blood and dirt to reveal a carp-and-waterfall design, lavishly rendered in gold. He separates the sections, one by one, to see what's inside. The bottom one holds an elegantly carved pipe, the next, some fragrant tobacco to smoke in it. Atop that, a segment containing an apothecary concoction. He sniffs it. Charred lotus root, a common aphrodisiac. If that woman wasn't his mistress, the man who stabbed the shōgun's retainer has one somewhere. The top compartment is a little tougher to get into; the lid fits tightly and blood has dried in the crack. He finally pries the sections apart, and a slender case drops out. Inside is an ivory signature seal, the kind that can only be used by its registered owner. He studies the name carved into the end.

Masatoki Koga.

He knows that name. It's a name he has cursed more times than he can count. Koga is one of three administrators who advise the Edo city governors on matters of finance. And procurement. Including construction procurement.

His fingers tighten around the slim stick of ivory and a smile curls his lips. Unless this seal's owner wants the shōgun to learn exactly who killed that foreigner, an impoverished branch of the Takeda clan is about to become a preferred supplier of timber for the rebuilding of the capital.

Only ten days have passed since the fire was halted by the Sumida River on one side and gangs of profane, tattooed firemen on the other, but the prospects of the man striding down the road that cuts through the blasted landscape have changed nearly as much as the city itself. Today, Takahisa Takeda is dressed like a man who's not to be trifled with, wearing a crisp new jacket and trouser-skirt he'd had made from the roll of fine silk he'd picked up along the road.

"You don't think the pattern a trifle bold?" he'd asked the tailor.

"On the contrary," the kimono maker replied smoothly. "It makes a statement, demonstrates the kind of confidence ordinary men can only hope to possess."

Whispers of smoke still rise here and there from caches of coals burning themselves out between the mounds of debris, but the blackened landscape is already alive with workers scurrying over the anthill of Edo, carting away baskets of burnt and scorched belongings. He takes it as a good omen that the artery leading to the seat of government is the first to be cleared, paving the way for the Takeda family fortunes to rise from the ashes, hand-in-hand with the shōgun's city.

Fingers drumming on the leather pouch hanging from his shoulder, he rehearses the words he'll need to get past the sentries as he advances onto the narrow causeway bridging the moat. The main gate looms ahead, its stout timbers and iron fittings looking more forbidding than he remembers. Are there more men guarding it than usual, or is he just noting their strength because he needs to get past them?

Halting before the sentries, he plants his feet and raises his chin as a pair of them step forward to ask his business. He clears his throat and tells them he has an appointment with City Administrator Masatoki Koga. Reaching into his pouch, he hands over a document requesting his presence at the castle, stamped with the seal he found inside Koga's bloodied *inrō*.

The first soldier examines it, frowns, passes it to his companion. They look him up and down, study his face, then nod and stand aside. He exhales, feeling their eyes on his back as he passes through the gate.

On the other side, he joins the military men and officials wending their way into the shōgun's administrative labyrinth, toward the center where spiders like Koga dispense their favors. Dark walls built of stone blocks tower over him on either side. He cranes his neck to squint at the top. Catching a flicker of movement, the skin tightens between his shoulder blades. Edo Castle may seem like a pleasant beehive of bureaucracy, but archers are keeping a steady bead on his heart as he passes below.

He swipes his sweating palms down the back of his new trouser-skirt before approaching the sentries posted at each bridge and gate, but as soon as they spot the distinctive red seal, they wave him past without question. The signature stamp is genuine, even if the invitation isn't.

A building wider than an entire block of shops swings into view. Even here, at the very portal to the shōgun's inner sanctum, the red stamp wins him entrance, unquestioned. He steps into a hall so cavernous it could swallow his entire family compound. Even in the deepest mountains of Kai, he has never seen trees massive enough to be hewed into the beams that support this roof.

His eye is drawn to an enormous golden screen floating above the bustle below, the figures painted upon its many panels eternally riding to victory alongside their Tokugawa allies at the Battle of Sekigahara. And... *there*. Galloping over a hill near the bottom: the Takeda bannermen.

Despite his recent pique at the meagerness of his family's reward for that long-ago service, he grows a little taller inside his fine new jacket. Turning to look for someone to direct him to Koga's office, he's surprised to find a fussy-looking man in extravagantly trailing green brocade trousers swimming toward him through the crowded room, his tall, black mesh hat cutting through the sea of clerks and guards like a shark fin.

"What business brings you here, vassal?" the man demands to know.

Vassal?

"I beg your pardon?"

"Why are you here? Whom do you serve?"

"The shōgun, like my ancestors before me." This foppish son-of-a-goat had taken one look at his crisp trouser-skirt and mistaken him for a mere retainer! "I am Takahisa Takeda, Head of the Kai Domain Takedas, here to see City Administrator Masatoki Koga," he thunders, extending the invitation, hand trembling with rage.

The man scans it, lips compressing to a thin line as he arrives at the red seal.

"Ah. My apologies." He bows, not deeply enough. "I'll take you to Koga-san myself."

Takeda is still fuming when they arrive at Koga's door. His nose wrinkles in distaste as they step into an anteroom that looks more suited to a woman than a warrior. It smells of incense and flowers and is plastered in a soothing greenish gold, an artfully scrawled poem displayed in the alcove.

"Wait here," his guide instructs, drawing Takeda's invitation from the folds of his robe.

"One moment." Takeda produces a second message. This one is sealed, for Koga's eyes only. "He'll want to see this first."

The man takes it with a curt bow and slips behind a golden screen painted with a scene from *The Tale of Genji*.

While his guide interrupts the low conversation taking place beyond the screen, Takeda paces, poem to door, door to poem. What happens next will make his fortune or break it. He pauses to listen to the snap of the seal, the silence while Koga reads. A few terse words send a hunched clerk with an armful of documents fleeing from the room, closely followed by his escort, who barely sketches a bow in passing as he—

"Who do you think you are?"

Takeda turns to find the icy voice belongs to a man who is nearly his age, but has the smooth, unlined face of someone who has never had a door slammed in it, and the manicured hands of a man who commands others to do the dirty work.

"Perhaps you'd prefer to discuss that in private?" Takeda gives him a feral smile. Dipping into his pouch, he produces the *inrō* with its ivory octopus.

The blood drains from Koga's face. He spins and disappears into his office.

It's all the invitation Takeda is likely to get. He follows, but before he has a chance to utter an ironic apology for intruding, the administrator snatches his note from the table and rounds on him.

"How dare you threaten me!"

Takeda doesn't flinch. For the first time in his life, he holds all the cards.

"Who was she?" he taunts. "Your wife? Your daughter? Your mistress?"

"I don't know what you're talking about."

"I think you do." He dangles the octopus and *inrō* before its former owner. "I found this beneath the body of the Tokugawa retainer you killed before fleeing on his horse."

"That's not mine," Koga lies.

"Then why was your signature seal inside? Did you hope the fire would get there before anyone found it? Did you count on the disaster erasing the evidence, so you'd never have to answer for your crime?"

Koga's fists open and close.

"Don't worry, nobody knows I have it. Not yet, anyway. I hid it somewhere quite safe." He cracks open the top compartment to show him it's empty.

Koga stares, face flushing an angry crimson. Then he closes his eyes, attempting to master himself. Turns to adjust a hanging scroll that's not crooked.

"Keep it," he says, feigning indifference. "I did lose a signature seal some time ago, but I replaced it as soon as I noticed it was missing."

"I'd be surprised if you hadn't," Takeda replies amiably. "But I doubt your new one has that distinctive little chip in the second character of your last name. The gap that shows up on every official document you stamped with it, right up to the day you—"

"All right," Koga cuts him off, face sour. "What do you want, Takeda?" No more honorifics.

"Don't look so worried, my friend." He switches to more familiar speech too, hinting at just how close they're about to become. "You have a capital in need of rebuilding, and my family has five hundred oxcarts of wood to sell. All I want is a contract with the city of Edo to buy our harvest. And," he hastily adds, seeing the fleeting look of relief on Koga's face, "a promise to renew that contract every year. In perpetuity."

"*Forever?*"

There's the outrage he was looking for.

"Impossible!" Koga barks. "We'll buy your accursed trees this time, but once reconstruction is complete, the shōgun won't be needing more timber than the relationships he has honored for generations can supply."

"I admire his loyalty. But I'm sure you can persuade him to make room for one more trusted source." Takeda pulls another document from his satchel. "Unless, of course, you'd like him to see your signed confession?"

"My *what?*" The administrator snatches it from his hand. His eyes dart over Takeda's eyewitness account of what happened on the street he'd believed was deserted. By the time he gets to his own vermilion signature with its distinctive gap in the final character, his hand is shaking. The page crumples in his fist.

"Go ahead, Administrator-san. Rip it to shreds, if that makes you feel better." Takeda can afford to be generous. "As long as I have your seal, I can make another one, and the shōgun will find it just as damning."

"All right," Koga agrees through clenched teeth. "You'll get your damned contract. And in return, you will return my property and give me your word you'll never speak of this again as long as you live. And that I will never, *ever*, have to see your face again."

"Oh, no." Takeda can't help but smile. "I think not. This is but the beginning of a long and profitable relationship."

1784

TWELVE YEARS LATER

Yoshiwara Pleasure Quarter
Edo, Japan

The twilight sky has deepened to the vibrant blue of a kingfisher's wing by the time the House of Treasures' procession finally makes it to Teahouse Street. Courtesans long for the privilege of entertaining their customers outside the small banquet rooms and less private sleeping arrangements at their own pleasure houses, but only first-rank oirans like White Pearl and her wealthy patron will be invited to stay until dawn at the elegant establishments just around the next corner.

Birdie stretches onto her toes to peer past the swaying white lantern being carried ahead of her on a long pole by one of the Treasures' manservants, but tonight the pleasure quarter is so crowded, she can't see a thing. Why do grown-ups have to be so tall?

Step. Wait. Step. Wait. The new thong on her *geta* is rubbing a sore spot on her right foot, but she learned the hard way not to stop and fix her shoe or make a face at Tiger, who is trying to make her laugh by making farting noises as he darts in and out of the crowd. A child attendant who delays an oiran's procession is a child attendant who will regret it. She and Flower have a job to do. An important job. The second-rank courtesans are there to look pretty—but not *too* pretty—so their oiran shines like a jewel amid a bouquet of flowers. But it's the innocent child attendants like her and Flower who make Pearl look so alluring by comparison that every man who sees her longs to possess her.

Step. Wait. Step. Wait. It's so much harder to walk slow than fast. None of them are allowed to move any faster than Pearl's oiran strut, which is designed for seduction, not speed. With every step, she kicks her ankle out to the side, revealing a flash of bewitchingly bare foot. It's harder than it looks (Birdie has, of course, tried it at home) because an oiran must manage the strut in *koma-geta*, the tall platforms that make Pearl more than three handspans taller. Tonight, she's also weighed down by seven layers of robes and the heavy brocade sash that was a gift from tonight's patron. The pink and gold checkered *obi* is tied in an extravagant knot over her stomach and cascades nearly to her toes.

Birdie and Flower are wearing outfits that match, of course. The current Yoshiwara fashion is for child attendants to be dressed as twins, even though she and Flower don't look much alike when they're not on procession. Flower is as pretty as the Bamboo Princess, but Birdie's eyes are too round to be fashionable and her pointy ears would inspire plenty of nervous warding against fox spirits if anyone caught sight of them. Lucky for her, her elaborate hair ornaments are excellent at hiding them. Today's have rows upon rows of silver strips dangling below. Birdie shakes her head and smiles at the swishy feeling and the merry tinkle, taking advantage of Auntie being too far away to scold her. She and Flower aren't expected to ignore the spectators as if everyone is beneath them—in fact, their job is to look around and report on everyone they see—but any fooling around that might damage the costly accessories would earn her a sharp word if Auntie weren't stuck at the back of the procession, where a drab house manager belongs.

A plume of smoke that's fragrant with charcoal and grilling chicken blinds her as they round the corner onto Teahouse Street. How long has it been since she ate that bowl of—

"... assure you I heard it on the very best authority."

Birdie's head swivels toward the familiar voice. Shouldn't the third magistrate already be at the Five Fans, enjoying his first flask of sake? Pearl won't be happy if her patron isn't waiting when she arrives. Why is he still standing outside the Camellia, talking to a man who—

Oh, dear. Even the boy they call Porridge Face didn't have the smallpox that bad.

She catches the third magistrate's eye and gives him a dimpled smile, but quickly looks away when the scarred man turns his gaze in her direction. She can't let him think she was smiling at him. Pearl won't like it if she gives the wrong kind of man reason to hope he'd be welcomed at the House of Treasures. An oiran gets to pick and choose who she entertains, and that man is definitely not her type. Too frowny, too ugly, too *old*.

She glances at Flower, gives her twin a nudge to remind her to at least pretend not to be tired. It's only a little farther, see? There's the Five Fans up ahead. All they have to do is make it inside, and the hardest part of their day will be over. But until they get to the teahouse, they must stand up straight and look around with pleasant smiles, even if they don't feel like it. They must pretend they're delighted to see every House of Treasures customer, even if they're not.

Because that's the way things are done in Yoshiwara. Nothing has to *be* true, as long as everyone *believes* it's true.

Takahisa Takeda bids the third magistrate good evening, keeping his pleasant expression in place as he watches that reliably indiscreet source of government information apologize his way through the throng toward the Five Fans. As the crowd swallows him, Takeda's mouth twitches into something that's nearly a smile. The magistrate let slip that a quarter of the largest fleet in Edo has been impounded by the government while the shōgun's minions search the boats for smuggled foreign goods. Whether they find any or not, it will delay their legitimate cargo from being unloaded, a situation the shipowner he's meeting tonight will certainly wish to take advantage of.

Twelve years ago, he'd never have believed it if someone told him he'd be inviting a money-grubbing merchant to enjoy his company at the most expensive teahouse in Yoshiwara. Back then, he hadn't yet grasped that when a samurai leaves his swords behind at the Great Gate, he also leaves behind the unspoken rules that keep his family in debt.

Witnessing that foreigner's murder during the Great Meiwa Fire had been the luckiest thing that ever happened to him. To this day, it remains unsolved, and to keep it that way, Masatoki Koga continues to make the introductions and award the contracts that have made Takeda what he is today. No fewer than seven samurai clans now rely on him to turn their timber crops into gold. His years of banging his head against the wall of bureaucratic indifference taught him just how much such access is worth. The proceeds from the trees his family grows on their land are a pittance compared to the fat percentages that pour in from making introductions on behalf of other clans. Takeda doesn't handle the details himself, of course—samurai are still forbidden to dirty their hands with commerce—but gone are the days when he had to count his coins and wonder if he could afford to indulge his desires. Now that he can spend with the best of them, he laughs at that stiff-necked samurai from the sticks who thought the pleasure quarter existed only to satisfy his basest desires.

Which reminds him—Priceless Jewel is waiting for him upstairs. Before going in, though, his eyes stray to the House of Treasures oiran now being welcomed across the street at the Five Fans. This one might even be pretty under all her makeup. He used to wonder why the most beautiful women in Yoshiwara pile it on so thick, until he saw one of them without it. These days, he insists on complete darkness when it's time to satisfy his manly urges. He doesn't want to see his woman's face up close, any more than she wants to see his. It doesn't matter to him that her beauty is all an illusion. In fact, that's the best part about the pleasure quarter. Nobody cares about his cratered face or his mediocre lineage. As long as he's a useful and profitable man to know, even the third magistrate, who far outranks him the moment they step outside the Great Gate, isn't wealthy enough to outshine him here.

He gives a small grunt of approval, then flips aside the door curtain emblazoned with the crest of the Camellia and goes inside.

"Dutch Learning," the shipowner says with a sly wink, tossing back the rest of his sake and holding out his cup for Takeda's oiran to pour him some more. "Your timber crop will keep your rice pot full, but supplying the shōgun with barbarian scribblings and foreign fripperies is the only way to make a real killing."

"Nonsense." Takeda stifles a yawn. "Novelties like that come and go. They'll never be worth more than good, solid timber."

"I disagree, my friend. I heard the Dutch have figured out how to cure the pox and turn lead into gold, and they even have a golden wand that makes things that are far away look close enough to touch. Mark my words, those goods are about to become the hottest commodity in Edo. And do you know why?" The shipping magnate lowers his voice to confide, "The shōgun finally found a new translator. His Excellency hasn't been able to take advantage of Dutch Learning since the previous one died in the Great Meiwa Fire, and without someone to turn their chicken scratches into something a civilized man can understand, they're useless. But now he's going to be making up for lost time, and he'll be eager to pay top price for even the silliest contraptions."

Takeda's interest stirs. "How eager?"

"Plenty," the boatman assures him. "What do you make on a shipment of trees? Ten percent? Fill the same boat with Dutch Learning, and you can name your price. Ten times what you paid. Fifty. A hundred."

Takeda blinks. Can that be true? If it is, it's the opportunity of a lifetime.

"Are you looking for a partner?" he ventures, motioning for Jewel to pour more drink.

"I am." The shipmaster accepts a refill. "But I'm afraid I'm already in talks with the Maedas."

Takeda bristles, silently cursing the Big Five samurai clans whose riches just keep making them richer.

"Why them?"

"Why not them? I need new ships; they've got the cash to build them."

"What's wrong with the ships you've got?"

"Too big, too slow. The shōgun only allows the Dutch to bring in one shipment a year, and once word gets around that he and his lords are willing to pay any price to get their hands on what's inside, every fleet in Edo will be waiting in Nagasaki to outbid each other when it arrives. But here's what they haven't figured out. It's not who gets there first, it's who gets back to Edo first. The first boats back will be able to sell every last trinket in their holds for premium prices before the worthies in the capital have any idea what else is on the way. I'm betting that my competitors will do the greedy thing and send their biggest boats, but I'm going to build small, swift ones that will get the goods back here so fast, my profits will be counted and earning interest before their lumbering oxcarts make it back to Edo harbor."

Takeda can't help but admire the son-of-merchant's craftiness. He wants in.

"Why not work with me instead?"

"Can you afford to build three ships?"

He can't. But small scrappy wrestlers rarely get the opportunity to take down reigning champions, and a chance like this may not come his way again. Bluffing about the size of his holdings while he scrapes together the cash and calls in favors isn't going to be an option, though. The man across the table moves every last stick of his timber and knows to the *mon* how much he makes on it. How can he tip this in his favor? What can he offer that the Maedas can't? Or . . . won't. If there was ever a time to sweeten the pot with the one thing even the richest merchant can't buy, it's now.

Takeda picks up the sake flask.

"I understand you have several daughters," he ventures, filling the shipowner's cup, then his own. "And I may not have mentioned it before, but I have a son..."

Takeda cries out as he battles up from deep sleep in the Camellia's upstairs room. What woke him? An earthquake?

Jewel shakes his shoulder again, whispering, "I'm sorry to disturb you, Takeda-san, but a messenger from your household is downstairs. He says it's urgent."

"Urgent?" He sits up. "What kind of urgent?"

"The mistress didn't say, just asked me to wake you."

Only a genuine catastrophe would prompt the night watch to dispatch a messenger all the way across town to drag him from his oiran's bed. He stumbles to his feet.

Jewel holds his robe for him, but he snatches it from her; it's faster to dress himself. He cinches up his sash and hurries to the entrance. Just outside, a young samurai paces back and forth, too impatient to take off his footwear and come in.

"What is it?" Takeda barks.

"There's been a break-in."

"A break-in? Where?"

"In Takebashi, sir."

Not his warehouse, his home. The fine house he'd built when he moved his growing business interests to Edo sits right across from the Takebashi Bridge, a stone's throw from the shōgun's castle. It's not where the bulk of his wealth is stored, though. Why would an intruder break into his home?

"Did they catch him?" he asks.

"I don't know, sir," his retainer replies, falling in behind him as he strides off toward the Great Gate. "The captain just told me to take a horse and fetch you without delay."

Takeda steers clear of a clutch of drunken revelers stumbling out of the last lighted doorway. The pleasure quarter never sleeps, but right now, it's at its emptiest. A few windows still glow on the upper floors of the teahouses and brothels, but those who thronged the streets earlier are now sleeping or doing things best done in the dark. But Takeda's mind is already across town, thinking about his high wall, his well-guarded gates. How did a thief get past his defenses?

They stop to retrieve their swords from the gatekeeper, slinging them into their scabbards as they clomp onto the bridge spanning the moat. Ignoring the drowsing palanquin bearers, they trot toward the stables, splashing through shallow puddles with their swords swinging. Takeda leaps onto his horse and tosses some coins to the groom, wheeling his mount and setting off with such speed that the young retainer has to spur his horse to a gallop to catch up. Clattering over the wooden bridges and through the deserted streets, they canter past dark houses and shuttered shops, the wind of their passage lifting the neighborhood watchman's cloak as he claps his sticks for the all's well.

Takeda's horse swerves as a cat streaks across its path; he urges it forward again, his worries chasing him like angry ghosts. If the thief wanted gold, he wouldn't have targeted his home. He must have been after something else. What does he own that's rare enough to tempt a burglar? The scroll painted by an artist from the school of Kōrin? The Chōjiro tea bowl? What else does he have that's rare and one-of-a—

Koga's signature seal.

"Hya!" he cries, digging his heels into his mount. Faster!

If that seal is missing, he'll be ruined. As long as it's in his possession, the mere threat of exposing the city administrator as a murderer allows him to extract the contracts and introductions he needs. But Koga's personal seal is the only evidence that he witnessed the crime committed during the Great Meiwa Fire. If it's stolen, it will be Takeda's word against Koga's that the city administrator was in Edo killing a foreigner that night, not visiting his wife's relatives in Odawara, like he told the investigators.

And it won't matter if the thief keeps it, gives it back to its rightful owner, or sells it to the highest bidder. The moment Koga learns he no longer has the seal, his connections—along with his reputation and his fortune—will wither faster than a morning glory in the noonday sun.

His gate swings into view. Hauling his horse to a halt, he leaps off and tosses the reins to the guard, pacing before the massive wooden door while the man inside drags it open enough to squeeze through. He crosses the stepping-stones two at a time through the mossy entry garden.

The captain of his guard awaits him before the front door.

"Well? What happened?" Takeda barks. "Did you catch him?"

"No, Master." He falls to his knees. "Please accept my sincere and abject apologies. This unworthy underling begs you to—"

"Stop. You can grovel later. Tell me what happened."

"The . . . the thief slipped in and out like a ghost, sir. Dressed head to toe in dark clothing. He must have been a professional."

A professional. Like someone Koga might hire to get his seal back?

"If you didn't catch him, how do you know he was dressed in black?"

"The night watchman heard a suspicious sound and surprised him crouching in front of your family altar."

He knew to search the altar room?

"What did he take?" Takeda croaks, mouth suddenly dry.

"We don't know yet. We're going through the house now, but we haven't discovered anything missing."

Worse and worse. Plenty of easily snatched valuables sit in plain sight, and if nothing obvious is missing, that means the thief came for something specific. It takes all of Takeda's willpower to resist pushing past the guard captain and running straight to the hiding place to see if Koga's seal is still there, but he can't risk revealing its location. Instead, he asks, "How did he get away?"

"Knocked out the watchman who discovered him. One of the guards saw a flock of birds spook into the sky by the servants' gate, but by the time he got there, it was standing wide open and there was no one in sight."

Which means the thief knew his way around. It's the only way someone could have navigated the twists and turns of his compound's corridors that quickly in the dark. Had someone in his household been *bought*?

A guard lurches to a halt before them, breathing hard.

"The cook's new assistant ... the one who replaced Old Okita ... he's ... he's missing."

"Send someone to report him to the police this instant," orders the captain. "And wake the rest of the men. I want them out of their beds and quartering the neighborhood. Now."

"You go with them," Takeda commands. He can't check the hiding place until he's alone.

"Yes, sir."

Takeda takes his time removing his footwear and cloak, listening until the clatter of men racing out the back gate grows faint. Then he grabs a lighted candle and strides to the room where the thief was discovered. A half-asleep maid pokes her head into the corridor.

"You," he growls. "Stand watch outside this door while I pay my respects to the ancestors. If I'm disturbed by anyone, even family, you'll be looking for another job before morning."

He eases the door shut behind him. Heart banging against his ribs, he ignores the elaborate black-and-gold altar, its doors flung wide and drawers hanging half open. Crossing to the simple shelves and cabinets affixed to the opposite wall, he drops to his knees.

They look like ordinary cupboards, but these were crafted to his specifications by a man who lives deep in the mountains of Kai, an artisan whose family has served the Takedas for generations. Sliding open the upper cabinet, he presses on the panel that unlocks the drawer below. With trembling fingers, he pulls it out and triggers the hidden spring that holds its false bottom in place. He fumbles it out. And—?

The seal is still there, just as he left it.

Snatching it up, he clutches it to his chest, weak with relief. When his pulse slows, he crosses to the altar and sets the ivory seal before the black-and-gold funerary tablets of the Takeda ancestors. Pokes a stick of incense into the urn. A thread of fragrant smoke curls up into the darkness as he knocks his forehead against the floor, thanking the dead

Takedas for protecting the one treasure the living Takedas can't afford to lose.

Then he sits back on his heels, turning the seal over in his hands. Koga must be behind the attempted burglary. He's the only one who knows he has it, the only one who would benefit by its theft.

Or is he?

He and Koga weren't the only ones on that street the night of the fire. What about the woman? He opens his palm and regards the precious stick of ivory. For twelve years, he has profited from witnessing a murder without knowing the reason behind it. He hadn't wasted much thought on why the woman was there, who the dead man was, or why Koga killed him. But now he wonders. If he's going to keep the seal safe, he'd better find out who wants it. And why.

But he can't do that tonight. He crosses the room to put it back in the drawer, then hesitates. He'd be a fool to continue depending on the dead to protect his family against enemies who are very much alive. But who can he trust? He has never shared the secret of his family's meteoric rise with anyone, and he's not about to start now. The only way to make sure Koga's seal is safe is to keep it with him at all times. He cracks open the top section of the carp-and-waterfall *inrō* he has worn every day since that fateful night and slips it inside, next to his own.

As Birdie steps out the House of Treasures' front door, the streets of Yoshiwara are still in shadow and sunlight is just beginning to inch down the front of the pleasure house across the street. She tips her face to the sky and draws her first breath. Smiles. The freshness in the air will soon be overwhelmed by a stew of roasting tea, tobacco smoke, charcoal fires, and moat water, but right now Yoshiwara still smells like a new day.

Hooking her basket over her arm, she skips off toward the fruit seller. Except for a few deliverymen and a trickle of street vendors plodding in through the Great Gate with their stands on their backs, she has the streets to herself. No hawkers call, no doors slam, no shouted greetings welcome customers into still-shuttered shops.

Cutting through the shrine garden, she stops to toss a few pebbles in the pond to fool the greedy carp into gathering around. The House of Peonies isn't on the way to the orange seller, but she goes that way anyway. Hopping over a trail of ants (which she and Flower agree are bad luck to step on and must be crossed right foot first), she pauses to examine the new samples on display at the hair ornament shop. If she were a first-rank oiran like White Pearl, she would buy the one with the long tassels of pink flowers.

She loiters outside the back door at the Peony, waiting for Tiger. Orphans and off-duty child attendants must earn their keep, and unless the sun reverses course to rise in the west, he'll soon be sent out to buy oranges too, so their overnight customers can continue to believe that Yoshiwara is a bottomless rice pot of luxury.

"*Ohayō!*" she chirps as the door trundles open, happy to see the boy with scrub-brush hair stepping out, rubbing the sleep from his eyes.

"'Morning," he yawns.

Tiger is the least enemy-like of the boys who live in Yoshiwara, even though he sometimes runs with the ragtag gang of prostitutes' spawn who live by the moat. When they first met, he told her he was called Tiger because he was born in the Year of the Tiger (which would have made him two years older than she is) but once she found out he's actually four months younger, he switched his story, saying his nickname is a testament to the fighting skills he inherited from his father, a supposedly high-ranking samurai who will return someday to offer him all the rank and privilege he deserves.

They tramp side by side in companionable silence as far as the first corner, when Tiger wakes up enough to remember Birdie is sure to know details about the hottest topic in Yoshiwara.

"I heard what happened to the apothecary the other night. Wasn't he Lucky Doll's patron? Did they really find him in her *bed*?"

Birdie looks up sharply.

"Who told you that?"

Auntie made everyone promise to say he keeled over outside. Nobody wants to visit a pleasure house where a customer just died.

"Is it true?"

When she doesn't answer, he wheedles, "Come on. I promise not to tell."

"Swear?"

"Swear."

"It's true. When she woke up to fetch him tea the next morning, he was just lying there. All *cold*."

She shudders. She'd had to take care of Lucky Doll that morning, instead of the other way around. Elder Sister had been so distraught that Birdie had to deliver the bad news to Auntie. The House of Treasures' manager didn't spare the messenger, then spent the next two days fuming while they shut down to observe the purification rites.

"That's too bad. But—" Tiger grins. "Now the night watchman owes me three *mon*."

"No!" Birdie yelps. "You can't tell anyone. You promised."

"Okay, okay, don't get your *fundoshi* in a fankle." He backs down. "I made a bet the other way with Cook for five *mon*, so as long as nobody blabs what really happened, I'll still be two ahead." He hesitates, then lowers his voice to ask, "Did you *see* him? When he was, you know, dead? Were you scared?"

"A little." Birdie bites her lip. To be honest, though, Dolly's face scared her more. She looked ten years older than when she went to bed. The apothecary was her last regular customer, and at her age, she's not likely to land another. It's only a matter of time before Auntie makes her give up her private room.

Lucky Doll had been a ten-year-old child attendant at the House of Peonies when Birdie's mother died giving birth to her. Three years later, after Dolly shot up to be a full handspan taller than most men, the Peonies' manager traded her to the House of Treasures, throwing in little Birdie for free. A courtesan's orphan like Tiger isn't so easy to get rid of, but girls are different. The Treasures' overseer was quick to see the upside in taking on a fresh, young, junior courtesan who could earn her keep with the perverse customers who prefer tall women, while also training a future child attendant and saving them the hefty broker's fee.

But Birdie doesn't want to invite bad luck by admitting that Lucky Doll's future looks shaky. That might make it come true.

Instead she asks, "Why are you limping?"

"I'm not limping." Tiger scowls.

She heard he fell off the shrine shed roof yesterday. Dolly forbids her to climb up there, but Tiger can't resist watching the jugglers and monkey shows on the street below for free.

"You fell off the roof, didn't you?"

She knows she's right by the way he ignores her question and tries to change the subject.

"Let's take the shortcut," he suggests, veering onto the street where the geisha live.

"You know there's a big wasp nest in the alley by their bathhouse, right?"

"I'm not afraid of a few bugs," he scoffs.

But he is—swells up like a water gourd if he gets stung—which means his ankle must really be hurting. She sighs and follows him onto the geishas' street, even though she'll get a scolding if anyone sees her. A child attendant from a top pleasure house like the Treasure must never be seen mixing with the dull sparrows who entertain patrons at teahouses while they wait for their oirans. Everyone at the Treasure feels sorry for them, because geisha aren't allowed to wear bright clothes or more than four hairpins, and Yoshiwara law forbids them to do more than amuse patrons from a distance. All the work, none of the reward.

She breathes a sigh of relief as they round the corner onto the tawdry street by the moat where the third-class pleasure houses squat. Fortunately, the smell isn't yet—

Wait. Is that . . . ?

She turns to squint at the man slinking out of the House of Cranes. It can't be. But it is. Only one man in all of Yoshiwara wears a cloak that color, and the only door Third Magistrate should be sneaking out of at this hour is White Pearl's.

"What?" Tiger asks, turning around to see why she stopped.

"Nothing," she says, catching up and hustling him toward the fruit stand.

But it's hard not to skip down the street in glee. Pearl will be overjoyed to hear Third Magistrate is cheating on her. Everyone knows a repentant patron is more profitable than a faithful one. If she lets Lucky Doll deliver the news, Elder Sister can pretend she saw him herself. That ought to remind Auntie not to be too hasty about pushing out a seasoned courtesan who can still produce the kind of information gold that keeps the House of Treasures in the black.

"That wasn't me!" Third Magistrate's goatee juts as he pompously adds, "And even if it was, am I not free to take a morning stroll anywhere I please?"

"That depends," White Pearl replies with a chilly smile, "on where you were coming from and what you were doing there."

The magistrate, his entourage, and the superior he invited tonight as his honored guest are lounging around a black lacquer table in the most elegant banquet room at the Five Fans, the one with the round window that looks out over their small garden and a poem by Edo's second-most-famous poet on the wall. But their tray of leftover sashimi has lost its gleam and the number of empty sake flasks outside the door could nearly form a regiment, which explains why their topknots are already askew and their fine robes rumpled.

"Is it not a bee's nature to taste the nectar of many flowers?" the magistrate wheedles.

"Not if he expects to taste any of mine." Pearl sniffs.

"In that case," he jokes, holding out his empty cup to be filled, "I hope whoever I was supposed to be bedding was pretty enough to be worth it."

"That's for you to decide," the oiran says coldly, ignoring his feeble attempt at humor. "But now that you're in violation of our sacred contract"—the three cups of sake a man drinks when he becomes an oiran's patron—"there's only one way you can get back in my good graces."

"Is that so?" He leers at her. "And what delicious punishment do you have in mind for me this time?"

"That's yet to be decided. At your oiran tribunal."

"My *what*?" He sits up.

"Oiran tribunal, Honorable Magistrate," Auntie says, appearing in the doorway on cue. She's dressed in her most formal kimono and bearing a regal purple cushion. "You're in Yoshiwara, so you must submit to Yoshiwara law."

"If you're found guilty," Pearl informs him, "you must pay the price."

"Ha!" The third magistrate's superior snorts, taking more of an interest than he's shown all evening. "You're in trouble now, young man. I've heard of such goings-on, but I never thought I'd see one. All I can say is, better you than me."

And suddenly Pearl's patron doesn't find this so funny. He'd arranged this evening to impress his boss with the wit and elegance of his oiran, not grovel before a queen of the night and suffer some gossip-worthy punishment.

"This is preposterous!" he blusters. Looks around for support. But his companions are all eager to see the promised theatrics and calling for him to be a good sport.

"What if I refuse?" he growls.

"Well, that would be an admission of guilt, wouldn't it?" Pearl purses her lips in disapproval.

The magistrate's boss leans in to advise, "You'd better do as she says, boyo. This isn't worth losing your oiran over, is it?"

It's not. The magistrate fumes. He didn't pay good money and jump through all kinds of hoops to become Pearl's patron just to be dismissed over something so trivial.

"All right." He gives in. "Let's get this over with."

Auntie calls for a pair of manservants to bring in the small dais the Five Fans keeps on hand for such proceedings. Pearl seats herself atop it on the purple cushion and points her patron to the thin straw mat that's been placed front and center for the accused.

Naturally, the women of Yoshiwara have only the vaguest idea of what a real trial entails, and since they are first and foremost entertainers, the "testimony" provokes hoots of laughter as Lucky Doll is called as witness, spinning a much-embellished tale of how she saw Third Magistrate emerging from the House of Cranes at dawn, singing "A Stranger in Yoshiwara" so off-key, she didn't recognize it at first. This is loudly decried as a crime against the ears of the good citizens of Yoshiwara, but she assures them his offense was brief. He only made it through one verse before hurrying into an alleyway to lift his leg, where he was bit by a wasp midstream and—just imagine!—his poor manhood swelled up like summer squash left too long on the vine.

This provokes gales of laughter from everyone but the man in question, because unfortunately, it's too close to the truth. He'd been so horrified and embarrassed by the price he paid for a fleeting moment of conduct unbecoming a man of rank, he'd told no one. Pearl only found out because she saw him in the buff before he'd entirely recovered.

Birdie shifts uncomfortably, watching the third magistrate's face flush dangerously red. Fortunately, Pearl notices too, and cuts Dolly's testimony short.

"I think we've heard enough," she proclaims. The onlookers quiet, leaning forward expectantly as she pronounces, "As magistrate of these solemn proceedings, I hereby declare the defendant guilty, as charged!"

The third magistrate leaps to his feet as hoots and catcalls break out, sputtering, "That's not fair! You can't declare a verdict before hearing my side of the story!"

"That may be true in Edo Castle," Pearl informs him in a prim voice, "but in the court of my opinion, any man who even looks at another woman doesn't deserve my regard or my time. If you ever want me to look upon you with favor again, you must now submit to a punishment of my choice."

He looks around for support, but this party has been all too successful, and his honored guest is having a far better time than he expected.

"All right." He grits his teeth and swallows his chagrin. "Have your sport. How must I atone, Most Honorable Magistrate?"

Pearl steps down from the dais and points to a spot on the tatami.

"Kneel here. No," she corrects him as he drops to his knees in mocking supplication, "turn around."

He shuffles into position, facing his guests.

Pearl holds out her hand. A gasp goes up as Dolly produces a freshly sharpened razor. Before her patron can twist around to see why everyone's mouths are hanging open, Pearl seizes his topknot and lops it off.

Bright morning sunlight slants across the smooth tatami mats of Pearl's private sitting room at the House of Treasures, while Birdie listens to the chatter about last night's oiran tribunal.

"Have you heard from Third Magistrate yet this morning?" Butterfly asks.

Pearl's humiliated patron had stormed out of the Five Fans in high dudgeon, but Pearl just laughed and poured another round for his guests. He'll get over it, she told them. They always do. She'd dispatched a next-morning message granting him full pardon and assuring him she'll welcome him on his next scheduled day, then turned her mind to more important matters, like the news that the Peonies' number one oiran will soon be marrying her biggest patron. Rumor has it he's a rich farmer. No, a silk trader, a smuggler, a lord. And he's not just buying out her contract, he's doubling it, tripling it, paying ten times the sum.

According to Tiger, of course, they're all wrong. He told Birdie that the House of Peonies is erecting a set of enormous scales in the reception hall, so the prospective bride can sit on one side and her future husband can pile gold coins onto the other until it balances. Tiger, however, is a born liar, so Birdie doesn't repeat that one to anyone but Flower.

What she does know is that the moment Pearl's chief rival retires from Yoshiwara, her well-heeled patrons will be up for grabs. For the next few weeks, Pearl won't be the only oiran finding excuses to parade her entourage through the streets in their most attention-grabbing outfits, hoping to lure at least one of the big spenders. She won't set foot outside the Treasure unless she's primped and plucked and polished from the tips of her toes to the elaborate winged hairdo that requires a whole pot of pomade, eight hairpins, two combs, three twisted paper ties, four ornaments, a pair of tassels, and an untold number of tears before it's done to Auntie's satisfaction. Which is why Pearl's attendants are all crowded into her private sitting room for the second day in a row to help get her ready.

"Ow!"

Birdie glances up, but the oiran's complaint is aimed at the hairdresser, not her. She returns to rubbing Pearl's toenail with a crimson petal. Today, she's working on the left foot, and Flower is doing the right.

"Can't you be more careful?" Pearl complains, as another long hank of her hair is pulled and twisted.

The stylist murmurs an insincere apology as she positions a wide tortoiseshell comb and shoves it in.

"Ouch!"

"It hurts to be beautiful," Auntie chides from the doorway, the wrinkles around her lips tightening around the stem of her pipe as smoke trails her into the room.

Birdie rolls her eyes. How many times has she heard that? It must be the house manager's favorite saying. It's Auntie's job to make sure her courtesans live up to the Treasures' reputation, but she gets a little too much satisfaction from watching the rest of them suffer as she suffered, now that she's long past the days when she was a first-rank oiran and sat before the tall mirror herself. Auntie's hands are as bony as a sack of dice now, and her scalp gleams through her hair in pale stripes when she washes it at the bath house. None of them can believe men actually paid to spend time with her.

Birdie glances at Flower, whose clever little fingers are already one toenail ahead. She speeds up, unwilling to let her fellow child attendant beat her, even at something as small as this. She and Flower are best friends and twins forever, but only one of them will get the chance to take Pearl's place when the time comes. Rolling her used petals into a ball, Birdie flicks it at her twin. Flower gives a small cry as it bounces off her cheek. Their eyes meet. Like reflections in a mirror, their hands fly up to hide their giggles.

Auntie's eyes dart their way and they quickly return to pinkening Pearl's toenails.

The hairdresser fusses with the final tie, then asks Pearl to bow her head, so she can shave the back of her neck. When she's done, she hands Pearl a hand mirror. The oiran turns this way and that, checking the angles of the long golden hairpins that frame her face like rays of the sun. Like most courtesans, Pearl isn't especially pretty before she puts on her makeup, but no pocks mar her skin, and her hairline frames her features in a pleasing curve that needs little plucking. Nodding, she hands back the mirror as her eyes sweep the room, searching for the courtesan who helps with her makeup.

"Where's Lucky Doll?"

"Lucky Doll is no longer with us," Auntie replies.

Birdie's head snaps up. What does she mean "no longer with us"?

"Feather will be helping with your makeup from now on."

Dolly is *gone*?

"Why?" Pearl frowns.

"Because that ninny's failing eyesight just cost you your biggest patron."

The color drains from the oiran's face.

"Not . . . Third Magistrate?"

"I hear he canceled all his official appointments," Auntie tells her, puffing furiously on her pipe, "and hid in his office until someone took pity on him and told him about the barber who specializes in topknot replacement. Turns out, he wasn't even in Edo that day. It was his son wearing that damned cloak, trying to impress some slag at the House of Cranes. You'd better find another patron soonest if you want to pay for those cherry blossom robes you ordered last month, and from now on, I'd be a lot more careful who you—"

But Birdie hears no more, as the devastating news about Dolly hits home. She just lost the closest thing she ever had to family. The woman who raised her, played with her, comforted her like an elder sister, is gone.

Her throat closes as her hand flies up to stifle a sob. Nothing has ever hurt like this. Nothing. Until it gets worse. Because this is all her fault. Dolly isn't the one who mistook the son for the father. She did.

"Birdie?" The cupboard door slides open a crack. "Are you in there?"

Birdie shrinks even farther into the shadows, but Flower is the only one who might not scold her for shirking her errands to weep for a courtesan who no longer belongs to the House of Treasures. She peeks around the folded futon and sees her twin peering into the gloom.

"Are you crying about Lucky Doll?" Flower asks.

Birdie nods, swiping at her wet cheeks.

Her twin offers a hand to help Birdie out of her cave.

"She's the only one who's known me since I was born," Birdie quavers. Dolly wasn't her mother, but she'd looked after her like an elder sister. Corrected her when she did something wrong, was proud of her when she did something right. "Does . . . does anyone know where she went?"

Flower shakes her head. "Auntie won't tell us. But she must still be somewhere in Yoshiwara."

That's true. No courtesan is allowed to pass through the Great Gate if she's still indentured to a pleasure house. It's small consolation, though—Dolly may still be in Yoshiwara, but she's been banished from everyone she holds dear. If Auntie knew who was really to blame for costing Pearl her patron, Birdie would be the one who woke up this morning in a strange place, not knowing a soul. It's the worst punishment she can imagine. But it's the one she deserves.

"You don't understand," she confesses to Flower, gulping back a sob. "It's . . . it's all my fault. I'm the one who saw the man in the cloak. If Auntie knew it was me who saw the wrong man cheating, I'd be the one who was gone." She doubles over, rocking and moaning.

Flower silently pulls a coverlet from the cupboard and wraps it around Birdie's shoulders as the waves of weeping ebb and flow. Through it all, Birdie is dimly aware of a small, warm hand on her back. It stays there until her tears run dry and her grief is spent, reminding her that she's not entirely alone. Her Elder Sister is gone, but she still has Flower.

Birdie looks for Dolly everywhere as she crisscrosses Yoshiwara, fetching face powder, rice crackers, and hairpins, desperate to unload the unbearable burden of apology and gratitude she owes the courtesan who shouldered the punishment that ought to have been hers.

She eavesdrops on the women waiting outside the apothecary, listens in line at the shrine, but no one mentions the name Lucky Doll. Every evening, she scans the faces of the courtesans in the other great Houses' oiran processions, but Dolly isn't among them. Hope curdling into dread, she begins to study the entourages of the second-rate courtesans. Still no sign. Where can she be?

On the night she finds out, Pearl's procession is on its way to the Nightingale, sandwiched between oiran parades from the Bamboo and the Pine. Birdie already knows Dolly isn't at either one, so she's doing as Pearl commanded, scanning the crowd and trying not to be distracted by the stain shaped like a cat's face (or is it more like a bear?) on the lantern-bearer's backside. The man hasn't been at the House of Treasures for very long, so he probably doesn't know you have to pay special attention to how you look from behind. Auntie has the sharpest eyes in the pleasure quarter and plenty of time to find fault as she trudges along at the back of the procession.

Step. Wait. Step. Wait. A snail would beat them to the Nightingale tonight. Do the Peonies' soon-to-be-available patrons really need this much time to appreciate Pearl's charms?

Flower tugs at her sleeve, points.

Birdie's eyes widen, her mission and sorrows momentarily forgotten. Teahouse Street has completely changed since they walked this way last night. Festive red lanterns now hang from every balcony, casting a pink glow on the blossoms of the brand-new cherry trees running down the center of the boulevard. The first time she'd seen them, she thought these trees appeared by magic. She'd been disappointed to learn they're stuck in the ground every year for the cherry blossom festival, and as soon as the last petal drops, they're dug up and replaced with next season's flowers.

"No one comes to the pleasure quarter to see cherry trees that aren't in bloom," Pearl had scoffed. "That's the first thing you need to learn if you're going to survive in Yoshiwara." Because inside the Great Gate, the flowers must always be in bloom. Men pay to be surprised by spectacle, entertained by excess, to feast their eyes on the famous courtesans who are confined to the pleasure quarter like songbirds in a gilded cage.

But tonight, those men are pressing so close Birdie can smell what they do for a living: horse trader, sake brewer, swordsmith, priest. It's time to scan the crowd for the men on Pearl's list. Or, rather, their *netsukes*, the big carved beads that keep the cords of men's tobacco pouches and *inrō* from slipping through their sashes. Paying famous artists to fashion exquisite little figures from rare materials is one of the more sophisticated ways merchants flaunt their wealth without courting fines from the shōgun's clothing police. Copying another man's *netsuke* is a social blunder that the players on today's potential patron list would never make, so it's the best way for Pearl to make sure Birdie and Flower report on the right men.

After the first block, they've spotted all but one, the man Auntie says is the biggest catch. His name is Takahisa Takeda, and much to Birdie's horror, he's the scarred man she saw with Third Magistrate last week. She won't have to spot his octopus *netsuke* to recognize those mismatched squinty eyes and the pockmarked face that his wispy moustache and beard fail to disguise. Pearl thinks he's the ugliest man in Yoshiwara.

"If I have to reel in one of the Peonies' patrons," she'd said, inspecting her freshly blackened teeth in the mirror, "I'd much prefer the poet. He's at least somewhat attractive, as older men go."

Auntie pounced on that like a hawk on a mouse.

"It's not your place to decide such things, missy. If Overseer-san tells you to go after Takahisa Takeda, it's the timber baron you need to charm. Courtesans' contracts can be sold as easily as they're bought, you know."

That made Pearl grudgingly agree to grant Takeda a smile if she sees him, but she'd rolled her eyes and made a face as soon as Auntie's back was turned.

Step. Wait. Step. Wait. Birdie shifts the oiran's ornate tobacco set to her other hand and glances over at Flower, who's carrying the writing box today. Her twin is drooping.

"Do you want to trade?" she whispers.

Flower doesn't answer, and she's got that faraway look in her eyes again. She's keeping her head up out of habit, but whatever she's thinking about, it's not *netsuke*. How long has it been since she stopped paying attention?

It's no use poking her twin when she gets like this. It's the one thing Flower hasn't outgrown. She's a year older than Birdie, but when she first came to the Treasure, she'd been frightened of the big phoenix painting in the receiving room, and thought the lattice-walled room downstairs where the courtesans are displayed every night must be the entrance to the shōgun's palace. When Pearl glided down the stairs wearing one of the old kimonos she throws on after her bath, she'd gaped like the empress doll from her village's Girls' Day display had come to life. Flower hadn't even noticed that Auntie was old until their house manager ordered the two of them to kneel in the light where she could see them, then sat down next to Pearl to discuss what to name their new pair of child attendants.

They'd both been called something else, of course, before the House of Treasures turned them into twins. Auntie had packed a pipe for Pearl, then one for herself, then the two of them sat there, smoking and studying her and Flower as if they were carp on a cutting board. Birdie's legs had been prickling pins and needles by the time they finished considering Sandpiper and Swallow, Moonflower and Peony, Little Jewel and Bright Jewel, before finally settling on Little Bird and Little Flower.

Flower turned out to be a quick learner, but no amount of elbowing can bring her back when she's staring into the distance like this. Birdie sighs, and begins to search both sides of the street for Takahisa Takeda.

Ah. There he is, on the upstairs balcony of the teahouse next to the Nightingale, chatting with a young man in a purple kimono. He's paying attention to the conversation, not his surroundings, but the dandy in purple looks down and sees them. An appreciative smile curves his lips as he takes in the junior courtesans, but as his attention shifts to Pearl, his mouth falls open. He shuts it quickly and glances around, hoping nobody caught him gaping like a fish.

Birdie's hand flies up to stifle a giggle. Direct hits like that are what an oiran relies on her child attendants to watch for while she's playing too exalted to notice.

The young man leans over to say something to Takeda, his eyes still glued on Pearl. The older man nods agreeably, turning his attention their way. It's hard to tell what he's thinking, behind those squinty eyes. He doesn't seem overly impressed, but he's a high-level patron at the Peony, so he must have seen countless oiran parades like this. The dandy in purple is a much more promising target. If he's one of Takeda-san's retainers, perhaps they can persuade him to steer his boss to the House of Treasures.

The lantern-bearer halts before the swooping roof crowning the Nightingale's entrance and the crowd parts to allow the teahouse mistress to welcome them. Birdie and Flower catch the edges of the linen door curtains to hold them open as Pearl and the rest of her entourage sweep inside.

A raucous drinking song is coming from somewhere upstairs as they file into the room where Pearl will freshen up before entertaining tonight's banquet patron. Birdie hears his braying laugh rise above the merriment. He's probably been here for hours already, enjoying the storytellers and the geisha music while he drinks with his guests.

The mistress withdraws; Feather and Butterfly maneuver the room's folding screen to block the door and give them a little privacy while Auntie casts a critical eye at sashes that need straightening and faces that need powdering.

Pearl sinks onto a cushion before the low table, wriggles her aching toes, finally free of the tall *koma-geta* she left behind in the foyer. Birdie opens the tobacco box to pack a pipe so Pearl can have a quick smoke while the junior courtesans smooth her hair and freshen her powder.

"All right, girls." The oiran takes a few puffs and turns to her child attendants. "Who came out to see us today?"

"The second governor was on the corner where the monkey trainer was doing his show, talking to an important-looking man with a big red mark on his neck," Birdie reports.

"The minister of coin." Pearl puffs thoughtfully. "Did he look... interested?"

"He was wearing his uniform, so he may just have been here on business," she replies apologetically. Samurai who visit Yoshiwara for pleasure leave their wide-shouldered vests and stiff, pleated, trouser-skirts at home.

"He attacked a girl in the crowd," Flower announces.

Birdie turns, astonished. "What are you talking about?"

"The new monkey. He charged a girl in a red kimono and the trainer barely caught him before he bit her."

Oh, no. Had Flower been off in her own little world all afternoon? Now Pearl is frowning, and frowning doesn't bode well for the evening ahead.

"I saw the man with the fox *netsuke* on the next corner," Birdie quickly says, to distract Pearl from Flower's gaffe. "He watched you both coming and going."

"Good." The oiran sparks another pipe. "If he liked what he saw, maybe the next time you see him, he'll be knocking at our door." She opens the lid of her tobacco set. "Who else?"

Birdie reports on the rest of the *netsuke* wearers, ending with Takeda.

"He was watching you from the balcony of the Camellia when we arrived."

"I saw him. I wonder if that's where Jewel usually entertains the old moneybags?"

"I wouldn't make fun of someone for being one of the richest men in Edo, if I were you." Auntie's ears are the sharpest in Yoshiwara. "Unless of course you'd prefer to wake up every morning in a geisha house."

"Sorry, Honorable Auntie," Pearl mutters. She knocks the ash from her pipe and begins pulling herself together.

"Did you notice that young guy he was with?" Peach moans.

Pearl pauses. "I saw him."

"Well, if you land Takeda-san, can I have *him*?"

Birdie winces. Even she knows that if Pearl has to settle for the ugly old geezer, she's not going to let her attendant make off with the handsome retainer.

"If that's the kind of patron you're setting your sights on"—Pearl skewers Peach with a disdainful look—"you'll never get your own room. Peacocks like that are rarely rich, because they spend all their money trying to *look* rich."

Auntie claps her hands for quiet.

"Who do you want tonight?" she asks Pearl.

They all perk up. The reason they call tonight's patron "Goldbelly" is that he keeps his tip money tucked into the folds of the sash wrapped around his prosperous paunch. After he's been drinking and lounging around for hours, some of it always ends up on the floor, and he forgets to pick it up when he goes upstairs with Pearl. Sometimes it's as much as two *bu*!

"Butterfly, you can go." Pearl knows this is the night her favorite customer usually visits. "Peach and Feather, you're with me. If Goldbelly's guests want company at the end of the night, you can escort them back to the Treasure."

Murmuring agreement, they gather their things.

Birdie pulls Flower aside. There's something she has to say before they go upstairs to help Pearl tonight. She doesn't fully understand Auntie's threats about "contracts" and "geisha houses," except they're about being sent away, to live somewhere else. The House of Treasures is their home, and the monkey blunder stirred up her fears again. If Flower keeps making mistakes like that, Pearl might get fed up with her and send her away. And if Flower is sent away, what will happen to her? They're twins now, so Pearl might very well replace them both. Birdie leans in, pretending to adjust Flower's collar.

"I know you're tired, but please, *please* do everything Pearl asks of you tonight."

"I do."

"No, you don't. When she asked us about what we saw on procession this afternoon, you told her that thing about the monkey."

"I didn't tell her about the monkey." Flower pouts. "I told her what the monkey did."

"That's what I mean. When Pearl asks you to be on the lookout for things that will help her, she doesn't want to hear about monkeys. She wants to hear about the men who might become her new patrons. That's what's important. The monkey's not important."

"The monkey *is* important."

"To you, maybe. But not to her. And she's the one who puts rice in our bowls." How can Flower not understand this? "If you want to get promoted to junior courtesan, you have to do what she says."

She might as well be talking to a stone lantern. Flower doesn't answer, just stands there, looking at her as if she were speaking some rural dialect from Aomori.

But there's no time to say more because Auntie is announcing, "Everybody up! Time to go."

They join the others filing from the room, chattering about the evening ahead.

But Pearl hangs back, catches Birdie's sleeve.

"Before you come upstairs, I've got a job for you."

"Boo!" Birdie leaps from the dark alleyway, and Tiger yelps in surprise, bumping into a passing tradesman who deals him a cuff on the head.

"Hey!" He glares at her. "Don't do that!"

"Got you." That'll teach him to hide a hateful sardine in her rice cake.

Birdie has been waiting for him outside the side entrance to the Camellia, knowing it was only a matter of time before the Peonies' oiran sent him out on some errand.

"I don't have time for games tonight," he announces, taking off down the street with a self-important swagger.

Birdie catches up to him. "Why not? Where are you going?"

"Takeda-san has a hankering for eel tonight, so . . ." He purses his lips and simpers, "'Tiger will fetch it, won't you, Tiger?'"

Birdie laughs. He sounds exactly like Jewel.

"Is Takeda the one with the, you know . . ." She crosses her eyes and pokes her fingers all over her cheeks.

"Yeah." Tiger laughs. "The pox didn't do him any favors, did it?"

They split to go around a noodle vendor.

"What about the handsome guy he's with tonight?" she probes. "The one in the purple kimono. I saw them standing together on the balcony at the Camellia while we were waiting to go into the Nightingale."

"You mean his son?"

She blinks. "His son?"

"Eyebrows plucked like a kabuki star?" Tiger makes a face. "He's so full of himself. You'd never guess he's got the smallest—" Snaps his mouth shut.

"Purse?"

"Yeah. He's got a really small . . . purse."

"Well, he sure acts like he's got a big one, the way he was gaping at Pearl when we went past."

"That one gapes at all the oirans."

"He doesn't have one of his own yet?"

"He's not even married yet. And like his father always says, 'What's the point of having a mistress if you don't have a wife?'" He snorts. "We're all looking forward to never having to laugh at that joke again."

Before she can ask any more, they arrive at the eel seller, and Tiger has work to do. He straightens his jacket and trots inside, tossing a "see you later" over his shoulder.

But that's okay, because her work is done. She'd found out everything Pearl asked for, and more. With a skip in her step, she turns back toward the Nightingale. It isn't even dark yet. She'll be back long before Pearl and Goldbelly go upstairs. She was afraid she'd miss out on the dropped coins, but she may be able to beat the teahouse maids to the spoils after all. How should she spend them? Rice cakes or a puppet show?

She slows beneath the window of a teahouse and listens to a performer telling a story she hasn't heard before. When gales of laughter and table pounding erupt, she moves on to the tobacco shop to do the other job Pearl gave her, in case anyone asks where she's been. Tucking the packet into her sleeve, she detours to join the crowd gathered on the next corner to watch the monkey trainer put his new one through its paces. It's wearing the old monkey's vest and a new red cap. What happened to the old monkey? This one can leap higher, but it doesn't know as many tricks. And it doesn't always do what the trainer tells it to. She moves on before he can pass the hat. Coins don't come her way very often, and she's not about to spend any on a monkey show unless it can do tricks she hasn't seen.

She ducks under the curtain at the entrance to the Nightingale, sketches a bow at the manservant on door duty (who is not forgiven for clearing away Goldbelly's sashimi tray last week before they had a chance to polish off the leftovers) then trips up the stairs to the banquet rooms. At the top, she pauses, listening. Hears singing coming from one room, peals of laughter from another. None of them sound like Goldbelly.

A maid appears from inside the nearest room, kneeling to slide the door closed behind her. As she picks up her tray, Birdie asks which room is Goldbelly's. The girl flips an elbow toward the one at the end.

That's what she was afraid of. That door stands open, meaning the party's over. And if the party's over, the teahouse staff will already have pounced on whatever dropped from his sash tonight. She checks, just in case, but the room has already been cleared, the floor disappointingly bare. Tonight's coins are jingling in someone else's sleeve now. There's nothing to do but go home.

Birdie scowls. Why did they go upstairs so early tonight? Pearl had been complaining of a headache all afternoon, but still. If *she's* promoted to oiran, she'll make sure her patrons have a good time, even if she has a headache. If *she's* promoted to oiran, they won't even think of going to bed before midnight.

At least now she can get to her own bed earlier than usual, so she can get up and practice her music lessons before Flower gets back. She hasn't even started learning this week's *shamisen* tune, and her twin already knows it by heart. Most of the time she can beat Flower at playing games, calligraphy, and poetry writing, but Flower is better at music. Tomorrow her twin will be stuck at the Nightingale until at least midmorning, so Birdie will have a couple of extra hours to catch up. Some men insist on being awakened before first light so they can make it out the door before the six o'clock bell and avoid paying another day's teahouse fee, but Goldbelly is considerate, as patrons go. Not only does he stay until after six, he tips everyone, upstairs and down, on his way out.

If only she'd gotten back earlier and been chosen to stay tonight, she'd be getting a tip in the morning, plus the—

"Oh!" As if thinking his name conjured him, Goldbelly lumbers up the last few stairs from the privy.

"Hello." He squints at her face. "Birdie, is it?"

"Yes, Honored Sir." She bows.

"Why such a long face?" he asks. "What's wrong, little one?"

Her cheeks grow hot. She can't very well admit she's disappointed she got back after all his dropped coins were scooped up.

"I didn't see you earlier," he says. "Did you come back after we went upstairs? Are you hungry? Because I could have them bring some—"

She quickly shakes her head. She *is* hungry, but she'd be in big trouble if it got back to Auntie that she'd revealed to a patron that she's an ordinary human being who needs to eat.

"Ah." He smiles. "I bet I know why you're sad. The others gleaned the field before you got a chance, didn't they?"

What does he mean by that?

"Hold out your hand."

Her heart hammers. Is he going to punish her?

"Come now, I don't bite."

Timidly, she extends her hand, palm down, the way Pearl taught her. Never reveal your palm, she'd said, except to someone who has earned the right to see it.

Goldbelly is digging around in the folds of his sash. Pulls out a large gold coin. Smiles and turns her palm up, then places the coin on it. Folds her fingers around it.

Her face burns with shame. A man has never touched her hand before. She has never held a gold coin before. It's heavy. She feels dirty. She feels rich.

"Don't tell the others, okay?" He leans in, lowers his voice. "Can't have them all expecting a gold coin every time they pull a long face."

She stammers her thanks, bowing deeper than she's ever bowed in her life, then stares after him as he mounts the stairs to the upper floor with a spring in his step.

She tucks the coin into her sash. Rubs her hand down her kimono again and again, as if that will wipe away her confusion. She tries not to think too much about what Pearl and Goldbelly do when they're upstairs together. Does she let him see the palm of her hand? She must. He's certainly earned it by now. He's her second-biggest patron. Does she let him touch it? The way he didn't think twice about grabbing hers and turning it over and—She shudders. It doesn't mean anything. And yet, somehow, she's afraid it does.

Like everyone who lives in a pleasure house, she has learned to ignore the noises coming from the rooms where the courtesans take their customers at night. The main sleeping rooms are divided by folding screens, with curtains over the entrances for privacy, but they're far from soundproof. She and Flower have many theories about what makes the courtesans cry out. They moan like they're in pain, but that can't be right, because if the customers are hurting them, why beg for more? Plus, the next morning they seem perfectly fine.

Naturally, they've dared each other to peek behind the curtains, but neither of them has been brave enough to take more than a quick look, so the wrestling that Butterfly and the tobacco vendor were doing under the covers raised more questions than it answered. The second time they got up the nerve, Peach caught them peeping and glared at them so fiercely over her customer's heaving shoulder they never tried again. It remains a mystery.

She races down the stairs, the gold coin burning beneath her sash like a live coal, and parts the curtain. There's a solid wall of well-dressed backsides lining the street outside the door. Why are they still here? Teahouse Street is usually empty by this hour—patrons are inside with their oirans, and the rest ought to have drifted over to the streets lined with lattice-fronted rooms to choose cheaper companionship for the evening. Birdie stretches onto her tiptoes, catches sight of a lantern bearing the House of Bamboo's crest swaying above the heads of the onlookers, followed by a red parasol that would have shaded the Bamboo's oiran had she been parading down the street while the sun still shone. Behind her, more lighted lanterns and parasols jockey for position.

So many oirans must be hoping to impress the House of Peonies' soon-to-be-available patrons that the processions are backing up. It will be easier to go the long way home instead of fighting her way through the crush. She turns her back on the central boulevard, setting out toward the moat instead.

The crowd thins. Slowing to greet the pawnbroker's assistant, she exchanges bows with another child attendant and passes a watchman clapping the "all's well" with his wooden blocks, keeping an eye out for troublemakers. Masa the pickpocket darts into a narrow alley across the street, just in time.

She rounds the corner onto the street bordering the moat and hesitates. On one side, crowds of men jostle for a view of the courtesans on display at the third-rate pleasure houses. In this part of Yoshiwara, child attendants dressed in the latest fashion are as rare as cherry blossoms in a pumpkin patch, and she's already attracting nudges and stares. She hurries to the side where a low stone wall is all that stands between her and the steep drop to the dark water below, reminding herself she's much too old to believe in the *kappa* demons who snatch little girls walking alone at night to drag them beneath the dirty water with their slimy fingers.

The wind tightens her skin into goosebumps, and she buries her nose in her sleeve to mask the smell of stagnant water. Head down, she skirts the noodle seller and hustles past the fortuneteller, trying not to admit that the real reason she's willing to take her chances with the water demons is that she's worried she might glimpse Lucky Doll in one of the tawdry streetside viewing rooms.

The pleasure houses here are so far beneath the House of Treasures that their courtesans don't cross paths at any of the same teahouses. The House of Cranes, the Golden Drum, the Red Plum; not a single ranking oiran among them. The House of Treasures' streetside lattice room is designed to offer only narrow, tantalizing glimpses of the courtesans inside, but the extra-wide gaps at these third-rate houses provide little relief from the men pointing at this one and that, debating their merits in the coarsest terms.

Even though losing Dolly has faded to a dull ache, being confronted by the grim reality of the down-at-heel Houses she hasn't yet searched floods Birdie with fresh guilt. Trying to outrun it, she hurries around the next corner to cut through the geisha quarter and avoid any more viewing rooms that might confirm her worst fears about what happened to Dolly.

Whew. Her footsteps slow to match the more sedate pace of geisha headed to the registry office to wait for work, trailed by servants carrying their *shamisen* cases. The rest of the modestly dressed women on this street are carrying folded cotton wrappers and converging on the street's public bath, hand towels slung over their shoulders and bran-filled washbags in hand.

Suddenly aware how much grander she looks, she lifts her chin, stands a little taller, slows to practice her sashay. Bobbing her head ever so slightly to make her hair ornaments twinkle in the moonlight, she thinks, this is what it feels like to turn heads! This is what it feels like to be an oiran! She pretends not to notice the admiring glances coming her way—that's what Pearl would do—but it's hard not to allow a tiny smirk of triumph as a woman across the street stops in her tracks at the sight of her, grabbing the sleeve of her companion and staring at—

Oh no, it's Lucky Doll.

Birdie spins around, hitching up her robes to trot back the way she came, praying, praying, *praying* she hadn't been recognized. Auntie would kill her if she saw her clopping along in her best *geta*, not caring if they get scuffed, but she'd seen the expression on Dolly's face as she turned.

However much Elder Sister loved her before, she hates her now.

Birdie finally makes it back to Center Street, where the bright lights of respectable pleasure houses invite men to consider a courtesans' charms, not appraise them like fishmongers. She bows her head to hide her red-rimmed eyes, still stinging from discovering Dolly has been doomed to a geisha house. Sore spots are burning on both her feet now, but the blisters don't hurt as much as the painful truth that no amount of apologizing or gratitude will make up for ruining Elder Sister's life. All she can do is stay out of her way, make sure they never cross paths, make sure they—

"Birdie!" Auntie pounces on her as she ducks through the Treasures' door curtain. "Where have you been?"

"I ... uh ..." The Nightingale feels like a lifetime ago. "Pearl sent me out for tobacco, and the streets were so crowded I had to come back the long way, and then my feet started hurting, and—"

"Excuses, excuses," Auntie grumbles. But she must be really swamped tonight, because she cuts her lecture short to say, "I need you to take this *koto* upstairs to Butterfly, but first, let me fix that collar. And your hair. Honestly—!" Lips pursed, she tugs here, smooths there. "All right, you'll do. Now, pay attention. I saw the man who requested her tonight going into the House of Peonies last summer, but this is the first time he's been to the Treasure. He and his guests have been ordering top-shelf sake and platters of fish from Uogoro, so he must be richer than he looks. See if you can get him interested in her. You know what to do."

She does. Auntie thrusts the ungainly thirteen-stringed instrument into her arms and she hauls it up the stairs. Making her way down the corridor, it's easy to figure out which room the big spenders are in, because so many empty sake flasks stand outside their door, and a manservant is arriving with a magnificent platter of sashimi from the restaurant that only their well-heeled customers can afford. Polite female laughter mixes with raucous guffaws from within.

"Excuse me . . . ?" she ventures.

Butterfly claps her hands with delight. "Look, the *koto* is here!"

Birdie performs a low bow accompanied by the standard "please show this humble person your favor." The four men roar a welcome—they've obviously been drinking for some time—and wave her into the room. They're lounging around a table crowded with dishes of pickles, salty drinking snacks, and the platter of raw fish that just arrived. Birdie's stomach growls. She hasn't eaten since before they set out for the Nightingale, and even then, it was just a bowl of rice with tea poured over it.

Two of the men pluck some choice tuna belly from the platter and resume a drinking game with their courtesans between bites. The third accepts a refill with one hand and unfurls his other toward Peach, who is predicting his remarkably lucky future.

"Have something to eat," the fourth man offers, in a jovial voice. "There's plenty."

Butterfly is glued to his side, so he must be the one paying. He's not much to look at. Not young, not old, his round face more comic than handsome, and his eyes crinkle at the corners as if he spends most of his time laughing.

"My name is Saheiji," he says, "but you can call me Jester. Everyone does." He pats the tatami in a friendly way. "Have a seat."

"Oh, I'm sorry, I really can't." She doesn't want to get stuck here all night. "I'm only a child attendant."

"But even children have to eat! Try some of this nice fish." He plucks a piece of sea bream from the tray with his chopsticks and gleefully swims it through the air toward her, squealing, "Hee hee!"

His face looks exactly like the fool's mask that townsfolk wear at festivals, and she can't help but laugh. Nevertheless, she must refuse his tempting offer. Butterfly will tell on her if she doesn't.

"I'm afraid I can't, honored sir, but please go ahead." Birdie smiles, displaying her dimple. "Before your friends eat it all."

"Ha! If they do, we'll just order more." Jester laughs and pops the bream into his mouth. "The sky's the limit tonight, right, boys?"

Amid a chorus of "Yes, boss!" and "Hear, hear!" they all raise their sake cups and drain them.

Pleasantly unfocused, Jester holds his out for a refill.

"Why don't you stay and play us a tune on that *koto*, then?"

"I'm afraid I'm still too young to have lessons, honored sir." She quickly pushes the instrument toward Butterfly. "But you should ask Butterfly to play 'Across a Bridge of Stars.' It always brings tears to our eyes."

Taking her cue, Butterfly plucks a couple of tuning notes.

Jester turns his attention to the music and Birdie slips out the door, kneeling to slide it silently closed behind her. She trots downstairs, making a beeline to the kitchen to scrounge whatever rice is left in the pot. Are there enough pickles in the crock for her to sneak an extra one without Cook noticing? Why yes, there are. She helps herself, rearranging the bran so it looks like the lower levels haven't been disturbed.

Then, with a yawn as wide as a badger hole, she creeps up the stairs to bed.

"Hold still, woman!"

Takeda grunts as he finishes with his oiran.

Stupid cow. Not only had Jewel failed him in the banquet room tonight, she had diminished his pleasure right up to the end by whimpering that the position he requested tonight was hurting.

What had he ever seen in her? She's pretty enough, but all women look the same in the dark. That's just one of the unwelcome lessons he's learned since he began paying an astronomical sum every month to possess her. Becoming her patron had delivered the admiration and envy of every social climber in Edo, but everything else has been a disappointment. How could someone so boring and unwilling to experiment become the top oiran in Yoshiwara?

He gazes at the ceiling as his heartbeat slows. It hadn't always been like this, but now that he thinks back, it wasn't long after she went from being an unattainable queen of the pleasure quarter to the woman he beds four times a month that her intelligence—and, frankly, her looks—began to go downhill. Now that she takes his generous monthly stipend for granted, she no longer bothers to make her eyes sparkle for him or lean close enough for him to smell the scent of her skin beneath her perfumed robes. He can't remember the last time she attempted to inflame his desire by flashing him a glimpse of the body parts only a patron is allowed to see. He's no longer aroused by such mundane enticements, of course, but she could at least show him a little appreciation by trying.

And tonight, she'd been so clumsy at helping him negotiate the details of the marriage match with the shipowner, it was as if she'd bungled it on purpose. Even that little bastard Tiger could have done better. Why should he pay the kind of money it costs to keep an oiran if she won't wrap his bluntness in a cocoon of pleasantries, so the men he does business with walk away congratulating themselves, thinking they got the better end of the deal? No thanks to her, that accursed shipowner bested him tonight. Not only did he have to pledge his son to keep the deal alive, he promised more of an investment than he can deliver.

Where's he going to find the shortfall? Trees are trees. They don't suffer from crop failure in bad years, but they never deliver a single *mon* more than expected in good ones.

Could he squeeze cash from Koga? It's not the first time that's crossed his mind, but he rejects it for the same reason he did before. That well just isn't deep enough. The city administrator is rich in influence, but the Kogas are an old family and their wealth is spread thin. He'd inherited the family compound that's just a stone's throw from the spot where he killed the shōgun's retainer on the night of the fire, but keeping up appearances on an official's salary can't be easy.

Was that why Koga was still on that street after everyone else had fled? Making sure nobody took what was his? That doesn't explain the woman, though. Since the night of the break-in, that question has been keeping him up at night. Koga is the only one who knows the answer, but he's made it clear he'll only meet Takeda's demands as long as he's never asked about that night.

It's exactly the sort of problem a skilled oiran should be willing and able to help with. How did he get stuck with this nincompoop who doesn't understand that she must make his interests her own if she expects him to keep her in fancy clothes?

Look at the lazy minx, just lying there, staring at the ceiling. He knows exactly what she's playing at, but her reproach still makes his skin shrink. She knows better than to turn away—that was the first lesson he'd taught her—but she's all too pointedly withholding the post-passion praise he expects from a courtesan. He knows it's all lies, but Jewel is supposed to be the best in Yoshiwara at telling them. What's the point of having an oiran if she's not going to deceive him in the way he wants to be deceived?

"Well?" he prompts into the darkness, tired of waiting.

But she's apparently not finished punishing him with her silence. She slips from the covers without a word and shivers off into the night to fetch the washcloth he insists upon, instead of the cheap paper wipes that remind him he need not pay this kind of money for the service just rendered.

Birdie doesn't wake up as early as she'd planned when she made that vow to practice "Bells of Edo" before Flower and Pearl return. She's halfway through tying her sash before remembering Dolly's predicament, but she can't afford to wallow in guilt and despair if she wants to stay in the running to become the House of Treasures' next oiran.

Creeping on little cat feet, she makes it as far as the stairs, but on her way down has the misfortune of encountering the upstairs maid, who ropes her into helping clear up the orange peels, ashtrays, and empty sake flasks that litter the hallway outside the occupied courtesan rooms. Customers who have been allowed the privilege (and paid handsomely) to stay the night will wake to find their clothes folded, tea waiting, and the hallways swept and gleaming for their departure, but it takes plenty of work to make it that way. She helps the maid tidy up but manages to escape before it's time to empty the ashes behind the customers' privy. You can smell it from all the way across the garden after a busy night, and not in a good way.

She chooses a *shamisen*, then sneaks toward the room that's nearly always empty. The debtor room is furnished with scruffy rice straw mats and a thin futon, reserved for the rare customer who overspends his means and must be jailed until his unpaid bill can be collected from friends or family. Thanks to Auntie's spiderweb of colleagues at other pleasure houses, the Treasure usually hears about such scofflaws before they get past the door curtain, so this room is rarely occupied.

But just as she's reaching for the latch, Auntie pokes her head out of her office, thrusting an empty basket at her.

"Good. You're up. We need more oranges."

Birdie sighs, but who is she to question the gods if they've decided she won't be practicing today?

She doesn't find a single dropped coin this morning, but her luck revives when Tiger emerges from the back door of the Peony at the exact moment she arrives. Whistling "A Stranger in Yoshiwara," he's toting the wooden bucket they use to fetch fresh tofu. The tofu maker is on the same street as the fruit vendor, so they fall in side by side.

"So? Was I right?" She picks up where they left off last night. "Did Takeda's son say anything about Pearl when you got back?"

"Ugh, the silly buffoon wouldn't shut up." He rolls his eyes. "He really didn't know when to quit." He leaps to swat a low-hanging cherry branch. "He finally annoyed his sire so much that he's been forbidden to set foot in the Treasure."

"Even if he's invited?"

"Especially if he's invited."

"Do you think he'll pick one of the Peonies' courtesans instead?"

"They live in hope. Someday that little rooster will be a very rich man."

That reminds her. "Do you remember a moneybags named Saheiji who came to the Peony last summer? Calls himself Jester?"

"How could I forget?" Tiger snorts. "But that joker's not rich. Far from it. We booted him out the back door the next morning with his hairy shanks sticking out the bottom of an old maid's uniform."

"You took his clothes?" That's not good. "Couldn't he pay his bill?"

"Not with the six *mon* he had on him. What we got for his kimono and tobacco pouch barely covered his sake bill. You'd think he'd be embarrassed to show his face this side of the moat after that, but less than a month later, I saw him capering about at one of those second-rate teahouses where geisha entertain, as if nothing had happened." He shakes his head in disgust. "Why do you ask?"

She tells him.

"Why didn't your manager stop him at the door?"

She doesn't answer, but she knows why. The one manager in Yoshiwara who Auntie isn't on speaking terms with is the Peonies.' Something happened in the distant past when Auntie was an oiran and the woman who manages the house where Tiger lives was a novice. They haven't spoken a word to each other since.

They arrive at the fruit seller. Tiger slouches off to pick up his tofu, and she goes inside to collect the Treasures' oranges. On the way home, she sacrifices one of her precious coins at the shrine to beg the gods to keep Dolly far, far away. She's still fretting about what to do if she runs into Elder Sister again as she sails through the door curtain at the Treasure and someone grabs her sleeve. She nearly drops the oranges.

"Where have you been?" Flower whispers. "Pearl's been looking for you ever since we got home. She's waiting upstairs."

Uh oh. The oiran usually goes straight to bed when she gets back from a teahouse—which makes no sense, because hasn't she been sleeping all night?—and if she doesn't get her "beauty rest," she'll be dealing out pinches and ear tweaks the rest of the day.

Birdie thrusts her basket into Flower's arms and hurries upstairs. Knocking timidly, she begs pardon before entering.

"About time!" Pearl sits before her dressing table, already changed into the cotton wrapper she sleeps in, sighing with relief each time she pulls another long pin from her hair.

"I'm sorry I wasn't here when you got home, Honored Elder Sister. Auntie sent me out for oranges, and I just got back."

"Well, I hope you brought me one," Pearl huffs. "I'm starving."

Birdie tosses the one she palmed from the basket before handing it to Flower. Pearl catches it and invites her to the table where her morning tea awaits. She pours two cups, slides one across.

"So?" The oiran digs a thumb into the peel. "Did you find out who he is?"

"Yes. He's Takeda-san's son."

"His son?" Pearl stares. "Are you sure?"

Birdie nods.

"Huh. He must take after his mother." She peels off an orange segment. Pops it in her mouth. "Who was he with? Which woman, I mean."

"Dunno. He might just have been there to keep his father company."

"Why do you say that?"

"I hear that every courtesan at the Peony has her eye on him, so he must not have chosen one yet. Besides, what kind of courtesan would let her patron moan on and on about some other House's oiran all night?"

"He was moaning about an oiran? Which one?"

"You."

Smiling like a cat that just raided the goldfish bowl, Pearl breaks her orange in two and hands half to Birdie.

"What's his name?"

"I don't know."

"Is he the eldest Takeda son? Or a younger one?"

"I don't know."

"Can you find out?"

Birdie swallows her bite of orange.

"Of course." She grins.

Pearl nibbles thoughtfully. "Who do you suppose he'll ask for an introduction?"

"He's not allowed to. His father told him he can't come here."

"Funny thing for a father to say, especially while they're entertained by his mistress. Isn't it a wife's job to say that?"

"He doesn't have one."

"A wife, or a mistress?"

"A wife."

Pearl stops chewing.

"Are you sure?"

"My friend at the Peony said his father is always telling him he doesn't need a mistress until he has a wife."

Pearl's eyes narrow as she finishes her orange, no longer tasting it. She turns to Birdie.

"Listen to me," she says, with an intensity that's a little frightening. "Don't say a word about this to anyone, do you understand? Especially Auntie. I'm not interested in Jewel's pockmarked old cast-off. That boy is going to be my next patron, and if I play my cards right, he'll make me his wife too. But I'm going to need your help."

Birdie's been lurking just inside the Great Gate since Pearl yawned herself off to bed. The only way in or out of the pleasure quarter is past the gatekeeper who makes sure that no weapons or horses come in and no women go out.

Tall timbers with a stout crossbeam frame the portal that's nearly as busy in the morning as it is at night. But if the evening crowds are like a sumptuous brocade, those arriving now are the riot of colorful threads on the underside. Vegetable vendors, fishmongers, eel-grillers, oil fillers, noodle sellers, fortunetellers, and monks with their begging bowls all stream in through the gate, dodging hand-pulled carts piled high with rice, sake, and all the luxuries that keep Yoshiwara humming along like the city within a city it is.

But it's getting late, and still no sign of Takeda's son. Birdie's been watching since the line of weary samurai collecting their swords from the gatekeeper stretched down the block, but now the gatekeeper stands idle and the sun is topping the fire tower. Did she arrive too late? The

Takedas didn't sound like the kind of tight-fists who are out the teahouse door before the six o'clock bell, but you never know. She steps aside for a servant staggering past with his arms full of sweets boxes. Wishes one was for her. Pearl sent her out before the morning rice was ready, and there's probably none left by now.

A man in purple raises her hopes as he exits the Harvest Moon, but he's too old to be the Takeda son. A young man in a gray cloak rounds the corner and she's about to dismiss him when she sees his face. Those eyebrows.

She runs up, tugs his sleeve.

"*Ne, ne,* third son of Mitsu Sano the rice broker, remember me?" She deploys her dimple.

He looks down, startled.

"Sorry, little sister, I think you're mistaking me for someone else. I'm not the third son of Mitsu Sano the rice broker, I'm the eldest son of Takahisa Takeda, and our clan deals in timber."

"But you look just like him," she insists. "Isn't your name Tadayoshi?"

"No." He laughs. "It's Kiyohisa."

"Oh no." She claps a hand over her mouth, eyes wide. "White Pearl will be so mad if she finds out I made such a fool of myself. You won't tell her, will you?"

"Of course, I—White Pearl? The oiran? Do you know her, little sister? Do you live at the—Wait!"

But she's already skipping down the street, mission accomplished. She has pilfered his name and birth order as deftly as any pickpocket and also managed to remind him of the woman he wants, but was told he can't have.

She can't deliver her report until Pearl wakes up, so she's practicing her calligraphy in the room next door when their head manservant marches Jester down the hall to Auntie's office.

"This bum can't pay his bill. When I went to collect this morning, his three friends were gone, and all he had on him was this."

Coins slap onto the table.

"Three *ryō*, one *bu,* and six *mon,*" Auntie counts. "How much is his bill?"

"Fourteen *ryō*, two *bu.*"

Birdie winces, even though she isn't sorry she decided not to tell Auntie what she'd learned from Tiger this morning. Last night's damage was already done, and in Yoshiwara, the bearer of bad news is seldom rewarded for it.

Auntie lets out a windy sigh.

"Where are your friends? Tell us where they work, and I'll send our man to collect from them."

"Well," Jester waffles, "there are so many kinds of friends, aren't there? Friends you've known since childhood, friends who will give you a loan, friends you just met while drinking in Yoshiwara..."

"Let me guess." Auntie sees where this is going. "Those were the kind of friends you just met while drinking in Yoshiwara."

"Yes."

"And you don't know their family names."

"No."

"Or what they do for a living."

"No. One of them writes poetry," he offers helpfully. "Although, judging from the verses he recited last night, that may be more of a hobby."

"I have no use for hobby poets!" Auntie thunders. "There's only one poet in all of Yoshiwara who can afford to spend fourteen *ryō* at a pleasure house, and that wasn't him. You realize you're giving me no choice, don't you? I'm going to have to send our collection agent to your family for the money. I hope for your sake they haven't disinherited you."

"Of course not. Not last I heard, anyway."

"Good. Where can I find them?"

"Aomori."

"*Aomori?* Goro-san, go fetch the constable."

"Wait!" Jester yelps. "If you turn me over to the police, you'll never get your money."

"At least you'll never drink in Yoshiwara again."

"Can't you just lock me in your debtor room instead?" he wheedles. "That way, you can see for yourself that I'm not enjoying my disgrace, not one bit."

Birdie nearly bursts out laughing. What an outrageous request!

"The debtor room is only for making sure grifters don't run off before someone comes to bail them out," Auntie replies with scorn. "And it doesn't sound like anyone is coming to bail you out."

"That's true," he concedes. "And I'm sorry about that, I really am. But," he adds in a cheerier voice, "maybe I could bail myself out."

"How are you going to bail yourself out if you're locked inside a pleasure house?"

"I'm really a very useful guy to have around. You'll see."

"What can you do?"

"I can teach your courtesans how to play 'A Stranger in Yoshiwara,' with the original words *and* the latest Yoshiwara verses."

"My girls don't need to learn street tunes with vulgar lyrics!"

"Well," he says, "you may be right. On the other hand, have you noticed how busy those teahouses next to the geisha street have become? The girls there play all the popular songs. In fact, that's how they become popular."

"That may be true," Auntie sniffs. "But the kind of patrons we attract at the House of Treasures have no interest in such unseemly performances."

"Could be, could be," he murmurs in a conciliatory way. "But you might be surprised. I heard Utamaro is featuring geisha in his next 'Famous Beauties' series."

"*What?*"

It's like Auntie sat on a tack. For months, she's been wearing out her *geta*, making the rounds of everyone she knows in Yoshiwara, dropping hints that Pearl would say yes if the famous woodblock artist needed another oiran to model for his popular prints.

She fumes in silence, but at last she grudgingly agrees.

"If you don't prove to be as useful as you say," she warns, "you can look forward to being paraded down Center Street wearing nothing but a barrel."

"Hee-hee!" Jester rubs his hands together with glee. "You won't regret it, Manager-san. Soon you'll be wondering how you ever got along without me."

Birdie stifles a giggle, imagining the fool's face he's certainly making right now as Auntie shoos him from her room, scolding him for wasting so much of her precious time. Jester dances a jig all the way down the hall, and Goro follows, trying not to laugh.

"Your meals will be added to your debt!" Auntie calls after him.

Takeda calls for more sake as Jewel empties the last drops into Masatoki Koga's cup, filling it for the umpteenth time and prattling on about the witless things courtesans care about. When the wisteria will bloom. The latest tunes. And does Koga-san plan to see the new kabuki play about the forty-seven *rōnin*?

Takeda knows this kind of tiresome chitchat is necessary to soften Koga up for the information she'll extract from him later, so he allows her to babble on while he absently rubs a sore spot on his thigh and mulls over the placement of the rocks in the garden he's building at his Takebashi house.

But as Koga suppresses a yawn, Takeda's attention snaps back. Isn't it high time his oiran got around to doing what he'd asked of her? He'd made it quite clear tonight that he expects her to do more than merely help them make it through the evening without revealing how much he and Koga loathe each other.

The second time he showed up at Koga's office in Edo Castle, he wore the carp-and-waterfall *inrō* with its octopus *netsuke*, and the city administrator had reluctantly agreed that it would be better if they were only seen together in Yoshiwara, where nobody would guess it had once belonged to him. But he's never been comfortable here and insists on wearing one of the deep-brimmed straw hats that nervous first-timers rent to hide their faces while violating the shōgun's edict against wasting their stipends on courtesans. The hat vendors laugh up their sleeves and take his money, knowing full well his secret would be perfectly safe without skulking around in silly headgear. It apparently hasn't occurred to him that nobody dares gossip about who they saw in Yoshiwara, because that would reveal the tattler is guilty too.

Takeda clears his throat, hinting that it's time to get down to business, now that Koga's discomfort has been dulled by enough sake. But his oiran takes no notice. Then he remembers she'd suggested he leave the room while she probes Koga for the information, so he'll be less wary of letting something sensitive slip. He staggers to his feet, excusing himself to "drain the dragon."

But the privy will have to wait until he hears what's said once he's gone. He flattens himself against the wall just outside, holding a finger to his lips to silence the maid who appears with sake for the party next door. What he hears next, however, is not at all what he's expecting.

Instead of using her wiles, Jewel blurts, "He wants me to ask you about the night of the Great Meiwa Fire."

"What?" Koga yelps. "Why now, after all these years?"

"I don't know. What do you want me to tell him?"

"Nothing! Isn't that what I pay you for?"

"You do. And I have no intention of breaking my word. But I have to tell him something. He knows there was a woman. Wants to know who she was."

"Who told him?"

"It wasn't anyone from the Peony. What do you want me to say?"

"Why are you asking me?" Koga sputters. "You're supposed to be good at this. Think of something!"

"Like what? That she was a courtesan?"

"No. We don't want him to connect her to Yoshiwara in any way. I can't be sure some old-timer won't remember seeing her here. Tell him . . . tell him she's dead. If he pushes, say I barely knew her, she meant nothing to me, end of story."

"All right. I'll try to find some way to make that sound like the truth."

Out in the hall, Takeda is seething. The two-faced whore! How dare she conspire against him?

"Here," she says to Koga. "Drink this."

Now she's pouring him more sake? Sake *he's* paying for?

"Thank you. Any chance we can wrap this up soon? I've had about all I can take for one night and I feel a headache coming on."

Takeda spins around and stalks to the privy. He manages to make it there without punching a hole in the teahouse wall, staying long enough to rein in his fury before he returns. But he can't stomach Koga's presence for one more minute.

"I'm sorry, I'm feeling a little indisposed," he announces with false regret, and Koga extends equally false wishes for a speedy recovery.

Performing his role as gracious host in front of the teahouse staff, Takeda bows his guest out the front door, then tromps back up the stairs, fuming. That cow of an oiran didn't just fail to help, she's planning to lie to him. Stupid woman. Stupid, stupid woman.

Jewel and her attendants fall silent as he fills the doorway, jaw clenched. What had he done to deserve such trickery?

She dismisses her women and leads him upstairs, nattering away as if she hasn't noticed how angry he is. He manages to keep his rage bottled until they're alone in the room where her bedding has been laid out, but the moment the door slides shut behind them, he grabs her by the arm.

"You idiot!" he growls, hauling her toward him.

"No!" She twists, wrenching her arm from his grasp. "Not tonight."

His eyes bulge. First, she betrays him, and now she defies him?

"I must regrettably inform the honorable Takeda-san that I have accepted an offer of marriage," she announces, drawing herself up to her full height. "Our long and mutually beneficial relationship must come to an end."

What? End? *Marriage?*

"On the twenty-sixth day of this month, I will be retiring from Yoshiwara. This will be our final night together."

Their final—? Wait, he's her patron. They have a contract. It's not even the end of the month yet! Doesn't he deserve more notice than this? She can't just—

She bows, with the kind of finality designed to silence objection.

He stands there for a moment, blinking. How dare she dump him before giving him the chance to dump her? He raises his hand to give her a taste of his outrage, but instead of flinching, she looks him in the eye.

"I'd think twice about that if I were you," she warns. "It would be a shame if I were to have any bruises tomorrow. My future husband would deserve to know the truth, and he's not a forgiving man."

She dares to threaten him? Takeda's nostrils flare like a maddened bull, fists clenching and unclenching. He's itching to teach her one last lesson, but he's been outmaneuvered. Now that she no longer needs his financial support, she has no reason to cover up what he does to her in private.

There's more than one way to exact punishment, though. A contract is a contract, and she can't escape this last night together. He'll make sure it's one she won't forget. He pushes her down onto the futon, welcoming the surge of anger that so often runs hand in hand with desire. Come on, woman, resist. Fight back. Add a little spice to the proceedings, for once.

But she doesn't. Just lies there, eyes fixed on the ceiling. Makes no move to untie her sash or part her many layers of kimonos.

Fine. Unwrapping her will only increase his desire. He rips at the layers like a burrowing animal, pushes her legs apart, hikes up his robe. But Jewel lies there as limp and lifeless as a puppet with its strings cut, and tonight his fury is not his friend. His anger turns to frustration, and when it finally becomes clear that nothing will revive his manhood enough to achieve satisfaction, he rocks back on his heels, cursing her. Scarlet with shame, he girds himself back up in silence, and without a single parting word, throws on his jacket and stalks to the teahouse exit.

With a terse excuse to the mistress, he escapes into the cold night air. Stands on the street outside, vibrating with unspent energy. Even the drunkest passersby give him a wide berth, sensing it would be a mistake to jostle an ugly man who's not having as good a time in the pleasure quarter as he expected.

He lurches toward the moat. It's the only place in Yoshiwara where he won't run into anyone he knows. Snatches of music and conversation escape from the lighted doorways of the increasingly shabby teahouses he passes, but he's deaf to their promises of earthly delights. It's not until he turns onto the lane lined with the disreputable buildings that house the most disreputable of women that he feels a stirring in his loins. His steps quicken. The best way to wash away the bitter taste of Jewel's betrayal is to spend the rest of the night with a woman who will refuse him nothing.

Birdie's basket feels heavier than usual this morning. Two more stops, then she and Flower can duck into the shrine garden to eat the extra rice cakes she wheedled from the seller.

"Why don't you pick up Pearl's new combs," Birdie suggests, to avoid the errand that's dangerously close to the street where Dolly lives, "and I'll fetch Butterfly's face powder. We can meet at the shrine afterward to eat our rice cakes."

They finish their errands in record time and are soon stepping through the shrine's gate arm in arm, looking forward to that first starchy-sweet bite in the shade of the giant pine.

But it's not to be. They hear Mosquito's sing-songy voice before they see her. "Tiger doesn't have a dad, that's 'cuz he was born bad . . ."

The lanky child attendant from the House of Wisteria is standing head and shoulders above a cluster of girls giggling into their sleeves on the far side of the pond. Mosquito's real name is Firefly, and she has never forgiven Tiger for bestowing the nickname that was far too perfect not to have stuck.

The scowling target of her taunts is chucking pebbles at the carp from the stone bridge and studiously ignoring her.

"Hey, Tiger!" Birdie waves. Digging deep into her sleeve, she calls, "Brought you something." He obviously needs a rice cake more than she does this morning.

"Thanks," he says, catching it with both hands. Emboldened by reinforcements, he cups his hands around his mouth to retort, "Mosquito, mosquito, can't hurt me, you suck blood but I sting like a—"

"Watch out!" Flower cries, pointing to the big pine. "Move!"

Then everything happens at once. A crow lands on the branch above Mosquito's head, flicks its tail, a white glop plummets. She shrieks, scrabbling frantically at her hair ornament, ripping it from her head. Flinging it to the ground, she claws at the mess in her hair, then looks daggers at Flower.

"You!"

Snatching up the defiled ornament by one long string of wisteria blossoms, she runs toward the bridge and whips it at Flower. It hits her front and center, leaving a smear on her kimono before bouncing to the ground.

Birdie steps in front of her twin.

"Leave her alone."

"My new hair ornament is ruined!" Mosquito shrieks, feinting right, left, trying to get past her. "And it's all her fault!"

"No, it's not. It's just bad luck." Birdie scoffs. "No one can control where birds poop."

"She can!" Mosquito points a shaking finger. "And it's not the first time. Today we all heard her, though, didn't we?" She turns to the others. "This time we'll make Poop Girl pay!"

"Poop Girl! Poop Girl!" her followers begin to chant.

"Ignore them." Birdie takes Flower's arm, propelling her toward the gate. "Come on."

Then from behind, an angry, "Ow!"

She looks back to see Tiger chucking pine cones at the advancing girl gang.

"Run!" he cries.

They do. Kimonos hiked to their knees, they flee. Across the grounds, out the gate, down the alley. No one follows, but the possibility chases them all the way to the weedy no-man's-land behind the House of Peonies.

"Thank you." Flower doubles over, panting. "For saving me."

"It was Tiger." *Huff, huff,* "Thank Tiger." Birdie swallows, catching her breath. "Did you and Mosquito have a fight, or something?"

"No, but—" Flower's eyes slide away. "Remember last summer, when Auntie told us to stop using shortcuts between buildings because a girl got bit by a centipede and her arm swelled up like a giant radish and she almost died?"

"That was *her*?"

Flower nods.

"I tried to warn her because I knew something bad would happen if she went in there, but—"

"Went in where?"

"The gap behind the old well."

Birdie knows it. You wouldn't catch her setting foot in that den of creepy crawlies for ten thousand *ryō*.

"I'd call that a win, wouldn't you?" Tiger slaps to a halt, then saunters toward them, raising his arms like a sumo wrestler acknowledging the cheers of an adoring crowd.

"Thank you for saving me," says Flower.

"Tiger! Where on earth have you been?" the Peonies' manager calls from the back stoop of the pleasure house. She obviously expected him back some time ago.

"Sorry, gotta go." He grins.

"See you later," Birdie calls after him, but gets only a fart in reply.

She returns her attention to Flower and the bird filth crusting the front of her robe. Depending on Auntie's mood, soiling a House of Treasures kimono is at least a going-without-supper offense. If the stain is permanent, Auntie might even dust the cobwebs from the bamboo cane that hasn't been used since they came to the House of Treasures, but is left propped by the back door to remind them it could be.

"I shouldn't have tried to warn them," Flower says sadly.

"We'll tell Auntie it was an accident. That you were standing beneath that branch, not Mosquito."

"What if the Wisteria's manager tells her what really happened?"

That could be a problem. Mosquito will certainly try to shift the blame for ruining an expensive hair ornament, and if she convinces her manager that Flower was responsible, the House of Wisteria might try to recoup the cost from the House of Treasures.

"Okay, then switch kimonos with me," Birdie suggests. As always, they're dressed alike. "I'll tell her Mosquito threw the hair ornament at me, because I stood up to her insults. If you save me half your rice at dinnertime, neither of us will go to bed hungry."

"But . . ." Flower bites her lip. ". . . we'll have to do it for twice as long."

That's unfortunately true. The punishment will be harsher if Birdie is involved. Auntie agrees with the shōgun that civilized society will go belly-up if the lowly are allowed to question the judgment of their superiors, and because Birdie can seldom resist trying to talk her way out of a scrape, Auntie punishes her twice as hard as a matter of principle. One penalty for the offense, another for not knowing her place.

"It's better if I take the blame and leave you out of it," Flower says.

They trudge back to the Pearl, and Birdie stands by silently as Flower stubbornly sticks to the story that Mosquito threw the bird-slimed ornament at her for no reason. She's sent to bed without supper, but Birdie wraps half of her rice in her handkerchief as promised, along with a handful of pickles from the briefly unguarded crock in the kitchen, so neither of them falls asleep with an empty belly.

But when she wakes up the next morning, the silly suspicion that troubled her sleep has grown into a question that demands an answer. She does her errands in record time, so she can knock at the back door of the Peony on her way home. Beckoning Tiger down the alley where they won't be overheard, she divides the square of sweet bean jam she'd finagled at the sweets shop, offering him half.

"Yesterday," she says, "that business with Mosquito and the bird poop. You saw the whole thing, right?"

"Mmgf," Tiger replies, his mouth full of bean jam.

"At first, I thought Flower just saw that crow coming before anyone else." She hesitates. "But why warn them a bird is coming, even if it's headed straight toward the tree they're standing under? Birds land in trees all the time. And seeing a crow fly toward them is one thing, but knowing it's going to sit on that exact branch and take a poop the very next second is—" She swallows, her throat suddenly dry. "Do you think she *knew*?"

Tiger tosses the last bite of bean candy into his mouth, eyeing Birdie's half, still in her hand, untasted. She hands it over.

"I think"—he takes a bite—"it's not hard to guess where birds like to roost. And what they do when they get there."

He nods toward the overhang shading the back door of the Peony, where the usual clutch of pigeons is perching. The ground below is white with spatters.

"Oh." Why didn't she think of that? Now she's sorry she gave up her bean jam.

"Tiger!" The manager of the Peony appears at the back door, hands on her hips, a murderous look on her face.

He rolls his eyes, heads back inside to finish shirking his chores.

On the way home, Birdie hesitates at the entrance to the shrine. Just to be sure, she makes her way to the pond to check the spot under the pine where the girls were standing.

There's not a speck of white on the ground. Anywhere.

When Birdie gets back from her errand the next morning, Takahisa Takeda's son is standing across the street, gazing at the House of Treasures. Again. She's seen him so often since the night he was forbidden to come here, they now exchange small bows of recognition.

When he begins to stroll past the Treasure more than twice a day, Pearl suggests Birdie allow herself to be recruited as a go-between. His fervent and slightly embarrassing poems to Pearl go unanswered, but after he figures it out and sends one wrapped around an expensive tortoiseshell comb, Birdie whispers that it might be worth his while to be outside the fruit seller tomorrow afternoon.

"We're going to look at the new season's fans," Pearl tells Auntie, but they go by the way of the fruit seller, which is not really on the way at all. They don't arrive until late in the afternoon—it never pays to look too eager—but she was right to gamble that Kiyohisa would still be standing there in his purple kimono. His eyes follow her like a devoted dog. A first-rank oiran like Pearl never stops to talk to a man on the street, especially a man who lacks a formal introduction. But as they pass Kiyohisa, she flicks him a glance and casts a fleeting smile his way.

The next day, a love letter as long as Birdie's arm is pressed into her hands, along with an extravagant hair ornament dripping strings of coral beads.

That night is Goldbelly's regularly scheduled evening. As the Treasures' procession approaches the Nightingale, Birdie checks the Camellia's balcony and marks both Takedas present. The son's adoring eyes are glued to Pearl all the way up the street. When they're almost there, his face lights up and he clasps his hands over his heart as if shot right through it. She must have given him another smile.

Then Birdie goes cold, right down to her toes. The elder Takeda is also watching Pearl, but no one could mistake his expression for love.

"I'm going to need everyone's help tonight," Pearl announces, as they tidy themselves in the Nightingale's dressing room. "Goldbelly sent word that his guests will be two brothers from Nagasaki, and he wants us to make a special effort to show them a good time, even though they aren't like the men we usually entertain."

"Which means," Feather snipes to Butterfly behind her fan, "they either chew with their mouths open or smell to high heaven."

She's wrong on both counts, but Birdie still has to poke Flower to remind her not to stare at the man who runs the Dutch trading ship auctions and the doctor describing a new gout remedy to Goldbelly. Because they're not Japanese.

They're not the orange-haired, furry-faced brutes depicted in the woodblock prints at the newsstand either. They don't feed themselves with crude knives and pronged implements, they're deftly plucking sashimi from the tray with chopsticks while debating the merits of amberjack versus bonito in politely elegant Japanese. Their silk robes are stylish, scented with cloves and sandalwood, their topknots dark and freshly oiled. The auction master has a neatly groomed goatee like Pearl's preferred apothecary and the doctor's clean-shaven skin is so pale it looks like he spends all his time with his patrician-looking nose in his books. It's only their eyes that are odd, the color of half-dried moss, and so round, they look perpetually astonished.

At the moment, however, their amazement might be real. If there's one thing Pearl excels at, it's making an entrance.

"Vandermeer-sensei has been in the shōgun's service for several months," Goldbelly confides with a twinkle, as she sinks into position at his side. "But this is the first time he's met a real Edo oiran. I've warned him that even the loveliest ladies in Nagasaki can't hope to dazzle him after spending an evening in your company. I'm counting on you to prove me right."

Pearl rises to the occasion, even though the brothers' Nagasaki accents are so thick she sometimes has to pretend they said something naughty, instead of something she didn't understand.

When the sake has been flowing long enough for personal questions, she asks the doctor, "Are you enjoying life at the castle?"

"It's not as bad as I thought it would be."

"You didn't want to move to Edo?" How could anyone not jump at the chance to move to the capital?

"You wouldn't either," he replies, "if it meant spending your days translating treatises on venereal disease and teaching the shōgun which end of a telescope to look through, instead of doing something meaningful."

"Such as . . . ?"

"The research I was doing with my father, back in Nagasaki. We've been using Dutch scientific methods to isolate the compounds that make Japanese herbal remedies so effective."

"My goodness," Pearl exclaims. "How did a Dutch doctor become learned in herbal lore?"

"He's not. That's my mother's specialty."

"Even more impressive. How did a foreign woman learn the secrets of Japanese medicine?"

"She's not Dutch." He sips his drink. "She grew up in Nagasaki."

You could have heard a mouse fart.

"Your mother is *Japanese*?" Pearl blurts.

"Yes."

"But how is that . . . ?"

"Possible?" He gives a short laugh. "Dutchmen aren't allowed to leave Dejima Island, but Japanese travel freely back and forth every day. He met my mother when she came to treat the Japanese staff during an influenza outbreak that his medicine couldn't cure. Their marriage was opposed by both sides, but Mother's family made peace with it once he agreed that any children be raised at the family compound in Nagasaki."

"And that's what makes my friend such a rare and valuable asset to the shōgun," Goldbelly boasts on the doctor's behalf. "He and his brothers grew up speaking both Dutch and Japanese. His Excellency has been trying to persuade him to move to Edo for years, and refused to give up, no matter how many times Vandermeer-sensei refused."

"What changed your mind?" Pearl asks, pouring more sake.

Vandermeer's brother guffaws. "He finally figured out he was trying to tempt the wrong man and made our father an offer instead."

"And that was . . . ?"

"If I came to Edo to be his Dutch Learning Expert . . ." Vandermeer sighs. ". . . he'd give me access to everything the investigators learned about our eldest brother's death. If there's one thing Father wants to find even more the cure for scurvy, it's the truth about what happened to Ichiro on the night of the Great Meiwa Fire."

"Your brother died in that fire?" Pearl shivers. "I was just a child, but I remember that day as if it were yesterday. The wind drove the flames through the city faster than a man could run."

"Ichiro didn't die running," Vandermeer says, his face grim. "And the fire didn't kill him."

"But if he didn't die in the fire . . . ?"

"Someone ran him through with a very sharp sword on a street that the fire spared. His killer was never caught." The doctor tosses back his sake. "I vowed I wouldn't return to Nagasaki until I find out who murdered my brother and see him punished."

Takeda ambles along the street lined with pleasure houses, stopping now and then to peer through the elegant lattices at the rows of women waiting to be chosen. Plump ones, skinny ones, lively ones, shy ones. Women with pouty lips and bored eyes, women with knowing glances. Too bad he can't allow himself to be tempted by any of them. Once a man is known as an oiran-level patron, no manager in her right mind would let him be entertained by a courtesan of lesser rank. The last thing he needs is to be tricked into a relationship with another expensive empty-head who will fail to meet his needs. He'll be far more careful when choosing his next one.

Strolling on to the next viewing room, he wonders—not for the first time—if one of the ladies inside could be the woman Koga brought to Yoshiwara on the night of the fire. He still doesn't know if she was a courtesan or not, only that Koga fears some old-timer might remember seeing her here. It's the only true thing Koga said on the night Jewel betrayed him.

It wasn't until Takeda had replayed the memory of that evening enough times to relieve it of its sting that he finally saw the pearls of truth Koga's wave of deception had left behind. He'd implored Jewel to lead Takeda astray, so everything he told her to say must be a lie.

Which means the opposite is true. The woman Koga brought to Yoshiwara the night of the fire is not dead. And she means so much to him that the mere possibility someone will learn her name throws him into a panic. Why is he so desperate to keep her identity a secret?

If she was a courtesan, she had no business outside the walled pleasure quarter, especially on the street where the *hatamoto* keep their lawful wives and children. But even if she was Koga's woman on the side, her presence so close to his family compound wouldn't be worth killing over. Everyone would be more surprised if a senior official like him *didn't* have a mistress. Which suggests she wasn't a courtesan. What if she's the wife or daughter of a *hatamoto*? Could Koga be protecting her from a father or a husband who must never learn she was involved in a foreigner's murder? Or maybe he's protecting *them*. Their honor and official appointments would be called into question if her involvement in a crime so sordid comes to light, and they might be willing to pay for his continued discretion.

Takeda needs the money. He always needs money. When he was poor, he had no idea how much good fortune costs, but the more he expands the Takeda empire, the more it costs to expand. He's dreading his next meeting with the shipowner, because the man's thirst for growth is still outpacing Takeda's ability to invest. Unless he finds a new source of funds, his partner will look elsewhere. Finding Koga's woman might very well provide the means to satisfy his partner's ambitions.

He looks up to find that his feet have carried him to the street by the moat. What better place to start looking for the "old-timers" Koga is so afraid of? He orders a bowl of buckwheat noodles from the soup vendor, studying the knots of men slurping at their own steaming bowls while they decide what—or who—to have for their next course. Who might remember the woman Koga brought here the night of the fire?

But his gaze soon shifts to the down-at-heels pleasure houses across the street. Yoshiwara is teeming with men, but few live here. A woman would be a better bet. Koga is bribing the Peony's staff not to tell, but what about someone who was there twelve years ago and has come down in the world? Any courtesan who'd been working at the time of the Great Meiwa Fire would be at least thirty now, and if she's still in Yoshiwara, her contract would have been sold again and again to lesser pleasure houses as her charms waned. Such a woman might no longer bear much loyalty to the House of Peonies. Or its secrets.

He strolls past the shabby pleasure houses lining the street, still doing a brisk business despite the hour. Their viewing rooms are nearly empty, only their most jaded courtesans still on offer. Fortunately, those are exactly the kind of women he's looking for. When he stops to enquire, though, none of the leftovers in the first three lattice rooms started out at the Peony. He moves on. One of the two woman sitting in lonely splendor in the Golden Drum's lattice room is far too young, but the other might very well have been in Yoshiwara twelve years ago. Her powder has settled into the lines around her eyes and she's bravely trying to look unashamed that she's so publicly unchosen. He studies her through the bars. She has fallen about as low as any courtesan can fall, yet her makeup is applied with care and she holds herself like someone who believes in her own worth, even if no one else does. He parts the curtain and goes inside.

"Excuse me," he says to the manager. "That woman in the corner—might she be someone I used to visit at the House of Peonies?"

"You have a good eye, sir," the manager smarms. "Willow is indeed a top-quality courtesan, trained by the Peonies' first-rank oiran."

Willow. That name rings a bell. The Peonies' junior courtesans still use "Poor Willow" as shorthand for some foolish courtesan who was dismissed for a reason that was memorably cautionary. Was it so cautionary that she might have little loyalty left for the house that chucked her out?

". . . be pleased to offer a man of your discernment a discount, on account of the late hour."

"I'm afraid I have pressing business elsewhere tonight," he demurs, with an unexpected stab of pity for the woman who's being offered for a cut rate behind her back. "I'll come back another time."

And when he does, he'll have his questions ready. He'll come early and pay full price. Choose her in front of the more popular women who are still trying to charm one of their uncouth admirers into paying for a few hours of their time. He'd been nobody's choice often enough to know that "Poor Willow" is much more likely to tell him what he wants to know if he plies her with sweet rice than if he pelts her with sour plums.

Pearl is barely back from her morning bath when Birdie hands her another impassioned missive from the Takeda son.

"Already?" She laughs. It's barely past noon, but this is the third one today. The oiran glances at the poem, drops it atop the others.

Indifference makes men's hearts grow fonder, and right now, she has an outfit to fret over. Jewel's marriage is now just ten days away, and men are crowding into the pleasure quarter every evening to ogle the oiran processions as the competition to attract her soon-to-be ex-patrons heats up. Pearl knows that owning a woman all men desire is the one sure way to drive a young man beyond mad infatuation to true commitment. If she becomes Yoshiwara's number one oiran, Kiyohisa Takeda will be hers.

Yesterday, the Peonies' number two oiran sallied forth in a frankly suggestive crimson-and-gold peony theme, so today Pearl chooses to clothe herself and her attendants in stylishly simple silver and blue.

It's a great success. Everyone agrees her cherry-blossoms-by-moonlight ensembles made the Peonies' Number Two look gaudy and overeager. The next day, the House of Bamboo and the House of Coral's oirans follow Pearl's lead, aiming for elegant understatement, but are dismissed as boring when everyone sees Pearl's next display, which turns her entourage into a cloud of dreamy, fluttering, cherry petals.

But all of this is mere jockeying for position before the event that could boost one oiran so far past her rivals, she'll have her pick of Jewel's ex-patrons. Lord Oda's moon-viewing party.

Every player in Yoshiwara is on the *daimyō's* guest list, and they've been invited to bring their oirans to share any talents that might amuse the great and good. It's not just a chance for the oirans to look pretty, it's a rare opportunity to display the accomplishments that are usually performed only for their patrons in the privacy of upstairs banquet rooms.

Birdie keeps her ears open at the tobacconist, the newsstand, and the apothecary, and reports that the House of Pines' oiran plans to demonstrate her skills on the *koto*, the Bamboo's will dance, the Wisteria's will play a hand drum and sing. Jewel from the House of Peonies has decided to make her final Yoshiwara appearance as the leader of the forty-seven *rōnin* in a skit casting her attendants as the famous warriors, armed with fans and sake flasks in place of swords. Tiger has been in a foul mood all week because everyone thinks it would be hilarious if he plays the one female role, and he hasn't managed to weasel out of it yet.

Now that Pearl knows how her rivals intend to impress, she decides to shine at the most challenging entertainment of all—the game in which cups of sake are floated down the garden's winding stream and the contestants lining the banks must compose a poem on the spot or drink the sake as forfeit. Few oirans dare to match wits with the learned officials and ambitious samurai who will be vying to outdo each other, but Pearl is clever. She's confident she can come up with verses that will be original enough to garner whoops of admiration, but not so brilliant they outshine the men she wishes to charm. The night's topic won't be announced until everyone is seated with paper in hand and brushes poised, but the fact that this is a moon-viewing party makes it worth her while to have several prewritten.

She adds one about the moon playing hide-and-seek with the clouds on the morning of the party, because rain is pattering on the roofs of Edo as the day dawns. The Yoshiwara shrine rakes in triple its usual offerings as everyone who is counting on the party to boost their standing begs the gods to clear the skies by nightfall. Birdie lets Tiger join her in line, and they keep dry under her parasol until it's time to step up together to toss their coins, even though she's pretty sure their prayers will cancel each other out.

The gods, however, are feeling perverse, and grant both their wishes. The heavens clear, and the first stars are gleaming in the cobalt sky as Pearl's procession pauses at the Great Gate for the minister of granaries' manservant to show the gatekeeper their signed travel pass. Jewel and her entourage are right behind, but Tiger is not among them. Unwilling to put too much trust in the gods, he'd eaten a pile of unripe plums from the tree in the Peonies' garden and monopolized the privy for long enough that everyone agreed they'd better not risk making tonight's performance memorable in all the wrong ways.

Pearl and Jewel are the last oirans to arrive at the *daimyō's* sprawling compound. The noblemen and high-ranking samurai officials have been pouring each other sake for hours, and by now have mostly forgiven each other for not knowing their proper place.

Sliding doors dividing the rooms bordering the garden have been shifted aside to turn them into one wide pavilion, with superbly painted folding screens set up at one end as a backdrop for the night's entertainment. As they emerge into the garden, Birdie's breath catches at its sheer magnificence. The gardens at top teahouses in Yoshiwara are just as pretty, but this one is so huge she can't see where it ends. The pond is big enough to be called a lake, and a lantern-festooned boat filled with musicians is being poled from one end to the other, filling the air with the twanging of *shamisens* and the breathy sighs of a *shakuhachi* flute.

It won't be fully dark for another hour, but the moon rising above the island in the lake's center bathes the guests' faces in a flattering light as they cross the arching orange bridge that anchors it to the shore. While Pearl asks the whereabouts of her patron, Birdie spots two of Jewel's soon-to-be-exes among the men standing on the banks of the lake, pointing out the eighty-eight views from famous poems that the garden is famous for. The music grows louder as the boat swings into view and the players launch into a sprightly tune. Pearl and her attendants stop halfway across the bridge to admire the boat slipping beneath their feet. One of the *shamisen* players looks up, and Birdie jerks back from the railing, afraid it might be Lucky Doll. It's not, but her heart doesn't stop pounding until they've safely melted into the crowd on the other side, where everyone is gathering to admire the *daimyō's* new toy. A telescope.

Pearl charms her way through the scrum to pay her respects to their host, who is wearing a smug smile at the consternation on everyone's faces as his guests peer through the eyepiece. Tonight's poetry topic will be one they hadn't prepared for, and the traditional moon verses stashed in their sleeves won't do them a bit of good.

The minister of granaries is looking especially anxious, and he welcomes Pearl's arrival with palpable relief, beckoning her over to join him in line. He takes only a brief peek through the device before relinquishing the lens to the oiran he's counting on to save him from embarrassing himself in a contest that's going to be more challenging than he bargained for.

All eyes are on Pearl as she playfully examines the tube from both ends and takes a good long look at the rising moon through the eyepiece, then follows her patron over the bridge to where the poetic combatants are taking their places along the meandering stream. After settling the minister into his appointed spot, she steers Birdie to the *daimyō's* chamberlain, volunteering her to join the other child attendants stationed along the stream to nudge the floating sake cups toward the next contestant with their long sticks. Pearl whispers something in the chamberlain's ear that makes him smile, and he gives her a nearly imperceptible nod. Before taking her own place downstream, she pulls Birdie aside.

"I got you a post nearest the minister of granaries. When you get the note saying he's next in line for the sake cup, come tell me."

For the next hour, Birdie hovers behind Pearl's patron with her steering stick, and when the runner finally thrusts a paper into her hand, she trots it over to Pearl. The oiran slips her the poem she'd just dashed off, and Birdie delivers it to the minister.

But it's Pearl's turn first, and her verse expressing astonishment that the telescope brings the moon so close she can "see the pockmarks beneath its powdered face" is met with an outburst of appreciative hoots and whistles. They aren't as loud as those that greet her patron's, though. The verse she wrote for him answers hers with the moon looking through the other end of the device and remarking how even Yoshiwara becomes a flawless jewel when rendered small enough to fit inside its narrow tube.

Pearl glows, as surprised and delighted murmurs in response to the minister of granaries' poem reward more than the lines alone. Anybody who spends time in Yoshiwara appreciates that she just pulled off a feat that only truly great oirans can deliver. She made the dullest patron at the party look good in front of men he seldom impresses. Basking in her triumph, Pearl demurely diverts the praise to the granaries minister, with a sideways wink at her admirers for being worldly enough to appreciate her art.

Now that Birdie's job is done, she's idly watching Pearl's patron duck his head and blush under the undeserved praise, wondering how hard it would be to snaffle a moon cake from the trays being passed by the maids. Then the man sitting next to Pearl's patron turns to extend a stiff "well done," and the moon cakes are forgotten.

His ears are as pointy as a fox spirit's. Just like hers.

"... then he turned, and that's when I saw them," Birdie whispers excitedly.

"Saw what?" Flower squints up at her, still half asleep.

"His ears. They're pointy. Just like mine. Don't you think that means he's my father?"

Flower frowns.

"Think about it," Birdie argues. "How many men do we see in Yoshiwara every day? A hundred? A thousand? In all the time I've been here, I've never seen a man with ears like mine. Have you?"

"What's his name?"

"I don't know. I asked around, but he must not be a Yoshiwara regular, because none of the other child attendants recognized him. Do you think..." She hesitates. "Do you think the reason he never came looking for me is because he doesn't know I exist? My mother died when I was born, so if he never comes to Yoshiwara, maybe he doesn't know he has a daughter here."

Flower opens her mouth, then thinks better of it.

"What?" Birdie frowns.

"Just... don't get your hopes up."

Pfft. That's not what she wants to hear. She flops back on her futon, rolling over and pulling her covers up around her ears. Unlike Tiger, she never wasted time lying awake at night, dreaming of finding her father. But now that she's seen him, a longing that's lain dormant all these years is stirring.

It shouldn't be hard to find out his name, maybe even figure out a way to meet him. When he sees her face for the first time, will he sense their connection? Maybe even recognize her as his own?

•

By the time Birdie returns from her errands the next morning, Pearl is up and pacing and demanding to know what she overheard while she waited in line for *shamisen* strings, sleeping powder, and oranges.

Birdie is pleased to report that word of Pearl's triumph at the moon-viewing party is igniting the pleasure quarter like a spark on a thatched roof, and even some of her keenest rivals are admitting grudging admiration. No one who knows the minister of granaries believes for a moment he's capable of writing such an inventive poem about the telescope. His verse and Pearl's are being quoted as if they already enjoy a place among the classics, and no man who's shopping for an oiran will fail to hear that it was Pearl of the House of Treasures who made her patron look so good. By the end of the week, all of Yoshiwara is in agreement. Pearl has taken Jewel's place as the number one oiran.

When Birdie tells her, "I just heard Kiyohisa Takeda is announcing to anyone who will listen that the two of you are bound together by the red thread of fate," Pearl decides it's time to reel in her catch.

Birdie is dispatched to wait for him by the Great Gate, and when Kiyohisa appears, she whispers that Pearl will be waiting for him under the Yoshiwara Shrine's famous willow tree at the Hour of the Boar. When she returns, the oiran sends her out again for a double dose of Auntie's sleeping potion.

"Since when do you need herbs to help you sleep?" Oirans seldom get more than four hours a night.

"They're not for me, silly. I'm going to put them in the minister's sake after dinner so he won't wake up while we slip out."

"You don't think he'll notice?" Even Auntie complains of the taste.

"Yes, but he'll drink it anyway, after I tell him it's a secret aphrodisiac known only to first-rank oirans."

Sure enough, by the time Birdie tiptoes in to tell Pearl it's nearly the Hour of the Boar, her patron is snoring like a laborer. Thanks to the "aphrodisiac," he must have finished his business in record time, because

Pearl's hair is already smoothed and her sash retied. Birdie hands her a plain green outer robe to cover her kimono, and they shroud their faces in traveling veils. Slipping down the back stairs, a coin buys the silence of the doorman.

Kiyohisa is pacing before the willow when they arrive. It's dangerous for Pearl to meet him in such a public place, since he hasn't yet performed the ritual that will make him her official patron, so Birdie's job will be to stand watch while they're within the circle of trailing branches.

Pearl begs him to keep his voice down, but he soon forgets. He's so overwhelmed at meeting the object of his desire face to face that she has a hard time persuading him to express his passion in words, instead of acting on them. She talks him out of a love-crazed scheme to give up his inheritance and run away with her if his father refuses to allow him to become her patron. Makes him promise that he'll find a way for them to be together that doesn't ruin them both.

As they part, he vows that the next time she sees him, they'll be sharing the three ceremonial cups of sake that will officially join them as lovers before mounting the stairs at the Camellia.

When Birdie drags herself back from her errands the next morning, yawning, she's not surprised that Kiyohisa is absent from his customary spot. He doesn't appear the next day either. Or the next. If Pearl is worried, she doesn't show it. She takes her dance lessons, writes her letters, and orders new hairpins to replace those that broke or disappeared in the past month.

Finally, the day of Jewel's wedding arrives.

"What do you think she'll be wearing?" Flower asks, as she and Birdie eel their way through the spectators lining the procession route, wriggling their way to the front. "I hope she's dressed like a bride."

So does Birdie. Brides are scarce in Yoshiwara, so neither of them has ever seen one, except in the woodblock prints at the newsstand.

Bouncing with barely contained excitement, they crane their necks to catch the first glimpse of Jewel in all her splendor.

The junior courtesans wait closer to the Peony. They'd dashed out early, racing each other to the best spot from which to find fault with the wedding gifts, ready to agree amongst themselves that Jewel isn't as lucky as everyone says she is.

And Auntie watches the proceedings from a second-floor window that has a bird's-eye view of the Great Gate. The moment Jewel passes beneath, her former patrons will be free to choose a new oiran.

Three days after Jewel's departure, Auntie summons Pearl to her office and shuts the door. Word races through the House of Treasures: the first proposal from a prospective patron has arrived. It's quickly agreed that Flower will get in the least trouble if she's caught with her ear up to Auntie's door.

Birdie waits with the excited courtesans in the common room, but before Flower has a chance to deliver her report, Pearl pokes her head in to say, "Birdie, I need you."

As Birdie follows her down the hall, the oiran's erect back and rippling hem give nothing away. Did she get good news? Or bad? It's not until the door is safely shut behind them that Pearl abandons her serene façade and grabs Birdie's hands, whirling her accomplice around her sitting room with unbridled glee.

The go-between was working for Kiyohisa's family.

A fortuneteller is consulted, and Pearl's first formal meeting with her new patron is set for the seventh day of the Fifth Month. Birdie is beyond excited to hear it will be at the Camellia, just as the Takeda son promised. To hear Tiger tell it, it's as close to the Western Paradise as Yoshiwara gets.

"The Camellia's garden doesn't just have a pond, it's fed by a waterfall that's the tallest in Yoshiwara," he boasts to her, like he's some teahouse expert. "It's got five stone lanterns and two bridges. There's even a boat for poetry parties."

Birdie refuses to give him the satisfaction of being impressed—she has, after all, seen Lord Oda's garden and he hasn't—but secretly she can't wait to get her first look.

The days fly by in a flurry of preparations. Pearl decides she has nothing to wear and spends the better part of an afternoon wheedling her favorite kimono maker into pushing aside his other commissions to make her something new. There's a tempest over whether she's still obligated to meet the minister of granaries on his usual night, but she loses that one.

In fact, her company has never been in higher demand. Pearl goes through the motions, but Birdie doesn't blame her for not expending any more effort than necessary to get through the evening. Why should she work hard at cultivating men she doesn't care about, now that she's so close to capturing the Takeda prince and living happily ever after?

The fact that Kiyohisa will soon be her patron is, of course, still a secret. No pleasure house in the midst of such delicate negotiations will risk jinxing it by letting the news slip before they've sipped the three cups of sake together and sealed the deal. Birdie hasn't even told Tiger.

Still, insiders can guess who's committing where, and rumors are flying. All Yoshiwara is eager to hear where Jewel's big spenders will land, and everyone is keeping an eye on the futon shop because a luxurious set of bedding is the traditional first gift sent by a patron to his new oiran. It's not long before word spreads that a coverlet of blue silk woven in a four-diamond pattern—which just happens to resemble the Takeda crest—is being embroidered with a scattering of white pearls.

The day of their First Meeting dawns glum and humid, but Pearl's fortuneteller pronounces the unpleasantly muggy weather an excellent omen for a warm relationship with her new patron. Birdie and Flower roll their eyes behind Pearl's back. A typhoon could be blowing the roof off, and this seer would find a way to tell Pearl exactly what she wants to hear.

But even the oppressive weather can't spoil Pearl's good mood. She doesn't make a single complaint as the hairdresser tugs a comb loaded with sticky pomade through her hair, and her smile glazes only slightly as the ornaments are pushed in, eight golden hairpins fanning around her face like a crown.

Pearl tucks her plain white hip wrap tight, then stands there, glowing with anticipation as layer upon silky layer is draped on her slender frame. One crimson and three golden underrobes, a purple one with a folded crane design, and finally, the new scarlet kimono embroidered with flying cranes. They're trussed in place and topped with a heavy gold brocade obi that cascades from Pearl's breast to her blushing toenails. She moves to the mirror to tuck in her fan, then raises her arms for Feather and Peach to lift the padded outer robe onto her shoulders, the one embroidered with a gold dragon flying through silver clouds.

She looks so radiant as she makes her way to the Camellia, even jaded Yoshiwara natives pause their conversations to watch her pass. She's too much of a professional to reveal her eagerness, but Birdie notices they make it to Teahouse Street a lot faster than usual. The lanterns aren't even lit yet, but it doesn't matter that they're unfashionably early. Her new patron has been waiting for hours, eating and drinking with his friends.

Birdie hates to admit it, but Tiger was right. The Camellia *is* nice. Better than nice. Even the dressing room has an elegant arrangement of flowering branches in its *tokonoma* alcove, and a seasonal scroll hanging above it.

But Pearl barely has time to smoke her first pipe before a manservant appears to usher them to the banquet room. Her new patron has heard she's here and can't wait another moment.

Up the stairs and down a wide corridor that's plastered in soothing green and punctuated with niches framing flowers and poems, Birdie's heart flutters with anticipation as the manservant slides open the door to announce their arrival. A hush falls.

Birdie steps through the door with Flower, then stumbles to a halt, her eyes saucering.

The pockmarked Takeda father is sitting in the patron's seat, a cruel smile on his face.

Is this some kind of joke? Where's Kiyohisa? Birdie's eyes rake the company, but she doesn't spot Takeda's son until he raises his head to throw back another cup of sake. He's slumped over his flask, unable to meet the eyes of the oiran he has been denied in the most crushing way possible.

Birdie stands aside, biting her lip while the rest of the procession files in. Pearl glides toward her place with an expressionless calm that might deceive someone who doesn't know her, but the moment she spots who's sitting in the patron's seat, Birdie can feel the rage ignite behind her eyes.

It's lucky no one expects an oiran to acknowledge her new patron at a First Meeting. Tea is poured; conversation resumes. Pearl sits amid her attendants across the room from Takeda, ignoring his smug glances.

In time, Birdie's stomach unclenches. This storm won't break until after they leave the Camellia. Any hope of putting a stop to this farce will depend on Pearl's position as the top oiran in Edo, and making a scene at the pleasure quarter's most elegant teahouse would topple her from that pedestal so fast, it would become the stuff of Yoshiwara legend.

The moment they cross the threshold at the House of Treasures, Pearl rounds on Auntie with a fury like Birdie has never seen.

"No! I refuse. I REFUSE!"

The other courtesans scatter like pigeons before a cat, but Birdie and Flower don't move fast enough. They're cut off from the safety of their room by Pearl and Auntie facing off between them and the stairs.

"I refuse to have anything to do with that... that... toad," Pearl shrieks. "This is not what I agreed to!"

"But it is." Auntie crosses the reception hall to gaze out at the garden. "If you misunderstood which Takeda was proposing himself as your patron, it's no fault of mine."

"Yes, it is!" Pearl stamps her foot. "You know that old goat is the last man on earth I'd want for a patron, and you tricked him into thinking—"

"On the contrary." Auntie turns to face her. "It was you who gave him the idea. In fact, the Treasures' overseer is quite impressed with your cunning. Takeda-san might never have approached us if you hadn't been so blatantly trying to snare his son."

Horror blanks Pearl's face.

"You think I didn't know about the little game you were playing?" Auntie snorts. "I have to give you credit—you're good. Takeda could never have been goaded into offering such a lucrative arrangement if you hadn't driven his son so crazy that he threatened to run away and marry you."

"No!" A sob escapes the oiran. "Kiyohisa loves me! And I—"

"Stop!" Auntie thunders. "Don't ruin my high opinion of you by claiming you love him back. Customers can afford to indulge their fantasies in Yoshiwara, but you should know better. Any father who allows his unmarried son to be trapped by an oiran is a damned fool. Takeda-san may not be the most handsome man in Yoshiwara, but he didn't become one of the richest by being a fool."

Pearl's face crumples, and now she's sobbing, tears streaking her white makeup. Auntie returns to stand before her, regarding her with detachment.

"If you know what's good for you, you'll keep Overseer-san happy instead of making him sorry he invested in you. Get out of those silks, or you'll end up paying to have them cleaned. Takeda-san would not be pleased to see tearstains on your sleeves the next time you entertain him wearing that kimono."

Face smeared and blotchy now, Pearl whirls around and lurches toward the stairs, stumbles up them, still weeping. They hear her footsteps pounding down the corridor above their heads, then a sharp crack as her door smacks shut.

Dusk lingers in the Yoshiwara sky as Takeda swings onto the street next to the moat, a spring in his step. His new oiran barely batted an eye when she saw him sitting in the patron's chair instead of his son, every bit as professional as he'd hoped. He'd watched her face closely when she saw she'd been duped, pleased to see the flash of anger deftly concealed. A good sign she'll be a vixen in the bedroom but won't let her personal feelings get in the way of doing her job.

Now that he's successfully concluded that piece of business, he can no longer postpone the one that's becoming more urgent every time he entertains the shipowner. The three ships he went so far into debt to build last year are racing back to Edo at this very moment, their holds filled with Dutch Learning. But his partner is already talking about next year, and even if profits exceed expectations, Takeda's half won't be nearly enough to build more ships if he's to pay back the money his partner doesn't know he borrowed.

He needs a new source of income if he's to prevent the shipowner from looking elsewhere, and it's time to resume his hunt for the woman who escaped with Koga on the night of the Great Meiwa Fire. Once he finds out who she is and who she's related to, he can decide who might pay the most to keep her involvement in the foreigner's death secret.

Which is why he's here unfashionably early tonight to request Willow's company. He orders a bowl of noodles from the stand across the street, waiting for the courtesans to file in and take their places in the Golden Drum's lattice room.

Ah, there she is now, sinking onto a cushion at the end of the line. The Drum's manager steps outside to ring the opening bell, and its echoes are still bouncing off the moat wall as he parts the door curtain.

She bustles up to greet him, her sharp eye totting up the cost of the finery he wore to meet his new oiran, then gives a small start of recognition.

"Honored sir! How pleasant to see you again."

"I'm here to request Willow's company for the evening, as promised."

Her smile stales, now that she knows he can afford better.

"Let me see if she's available tonight, Mister...?"

"Matsuyama," Takeda says, giving her the name of his old timber broker.

Holding his hands over the coals in the waiting room's big bronze brazier, he waits while the manager makes a show of checking with Willow.

"I'm pleased to say you're in luck tonight, Mr. Matsuyama," the manager purrs upon her return. "Will you be with us just for just a few hours this evening, or do you plan to stay until morning?"

"I'll pay for the whole night."

"Very good, sir. Our steward will show you up to Shining Willow's nook in the Grand Room, and—"

"She doesn't have her own room?" That won't do.

"I'm afraid she doesn't enjoy that privilege, good sir, but if it's privacy you desire, perhaps I can interest you in one of our other lovely ladies? Pear Blossom, for example, has a fine suite that—"

"Fine. Send her up too."

That shocks her a little, but she says nothing to discourage a customer who's willing to pay two courtesans' fees for the entire night.

The room is up the Drum's worn stairs, near the back. Judging by its placement, it's one of their more premium rooms, but it's a sorry sight compared to the luxury he's used to. The tatami mats at the Camellia are never grubby or smell of mildew. And the bedding, ugh. One glance at Pear Blossom's stained coverlet makes him glad he has no intention of touching it. The room is barely big enough to go through the motions of entertaining, but there's a low, black table crammed into the corner for the sake drinking that customarily precedes the main event. The servant leaves him with a flask, then bows himself out to order the sashimi platter and barbequed eel he requested on the way up. Hopefully, that extra coin will ensure it actually comes from Uogoro, not their usual back-alley hole-in-the-wall.

His wait is short. In a fraction of the time it used to take Jewel to primp and preen, a courtesan who's young enough to be his daughter appears, trailed by the woman he came here to see.

"Welcome to the Golden Drum, my lord," warbles the girl, sinking into a deep bow. She's undoubtedly been told it's her lucky day, but that could change in an instant if she fails to secure this big spender as a repeat customer. "You can call me Pear Blossom, and this"—with a dismissive gesture at her companion—"is Shining Willow."

Willow straightens from her bow and does a doubletake at Takeda's face, but it's a hitch of recognition, not revulsion. She'd been long gone by the time he became an oiran-level patron at the Peony, but she knows who he is and is flattered that he requested her, even if she does have to share him with Pear Blossom.

The girl aims herself at the seat beside him, but he waves her off with a, "Thank you, you can go now."

"Go?" Pear Blossom looks at him blankly. "Go where?"

"Anywhere but here," he snaps, then remembers he's here to cajole, not command. "I came to see Willow, but I require your room for privacy."

The girl stands there, unclear on the concept, so he produces a small silver coin and slides it across the table.

"Go buy yourself some rice cakes. Watch a monkey show. I don't care how you spend this, just occupy yourself elsewhere until morning."

Willow leans in to whisper in the stunned girl's ear, tucking the coin into her sash as she propels her out the door in the direction of the back stairs. When the aging courtesan returns, she stands in the doorway for a moment, uncertain.

"Takeda-san, I—"

"Matsuyama," he corrects her. He gestures for her to take the seat across from him, then changes his mind. "On second thought, you'd better sit next to me until the food arrives. As if I were here for the usual reasons."

Her smile falters a little at the confirmation it wasn't her charms that brought him to the Golden Drum tonight, but seats herself on the proffered cushion while two maids deliver the food.

"Curtain," he prompts, and Willow gets up to unhook the length of cloth that serves as a do-not-disturb sign, while he lifts the lid of his lacquered box to give it a cautious sniff. It came far too quickly to be from Uogoro, but it doesn't smell too bad. Might actually be eel.

"Help yourself," he says, picking up one pair of the chopsticks and nodding toward the sashimi tray.

"Oh, I couldn't possibly—"

"I insist," he says. "I won't tell your manager, and I'd prefer your memory not be dulled by an empty stomach."

She looks at him for a long moment, then cautiously picks up the second pair of chopsticks.

"Thank you, uh, Matsuyama-san. I don't know what brings you to the Drum tonight, but..." Whatever it is, she'll do her best to provide it.

At first, she tries to make conversation, but his one-word answers make it clear he'd rather work through the food in companionable silence, so it's not until she has moved their empty dishes to the hallway and procured another flask of sake that he eases into his reason for being there.

"How long has it been since you left the House of Peonies?" he asks.

"Twelve years." She sighs.

"You were there the night of the Great Meiwa Fire?"

She nods.

"Do you remember anything unusual that happened that day? Besides the fire, of course."

"It would be easier to tell you what *wasn't* unusual about that day," she says with a short laugh.

"Take your time. We have all night."

She tips the flask over his cup and he pushes the second cup across the table, inviting her to pour for herself.

"Start in the morning and don't leave anything out," he says, then shows he means it by interrupting almost immediately to ask how *many* patrons were still there when the morning bell rang. And can she recall any of their names? She's not the smartest pigeon in the flock, but she diligently walks him through the hours. It's obviously been a dragon's age since anyone listened to her instead of the other way around. He sips and nods as she warms to her task, pouring out a stream of useless details. The junior oiran's rage over a moth hole, the burned rice, the other omens that in hindsight had predicted the disaster. He lets them flow in one ear and out the other until she gets to the point midafternoon when someone noticed the column of smoke rising above the Great Gate.

He leans in.

"What happened then?"

"The world turned upside down."

She tells him of the opening bells ringing in eerie discord, and instead of the streets emptying and the pleasure houses filling, the crowds flooding into Yoshiwara dwindled to nothing, and the line of men retrieving their swords on their way out stretched halfway down Center Street. The shades that had been lowered at every teahouse to protect patrons' privacy were flung wide by anxious customers elbowing each other aside to see if they should stay and enjoy their investment or take the loss and flee.

"Did any of the Peonies' customers stay?" he asks.

"No. The fire veered toward Yoshiwara around dusk, and everyone left."

"And later? When the wind shifted away again, did any of them come back?"

"Some," she said.

"Who?"

"Our oiran's biggest patron sent a servant to collect her and take her to his country estate. And Manager-san learned which girls were keeping a boyfriend on the side, because men who weren't customers began knocking on our door to find out if they were safe."

"What about women? Do you remember any women showing up that night?"

Her face clouds.

"Tell me everything you remember about her."

Willow sighs, rotating her sake cup on the table in silence.

"What was her name?" he probes.

"Manager-san said it was Sakura, but I'm sure that's not her real one. Sakura is the kind of name courtesans call themselves, not the kind given to ladies by their families."

"She wasn't a courtesan?"

"No."

"Then why would she come to the Peony?"

"A patron brought her."

A *patron*? Takeda's head snaps up. He knows who brought her to Yoshiwara that night—the man who hides himself beneath a novice's hat.

"Masatoki Koga was a patron at the Peony?" he asks in disbelief.

"Yes," she replies, puzzled. "How did you know his name?"

"Was she Koga's mistress?"

"I don't know. If she was, they must have been fighting, because he stormed out."

"They didn't stay the night?"

"She did, he didn't."

"You're sure?"

"How could I forget? Bringing a woman to a pleasure house is like bringing food to a restaurant. And," she adds sourly, "I was tossed out of my room so she could move in."

"For how long?"

"I don't know. Ten days after Manager-san made me go back to entertaining my customers in the common room, I was sent packing—" A grudge she obviously still bears. "—for something that wasn't even a crime."

"Which was . . . ?"

"Telling that loose-lipped apprentice at the newsstand that Sakura was pregnant."

Takeda slides his sword into its scabbard with a satisfying *snick* and strides out the gate, elated that his hunch about Willow had paid off so handsomely.

Why has Masatoki Koga been lying to him for all these years? The man who wears a silly hat to pretend he's a newcomer wasn't just an occasional Yoshiwara customer, he was a patron who ran a big enough tab at the House of Peonies that he could ask the manager to house his pregnant mistress in one of their precious money-making rooms, and insist she fire one of her courtesans for gossiping about it.

He tosses a larger coin than usual to the groom, mounting his horse with growing excitement. A man like Koga doesn't have to hide the fact he has a mistress. In fact, the higher the official, the more he brags. Unless she's a woman of rank like himself. If this so-called Sakura was from a *hatamoto* family, neither of them had any business being in a relationship that wasn't arranged and approved by their clans. And if Koga was the father of her child—not her rightful husband or a man her family had chosen as a desirable match—that would have been a big issue for both of them.

Especially if she insisted on having the baby. Did she? And if so, where is the child now? If he can find living proof of her infidelity, the funds required to meet his partner's future ambitions will be practically in his pocket. Then all he'll have to do is decide whether it's her husband or her family who are most anxious to avoid the kind of censure that would taint their reputations into the next generation.

The woman's trail ends at the House of Peonies, so that's where he'll start digging. No one who's still there will give him the time of day after he deserted them for the House of Treasures, but this is exactly the sort of thing he hopes his new oiran can help him with.

"Hya!" he cries, urging his horse to a canter. He's looking forward to seeing how Pearl exercises her wits outside the bedchamber as well as in it.

1785

Frost sparkles on the blossoms of the plum tree next to the shrine gate as Birdie stands outside, fingering the coin she just found. Should she climb the steps to the offering box, or buy a rice cake instead? She'd been stuck assisting Pearl until the wee hours last night, so the rice pot in the kitchen had been scraped clean by the time she had a chance to check it. Her stomach growls. The rice cake wins.

But the gods must have spotted her turning her back, and retribution is swift. As she rounds the corner by the fan maker, she's startled to find Lucky Doll standing right in front of the store.

Stumbling back around the corner in a panic, she slips through the shrine's back gate to clamber up a stack of crates to the garden shed roof. Creeping to the ridge to look down on the street below, she flinches back as Dolly tips her face skyward, holding one of the new plum blossom designs up to the light.

It's been a year since Elder Sister took the punishment that ought to have been hers. The loss that used to ambush her afresh every morning has subsided to occasional pangs, because Auntie made sure their disgraced courtesan didn't land anywhere that shared customers or teahouses with the Treasure. But Yoshiwara is only six blocks long and three streets wide. Birdie should have kept up her guard, knowing it was only a matter of time before she chanced across the woman who is now standing below, longing to possess the same fan she and Flower admired last week.

She watches from her perch until Dolly reluctantly replaces it and saunters off, then climbs down. Hooking her basket over her arm and hurrying back toward the Treasure, she hopes Flower remembered to wait for her outside instead of delivering her half-filled basket to Auntie and revealing that Birdie does more than her share of the errands. Seeing Dolly has stirred up her old fear that if Flower is found wanting, Auntie might send them both away. She has to make sure that never happens.

"Oh no, Flower, you got the wrong kind!" Birdie regards the package in her twin's basket with dismay. Yesterday Pearl declared she now prefers sweet rice crackers to salty ones.

Flower's face pales. Whoever delivers the wrong crackers will get a hard pinch, or worse.

"Let me." Birdie plucks the offending package from her basket. She has no intention of delivering them herself, of course, but she's better at ducking punishment than Flower. She trots to the kitchen in search of Jester. Pearl wouldn't dare lay a hand on a man, so he's her best hope of heading off the oiran's bad mood before today's robing session turns into a festival of faultfinding.

"And then," she hears him delivering a punchline as he scrapes the last bite of rice from bowl to mouth, "the mother says, 'Your father may be the girl next door's father, but it's fine if you marry her. He may be Osaki's father . . . but he's not *your* father.'"

Guffaws all around. Knives resume chopping and Jester helps himself to more rice behind Cook's back.

"Birdie!" he cries, spotting her. "Are those rice crackers for me?"

"No." She beckons him into the hall. "Can you take them up to Pearl for me? Flower bought the wrong kind, and . . ." She sees the look on his face and adds, "it would be a shame if you're napping the next time the privy needs cleaning, and I happen to mention to Auntie where to find you."

"Ah, Little Bird—" He takes the rice crackers with a rueful smile. "I've taught you too well."

And just as she'd hoped, by the time she and Flower arrive at Pearl's rooms to help her choose her accessories for tonight, the Treasures' prisoner has worked his magic. Pearl is tossing her old favorite crackers into her mouth, laughing at the story he was just telling downstairs.

Jester has made himself a fixture in the nine months since Auntie confined him to the pleasure house until he pays his debt. At first, he just pitched in to fetch sake refills and extra soy sauce, then he began amusing waiting patrons with comic stories until their courtesans were free to see them (enjoying their sake and sashimi while he's at it). Pleasantly surprised to find jovial and slightly drunk customers awaiting their arrival instead of surly and jealous ones, the courtesans reward Jester with their gratitude and generous tips. Everyone suspects that his gift for being at the right place at the right time must have produced a sizeable nest egg by now, but whenever he's asked if he's saved enough to buy his freedom, he shakes his head sadly and claims to be poorer than a graveyard cat. Auntie even allows him to accompany Pearl to teahouses to help entertain patrons now, since his reluctance to pay off his debt and his talent at heading off Takeda's bad moods make him more of a valued asset than a flight risk these days.

"You should tell that one tonight at the Camellia," Pearl advises him. The most popular kabuki actor in Edo has promised to stop by her banquet this evening. "But wait until Takeda-san goes to the privy. He thinks samurai should be above jokes like that, and it gives him indigestion when he can't help laughing."

Birdie can't believe how much has changed since the day Pearl set out for the Camellia to become the Takeda son's oiran and went home as the father's. The first month had been awful, of course, and Pearl had made everyone suffer with her. One day she'd refuse all food; the next, she'd round on them in a fury for not guessing what she craved. Sympathy for her wilted as fast as a cut flower in a dry vase.

"Don't get me wrong," Butterfly had groused, sponging a few sticky grains of rice from her robe after Pearl threw a bowl at her. "I don't like entertaining ugly old men any more than she does, but isn't it about time she quit sulking?"

"I couldn't agree more," Peach huffed, eyeing the small pile of coins that represented her entire savings. "He *is* one of the richest men in Edo."

Birdie is the only one who wasn't surprised by the depth of the oiran's disappointment. Only she knew that Pearl had been hoping Takeda's son would spirit her away to the life of her dreams.

Fortunately, Pearl hadn't tortured them for long. In fact, she recovered with remarkable speed. Heartbroken weeping had subsided to tragic sighs within a week, and by the end of the month, she was privately admitting that she'd been more in love with the chase than with the purple peacock himself. She would have vastly preferred landing a young and attractive patron to an old, ugly one, of course, but being kept by the elder Takeda is turning out to have its advantages. She finds it surprisingly easy to bend his ambitions to suit her own, and if she can't escape Yoshiwara, at least now she's the queen of it. A year ago, no kabuki star would have graced her evenings with his presence, but now that she has a patron who craves prestige even more than she does, the top actors, artists, and writers of Edo can't resist the superb food, drink, and entertainment Takeda offers in return for their company. Those fickle moths flock only to the brightest candles in the pleasure quarter, and thanks to Takeda, Pearl can now afford to burn brightest of all.

Jester excuses himself, and Birdie sits down with Flower to help Pearl choose hair ornaments that will go with tonight's outfit. Takeda's guest this evening will be a merchant with the third biggest rice warehouse on the Sumida River, and he's a rabid kabuki fan. If they can maneuver him into becoming a substantial patron of the actor who'd promised to stop by tonight, the kabuki star will return the favor the next time Takeda wants to impress someone by taking them backstage.

"What do you think of these?" Flower holds up an ornament adorned with plum blossoms of carved coral and ivory.

"Or these?" Birdie offers a pair topped with golden fans.

Pearl doesn't reply. A carved comb lies forgotten in her hands and she's staring out the window, lost in thought.

"Have you noticed something about the men who keep oirans?" Pearl turns to them, awaiting an answer.

"They... have a lot of money?" Birdie guesses.

"People always give them what they want?" Flower ventures.

"Yes, but there's more to it than that. Men who keep an oiran already have more money, more power, more everything than they'll ever need. But they still want more."

"Why?" Birdie asks.

"Good question," Pearl replies. "But it's the wrong one."

"What's the right one?"

"What does a successful oiran do, once she figures that out?"

And suddenly Pearl has all her attention.

"Well?" Birdie asks. "What *does* she do?"

"She helps them get it."

She helps them get it. Just like that, five words change Birdie's life. Lying in bed that night, she turns Pearl's words over and over in her mind, like golden coins. If she learns how to give rich and powerful men what they want, she can be as successful as Pearl. And if she's as successful as Pearl, she'll be so valuable to the House of Treasures, Auntie will never let her go. All she has to do is pay attention to what Pearl does. Not just the skills she'll need to become an oiran, but the small flatteries, the cunning subterfuges, the way Pearl bends a conversation in a profitable direction. She'll take note of what works and start practicing it herself.

She begins the very next day. And lucky for her, she has more opportunities to watch Yoshiwara's top oiran at work than ever before. Pearl's talent for devising ever more beguiling entertainments has finally been matched by Takahisa Takeda's ability to pay for them, as long as they deliver the desired results. Their invitations are seldom refused. The illustriousness of his guests is matched only by the quality of entertainers who flock to impress them. And Birdie is right there at Pearl's side, watching, learning, and helping her get Takahisa Takeda more of everything.

"What a buffoon!" Takeda groans, returning to the banquet room after bidding his guests farewell.

Birdie isn't sure if he means the rice merchant or the kabuki actor. It had taken more than one meeting for Takeda to secure the eternal gratitude of both parties, but tonight they'd left arm in arm, one-upping each other in fawning disagreement over who was more enamored—the merchant who had drunkenly pledged his "support" to ensure he'd be recognized by his idol the next time they meet, or the actor who is trying to pin down a sizeable monthly commitment before his mark sobers up.

Pearl must not know which one he's talking about either, because she murmurs, "Takeda-san deserves a reward for being so patient with both his guests tonight."

She beckons him over, and Birdie is relieved to see her draw back her sleeve to give him a glimpse of her white wrist as she pours him more sake. She does that sort of thing right before they go upstairs, which means Birdie might get more sleep tonight than expected.

But when Takeda sits down, he just sits there, turning his refilled cup on the table.

"Now that they're finally gone," he says, "I have a favor to ask."

Pearl tilts her head attentively.

"I'm looking for a missing child. Not my own," he quickly adds, noticing the slight downturn of his oiran's lips. "I'm asking for a... friend. Many years ago, his mistress told him she was pregnant, but she disappeared. She arrived on the Peonies' doorstep on the night of the Great Meiwa Fire, calling herself Sakura. They took her in that night, but by the time he discovered that's where she went, she was gone. He doesn't know if she had the baby or if it survived, but if it did, he's hoping to find it. Last year's influenza outbreak took his wife and both his children, so he's eager to acknowledge this one as his new heir. The problem is, he asked for my help when I was still Jewel's patron. The ladies at the Peony will be less than eager to answer my questions since I moved on to an oiran"—he smiles at Pearl—"who is smarter and prettier."

Pearl nods, pleased. "How can I help?"

"I think the best way to find the child is to find the mother."

"Is she still alive?"

"I don't know. Our first task is to find out, then we can track down where she went after she left the Peony."

Pearl sits back, thinking.

"I was one of Jewel's biggest rivals," she says slowly, "so I won't get a straight answer from them either. However . . ."

She turns to Birdie.

". . . I know who will."

"Tiger! I was hoping to run into you." Birdie has been loitering on the bridge over the shrine pond for nearly an hour, hoping he'd cut through on his way home so she can ask about the woman Takeda is looking for.

"I've been looking for you too," he says, waggling a slightly squashed rice cake at her. "I'll share this with you if—Remember that cricket cage I gave you?"

"You mean the cricket cage you *sold* me?"

"Well, I kind of need it back."

"Why?"

"Young Pine wasn't quite as done with it as I thought she was."

Last month, Birdie's passion for collecting pretty crab shells from the moat had been abruptly terminated by Butterfly and Peach after they sniffed out the source of the smell and threw them out. Tiger had cheered her up by suggesting she collect crickets instead.

"I thought you found that cage in the trash," Birdie says, eyes narrowing.

"Well, it was *near* the trash," Tiger waffles. "Can you give it back?"

Birdie frowns. She won't just be losing the cage, she'll have to let Jumpy and Hopper go.

"Okay," she reluctantly agrees. "But I want something in return. *Besides* what I paid you."

Tiger makes a face, but he can't very well refuse.

"Is there anyone still working at the Peony who was there on the night of the Great Meiwa Fire?"

"Dunno. Wasn't that before we were born? Why are you so interested in ancient history?"

"One of Pearl's patrons wants to know about a woman who came to the Peony that night."

He clamps his mouth shut. How dare she ask him to spy on his own house?

"You owe me," she reminds him.

He can't argue with that.

"Okay," he reluctantly agrees. "I'll find out if anyone who was working back then is still there. Meet me back here at the Hour of the Monkey. And don't forget the cricket cage."

Birdie gets there early to set her pets free, hoping they will enjoy a long life in the nice moss beneath the pine tree and have the sense not to go anywhere near the carp patrolling the overhanging grasses by the shore, mouths gaping.

"Hey," Tiger says, sauntering to a stop beside her, trying to conceal how relieved he is to see the cricket cage that Young Pine will soon be discovering at the back of her cupboard.

"Did you find out what I wanted to know?"

"All the courtesans who worked at the Peony then are gone," he reports. "Jewel was the last, except for Manager-san." Who, it goes without saying, would refuse to give out information that might benefit another pleasure house.

"What about the servants?"

"The only ones who've been there that long are Cook and Back Door Watchman."

He reaches for the cage.

"Not so fast." She whisks it out of reach. "Was that watchman on duty the night of the fire?"

"No, he started out on privy duty. I've never seen anyone so grateful for a promotion."

"Then I need to talk to the cook. Go get her."

"Now? I can't get her now! What if she's busy? What if she won't—"

"Tell her . . ." Birdie stops to think. "Tell her it's about the baby."

"Baby? What baby?"

Suddenly, he's all ears.

"None of your business. Just go get the cook."

He dithers, looking like he might refuse, but his need for the cricket cage wins out.

Tiger is every bit as persuasive as she hoped. He reappears, towing a stormy-faced woman wearing an indigo head wrap and wiping her hands on a long apron.

"What are you playing at, missy?" she snaps. "Wait." She holds up a hand. "Don't answer that."

She turns to Tiger and points toward the gate.

He scowls.

"Thank you, Tiger," Birdie says sweetly, handing him the cricket cage. "You can go now." She doesn't want him to hear the cook's answer either. It would be all over Yoshiwara before she has a chance to tell Takeda.

"But—"

"You can *go* now."

Heaving an aggrieved sigh, he slouches away, dragging his feet. Birdie follows him to the gate and watches him cast reproachful looks her way until he rounds the corner.

"I'm sorry we have to meet like this, Most Honorable Cook," she says, returning to make an apologetic bow. "But I have a question only you can answer. What happened to the woman who came to the Peony on the night of the Great Meiwa Fire?"

"Why do you want to know?" The cook's eyes narrow. "It's been thirteen years. Why now?"

"I heard the baby's father is looking for her."

"I thought he was dead."

"No, he's very much alive."

"You've *met* him?"

"Well, no. His friend told me he's looking for her."

"Why didn't he tell you himself?"

"We're not exactly on speaking terms." Why would she be acquainted with a patron's friend?

"So, it's some man who wants to find her." The cook folds her arms across her chest. "What do *you* want?"

"I want to find her too. If she's alive."

The cook studies her face, then gives in.

"I can't tell you if she's still alive," she says, "but she certainly was on the day her brother came to take her away. We tried to tell him two months isn't long enough to recover after giving birth, but—"

"Take her away? Where?"

"Odawara."

"Why?"

"He'd arranged a match for her with a *hatamoto*."

A match? Takeda's missing woman had her baby, then turned around and married a government official? That makes no sense. What kind of *hatamoto* would marry a woman who had just given birth at a pleasure house? Unless . . .

"Was the *hatamoto* her patron?"

"Good heavens, no. She wasn't a courtesan. She was a lady."

A *lady*?

"Was the Odawara *hatamoto* the father?" It's the only other explanation that fits.

"No." The cook shakes her head sadly. "If he had been, she wouldn't have left her baby behind."

"Did you find out her name?" Takeda interrupts Pearl's little attendant.

"The cook called her Sakura," she reports, shaking her head, "but I doubt that was her real name."

"Who did she marry?"

"I don't know his name either," she admits, shifting nervously from foot to foot. "Cook just said he was an Odawara *hatamoto*."

Takeda sips his sake, thinking. It's not much, but it might be enough to track down the missing woman. Odawara is a castle outpost, not a sprawling city like Edo, and most of the samurai who serve there are members of the Ōkubo clan. The bureaucrats assigned to oversee the shōgun's interests—collecting taxes, awarding government contracts, and so forth—would be outsiders from other families. There can't be many of them. If he can learn which one she married, he can find out her real name. And her brother's, since the girl just confirmed she came from a family with enough standing to marry her to a *hatamoto*. And he must have done it on false pretenses, since a marriage between families of rank would never go through if hers hadn't concealed she'd borne another man's child. Even thirteen years later, her brother could be stripped of his post—and his income—if that comes to light.

Now all he needs is proof.

"What happened to the child?" he asks. "Was it a boy?"

"Cook didn't say."

"Where is it now?"

"I'm sorry," she says, shaking her head apologetically, "but I didn't get a chance to ask. Someone started calling for her, so she had to go."

Takeda turns to Pearl.

"An orphan born in Yoshiwara might still be here, so perhaps it will be easier to find the baby than the mother. It wouldn't be a baby anymore, of course. What year was that fire? Meiwa Ten?"

Meiwa Ten? Birdie's brow furrows. Isn't that the year Tiger was born? Could this woman be his mother?

"No," Pearl recalls, "the fire broke out during cherry blossom season, shortly after I came to Yoshiwara as a child attendant. That was the Year of the Dragon, Meiwa Nine."

Oh. Too bad. The baby wasn't Tiger, it was a Dragon, like her.

"That would make it how old now?" Takeda muses. "Thirteen?"

Yes, Birdie thinks. Thirteen. Just like . . . her.

She stiffens. Could this woman be *her* mother? Pulling her hands inside her sleeves, she reckons on her fingers. If cherry trees bloom in the Fourth Month, and she was born in the Ninth... It's possible. *More* than possible. But if her mother left the Peony to marry some *hatamoto*, why did everyone tell her she'd died when she was born?

Even as she asks herself the question, she knows the answer. Courtesans can be heartless when it comes to men, but they take care of their own. Learning her mother abandoned her to run off and live her life as if she'd never been born might be the worst piece of news a daughter of Yoshiwara could ever hear.

Her skin as bumpy as a plucked chicken, Birdie sluices off the soap early the next morning, hoping a soak in the public bath will revive her after tossing and turning all night, questions buzzing in her head like a swarm of bees.

When she'd believed her mother dead, there'd been no reason to ask why she'd been left an orphan, but all kinds of uncomfortable questions are now rearing their ugly heads. Has her mother really been living just a half-day's ride away in Odawara all this time? What kind of woman would leave her baby behind?

It wasn't by choice, Birdie tells herself. No woman in her right mind would go through all the pain of giving birth and then—

"Birdie?"

Her head snaps up. She hasn't heard Dolly's voice for a year, but she'd know it anywhere. She leaps to her feet in a panic, but there's no escape. Neither of them is wearing a stitch of clothing. All she can do is throw herself to the bathhouse floor, knocking her forehead against the tile and crying, "I'm sorry, Elder Sister! I'm so sorry!"

"What? Why?"

Now Birdie's confused.

"I'm sorry because you... you didn't tell Auntie it was me who made the mistake about the third magistrate, and then you took the punishment instead of me, and you got banished to a geisha house and... and... it's all my fault!"

"Is that why you've been avoiding me?"

"I don't blame you for hating me," Birdie wails. "Or if you can't ever forgive me."

"Silly girl." Dolly laughs. "There's nothing to forgive. Stand up, sweetie. Dry your eyes."

She looks up to find Elder Sister regarding her with that little half smile that puts a dimple in her cheek, offering her hand. Birdie hesitates, then takes it.

"Why would I hate you?" Dolly pulls her to her feet. "Moving to the Nomura is the best thing that ever happened to me."

"But—" How can anyone be *happy* to be banished to a geisha house?

"Can we talk about it in the bath?" Dolly shivers. "It's cold out here."

Clutching her hand towel to her chest, Birdie hunches after Dolly into the cavernous bathhouse filled with the fragrance of the big cedar tub. Today, the steam rolling off the surface nearly obscures the painting of Mount Fuji on the far wall.

"Over here." Dolly steers Birdie to the side farthest from the women already lounging in the waist-deep water. The others cast a few curious glances, then resume gossiping as soon as the newcomers are dismissed as no one of importance.

Birdie sticks a toe in, winces as she lowers herself into the nearly scalding water. Lucky Doll eases in beside her.

"I . . . I thought you were angry," Birdie blurts. "When I saw you that first time, on the geisha street, you looked . . . mad."

"Not mad," Dolly replies with a rueful smile. "But seeing you in all your procession finery reminded me of everything I'd lost, and I hadn't yet realized how much more I'd gained."

Gained?

"Now I strum my *shamisen* at lecherous old geezers from across the room," Dolly explains, "instead of finding them dead in my bed."

Birdie can't deny that sounds like an improvement.

"But if you don't have patrons," she points out, "you can't get rich."

"Who needs to be rich? Haven't you noticed that the main reason courtesans always need money is to pay for the expensive clothes that they only need so they can get more money?"

Birdie never thought of it that way. But Auntie wouldn't threaten her courtesans with waking up in a geisha house if there was anything good about—*Auntie*. What if someone from the Treasure sees her talking with a courtesan she banned in disgrace? Auntie will make her go without supper for a week.

"Sorry," Birdie says, boosting herself out of the bath. "I didn't realize how late it's getting. I have to go."

But Dolly is rising from the water too.

"I'm glad I ran into you here this morning."

"Me too," Birdie agrees, toweling herself off as fast as she can.

"If you ever need me," Dolly says, "you know where I live."

Birdie freezes. Lucky Doll knows where she lives too. Now that they're on good terms again, what if Elder Sister comes to see her? Or stops to talk to her in public?

"Don't worry." Dolly sighs. "I'm the one who taught you that courtesans and geisha don't mix, remember? If I see you on the street, I'll pretend I don't know you."

Birdie stares at her feet, ashamed. It's the right answer, but it makes her feel worse than she expected. Now that she knows Dolly isn't mad at her, she wishes it didn't have to be this way.

Takeda slows his mount to cross the stone bridge spanning Odawara Castle's moat and announces himself to the sentry. The high walls on either side are pierced with arrow slits, designed to give a killing advantage to those defending against marauders who cross the water with conquest on their minds. But now the enormous copper-clad gate stands open. These days, the biggest threats to Odawara Castle are typhoons and earthquakes, not the armies of rebellious warlords.

"Where would I find the commissioner of protocol?" Takeda asks the man on duty. His wife finally proved useful for something besides producing daughters—her second cousin is wed to the man he's here to meet.

"That office would be in the castle itself, sir," the gatekeeper tells him, scanning his letter of introduction and handing it back. Doesn't need to add, "you can't miss it," because the white, seven-story keep sits atop a tall, sloping, stone foundation so its magnificence can be seen (and impress) from afar.

Takeda squints up at the stout white walls, its triple layers of peaked gables looking out in every direction, the tile roofs guarded against fire by leaping dragon-fish. He urges his horse forward to where it will be stabled while he hunts down the woman Koga brought to the House of Peonies on the night of the fire. He's hoping his wife's in-law can tell him which of the other *hatamoto* outsiders had married a woman from Edo thirteen years ago.

He has barely settled himself onto a cushion in the man's anteroom when he's summoned to the inner sanctum, much to the silent chagrin of the other waiting petitioners.

"Come in, come in." The protocol commissioner beams. Obligatory small gifts and pleasantries are exchanged, then the man asks what he can do for him.

"I'm looking for a woman from Edo who married an Odawara *hatamoto*, back in Meiwa Nine."

"A woman?" He sits up with interest.

"It's about a minor inheritance matter," Takeda lies.

Disappointed, the man sits back, stroking his goatee.

"There are three who might have been looking for a wife thirteen years ago," he says, thinking aloud. "The construction administrator—No, his wife came from Morioka. And the man in charge of castle repairs stayed single until three years ago. The commissioner of provisions did marry around then, but I don't think his wife is from Edo. Honorable Clerk?" he calls toward the anteroom.

The clerk pushes aside the blinds screening the office from the waiting area and steps in.

"You used to work for the administrator in charge of building supplies, didn't you?"

"My first posting," the clerk confirms.

"Do you remember anything about his wife? I seem to recall Maeda-san married around that time, but I can't remember if she's from Edo or not."

"She's not," the clerk replies. "He married a woman from Odawara after the, er, incident."

"What 'incident?'" Takeda asks.

"With his first wife, sir."

His *first* wife? Takeda's interest sharpens.

"What happened?" he asks.

The clerk glances at his boss.

"It stays within this room," the protocol administrator assures him. "What happened to Maeda's first wife?"

"Well, that's the thing," the clerk replies. "Nobody knows. She disappeared. On his first day back to work after the wedding, Maeda-san went home and she was gone. Took his best horse."

"Any idea where she went?"

"Everyone assumed she ran back to her family in Edo, but her brother sent word that she wasn't there either, which made it an embarrassment on both sides. They searched for her from both ends, with no luck."

"She was never found?"

"Vanished into thin air. Maeda-san stopped looking and remarried after the dowry was returned and the *umeboshi* contract signed."

"What *umeboshi* contract?"

"The contract to supply all the shōgun's troops with the pickled plums in their daily rations. The runaway wife's brother arranged for it to be awarded it to Maeda-san's family. As reparation."

Takeda wearily climbs back into the saddle for the long ride home. Spurring his horse toward Edo, he curses the woman who continues to evade him. It's not until he has galloped away some of his frustration and is once again chewing over the conversation that he finds a thread to pull.

The clerk couldn't recall the runaway wife's name, but her family has connections high enough in the shōgun's bureaucracy to deliver a lucrative pickled plum contract as an apology. They obviously value their honor and have already demonstrated that they're willing to pay to conceal her treachery. If the jilted administrator were to discover that his bride had not only abandoned him at the first opportunity, but that she'd been spoiled goods, the outrage of the rich and powerful Maeda clan would descend on her family with a vengeance that few could survive. If Takeda can find the brother, he'll have no choice but to pay whatever it takes to keep them in the dark.

But he needs proof. From now on, he'll concentrate his efforts on finding that child.

Birdie kneels, packed pipe at the ready, while Feather touches up Pearl's makeup. When she finally sits back to put away her brush, the oiran takes the pipe and inhales a few blissful puffs before calling her attendants to silence.

"We have a big night ahead of us," she announces, blowing smoke toward the ceiling. "Takeda-san sent word that he's bringing a very important guest for the first time and is counting on us to make the evening a pleasant one. The man is one of Edo's highest government officials, but he's a difficult fellow and has never been comfortable in Yoshiwara. I have assured Takeda-san that the ladies from the House of Treasures will change all that."

Everyone murmurs their support, excitement fizzing at the opportunity to entertain such an important man. Straightening their robes and tugging their sashes into place, they follow Birdie and Flower to the banquet room, assuring each other that by the end of the evening, the reluctant reveler will be a Yoshiwara devotee.

As Birdie catches sight of Takeda's guest for the first time, though, she has her doubts. The city administrator Takeda introduces as Koga-san isn't just wearing one of those ridiculous straw hats that looks like an overturned laundry basket, he refuses to take it off. Pearl gamely ignores it at first, plying him with the kind of questions that tempt most men to unbend and expound upon their interests with increasing enthusiasm as the sake flows. Despite his cup regularly disappearing beneath the hat and coming back empty, Koga answers with little more than a single word.

In desperation, she resorts to drinking games, and at last he finally shows some interest. Few men reach the highest ranks of government without a competitive streak, and the city administrator's desire to beat Takeda lights a fire under him. Unfortunately, Takeda also hates to lose, so every forfeit is followed by a bellow for another go. The drinking escalates so fast, with both sides swinging between triumph and defeat, Pearl must reach into her sleeve long before midnight.

"*Ne ne*," she interrupts, rattling a pair of dice in her hand suggestively. "I think we should start playing for higher stakes, don't you?" Before either of them can object, she announces, "It's time for Truth or Dare. Flower, fetch me my dice cup?"

As the rules are explained, Birdie studies the men, admiring how Pearl is making Takeda's eyes gleam and his guest lean forward, listening intently. She's never seen two men more eager to make each other perform an embarrassing feat or reveal something about themselves they'd rather not.

"Koga-san, you're the guest tonight, so I'm sure Takeda-san will agree that you ought to get first roll."

He wins that round, Takeda comes second, and Pearl loses. She chooses "truth" and Koga makes her admit that before she became White Pearl, her name was Little Daisy. They all marvel that she could ever have been known by such a common name. It's not true, of course. Pearl is the top oiran in all of Yoshiwara, and she didn't get there by admitting that anything about her is as ugly and vulgar as being named Bear Child until she was six.

Koga loses the next round to Pearl, and chooses "dare" instead of answering a question. After the city administrator demonstrates a hidden talent for playing the shamisen badly, the tables are turned. Takeda loses to him and also chooses to take a dare.

"I was hoping you'd say that," Koga says. "I've been admiring that octopus *netsuke* of yours all night. It was carved by Masanao, was it not? So was mine." Grabbing his exquisitely carved ebony monkey in his fist, he pulls it through his sash, along with the *inrō* it's attached to. "I dare you to trade."

"*What?*" Takeda looks like he's been slapped.

"Ooo, Takeda-san," Pearl squeals, heading off the refusal she sees coming. "I think you're getting the better end of this dare. It's ever so much nicer than your old—"

"Absolutely not!" Takeda sputters, clutching the octopus in one white-knuckled fist.

"Oh, Takeda-san," Pearl trills, the kind of laugh that conceals a warning, "don't be silly. What's the big fuss? Let him try it on. Need I remind you that in Yoshiwara, the rules of the game must be observed as strictly as the rule of law?"

Takeda still refuses.

"Is this how a man of honor behaves?" Pearl chides. If she allows him to back out, he'll blame her later for letting him make a fool of himself, and Birdie will be patching her up in the morning.

"Very well," she relents. "Let me ask the question again. Would you prefer to tell a truth instead?"

He wouldn't. And now they're in a bind.

Pearl lays a conciliatory hand on his arm, whispering in his ear, "Be a good sport, Takeda-san. Take it as a compliment that your guest admires your good taste so much. Your precious octopus isn't going to leave this room. I promise to get it back before the end of the evening."

Still scowling, Takeda allows Pearl to relieve him of his *inrō*.

"It looks very handsome on you." Pearl twinkles at Koga, pulling the octopus through his sash. "But I wouldn't get too attached. It's Takeda-san's turn to roll the dice next, and I have a feeling his luck is about to turn."

Birdie watches her stealthily swap the dice they'd been using for an identical-looking pair in her sleeve before handing Takeda the cup. No surprise, Takeda's dice come up unbeatable. Pearl swaps the old pair back in, and Koga loses. With visible relief, Takeda threads the octopus *netsuke* back through his sash and rises, muttering about the privy.

Birdie ushers him downstairs, wondering why letting Koga try on his scratched old *inrō* got him so flustered. Is it because the octopus was made by a famous artist? She holds her breath outside the latrine while

Takeda goes in, and is relieved that he seems to have recovered his equilibrium by the time he comes out.

As they approach the upstairs banquet room, it's clear the others have continued to play, because they hear Pearl give a crow of victory. She's chivvying Koga to pay up, and is snatching the hat from his head as they walk in. Her attendants erupt in a tumult of exclamations. They never guessed he was such a good-looking man! What a shame to hide that handsome face under a silly hat!

But all Birdie has eyes for is his ears. As he wrestles his hat back from Pearl, she can't help but see they're as pointy as a fox's. Just like hers.

"You saw them too, didn't you?" Birdie asks Flower excitedly, as they pull off their finery before bed.

"Saw what?"

"Koga's pointy ears! He's the man I saw at Lord Oda's party. I'm sure of it."

Flower says nothing, just keeps folding her robes.

"I know, I know," Birdie rolls her eyes, wishing her twin could just be happy for her instead of reminding her not to count the rice bales before they're threshed. "He didn't show any sign he recognized me, but doesn't that prove he has no idea he has a daughter in Yoshiwara?"

Flower folds and stacks.

"What? Spit it out," Birdie snaps, fed up with her twin's loud silence. "How could he know about me, when he's such a Yoshiwara novice he wears a hat?"

Flower sighs. "Maybe that's why he wears it."

"What do you mean?"

"I'm pretty sure he's the man I saw giving something to the Peonies' manager at their back door."

"What? When?"

"The last time I delivered the Treasures' monthly shrine offering."

"How do you know it was him?"

"He was wearing a hat, just like the one he had on tonight."

"Anyone can rent one of those."

"He was also wearing that monkey *netsuke*."

Oh.

"When did you see him?" Birdie asks.

"Last week." Reluctantly she adds, "But that wasn't the first time."

"He's been there before?"

"Yes, but I didn't know who he was until tonight."

"What was he giving her?"

"I didn't see. Something small."

"A payment?" Birdie guesses. The House of Treasures' regular customers settle their bills on the first of the month, the same day the shrine offering is due.

"That's what I thought," Flower admits. "But now that we've met him, he doesn't seem the type to be a regular Yoshiwara customer."

"No," Birdie agrees. "But if he's not a customer, what's he paying for?"

Flower says nothing, but she doesn't have to. The manager of the Peony has nothing to sell but courtesans' time . . . and information. If Koga isn't paying for a woman, he's either getting information or stopping her from giving it to someone else. What kind of secret would a man who hates coming to Yoshiwara be paying a pleasure house mistress to keep?

Then Birdie's heart sinks, as she sees what Flower has been trying so hard not to say. Maybe Koga hates coming to Yoshiwara because he knows he has a daughter here. And he wears that stupid hat so she never finds out.

The next morning, the only way she can cope with her father's devastating lack of interest is to put away her desire to reunite with him and work on finding her mother instead. Slipping the packet of tobacco into her sleeve, she looks both ways before leaving the tobacconist and takes the long way back to the House of Treasures, hoping Takeda won't be lying in wait for her somewhere along the way. Since he returned from Odawara with the disappointing news that the woman she believes to be her mother vanished soon after she got there, he has shifted his interest to the baby. He's been badgering her to go back to the Peonies' cook and ask whether it was a boy or a girl. And where the child might be now.

Birdie knows the answers, but until she sorts out her own feelings, she doesn't want to share them with anyone. Especially Takahisa Takeda. Once she pieced together that the "friend" whose mistress gave birth to their child at the House of Peonies was her father, she knew Takeda was lying. He and Masatoki Koga are anything but friends, and until she figures out the real reason Takeda is so eager to find her, she's not about to help him do it.

There must be a reason—a *good* reason—her mother abandoned her, and there's only one person who can tell her what that was. If her mother is alive, she's got to find her.

But how? She doesn't even know her real name. Birdie needs help from someone who can get information from outside the Great Gate, someone who's not Takahisa Takeda. It'll have to be a man, and there's only one man she trusts enough to help her.

After delivering Pearl's tobacco, she puts her ear up to the debtor room door. Hears a plaintive variation of "Teardrops on My Sleeve" being casually plucked inside. Jester is the only person she knows who hears everything and tells no one. Everyone trusts him with their secrets, even customers. His wide range of acquaintances spans from peddlers to lords.

She knocks.

"Come in," he calls, looking up as she hesitates in the open door. "Birdie! What brings you here today?"

"I'm trying to find my mother."

"Your mother?" He sets down the *shamisen* and pats the cushion beside him. "I thought she died when you were born."

Birdie closes the door behind her and explains.

"So," he says, "the Peonies' cook told you she was still alive two months after you were born. She left to marry an official in Odawara, ran away the next day, and nobody has seen her since."

"Yes. So, she might still be out there somewhere, but I don't know where to look. I don't even know her real name. Do you have any idea how I could find out?"

"Hmm." He thinks for a long moment. "If I were you, I'd ask Shinjō-san."

"Madame Truth? Who is Madame Truth?"

"The only fortuneteller in Yoshiwara who deserves to be called by that name."

Birdie has her doubts, never having met a fortuneteller who deals in the truth.

"If she's so great, how come I've never heard of her?"

"Because not many in Yoshiwara really want to hear the truth. Once she consults her divination sticks, she feels honor bound to tell the bad along with the good. You don't get one without the other." He picks up his pipe to pack it. "But if the truth is what you're after, she's the one to ask."

"Is she . . . expensive?"

"Five *mon* for a reading. You only get one question, and you must pay for the answer, whether it's what you want to hear or not. If the divination sticks tell her nothing, she won't lie to you and make something up. But she's never wrong." Jester grins. "She advised me to come to the House of Treasures, didn't she?"

On the first day of the Seventh Month, Birdie stands with Jester outside the place where Shinjō practices her art, five coins jingling in her sleeve.

She regards the warped steps leading up to the shabby shack with suspicion, wondering—not for the first time—if this is a mistake. Like the rest of the rundown buildings across from the moat, Madame Truth's is weathered a silvery gray, the wooden sidings oiled once when they were new and neglected ever after. The frayed linen curtain flapping over her door must once have been a deep indigo, but it has faded nearly as white as the character for "fortuneteller" dyed into the center.

"Are you coming?" She twists around to find Jester still standing in the street.

"No." He laughs. "You go ahead. I'm not in the market for the unvarnished truth today."

Turning back to the door, she squares her shoulders and knocks. A woman's voice bids her enter, and the fragrance of sandalwood envelops her as she steps through the door. It takes a moment for her eyes to adjust to the dim room, the only light streaming from a doorway in the far wall, throwing the fraying patches in the tatami mats into ragged relief as a thread of smoke curls from the incense burning on a low table.

Behind it sits a woman wearing a plain kerchief over her hair, looking more like a shopkeeper than an oracle. Her deep indigo kimono is cheap homespun, but the undercollar showing at the neckline is snowy white; Shinjō may be poor, but she refuses to give in to the petty indignities of poverty. Her face is as austere as a nun's, neither kind nor unkind, and it's hard to guess her age. Fine lines radiate from the corners of her eyes, suggesting she's older than Pearl, but not as old as Auntie. Kneeling behind the table, back straight, her lips soundlessly form the words of a sutra, one hand telling the beads of a Buddhist rosary.

As Birdie slides the door closed and turns to face her, the seer's eyes widen, and Birdie takes an involuntary step back. Does this woman *know* her? The moment passes, the startled connection replaced by a professional smile and a gesture toward the flat cushion on the other side of the table.

"Please sit."

The silence stretches. Now what? Birdie squirms a little as the seer studies her face. Should she introduce herself? Maybe explain why she's here?

She opens her mouth, just as the fortuneteller asks, "What brought you here today, Birdie?"

How did she—? Oh. Of course. Jester must have mentioned she was coming.

"I—" Birdie swallows. "I'm trying to find my mother."

A line deepens between Shinjō's brows.

"I was born at the House of Peonies," Birdie blurts, "and they told me she died when I was born. Only... I just found out that she didn't. She left two months later to marry a *hatamoto* in Odawara. I'm sure she didn't want to leave me," she adds quickly. "But I can't ask her, because she's not there now. She ran away from her new husband right after the wedding and no one has seen her since."

Madame Truth's lips tighten in disapproval.

"But she must have had a good reason," Birdie insists. "When I find her, I'll ask her. If she's still alive, that is. That's why Jester told me to come. He said you were the only one who might be able to help me. Can you tell me if she's still alive? And where to start looking for her?"

Shinjō studies her face for a long moment then says, "That . . . depends."

"On what?"

"What do you plan to do when you find her? After all these years, why is it still so important?"

Birdie stares in disbelief.

"She's my *mother*."

"But she left you," the fortuneteller points out. "Doesn't that make you angry?"

"A little," Birdie admits. Now that she mentions it.

"Wouldn't it be better to have no mother than one who abandoned you?"

"No." Absolutely not. "Any mother would be better than no mother. Will you help me? At least tell me if she's alive?"

The fortuneteller closes her eyes. Sits there long enough for the curls of smoke rising from the incense to straighten into a thin, wavering stream.

"I won't give up trying to find her," Birdie adds stubbornly. "Whether you help me or not."

Shinjō opens her eyes with a sigh and rises to fetch her bundle of yarrow sticks. When she returns, Birdie watches in silence as the divination sticks click back and forth between her hands and she counts under her breath, occasionally picking up one of the coins she'd brought from the back room, turning it heads or tails. When all six are arranged in a line along the edge of the table, she studies them, then sweeps them aside and repeats the process. Birdie looks on, puzzled. Jester told her she only got one question, so why is she doing it again? Didn't she like what the sticks told her the first time?

Outside, a vegetable vendor calls out his wares. A child runs past, wailing, "Wait for me!" as Shinjō turns the final coin, then gathers the sticks into a neat bundle and sets them aside. She reads the second answer, the corners of her mouth tightening.

"What is it?" Birdie blurts.

"The first hexagram is 'Brightness Hidden,' changing to the second hexagram, 'Confinement.'"

That doesn't sound good.

"Does that mean she's dead?" Birdie asks in a small voice. "Confined in a . . . a tomb?"

"No. 'Brightness Hidden' means she's hiding from an evil person or situation. 'Confinement' tells us where she's hiding." The next words drop from Shinjō's lips like coins she's reluctant to part with. "The character for 'confinement' represents a tree, completely surrounded by walls."

Birdie knows only one place where living things are confined by walls.

"Are you saying she's here? In Yoshiwara?"

Shinjō doesn't deny it.

"How is that possible?" Birdie cries. How could her mother have been living right under her nose all this time?

"Five *mon*," the seer says, closing her eyes and picking up her rosary.

The moment she leaves Madame Truth's shack, she begins studying every face she passes on the street. Could her mother be the courtesan ahead of her in line at the fruit seller? The geisha buying *shamisen* strings? The teahouse mistress welcoming men into the Red Lantern?

Her renewed quest occupies her so thoroughly that she doesn't notice she's bigger than Flower until her twin asks for help hanging her Tanabata wish on a branch of bamboo that's just out of reach. And when it's time to get dressed in the dragonfly kimonos that match Pearl's favorite midsummer outfit, Flower's still fits the way it should, but Birdie's ankles poke out the bottom like bird legs. She tugs it down as far as it will go and hunches her shoulders to seem smaller, but Auntie scolds her so much about her posture, she gives up the slouching that just draws attention to how much bigger she is now.

By the beginning of the Eighth Month, Birdie has even more to hide. She holds her hand towel over her budding breasts at the bathhouse and tries not to look startled every time she catches a reflection of herself in Pearl's mirror. Her face will never be as pretty as Flower's, but it's becoming more womanly, the childish roundness slimming to an oval. And her lips are beginning to remind men of less innocent things than flower buds now.

It's not until the Ninth Month that the worst thing of all happens. She's heading to the door to refill the teapot at the rice merchant's monthly banquet, when Pearl leaps to her feet and hustles her down the hall.

"Why didn't you take precautions?" she hisses, stooping to examine the back of Birdie's kimono. "If this doesn't come out, Auntie will have your head."

Birdie twists around to see a hideous red flower blooming on the back of her robe. She has lived among the women at the Treasure long enough to know why bloody rags get hauled to the laundress on a regular basis, she just didn't imagine the dreadful thing would happen to her so soon. She'd longed for the day she'd leave the restrictions of childhood behind, but growing up turned out to be one of those ideas that was only good until she started doing it.

By the time an early snow puts white caps on the stone foxes at the shrine, though, this uncomfortable development is more inconvenient than alarming, and she's relieved to learn that the pain the courtesans complain about every month is more like a stomachache than the kind of cut that produces that much blood. The worst thing is that she's expected to smile and go about her business without complaint, even though she's wearing soggy rags between her legs like a baby. It's hard not to be cranky about that.

But now it's becoming increasingly impossible to hide that she's more woman than child. Customers now make the kind of comments that fill her with the same confusion and dread she felt when Goldbelly pressed that gold coin into her hand. She can still get away with blushing and stammering and making a hasty exit, but Pearl warns her that if she doesn't want them to be mad instead of laughing it off, she'll need to come up with better ways of deflecting unwanted attention.

And she can no longer ignore the fact that when she gets too big to be a child attendant, attracting that kind of attention will be her job. Only the luckiest girls, a handful in all of Yoshiwara, are chosen to become apprentice oirans and skip straight to being a first-rank courtesan. No fourteen- or fifteen-year-old girl has enough experience to make fascinating conversation, so it's only the stunningly beautiful ones who can hope to attract a sponsor willing to pay oiran-level fees for a girl who has never even gone upstairs with a man. Sometimes she hears people wondering if Flower might be chosen, but no one ever predicts it might be her. She'll be occupying a cushion at the lowliest place in the lattice room and assisting the other courtesans until she attracts her first regular customer and begins working her way up the ladder.

She sets her sights instead on making herself indispensable to Pearl, so if Flower is elevated to oiran apprentice, she'll be promoted to junior courtesan instead of being traded to another pleasure house. Or worse. She knows where the unluckiest girls of all end up. In a geisha house.

The last day of the Eleventh Month starts out bad and goes downhill from there. Pearl wakes up grumpy, with a hangover, Cook has a headache and scorches the morning rice, then it starts to snow. No one wants cold, wet feet, so the courtesans all dump their errands onto Birdie and Flower. Their frozen toes barely carry them back in time to help Pearl get ready for the evening, then the snow turns to sleet just as they set out for tonight's teahouse. Pearl enjoys the luxury of being carried on a manservant's back so she doesn't arrive in wet, muddy robes, but everyone else must slog through the slush with chattering teeth and pained smiles on their faces. Worst of all, Takeda is the patron waiting for them upstairs at the Camellia tonight, and the teahouse mistress whispers to Pearl as they arrive that his guest for the evening canceled at the last minute. He's in a mood.

They all know what that means. Like a cat that's a known biter, Takeda-san lashes out with little warning. They've learned to read the signs, of course, so they manage to duck his sharpest barbs, but Pearl is all too aware that she must go upstairs with him at the end of the night, no matter what kind of mood he's in. As the evening draws to a prickly close, she has no choice but to goad him into exploding before they're alone.

She suggests a game of *sugoroku*, a board game that even the drunkest patrons can play. It requires no skill, just lucky rolls of the dice, and fortunately, luck is with her tonight. It's much easier to get him to blow up when she's winning.

As soon as she draws comfortably ahead, Pearl begins to tease him, saying they should bet on the outcome. That she'd wager her carved amber hair comb against his battered *inrō*. She's been after him to replace it for ages and knows he will resist wagering it, but tonight she refuses to back off.

"I don't understand why you insist on wearing that old thing everywhere," she complains. "What's inside it, anyway? Show me."

She reaches for it, but he twists out of reach.

"What is it? Something you don't want me to see?" she needles. "Your baby teeth? A naughty picture? No, it must be a keepsake from your old oiran! Yes, I'm sure that's what it is"—she pouts—"since you won't show me."

He leaps to his feet, fists clenched.

"What's in there is none of your business, woman."

"Why not?" she retorts, rising to face him. Half playfully she lunges for the *inrō*, as if to pull it through his sash, but instead of taking the opportunity to wrap her in his arms and laugh it off like her other admirers would, he grabs her wrist. She cries out as he twists it and gives her a push as he lets go. Tumbling to the floor, she sits there cradling her arm as her eyes fill with tears and shock that he dared abuse her in front of the others.

But Takeda isn't moved.

"When I tell you not to touch something, woman, I mean it," he growls. With a face like the god of thunder, he demands someone fetch his jacket, because he's not staying. Strides out, without a backward look.

Which is lucky, because if he had, he might have seen the hatred in Pearl's eyes.

They trudge back to the Treasure but no one gets much sleep, because even if they hadn't been able to overhear every word of Auntie's ear-blistering response to Pearl's report on the evening, they'd have been awakened by Pearl herself, stomping down the hallway and throwing her door shut with a crack that would wake the dead.

The next morning, Birdie's first dread-filled thought is to wonder what Pearl will write in her next-morning note. Will she try to patch things up, like the other times Takeda "taught her a lesson?" Or will she add insult to injury?

No one dares ask her, but whatever she wrote, the day drags by without a reply. So does the next. And the next. A week goes by, and still nothing from Takeda, including his monthly stipend. He hasn't sent word to sever their relationship, so everyone is hoping he's just taking longer to cool off than usual, but the worry is casting a shadow over all their New Year's preparations.

"*Ne, ne*, Jester! In here!"

Wrapped in two shawls to foil winter's chill fingers as they probe the cracks and knotholes, Birdie beckons him into the debtor room, where she's secretly been practicing the songs the courtesans' customers keep asking for, but Auntie forbids them to learn.

"Okay, Little Bird." Jester smiles, sliding the door shut behind him. "Surprise me."

"Listen to this." She picks out the melody of "Teardrops on My Sleeve," adding the flourishes he assured her would make people think she's better than she really is.

"*Waah*, that's great!" His eyes crinkle approvingly in his good-natured face. "But"—he sobers—"if Auntie catches a girl like you playing a grown-up tune like that, she'll know where you learned it, and I'll be finding her pipe ashes in my rice. So do me a favor, Birdie. If you're going to play 'Teardrops on My Sleeve,' play it like this."

He takes the instrument from her, pulls a long face like a shrine musician accompanying a solemn festival, and turns the lovers' lament into such a droning paean to doom that she's giggling into her sleeve by the time he finishes.

"Now, young lady—" He glowers, handing back the *shamisen*. "—don't let me catch you having fun again, when you're supposed to be suffering for your art."

"Wait." Birdie catches his sleeve as he rises to leave. "Is there any sign of a package from Takeda-san yet?"

He frowns.

"Not yet."

Neither of them needs to tell the other what bad news that is. Pearl is the top oiran in Yoshiwara, but that's more a matter of fame than fortune. Fame doesn't put tea in their teapots or socks on their feet.

"Birdie." Feather pokes her head in. "Pearl is asking for you."

"You'd better not keep Her Highness waiting," Jester advises.

She finds Pearl standing in her sitting room, hands on her hips, surrounded by kimono wrappers. She's not smiling.

"Anything from Takeda-san?"

"Sorry, Honored Elder Sister."

"That petty so-and-so!" Pearl stamps her foot. "How dare he go stingy on me, right before New Year's, the one time of year I can't afford to be?"

Birdie says nothing, because she knows no words that can conjure tips and gifts from thin air. New Year's is when faithful suppliers are rewarded, go-betweens' loyalty secured, and those who bend the rules for Pearl are given generous encouragement to keep doing so. Failing to top last year's largesse would be fatal to her reputation and her ability to wheedle the goods and services that keep her patrons happy. She needs Takeda to provide the means.

"It's still ten days before the new year," Birdie points out, trying to sound more hopeful than she feels. "It's not too late."

"It is, for our Second Day robes." Pearl pouts. "We were supposed to get our order in two days ago, and now it'll be impossible for everything to be ready in time. We'll have to think of a new idea."

Birdie is sorry to hear that. Visitors from all walks of life crowd into Yoshiwara on the second day of the new year to admire the inventiveness of the pleasure house processions and take notes on the latest fashions. Last year, Jewel from the House of Peonies caused the biggest stir when she dressed her entourage in original kimonos that conjured memories of favorite childhood sweets, which her child attendants handed out as they made their way down the main boulevard.

Pearl had planned to top that this year by ordering special outer robes covered with pockets and filled with the more manly indulgences of pipes and tobacco, which would be given to her fans along the parade route. Now she'll have to scale back to something more modest, and if Takeda's payment doesn't arrive, she'll have to scale back to nothing at all.

"The other houses will have their orders in by now," Pearl frets. "Take Flower and see if you can find out what they're up to. If we have to scrimp, at least let's not copy a house that can afford to do it better." She returns to half-heartedly sorting through her kimonos.

By the time Birdie meets Flower at their favorite shrine bench later that afternoon, she's glad they're rethinking their Second Day idea. Every pleasure house in Yoshiwara is planning variations on last year's winning strategy. The apprentice at the toy shop was packing up a large box of gaily painted wooden tops for the House of Bamboo, the Wisteria had the same idea as the Treasure and is about to take delivery of two dozen pipes, and even the Peony is copying the Peony. They're doubling down on last year's sweets triumph with a more flamboyant version.

They return to Pearl's room to find that Peach, Feather, and Butterfly have been recruited to help, but they're still headed in the wrong direction.

"... everyone loves dried squid snacks," Feather is saying, "and they're much cheaper than tobacco. What if we give those away instead?"

"That would certainly make an impression." Pearl wrinkles her nose in distaste. "They'd smell us coming before they even set foot inside the Great Gate."

"We shouldn't be giving anything away," Birdie announces from the doorway.

"Why?"

"Because every pleasure house in Yoshiwara is in a race to shower gifts on their followers." She doesn't have to add that without Takeda's payment, that's the kind of race the Treasure can't win. Can't even afford to enter.

"All right," Pearl replies, in a voice as sour and hard as a green plum. "Have you got a better idea?"

"Not yet," Birdie admits. "But if we want to stand out, we'll have to do something really different. Something no one has thought of."

Easier said than done. Not only does the new idea have to be cheap, it has to send the message that their oiran is the most desirable in all of Yoshiwara. It's a message that has been said a thousand times, in a thousand different ways, and outspending their rivals is no longer an option. Auntie sticks her head in to remind them it's past time to get ready for tonight's entertaining. Silently, they file out, the problem still trailing them like a wet dog.

But later that night, while Birdie is playing "Bells of Edo" on one string to amuse a waiting customer, inspiration strikes. She thrusts the *shamisen* into Peach's arms the moment she arrives and runs up the stairs to Pearl's rooms.

This is the only "double fee" day the oiran hasn't persuaded a patron to cover this month, and until she finds another man willing to pay double on the five days a month Overseer-san cranks up her rates to take advantage of her popularity, she has to cover the extra fee herself. Tonight she's getting her money's worth by sipping roasted rice tea in an old robe, answering one of the many messages that arrive daily from her admirers.

"Oh, it's you," Pearl yawns. "What are you doing here? Is it slow tonight?"

"No. But I had an idea."

Pearl sets down her brush.

"I remembered what Jester told me on the day he taught me to play 'Bells of Edo' on one string. 'Impressing people with less than they expect is more memorable than impressing them with more.'"

"Go on."

"Well, every pleasure house in Yoshiwara is trying to spend more money and give away better gifts than the others, right? So—" She takes a deep breath. "What if we do the opposite? Remember how you made the House of Peonies' fancy red-and-gold outfits look flashy and cheap?"

"By wearing the 'cherry blossoms by moonlight' kimonos the next day," Pearl recalls. "You think we'd stand out by holding back?"

"It's cheaper too," Birdie points out, nervously rocking back and forth, heel, toe, heel, toe. Does she think it's a good idea? Or a bad one?

"That"—Pearl tosses her one of the oranges sitting on her writing table—"is the best idea I've heard in a long time."

By late morning the next day, there's still nothing from Takeda. Pearl can afford New Years' tips or new Second Day outfits but not both, so she sends one of the manservants to search the storeroom for the bedding an ex-patron gave her as a customary first gift. The futon pads and comforter had long since been cleaned and aired and recycled to the staff, but the red silk coverings were too expensive to throw away, too intimate to sell. Perhaps they can be cut up and sewn into an outfit.

Birdie scrambles to her feet to help push the table and cushions out of the way so Pearl can spread the heavy red silk over her smooth tatami mats. The oiran and her attendants gather around, contemplating the enormous golden characters embroidered on the top. Merchants aren't allowed to have family crests, so her ex-patron had commissioned the characters for *dai-kichi* instead, which means "greatest good luck."

"There might be enough to make a kimono or a padded outer robe from the parts that aren't embroidered," Butterfly estimates. "But not both. Too bad it has those enormous gold characters on one side."

Birdie giggles. "It really does look like the biggest new year's envelope I've ever seen."

"Birdie!" Pearl shrieks, spinning around to grab her hands. "You're a genius!"

Then the others see it too. What man wouldn't think it the greatest good luck to unwrap a traditional red envelope with Pearl from the House of Treasures inside?

Birdie wakes in a flutter of excitement every morning as Pearl's Second Day robes take shape. She doesn't even mind pitching in to sweep the rooms and fetch the tea, doing her part to free up the maid who used to sew for a kimono maker before she came to work at the Treasure.

At last, it's done. She helps Pearl slip the outer robe onto her shoulders and watches her swivel this way and that before the mirror, looking pleased. The padded crimson robe with the giant golden *dai-kichi* characters on the back will certainly remind everyone of opening new year's gifts with childhood joy.

What she didn't expect is the color in Pearl's cheeks, and the kind of sparkle she hadn't seen in the oiran's eyes for a long time.

1786

On the first day of the New Year, Birdie gives Pearl's toenail a final buff and yawns. The bathhouse men had roused them well before dawn, trotting through the streets and exhorting one and all to come take the First Official Bath of the new year.

Now Birdie and Flower are scrubbed and dressed in their traditional pine branch kimonos, helping the others get ready for the First Official Shrine Visit and listening to the courtesans' unofficial first complaints.

"I keep hoping Overseer-san will give us a robe I'd ever wear again," grouses Feather, glowering down at her kimono. "But they just keep getting worse."

"Maybe it's his eyesight that's getting worse," Butterfly gripes, displaying a sleeve emblazoned with a gaudy House of Treasures crest as big as a peach.

"Look what just arrived," Auntie crows, sweeping in the door. Jester trails behind, lugging an ornate black and gold lacquered chest.

Pearl lifts the lid. It's filled with coins, both gold and silver. She raises an eyebrow at Auntie.

"From Takeda-san," the house manager confirms, handing her the note that came with it. "It's twice the usual sum." She's already counted it, of course.

Birdie sidles around behind Pearl to see what's narrowing her eyes as she reads. The note is a formal greeting for the new year, written by a professional scribe and stamped with Takeda's red seal. The same note he probably sent to his head gardener, his captain of the guard, and his tobacconist.

"I'll write to thank him after we get back from the shrine," Pearl says in a flat voice, handing it back to Auntie.

The others crowd around to admire the riches as Pearl turns back to the mirror to adjust her hairpins. Birdie catches a glimpse of her reflection and feels her First Misgivings of the new year. If Takeda-san thinks he has bought his way out of making an apology for his recent bad behavior, he's dead wrong.

The oiran processions set out bright and early the next morning, but since that's closer to noon for those who don't live on Yoshiwara time, plenty of spectators line the boulevard by the time the first pleasure house sallies forth.

Pearl makes Birdie and Flower put on their plain gold kimonos early and sends them out wrapped in everyday shawls so they can run back and forth to the Treasure, reporting on the other processions while the rest of them get ready.

The wintery breeze cuts like a knife and Birdie is already sniffling from the cold, but she decides she should be the one who stays outside to observe, while her twin runs back to describe what the other houses are wearing. It would not be a good day for Flower to drift off into her own little world.

The lesser pleasure houses hurry their courtesans out first, so their modest displays won't disappoint spectators already dazzled by top houses' extravaganzas. They're still dressed in layers upon layers of checks, patterns, and stripes, attempting to impress the onlookers with a riot of colors and seasonal motifs, and Birdie hears plenty of oohs and aahs from the samurai wives all around. By next week, kimono makers all over Edo will be busy copying them.

Flower returns, and they hop up and down to keep warm, watching the House of Bamboo and the House of Wisteria give out their wooden tops and pipes. She sends Flower back to the Treasure to report, then stretches up on tiptoe to see what's causing titters of laughter to ripple through the crowd. The House of Seashells' sea life theme is making quite an impression. The wrong kind. The last tentacle is just swishing past when Flower reappears.

"Auntie says to come back. They need our help."

That morning, Pearl had surprised everyone with her plans for Takeda's bonus money. She put everyone at the Treasure to work stuffing coins into red New Year's envelopes to hand out to spectators. If the kind of fame and goodwill she buys herself with her generosity doesn't make every man in Edo long to become her patron, nothing will.

Resting her basket of wrapped coins on her hip, a small breeze sends Birdie's sleeve ties fluttering as she waits for Pearl to signal it's time to step onto the promenade. How many times have she and Flower waited like this since they led the Second Day procession that very first time? Four? No, five. With a jolt, she realizes she's not twelve anymore. Yesterday was New Year's Day, when everyone became a year older. This may be the last time she and Flower lead the Second Day procession as child attendants, because in Yoshiwara, girls of fourteen are no longer considered children.

Auntie claps her hands. "It's time."

Birdie shifts her basket onto her arm as the manservant in front hoists the House of Treasures' lantern high. Halfway down the first block, he halts to announce, "First-rank Oiran White Pearl of the House of Treasures wishes you great good fortune in the New Year!"

That's their cue to hand out the wrapped coins. Spectators crowd in as word spreads that the House of Treasures is giving away more than new year's greetings. Most of the packets contain but a single tiny *mon*, but it's money the onlookers weren't expecting, so it buys Pearl far more appreciation and approval than a tip they deserve. A lucky few are already receiving the random packets Jester suggested they seed with silver *bu*, to spread the news of her generosity farther and faster.

At the second stop, Birdie passes them out right and left, saving the last of her one-*mon* gifts for Tiger, who melts back into the crowd and reappears at their third stop with a winning smile, where he accepts another from Feather.

When they stop for the fourth time, she's watching Butterfly approach a group of young *rōnin* who are supposed to be keeping an eye out for troublemakers but are enjoying the monkey show instead, when she catches a streak of movement from the corner of her eye.

Then everything happens so fast, all she can do is shriek, "Watch out!" as the monkey breaks free of its trainer and hurls itself in Pearl's direction, teeth bared. Feather recoils, Peach stumbles, and the young *rōnin* Butterfly was flirting with dashes into the street to intercept the angry monkey just as it takes a flying leap at Pearl. Gripping the flailing, screaming animal at arm's length, he hands it back to the trainer, who arrives on his heels, babbling apologies.

Then the young man turns to Pearl, asks if she's all right.

Pearl's eyes are still dark, brimming with fear. Right now, she doesn't look like an unattainable oiran at all. Her face softens in gratitude to the stranger who saved her from a biting, and the smile she gives him as she bows and thanks him isn't the practiced one she uses on customers, it's the real one Birdie only sees in the privacy of the Treasure.

Pearl looks down at the new year's gift in her hand, a heavy one, with a silver *bu* inside, and extends it toward the bowing *rōnin* with both hands. He looks up, surprised, and shakes his head, refusing. The young man's smooth cheeks redden. He murmurs something only she can hear and drops to one knee, lifting the padded hem of Pearl's outer robe to his lips. As he rises, she chooses an ornament from her sash and offers it to him.

By the end of the day, the story of the hero who saved the oiran has improved with every telling. Everyone knows someone who knows someone who died of a monkey bite, and all of Edo is convinced that the bauble Pearl bestowed on the penniless *rōnin* must have been made of gold, encrusted with pearls, costly beyond measure. You could tell, they nod sagely, by the look on his face.

"The thing is," Birdie tells Tiger later, "Pearl really did give him one of her most treasured possessions. It's not valuable in the way people think—the little tiger is just made of boxwood—but it's one of the few things she's had since before she came to Yoshiwara. She's worn it every new year's since she was a child."

Later, at the Treasure, they all compare notes. A horrified Feather holds her hands apart to show how close she came to the monkey's bared teeth. Peach doesn't remember her ankle hurting when she twisted it, but now it's swelled up like a fat white radish and she can barely stand. Butterfly was annoyed that the handsome *rōnin* ran off without an apology, until she saw why.

The only one who says nothing about what she was doing during the most talked-about incident in Edo is Flower. But that night, before they fall asleep, she turns to Birdie and smiles.

"See?" she whispers. "I told you the monkey was important."

Birdie stares at the ceiling a long time after that. The next day, she makes Flower promise not to say the monkey thing to anyone else.

Like many small twists of fate that change the course of peoples' lives, Birdie and Pearl have no idea how profoundly a chance encounter with a monkey is about to change theirs.

Pearl is showered with gifts and adoration every day by some of the wealthiest and most powerful men in Edo, but she'd trade them all for a kiss from a man who truly loves her. Which is why her pale cheeks are still flushed with possibility the next morning, when she asks Birdie to find out the name of her rescuer.

Tiger tells her it's most likely he's one of the young men who were hired as additional security for the day. (He tried to get hired too, but even the age he lied about was too young.) Most of the temporary hires were from disgraced samurai families who were stripped of their land and rank for fighting against the Tokugawas in the Battle of Sekigahara.

They'd lost their social standing, but kept the privilege of wearing two swords, so most of them make a living as guards and watchmen. Maybe Pearl's *rōnin* does too.

Three days later, Birdie is on her way to collect a fresh pot of Pearl's face cream when she spots him coming through the Great Gate, guarding a cartload of rice bales. She steals close enough to note his family crest (Yamada clan), the quality of the kimono he wears under his trouser-skirt (once splendid, now threadbare), and the proud profile that even his poverty and his family's lowly status can't cheapen. He obviously belongs on a prancing horse, defending a noble cause, not guarding a merchant's wagon in the pleasure quarter. It's too bad noble causes are few and far between in this age of peace and prosperity, and heroes no longer in as much demand as guards.

"He comes to Yoshiwara every Day of the Rat, with the wagon from the Matsui warehouse," Birdie reports to Pearl. And according to the talkative clerk, he usually arrives around noon, interrupting the man's lunch and annoying him greatly. His name is Yasunori Yamada.

Within a month, Pearl is sneaking out to meet Yasu at every opportunity.

"To another year of record profits!" the shipowner toasts.

Takeda raises his cup with an indulgent smile, as if it were beneath him to celebrate crass victories like beating the other Tokyo fleets back to Edo for the second year in a row. He takes a polite sip, mustering his arguments for the discussion to come. The man across the table is a brilliant fleet manager, but he thinks the only way to double their profits is to double their ships. This now means building six additional craft, and Takeda's coffers are bare. It would be tricky for the man across the table to ditch his partner in favor of a richer one after marrying his daughter to Takeda's son, but at the end of the day, merchants are merchants. He'd be a fool to expect honor or loyalty from a man who's never been bound by the samurai code.

"... think of how much we could make if we double our capacity yet again!" the shipowner crows.

That was fast. They haven't even finished the first flask of sake yet.

"Hold on," Takeda says, nudging Pearl to keep his companion's cup brimming at all times. "I'm as eager to increase profits as you are, but let's think this through. Our success the first year was due to having three small, fast ships instead of one big one. Our success this year was adding three more, and"—he raises his cup to salute the cunning ploy the merchant had suggested—"tying up all the sailmakers with orders for spare sails so our rivals' new ships were left wallowing at the Edo docks when it came time to sail for Nagasaki. But by next year, everyone will have fast ships and a sailmaker in their pockets. If we want to stay a step ahead, we'll need a new idea."

"Like six more ships," his partner stubbornly insists.

"Or increasing the value of our cargo, instead of our capacity."

"We're already filling our holds with the most valuable cargo there is," the shipowner objects.

"With all due respect, that's not true. We've been getting top prices for the auction lots we manage to win, because we're the first to return and dazzle Edo buyers with novelties they've never seen before. But the Maedas rake in far more than we do. Not by bringing back more, or bringing it back faster, but by outbidding us for the best."

"They're just lucky," the shipowner scoffs.

Takeda disagrees. "It can't be pure luck that they knew to bid on those unlikely looking contraptions for navigating at sea, and were able to pluck the cure for night blindness from the reams of untranslated writings."

"Well, if it's not luck, what is it?"

"I think they have an agent who tips them off to the good stuff."

"Impossible!" The shipowner snorts. "Do you know how few Japanese can speak their barbarian claptrap, much less understand their magic? It took the shōgun twelve years to find one! Show me a man who can do all that, and I'll eat my pipe."

"Well, Honorable Shipmaster," Pearl interjects with a smug smile. "I hope you enjoy the taste of tobacco."

Both men turn to stare.

"You know someone who speaks Dutch?" Takeda asks, surprised.

"I do. He understands Dutch Learning too."

"Is he here? In Edo?"

"Yes, he comes to Yoshiwara as a guest of a silk merchant who's a . . ." She hesitates, because it's bad form to remind one patron that she has others. "A frequent visitor to the pleasure quarter."

"What's his name?"

"Vandermeer."

"He's a *foreigner*?" The shipowner wrinkles his nose. "How does His Excellency stand the smell?"

"He doesn't smell," Pearl corrects him primly. "Vandermeer-sensei orders his scent from the shōgun's own incense blender."

"What brings him to Edo?" Takeda asks.

"He's the shōgun's Dutch Learning Expert and translator."

"Could he also be the insider tipping off the Maedas?" Takeda wonders. "And if so, do you think he could be persuaded to work for us instead?"

"You'd have to ask him."

"Can it be arranged?"

"Well . . ." Pearl shoots him a sly look. "If Takeda-san were to host that moon-viewing party I've been suggesting for ever so long, I might be able to talk him into accepting an invitation."

"But moon-viewing isn't done until the Ninth Month," Takeda objects. "It has to be sooner."

"All right, when would be the best time to make his acquaintance?"

"The Ninth Month is too late if we're to outbid the Maedas for his services before the trading season begins, but if we move too soon, it might set off a bidding war. What about the sixth month? Can you arrange an introduction around the beginning of the sixth month?"

"Yes, but . . ." She hesitates. "It would be difficult"—meaning impossible—"to introduce Vandermeer-sensei to you directly."

Yoshiwara etiquette requires he extend the invitation to the silk merchant, then rely on Pearl to work her magic behind the scenes to suggest that his foreign friend would be most welcome to accompany him.

"Perhaps a grand firefly-catching and poetry party here at the Camellia," Pearl proposes, "so it would be natural for you to invite a wide circle of acquaintances."

Takeda grimaces, and not just because of the expense.

"Does it have to involve poetry?"

"It does," she insists. "And a boat. With musicians. And painted lanterns." As he opens his mouth to protest, she adds, "If Takeda-san wishes to ensure that the influential man who brings the translator will accept his invitation, the party must be both novel and lavish."

Takeda groans inwardly. Typical oiran grifting. He's never known any courtesan to suggest that he might achieve his goals without spending the maximum. She's his only connection to the translator, though, so she's got him by the balls.

"Very well," he concedes. Turns to the shipowner. "Are we agreed?"

They are.

But he's already fretting about spending more money he can't spare, even though he knows that throwing a poetry party and bribing the translator will certainly cost less than six ships. He tells himself that enduring an evening writing some accursed verses can't be any worse than entertaining that oafish rice merchant he'd borrowed from before. He raises his cup with false enthusiasm to seal the deal.

Takeda had planned to stay at the Camellia until morning, but he tosses and turns, can't find a comfortable position. Even satisfying himself with his oiran hadn't dissipated his money jitters—which are now going to get worse before they get better—and the more serious concern that can't be solved by throwing a party: Koga's increasingly erratic behavior.

He throws on his clothes as Pearl pretends to sleep, then stalks downstairs and flips aside the Camellia's door curtain. Striding off toward the moat, he replays the bitter memory of Pearl pulling that *inrō* through his adversary's sash on the night he'd nearly been undone by a courtesan's game. Does Koga know that's where he keeps the precious name seal? No, he's sure the scoundrel took it just to needle him, to show he was annoyed at being asked for twice as many introductions that month.

That's when Takeda began to worry that his days of enjoying unlimited access to the officials who sign government contracts were numbered. For the first time in fourteen years, Koga had refused. Takeda can't really blame him—he'd think twice before recommending a colleague do business with his ne'er-do-well son too—but this is the only way Kiyohisa will be able to obtain his own set of officials to cultivate for the good of the family fortunes.

Takeda walks faster, unhappy at the reminder that his family's future hangs by the single, fraying thread of Koga's influence. Why is their arrangement suddenly falling apart? Is someone putting pressure on Koga to make the threat of exposure go away? Had his quizzing of Willow or poking around Odawara gotten back to the woman who'd been with him on the night of the fire? Or perhaps her brother has heard he's asking questions.

He has to find that child. Takeda pauses across from the dark lattice room at the Golden Drum, then walks on. Willow was long gone by the time the missing woman's baby was born. It's that pack of professional liars at the House of Peonies who hold the key to finding it.

Time to deploy the little attendant from the House of Treasures again. But Birdie works for Pearl. She'll only help him if it's in her oiran's interest, and his faith in Pearl's loyalty has been shaken by her suspicious attempt to get Koga's *netsuke* and *inrō* away from him. He needs to come up with a way to make the girl so beholden to him, she'll do his bidding behind Pearl's back.

Lucky for him, that shouldn't be too hard. Everyone in Yoshiwara has her price, and it's not hard to guess what a child attendant wants more than anything in the world. She's a bit plain, but that might work in his favor. People probably underestimate her the same way they underestimate him. They're so busy admiring the beauties, they don't notice the mousy ones picking their pockets. The fact that she doesn't expect her wildest dreams to come true will make her even more grateful to him.

Smiling to himself, he turns around and strides back toward the Camellia. He's looking forward to turning Birdie into the best tool he ever had.

On the morning that the last patches of dirty snow have finally disappeared from the deepest shade, Birdie cracks open the common room's shutter, pokes her nose out, and gives a sniff. The air is crisp, the sky clear. Is it warm enough to do her errands without a wrap? Probably not. Her blue one won't look good with this kimono, though. Can she borrow Feather's green one and put it back before she—

"Auntie wants you," a maid announces from the doorway.

Birdie groans. Regretting she dithered over the shawl, she hooks her empty basket over her arm and trudges down the hall to be saddled with even more chores.

"Excuse me for intruding," she mutters as she slides open the door to Auntie's room, sounding as un-sorry as she feels.

And instantly regrets it, because Auntie is not alone. The House of Treasures' overseer is sitting at her table, smoking, dressed in the bold blue-and-red checkered silk kimono that he'd won off a kabuki actor in a dice game. There's a woman at the table too, with the look of an ex-beauty, her habit of haughtiness at odds with the way her face sags now. Her hair has been carefully puffed in a vain attempt to hide that it's thinning from too many years of pulling and pinning and pomading, and she looks vaguely familiar, but Birdie can't quite place her. Who is she? Why is she here? Her kimono is of good quality silk, but it's a muted gray, like Auntie's. She's not quite as old as Auntie, but the line dividing her brows is just as deep.

Oh, no. Could she be the manager of another pleasure house? No, she's only wearing two hairpins. Surely she's not from... a geisha house?

Heart racing, Birdie drops the basket, throws herself to the floor, presses her forehead to the rice straw mats, bowing like the kind of child attendant who would become a model junior courtesan if only she were given the chance, not the kind who would eat more than her share of pickles or practice popular songs when she's supposed to be learning the classics.

"It looks like you know why you're here," Auntie begins, puffing on her pipe.

"No, ma'am," she squeaks. Maybe if she doesn't say it, it won't be true.

"Stand up, so Mistress Moon can see you."

She rises to her feet staring at the floor, blinking back the urge to weep.

The woman stands and crosses the room. Lifts Birdie's chin.

"Look at me, girl."

The woman's face swims as tears spill down Birdie's cheeks.

"She certainly cries very prettily," the woman says, with a dry laugh. "I think I can work with that." She turns Birdie's face one way, then the other, then steps back to look her up and down.

"How long have you been bleeding?"

Birdie flushes with the shame of saying it in front of Overseer-san.

"Since the Ninth Month, Honored Madame."

Mistress Moon turns to Auntie.

"Do you think she'll get much taller?"

"Pearl was the same height at her age."

"Let's hope that means she'll be able to get some use out of Pearl's old kimonos, then, instead of requiring a whole new wardrobe."

Why are they talking about Pearl's kimonos?

"What do you think?" Auntie asks.

Please don't let her take me away. Please.

"I think we can make something of her." Mistress Moon nods. "If Pearl does her part, I can do mine."

"Little Bird," Auntie says, using her full name, "today is your lucky day. I suggest you thank Overseer-san and Mistress Moon for helping you become the House of Treasures' new apprentice oiran."

What . . . how . . . ? Birdie stumbles toward the common room. She must have somehow thanked everyone who needed thanking, because here she is, out in the hall, by herself. Her head is spinning. She can't believe the last half hour just happened.

Her first thought is to run down the hall and tell Flower, but as she thinks of the words, a fist of dread tightens around her heart.

"Flower, guess what? I'm the new apprentice oiran!" *And you're not.*

Something about this is not right. Nobody has ever suggested she's apprentice oiran material. Nobody. There must be some mistake. Or it's a prank. Someone playing a cruel game she's too young to understand.

Pearl pokes her head out of her rooms, like she's been waiting for her.

"Birdie!" The oiran pulls her inside and shuts the door. "Well? Did they tell you?"

"You *know*?"

"Of course I know!"

"But—" Is Pearl the one who chose her? "Why me?"

"Why not you?"

"Because—" Flower is prettier. Flower is better at music. "Everyone always said it would be Flower."

"Did Flower think of the idea for our Second Day procession? Did Flower find out Yasu's name and help me steal out to meet him?"

"Well, no. But—"

"You were picked because you think on your feet, and you can keep a secret. And"—her eyes narrow—"you know how to be grateful. In fact, shouldn't you be showing some gratitude right now?"

Yes, she should. For the second time that day, she drops to the floor, pressing her forehead to the tatami, babbling her confused thanks.

"Oh, get up, silly. I was joking. You don't really have to do that."

Doesn't she? She raises her head and watches Pearl cross to the table and pour two cups of tea. She waits for an invitation, but when the oiran looks up, cocking an eyebrow at her, she realizes one won't be coming. Her status has changed, and for some reason she doesn't yet understand, she no longer needs one. She sidles across the room, watching Pearl as one might keep an eye on a bee. Failing to show due respect to everyone who outranks her has always resulted in a swift and painful reminder that nobody survives long in Yoshiwara if they don't know their place. It's hard to ignore the lesson that has been drilled into her so painfully.

She warily lowers herself onto the cushion opposite and, just to be safe, waits for the oiran to take a sip before lifting her own cup.

"From now on I'll help you, and I expect you to help me." Pearl studies her face through the steam curling from her tea. "But first, there are some things you need to understand. Surely you've noticed that you're getting too big to be a child attendant anymore."

Birdie nods, swallows.

"Auntie has been looking for a new pair of girls since last fall." The oiran sips her tea. "They're arriving next week. You can thank me for making sure she didn't sell your contract to another house before then."

"She wasn't planning to promote me to the lattice room?" Birdie squeaks.

"She might have." Pearl gives an airy wave, as if it weren't a life-or-death matter. "But then you'd be stuck downstairs every night, when I need you helping me instead."

Helping her do what? Meet Yasu? How can her help be worth the huge sum Pearl will have to pay for her debut? Unless they find her a patron, Pearl will continue to be on the hook for her expenses as her attendant. She bites her tongue. If she says anything about the money, Pearl might change her mind.

"I'm honored to be chosen," she says instead, bowing low over the table. "I'll help you in every way I can, Honored Elder Sister."

"Good. See that you do. And never forget who's making you worthy of your promotion."

"I won't."

She straightens, no longer a fashion accessory, but an apprentice.

Birdie didn't expect her new job to begin right away, but it does. Pearl tells her to take off her clothes. From now on, Birdie will be dressed in the robes Pearl wore when she was an apprentice oiran.

Even her new underwear is a revelation. Birdie has never worn silk next to her skin before. So cool and slippery! She shivers in delight as

Pearl guides her arms into layer after layer of slithery underrobes that drape around her with the kind of luxury only oirans can afford. Each layer adds another sliver of color at the edge of her neck and sleeves—red, pink, gold, green—until they're topped with a glorious peony-patterned kimono that ties them all together. By the time one of Pearl's heavy brocade obis has been knotted over them all, she's beginning to understand why oirans walk so slowly. She can barely move. Not only are the clothes a lot heavier than she's used to, the sleeves are so long they trail on the floor.

"Don't you dare shame me by letting them touch the ground, or you'll find yourself peeling radishes instead of pouring sake," Pearl warns. "Hold your arms like this." She demonstrates.

As soon as Birdie has mastered the sleeves, Pearl re-twists her hair into a simple but more grown-up style, then unwraps an ornament with dangling tassels of coral and silver beads. Birdie winces as Pearl slides it in, but her tender scalp is forgotten the moment the oiran pulls her in front of the mirror.

She barely recognizes herself. She looks like a princess. She *feels* like a princess.

"Are you coming?" Pearl is already at the door. "Do you think I got you all dolled up for nothing?"

Birdie maneuvers herself down the steep stairs, gripping the rail hand over hand so she doesn't fall. Pearl has already ordered the front door maid to put out two pairs of glossy black *koma-geta*.

"The ones with the pink thongs are for you."

They're not nearly as tall as Pearl's, but when they step into the street, Birdie has to concentrate so hard on not tripping that Pearl has to remind her twice to walk next to her, not lag behind.

At the end of the block, though, she gets her first taste of being a first-rank courtesan. Pearl is used to turning heads, but now passersby are looking at her too. Not with a cheery wave, but with admiration. Respect. Like she's *somebody*.

"Stop grinning like a festival fool," Pearl hisses.

Up one street, down another. Smile, but not too much. Don't stumble. Don't let your sleeves drag. When Pearl is satisfied that they've started the rumor mill grinding, they turn toward home.

And not a moment too soon. Birdie's so tired she could weep. It's hard to remember so many new things while walking in a whole new way. As thrilling as it is to command the kind of attention that's showered on an oiran in public, she can't wait to shed her borrowed plumage and turn back into plain, old, invisible Birdie again.

But that's not to be. When they reach the Treasure, Pearl tells her to ask Cook for a bowl of rice, because she won't have time to eat later. She must spend the evening at her oiran's side, letting everyone get a good look at her in the robes and ornaments that haven't been seen since Pearl was an apprentice herself. She's to say nothing about her changed status, just lower her eyes and murmur the usual "please show this humble person your favor" in answer to their questions. By tomorrow, the news should be all over Yoshiwara.

The hours slip by. Much to her astonishment, Pearl's clothes possess a near-magical power to turn her into someone who doesn't stammer and blush, who doesn't feel like hiding under the table when men speak of her new allure. By the time they bow farewell to the last guest, she's both exhausted and exhilarated.

After Pearl and her patron retire upstairs, she walks back to the Treasure with the courtesans and guests who will continue their revelry there. But as they draw near, her feet begin to drag. She'll have to face Flower now. She's been dreading that all day.

Slipping past the drowsing manservant supposed to be guarding the back door, she creeps up the stairs, praying that Flower is already asleep.

But she's not. The room is empty. The floor is bare.

Birdie runs to the cupboard and throws it open, finds Flower's futon still folded up inside, her few possessions gone. She whirls around, runs back to the hall, looks both ways. Scrambling down the stairs to the back door, she bursts out into the alley.

"Flower!" she calls.

No reply.

"Flower?" she whimpers. The plaintive notes of "Teardrops on My Sleeve" drift from the pleasure house next door. Her throat closes. Had Flower run away after hearing Birdie was the Treasures' new apprentice oiran? Or had she been *sent* away?

It doesn't matter. She's gone. Tonight, her twin is sleeping in a strange futon, on a strange floor, without a friend, alone. And so is she. Birdie slumps against the back door, swipes her wet cheek on her shoulder before she remembers she's still wearing Pearl's fancy clothes.

But all the magic has gone out of them. She may look like the Treasures' next oiran, but inside, she's just a child attendant who has lost her other half. Two men stagger past the end of the alley and one grabs his companion's sleeve, pointing. They're too far away to see her swollen eyes and blotchy face, and their admiring catcalls ring like mockery in her ears. How dare they enjoy themselves, when her world just cracked in two?

Chased back inside by their bawdy hoots, she wakes the doorman.

"Have you seen Flower tonight?"

He shakes his head.

Dragging herself upstairs, she hears a few muffled cries coming from the courtesans' rooms, but she knows better than to interrupt and ask if they know where Flower is. Shedding Pearl's finery in a heap, she crawls into bed, shivering. The nook she's shared with Flower for four years is too big, too quiet, too empty. She pulls the covers up to her quivering chin in the darkness. Tears leak from the corners of her eyes, trickling through her hair, wetting her pillow. She has never felt so alone.

From the moment they knelt before Auntie and Pearl to receive their new names, she and Flower have always had each other. They covered for each other, stood up for each other, shared everything by halves. Who will she share those things with now? The Treasures' courtesans are like sisters to her, but tonight she heard the envy in their congratulations, the barbs in their banter. How can she blame them, when she just cut in line before them all?

As for Pearl's assurance that they're going to help each other from now on, trusting her would be as foolish as trusting a cat.

The next morning, Auntie refuses to tell her where Flower is, and the others either don't know, or have been warned not to say. For the next few days, Birdie won't be allowed to leave the House of Treasures.

Pearl and Auntie keep her so busy she has little time to think of Flower until she crawls into her futon at night, too exhausted to cry. Becoming the Treasures' new oiran apprentice is not all silk underwear and grown-up hairdos. If she doesn't want to suffer the same fate as Flower, she must change how she looks, how she walks, how she speaks.

"Good heavens, are those caterpillars or eyebrows? Pluck them at once. Now redraw them higher, so you'll look interested in what a man is saying, even if you're not."

"And those teeth! They'll look much better once they're blackened. See how yellow they look, compared to your white makeup? Once we let the stain set for a few hours, they'll recede into the shadows where they belong and men will focus on your lips instead."

Tea ceremony, *koto* playing, and dance are added to her other lessons. There are never enough hours in the day to practice them all, because she still has to run errands and help entertain guests before Pearl and her patron go upstairs. Where, she's now learning, they do more than sleep.

Mistress Moon turned out to be the House of Treasures' assistant manager. Even though she's usually hidden away in a back room attending to the books, she does double duty as the ex-courtesan in charge of teaching the secrets of pleasing men. Not the sort of pleasing depicted on the naughty woodblock prints Tiger refuses to show her (even though she offered to pay him), but the wiles she will need in order to snare men as patrons.

When to make them laugh and when to make them cry. How long to make a man wait to see the palm of her hand, or the inside of her wrist, or be allowed to pull the pins from her hair. How to play men like a *shamisen* to get what she wants. But those skills aren't really so different from the arts she's been copying from Pearl for years. It's not until her new instructor decides it's time she explained what will be required of her when a man takes her upstairs that Birdie finds herself in over her head.

"The first thing to know"—Mistress Moon lights her pipe—"is that once you're alone with a man, you needn't worry about memorizing the 'forty-eight positions' and such. It's the man's job to tell you what he wants, and your job to do it. Obedience is what men desire, not fancy techniques. Do you understand?"

"Yes, Honored Assistant Manager. But what exactly—"

"I'm getting there," she says testily.

But once she explains, Birdie wishes she hadn't. Walking around Yoshiwara afterward, she's repelled and fascinated by what lurks beneath the robes of every man she sees. Not just the pleasure house customers, but the fishmonger, the comb carver, even the temple priest chanting his sutras. She can't stop thinking about it. And now that she knows what's going on, she can no longer ignore the sounds coming from the courtesans' rooms at night. The more she tries not to think about what's happening in there, the more details her imagination supplies. At the bathhouse, she sneaks glances at the other women while scrubbing herself. How many times has the one with the saggy bottom done The Thing? What about the one with the mole on her chin? The one with the crooked toes?

She lowers herself into the bath. If only she had someone to talk to, to compare notes with. But the second-rank courtesans are so grown up, all they do is make jokes she can't understand, and the new child attendants are little more than babies.

If only she could talk to Flower. If only she could *find* Flower. She tips her head back and closes her eyes. Yoshiwara is only twelve square blocks, but nobody has seen her, not even Tiger. He's apprenticing to become a pleasure quarter guide now, so he's in and out of all sorts of places he didn't used to be, but he hasn't spotted Flower in any of them.

Sometimes Birdie can go hours without thinking of her twin, but then she catches a glimpse of the gatekeeper's lucky white cat, and there's no one to make a wish with. Or Auntie pretends someone else made that bad smell, and there's no one to giggle with. Or she finds a dropped coin that's enough for a rice cake, but there's no one to share it with.

And that always leads to the question she can't help worrying like a loose tooth. Why had she been chosen, not Flower?

The explanation Pearl gave her can't be right. Oiran apprentices aren't picked because they're clever and helpful. The ones from the other pleasure houses are all as pretty as Bamboo Princesses, and not at all smart or nice.

Was it just luck? Maybe. But Auntie always cackles that the luckiest courtesans are the ones who work the hardest, and she didn't work harder than Flower. Far from it. Besides, if it's hard work that brings good luck, why does Auntie waste so much money at the shrine? She's constantly throwing coins to the gods, begging them to—

Birdie sits up so fast, her towel topples off her head.

How many times had she watched her coin clatter into the offering box? A hundred? A thousand? How many times had she folded her hands to pray, "Please don't let them send me away from the Treasure." Not *us*. Always *me*.

The gods have played a terrible, terrible trick on her. They'd given her exactly what she asked for.

Climbing unsteadily from the bath, she tries to convince herself it's not her fault. She hadn't asked to be the Treasures' apprentice oiran. Hadn't even dared dream of it. And it's not like she had a choice. Everything was decided by Auntie. By Pearl. By Overseer-san. Nobody gave her a chance to refuse.

But ... what if they did? What if she'd told them she didn't want to be the Treasures' apprentice oiran? Would she and Flower both have been sent away? Or would Flower be the apprentice oiran now, and she'd be wherever Flower is? If she was given the chance to go back and do it again, would she trade places with Flower?

Her hesitation tells her all she needs to know. The guilt hardens into a little knot that she carries next to her heart, every hour of every day. Most of the time she's too busy to notice it, but at night it makes her toss and turn. The only way she can fall asleep is to promise herself she'll find some way to make it up to Flower, to balance the scales. If she can find her.

Spring ripens toward summer, and the day of Takeda's big party draws near. Inviting friends to eat and drink while pretty women flit about collecting fireflies in painted lanterns is one of the most time-honored ways a man can establish himself as a top-tier Yoshiwara player, and no one at the House of Treasures can figure out why Takeda resisted for so long. Musicians are hired, trays of seasonal delights ordered, and sake barrels are stacked, waiting to be tapped. Pearl dispatches her new child attendants to check the Camellia's garden every time they arrive, looking for the lightning bugs to emerge.

Birdie is relieved when the twins report the first few flitting among the reeds at the end of the Fifth Month. By the day of the party, so many will be flashing in the bushes and twinkling over the pond, there will be plenty to illuminate the lanterns that will charm Takeda's guests like tiny, captive fireworks.

The day of the party dawns warm and clear, but when Birdie goes to Pearl's rooms at noon, she finds the oiran curled in her covers, rocking in pain. She'd been afraid of this; in a house full of women, they can't help but be aware of each other's monthly ebb and flow. Without a word, she fetches a basket and fills it with clean rags.

"Can you brew up some gingko tea for Pearl?" she asks Cook, stopping by the kitchen on her way to the apothecary to fetch more packets of painkiller. "Make it extra strong."

They're going to need it. A patron must never be inconvenienced by the demands of his oiran's body, and Takeda has invited too many important people to postpone tonight's party. The future of his clan's business depends on meeting the shōgun's translator, and nothing must derail that introduction.

In between fetching Pearl hot drinks and warm towels to soothe her cramps, Birdie gets Auntie's permission to beg Peach and Butterfly to join the party tonight. They've been grousing about not being invited to go out on the boat and meet the kabuki star who's coming, so it doesn't take much persuading.

Now all she has to worry about is Takeda. It's too dangerous to give anyone else the job of distracting him from the fact that Pearl isn't feeling her best; she'll have to do it herself. It hasn't escaped her attention that Pearl's time of month too often coincides with their worst fights, and tonight a poorly timed tart retort could spell disaster for them all.

By the time they're dressed and ready to set out for the Camellia, Pearl has managed to pull herself together enough to endure the procession, and now that her face is painted to perfection, no one will guess how wan she looks under her makeup.

They reach the teahouse at dusk. Birdie bolsters her with another dose of gingko tea while Auntie unpacks fresh bleeding cloths and helps the oiran change them.

Goldbelly and his friend Vandermeer aren't expected to arrive until later, but Takeda, the shipowner, and their cronies have been here since midafternoon. By the time Pearl and her attendants make their grand entrance, there is already a drunken and merry crowd working their way through platters of fish and flasks of sake. The Camellia's courtyard garden isn't as big as Lord Oda's, but Birdie can't help but be impressed by how charming it looks. Fireflies flit among the reeds at the water's edge, and the familiar paths are lit by torches that make her shadow dance. A boat bobs at the landing stage, festooned with lanterns and stocked with brushes and slips of fine paper for the poetry contest.

They arrive just in time to lead the first group of revelers on board, and as Birdie watches Takeda and his guests cross the stepping-stones to the pond's edge, her spirits lift. The air is balmy, and the Camellia's clipped pine trees are black against the indigo sky. As they step aboard, the professional poet Pearl invited draws their attention to the way the moon is silvering the top branches and painting a shimmering path across the pond.

The boatman pushes off, and Jester steps in to entertain them with comic impressions of people they all recognize. Wily denizen of Yoshiwara that he is, he knows which guests can laugh at themselves, and which ought never to be poked—however good-naturedly—with his sharp tongue. (His wickedly hilarious impression of Takeda, for example, will never be performed outside the debtor room at the Treasure.)

Birdie keeps an eye on Pearl. So far, the herbs are dulling her discomfort enough that she's able to nod in response to Takeda's comments and make sure he gets his share of the delicacies from Yoshiwara's best eel restaurant and sake vendor. As they're poled around the pond, the other courtesans cover for her, and no one has yet noticed the absence of her skillful guidance.

Luckily, Takeda seems to be having a better time than he expected. He likes to bask in his oiran's reflected radiance, and as the evening progresses, he takes small liberties to remind everyone that the top courtesan in Yoshiwara belongs to him.

By the time the second circuit of the pond begins, the moon is higher in the sky, the guests pleasantly sated and more than a little tipsy. A servant passes out brushes and paper for the haiku competition, and Pearl rouses herself to playfully bully the poet into being the judge, because otherwise he'll wipe the deck with them all.

Birdie dashes off the poem she'd been revising all week in anticipation of this moment, then lifts her brush. Does Pearl need help remembering hers? She sneaks a glance. Her face looks a little pinched—how long has it been since her last dose of herbs?—but her brush is making its way diligently down the page.

It's Takeda who's not making any progress. He keeps glancing at Pearl, expecting her to save him the way she saved the minister of granaries at Lord Oda's party, but if she'd prepared any verses for him tonight, she's in no shape to recall them. Brows beetling, he reluctantly scrawls a single line, and it's not a very good one. Chatter breaks out as the others finish. The courtesans top up sake cups, coquettishly taunting, "I'll show you mine, if you show me yours."

And still Takeda's brush doesn't move. His frown deepens, but Pearl doesn't notice. If Birdie doesn't help him, no one will.

"What a promising first line, Takeda-san!" She leans in. "Will you let me guess what you're about to write?" In a low voice, she prompts, "Moon on the water, a fish jumps, shatters the sky."

"Why, you must be a mind reader, Little Bird." She hears the relief in his voice. "That's exactly what I was thinking."

He dashes off the lines, finishing just as the poet calls out, "Everybody finished? Time's up! Jester, yours is going to be the worst, so you go first."

Titters of laughter greet his tongue-in-cheek verse, then good-natured hoots of appreciation as the other poems are read. Nobody is surprised when the poet announces that their generous host has captured tonight's honors. Takeda accepts as graciously as his gruff nature allows and orders a fresh round of sake.

Pearl pours for her patron, but as he drinks, his eyes stray to Birdie. He regards her for a long moment, then murmurs to Pearl, "Our little Birdie is really growing up, isn't she?"

Birdie hides her discomfort at his unwelcome compliment by leaping up to steady the guests as the boat bumps up against the landing stage.

"Oh! Look!" She draws Pearl's attention to a wide man and his slender companion silhouetted against the glowing windows of the Camellia's courtyard rooms.

Pearl excuses herself to welcome Goldbelly and Vandermeer while Birdie searches out Takeda and tugs his sleeve.

"*Ne, ne,* Takeda-san," she whispers, nodding toward the secluded pavilion where Pearl is settling Goldbelly and Vandermeer onto silk cushions.

Takeda excuses himself and follows Birdie along the path as Butterfly and Peach step in to distract the other revelers by pressing firefly-catching lanterns into their hands, exclaiming there are far too many to catch all by themselves.

Birdie prays Pearl can hold it together through the introductions. After that, Goldbelly's jovial nature and Takeda's eagerness for the plan to succeed will achieve his goal of being officially introduced. After tonight, Goldbelly and Vandermeer will be obliged to reciprocate, and once the relationship is established, Takeda will be able to invite the translator by himself and broach matters that may be to their mutual advantage. All Birdie has to do is ensure the next half hour goes off without a hitch, and Takeda will agree that this expensive evening was worth every *mon*.

Pearl and the two men rise expectantly as they arrive at the pavilion, their faces illuminated by the full moon. Birdie steps aside to introduce Takeda, but when she turns to find out why he's not bowing and welcoming his guests, she finds him standing there speechless, staring at Vandermeer as if he'd seen a ghost.

It's *him*. But it can't be. He's dead. Takeda can't take his eyes off the face he last saw staring sightlessly up at the sky on the night of the Great Meiwa Fire. He bows to hide his confusion. Get a grip. It's not him. It can't be. But those *eyes*.

Despite Pearl's assertion that Vandermeer could almost pass for Japanese, Takeda had still been picturing a towering, red-furred monkey who'd been trained to impersonate a civilized man, not someone who's a dead ringer for—

"Takeda-san?" Birdie whispers.

He snaps back. Remembers his lines.

"Welcome to the Camellia, Honorable Gentlemen." He bows deeply. "Thank you for gracing this insignificant entertainment with your august presences."

Pearl takes her cue and introduces the silk merchant, who actually needs no introduction. Despite his easygoing nature and generosity of spirit, Goldbelly is well-known as one of the shrewdest silk traders in Edo.

"... and this is Doctor Vandermeer," she says, "the shōgun's translator."

As Vandermeer straightens from his bow, she leans in to impart, "You might be interested to know that Takeda-san shares your interest in Dutch Learning. In fact, he's responsible for bringing many Dutch marvels to Edo."

Pearl pours another round, and Takeda is reminded he ought to toast his new friends. But as pleasantries are exchanged and mutual acquaintances established, Takeda is frantically trying to guess how a dead man's shade can be sitting across the table from him. Is this a demon come to haunt him for profiting by that man's death for so many years? Or is his resemblance something more mundane? Could he be a relative? But what are the chances that one of the rare foreigners in Tokyo also happens to be related to the very man Koga killed fourteen years ago?

Takeda waits until enough sake has been poured and mutually entertaining anecdotes shared, then turns to Vandermeer and ventures, "Where did His Excellency manage to find a man of your rare talents?"

"He didn't have to look far. My brother had the job before me."

His *brother*?

"Why did he give it up?" Takeda asks, even though he's pretty sure he knows the answer.

"He didn't. He died on the night of the Great Meiwa Fire."

So that's why the dead man was dressed as a Tokugawa retainer! He was the shōgun's translator. But now Takeda must tread carefully. How much does Vandermeer know?

"I'm sorry to hear that," he commiserates. "So many lost their lives that day."

"Ichiro's life wasn't lost." The translator tosses back the rest of his sake. "It was taken."

"By the fire?" Takeda suggests, feigning ignorance.

"No, with a very sharp sword." He hesitates, then adds, "On the street where the highest officials in Edo live."

The back of Takeda's neck prickles. It sounds like he doesn't think this was an attack by a random *rōnin*. He suspects someone who lives nearby. Koga may be unstable, but until he can be replaced by another source of influence, Takeda can't risk anyone exposing his pet administrator's crime.

"Do you know who did it?" he probes.

Vandermeer hesitates. "No, but—"

"If the *hatamoto* are left to their own devices," Goldbelly finishes for him, "we never will."

Takeda sips his sake to conceal his surprise. Why are these two powerful men admitting they have little love for the ruling class their livelihoods depend on?

"I hear you're not originally from Edo either," Vandermeer ventures, studying his face. "So, when I say that the stone walls of Edo Castle will admit to wrongdoing before men from the *hatamoto* clans allow justice to come for one of their own, perhaps you understand."

Takeda nods cautiously, motions for Pearl to pour more sake.

"When I read the investigator's report," the translator continues, "it quite clearly describes the single, clean stroke that ended my brother's life. Only samurai are allowed to carry the kind of weapon that could deal such a blow. Yet somehow, the crime remains unsolved."

"That's why I urged Vandermeer-sensei to join me when I received your invitation," Goldbelly confides in a low voice. "I know you by reputation as a man of wide acquaintance, who moves among merchants and lords alike. If you were to hear anything that might help him get the justice he seeks, I would consider it the greatest of personal favors." Folding his hands before him, he leans in to emphasize, "You would have my eternal gratitude."

"And mine," adds Vandermeer.

Takeda blinks. Did he just hear what he thought he heard? Did one of the richest merchants in Edo and the man who recommends Dutch Learning purchases to the shōgun just say they will owe him a favor if he helps them find out who killed Vandermeer's brother? His pulse quickens. With men like these two in his debt, he would no longer need that increasingly troublesome snake-of-a-Koga.

"I'll keep my ears open," he promises, wondering how he might deliver that dirty little secret without splashing any mud onto himself.

It's not until nearly midsummer that Birdie has time to do anything but put one foot in front of the other. She hasn't visited the shrine in weeks, so on the first day she can carve out a little time between lessons, she opens her new red parasol and makes her way through the pleasure district. She hopes that the coins jingling in her sleeve might persuade the gods to tell her where to find her missing twin.

She and Tiger have looked everywhere, with no luck. Sometimes she glimpses girls who could be Flower—girls with a certain grace in their walk, a certain tilt to their heads—but they either turn out not to be her, or they disappear before she can be sure.

She's got to be somewhere in Yoshiwara. The Great Gate is guarded day and night, and no woman can pass without official papers, but the biggest reason she's so sure her twin must still be here is that Flower has nowhere else to go. Returning to the muddy village she came from would be as absurd as a white crane trying to make its home in a nest of sparrows. She would not be welcomed. Not by her family, not by anybody. Even in her plainest kimono, she would be gawked at, whispered about, desired by the men, resented by the women. In Yoshiwara, people may not be related by blood, but everyone is connected by obedience owed, favors done, minor crimes overlooked, property loaned. Outside the walls, who would make the introductions necessary to find a husband, a job, a place to live, a fresh start? Someday Flower will come to the shrine, or be standing in line at the sweets shop, or—

Birdie looks up, startled to see a familiar figure approaching the shrine gate from the opposite direction. But it's not Flower, it's Dolly. They've run into each other a few times at the bathhouse and exchanged news when nobody was looking, but this is the first time they've seen each other on the street since Elder Sister began performing at teahouses.

Even though Dolly is just a geisha, she's surprisingly pretty today in her blue and gray striped kimono. Her purple *obi* is tied in a modest drum knot in back and she wears only two hairpins in her upswept hair, but the simple style suits her. Birdie's own outfit is nothing fancy today. She's dressed for lessons, not entertaining, but it's still a riot of summer color, with layers of bright silk showing at her neck and sleeves and hair ornaments that shimmer as she walks. She shrinks a little, in a vain attempt to reduce the gulf between them.

Dolly lowers her eyes first. Honoring their pact not to greet each other in public, she performs the small impersonal bow of a stranger. Climbing the stairs to the offering box, they stand politely side by side, toss their coins, clap, and fold their hands in prayer. Dolly bows before turning to go.

"Wait," Birdie whispers. Had the gods brought Elder Sister here for a reason? Maybe she knows where Flower is. "Meet me on the bench by the shrine shed?"

Dolly nods. Descending the steps, she strolls off in that direction.

Birdie finishes reciting her prayers, then picks her way through the shrine grounds to the quiet corner that's more crowded with mops and cleaning buckets than visitors. They greet each other with all the affection they can't show in public, then trade news of what's happened in their lives since they last met. Dolly tells of the new songs she has learned, and Birdie complains about her stuffy *koto* teacher, who scolded her for adding Jester-like flourishes to the classical tune she's been practicing.

Then Birdie asks the question she'd just asked the gods.

"Have you seen Flower lately?"

"No. Why?"

"Well, the thing is..." Why is this so hard to say? "When I was promoted, she... wasn't. She went to live somewhere else, but nobody will tell me where. I was wondering if you'd seen her in the past few months. Maybe while you were entertaining on Teahouse Street?"

Dolly starts to shake her head, then a shadow crosses her face.

"Where did you see her?" Birdie cries. *Don't say geisha house. Please don't say geisha house.*

"She was at a party," Dolly replies reluctantly, "with some horse traders at the Red Lantern."

The Red Lantern? That's one of the shabbier teahouses near the moat. Birdie has never been inside. No patron of the House of Treasures would be caught dead entertaining there.

"I saw her with a couple of the courtesans from the House of Cranes."

Worse and worse. The Crane has no courtesans who rank anywhere near an oiran. Even their top entertainer wears hair combs made from horse hooves, not real tortoiseshell. How could any of them deserve a child attendant as pretty and talented as Flower?

"At first, I thought she might be the senior courtesan's child attendant, except"—Dolly makes a face—"at the end of the evening, she went upstairs with one of the horse traders too."

"What? Flower went upstairs? With a man? No." Birdie is shaking her head. "You must be mistaken. It couldn't have been her."

"I'm afraid it was."

No. She's wrong. Elder Sister is old. Her eyesight is failing. A comforting hand reaches for her arm, but she spins away. Can't believe it. Won't. Robes bunched in her fists, she runs all the way home, not caring that tales of an oiran apprentice clopping down the street with tears streaming down her cheeks will enliven plenty of banquets tonight.

Birdie goes through the motions at Pearl's side, but the smile she pastes on to reward the minister of graneries' compliments is wooden, and even the luxuries that surround the oiran wherever she entertains seem no more than gaudy props meant to distract from the ugly truth of what happens when the lights go out.

Because love is not the only passion men come to Yoshiwara to indulge.

"She won't be able to work again until her nose shrinks back to normal size," Birdie tells Tiger the next day, outraged at the tea trader from Nihonbashi who slapped Feather around when she refused to submit to his demands.

"I know that bastard." Tiger's lips twist in disgust. "Last month, I helped toss him out the back door of the Peony for spraining Young Pine's wrist. I'm sorry to hear he moved on to the Treasure."

"Why didn't you report him?"

"We did."

"Then why isn't he banned? The man is dangerous. If Jester hadn't stopped him—"

Tiger snorts. "The reason he isn't banned is because he can afford to pay."

"What do you mean, 'pay?' There's a *price* for abuse?"

Of course there is. The House of Treasures reports him too, but the tea trader gets off with a fine and must compensate the Treasure for ten days of Feather's time. Auntie, of course, sends her back to work in six.

But even though violence may be compensated, it's not always reported. Far from it. Pearl absorbs Takeda's anger without complaint, because every bruise or slap buys her an unspoken apology the next morning, in the form of a doubly generous tip. She drinks painkilling tea like water and adds Takeda's guilt money to the nest egg that she and Yasu will use to start their new life together.

Which is one more reason Birdie is doing everything she can to master Mistress Moon's lessons and defuse Takeda's anger before it erupts. Every insult makes Pearl more eager to leave Yoshiwara and live happily ever after with Yasu, and every extra tip brings her closer to her dream. As the oiran's savings grow, so does the danger to Birdie's future. When Pearl has saved enough, she will pay off her contract with the House of Treasures and leave Yoshiwara.

But Birdie can't let that happen before her debut, and her debut can't happen until Pearl finds her a patron to pay for it and makes the formal teahouse introductions that will launch her career.

In the meantime, Birdie is up before dawn to bring her morning tea and can't count on pulling the covers over her own head until well past midnight. In between, she learns how to shape her eyebrows, admire a tea bowl, take a compliment, hide her dismay, mix tooth blackener, walk in tall geta, and choose an ensemble. She cries every day, because in Yoshiwara, tears aren't just for calamities or mourning, they're for getting what you want.

"Some men will do anything to avoid a woman's tears," Mistress Moon informs her. "Make your lip tremble, just so. Good. Most of the time, you won't need to do more."

But if stronger measures are called for, there's an alum concoction she can paint on the inside of her collar. All she has to do is hide her nose and take a sharp sniff to make the waterworks flow. For three days,

Birdie's eyes are red from practicing, but soon she can reliably perform the entire range of weeping, from a mere lip quiver to abandoned sobs.

"Good." Mistress Moon nods. "Now, look pretty while doing it."

That's not always possible. The more Birdie watches Takeda and Pearl together, the more she understands that even oirans can't manage the pretty part when the crying is not an act.

The year slides toward winter and the temperature dips right on schedule, turning the gingko trees across the moat into torches of gold overnight. Flaming red leaves are plucked from the maple trees by curls of wind that whisper of snow, swirling around the feet of the stone foxes at the shrine. Everyone in Yoshiwara shakes out their padded jackets, and the courtesans in their lattice rooms huddle close to the brazier, hoping to be invited upstairs sooner rather than later.

On a day when the wind is blustering in that infuriating way that makes Birdie feel like it's against her both coming and going, it's her bad luck to return to the Treasure just after Auntie discovers one of the *shamisens* is missing a tuning peg. Before she has even slipped out of her *geta*, she's sent trudging back out again. It's not until midafternoon that she has a chance to stop by Pearl's rooms with chapped lips and windblown hair to ask if she needs help with anything before it's time to get ready for the evening.

She finds the oiran pacing back and forth, checking her hair in the mirror, muttering under her breath. Thinking it best not to interrupt, she withdraws, but Pearl spins around and catches her.

"Birdie! Where have you been? I was afraid I wouldn't have a chance to tell you the good news before I talk to Auntie."

Good news?

"I've saved enough money to pay my debts."

Oh no. That is *not* good news.

"Con... gratulations?" she stammers.

"Thank you, I knew you'd be happy for me." Pearl turns back to her mirror, checks her teeth. "It's a lucky thing I went to the fortuneteller this morning, because she said today is the last auspicious day for fresh starts before the New Year."

"You're leaving *today*?"

"As soon as Auntie signs the papers."

No. This can't be happening.

"Wish me luck?"

"Good luck, Honored Elder Sister," Birdie parrots numbly. What about *her* future? What about her debut?

Blind to her apprentice's dismay, Pearl lifts her chin and sails down the hall toward Auntie's room.

Birdie stares after her. Pearl wouldn't really leave before doing right by her apprentice, would she? Pearl chose her. She's been loyal. And helpful. If she didn't intend to . . .

Birdie's stomach does a flip-flop. What *if* she didn't intend to be here for her apprentice's debut? What if she'd *never* intended to be here for her debut? What if all she wanted was an accomplice she could trust not to betray her affair with Yasu? Someone who was so grateful for the unexpected opportunity that she'd be blindly obedient right up to the moment Pearl rewarded her loyalty by abandoning her?

No. She wouldn't do that. And Overseer-san and Auntie would never allow it. But if Pearl really has the money, how can they stop her?

There's only one way to find out. Birdie pokes her head out and looks both ways to make sure no one is coming, then tiptoes down the hall and slides Auntie's door open just a hair, on the track that the maids are bribed to keep well waxed.

". . . time for me to leave the House of Treasures," Pearl is announcing.

Silence.

Then, "I see."

Tell her no, Auntie, please tell her no.

But she doesn't.

"I'll ask one of the maids to fetch Mistress Moon."

Birdie scrambles into the servants' sleeping room across the hall until the assistant manager sweeps past with an armful of ledgers and her abacus, then creeps back to listen.

"According to your contract," Auntie says, pages flipping, "you were indentured by your uncle on the fourteenth day of the Third Month in the year 1772 and he agreed to a ten-year extension when you became an apprentice oiran seven years later."

"That sounds about right," Pearl agrees. "There should be three years left in my contract."

"Correct."

"So, if I pay back three years of the 'salary advance' my uncle received, I'll be free to go?"

"Well," Auntie says slowly, "not quite. Your contract is a little more complicated than that. Mistress Moon, can you tell Pearl where she stands?"

"Of course," the assistant manager replies. Something thumps onto the table. "This ledger is the record of all your earnings and debts since you came to the House of Treasures. The good news is that in addition to the ten years' salary we paid your uncle when he signed the contract, you're also entitled to ten percent of your earnings."

"Ten percent?" Pearl sounds surprised.

"Yes." A turning of pages, a clicking of abacus beads. "The total you earned in the past six years appears to be twenty thousand, four hundred *ryō* and three *bu*." More clicking. "Your ten percent comes to two thousand forty *ryō* and thirty *mon*."

Pearl gasps.

So does Birdie. Two thousand *ryō* is a fortune! Maybe Pearl won't have to betray her after all. That's more than enough to pay for her debut, with plenty left over for—

"Of course," Mistress Moon adds, "your expenses must be deducted from that."

"For my clothes and attendants, you mean?" Pearl expected that.

"Yes. But in addition to the kimono maker's bills and providing for your entourage there are the *obi* cords"—the abacus clicks—"scarves, pads, hair ornaments, underwear and socks you ordered for both you and your dependents. Plus"—*click, click, click*—"new tatami mats for your rooms, ten years' worth of cleaning and repair fees, sick days, double-fee days when no patron picked up the tab, medical fees and apothecary expenses, tobacco, makeup, rice crackers, sweets, hairdressing, and"—*clickety, clickety, click*—"footwear. That brings your grand total of expenses to two thousand nine hundred sixty-seven *ryō* and one *bu*."

"What?"

Neither Birdie nor Pearl can reckon such huge numbers in their heads, but they both know what it means when the second number is bigger than the first.

"Minus your income"—the abacus clicks some more—"your current debt amounts to nine hundred twenty-seven *ryō*, three *shu*, one hundred seventy-seven *mon*. Plus, of course, the three years' and two months' salary you'll be paying back."

"No!" Pearl cries. "That can't be right. Let me see that!"

Birdie sits back on her heels, stunned. Pearl expected to owe the Treasure for her clothes and her attendants' support, but it sounds like that's only a fraction of her debt. She's been saving every *mon* since she met Yasu, but it can't be anywhere near the sum she owes.

Birdie hardly dares breathe while the oiran pores over the contract her uncle signed on her behalf when she was a little girl, searching for some loophole, some mistake. After several long minutes, she hears a sniff. Then another.

"For heaven's sake, pull yourself together and save your tears for the customers," Auntie scolds. "I don't know what you expected, but if you'd asked to read your contract once you were old enough, none of this would come as a surprise. If you work hard, you should be able to pay off your obligation in three, maybe four, years."

Three or four *years*? Four years is *forever*.

It's no consolation to Pearl, either. With a choking sob, she throws open the door and runs down the hall, leaving Auntie and Mistress Moon staring at Birdie, crouching in the corridor.

Sneaking past Pearl's closed door, Birdie hears an angry sob, then flinches as something hard hits the wall. This would be a bad time to be the most convenient target for her disappointment.

The other courtesans are, of course, all ears. Seated at the row of shared dressing tables in the common room, they pepper her with questions as they put on their makeup for the evening. *How* much had Pearl managed to earn? And her debt is *how* big? They're not surprised to hear she's expected to pay for her attendants' expenses and the double-fee days when she couldn't trick a patron into footing the bill, but... room maintenance? Medical expenses?

"Her medical expenses can't be very big, though," Birdie points out, passing Butterfly a comb. "Pearl is hardly ever sick. She only needs herbs when she gets her bleeding."

Butterfly and Peach exchange glances.

"It's the herbs for when she doesn't get her bleeding that really add up," says Peach.

Everyone seems to know what that means but her.

"If Mistress Moon hasn't explained that part to you yet," Butterfly says, holding a hand mirror to check if the nape of her neck needs shaving, "you'd better ask her."

She will. She'll add it to the questions that have been pestering her like a swarm of gnats since hearing the hard truths escaping from Auntie's door this afternoon.

What about *her* contract? What had the House of Peonies promised the Treasure when they threw her in with Lucky Doll, like an extra rice cake? Like Pearl, she never thought to ask. When will her ledger start filling with debts? Has it already started? No, Pearl must still be responsible for her expenses, because nobody has mentioned any suitably rich gentleman stepping up to sponsor her debut. It's depressing confirmation that Pearl had been so sure she'd be long gone, she hadn't bothered to look for one. But now that she's stuck in Yoshiwara, she'll be searching for a man to take Birdie off her payroll as soon as possible.

Who will it be? Biting her lip, Birdie follows Butterfly and Peach downstairs to survey the men peering hungrily through the lattice screen as the opening bell rings.

What if it's Doctor Death Breath? He's safely on the other side right now, but if they were in the same room, she'd be breathing through her mouth. How could she bear to be face-to-face with him for an entire night without gagging? She shudders, swivels her gaze to the man with bristles growing out of a big brown carbuncle on his jaw. He scratches his wrinkly neck, eyes resting appreciatively on each courtesan before making his choice.

"What's wrong with you tonight?" Butterfly elbows her. "If you're going to look like your cat just died, go back upstairs and don't spoil our chances."

"Sorry."

It's a good thing she excused herself and took the opportunity to visit the privy when she had the chance, because for the next few hours, she's so busy that both her head and her feet are aching by the time she finally drags herself to bed.

But now she can't sleep. She'd never really noticed if the Treasures' customers were fat, wrinkly, bald, or stinky, but tonight she'd become keenly aware that the less attractive a man is, the more likely he's the one paying. Her future patron is not going to be that smooth young swordsmith who went upstairs with Butterfly, he'll be the sixty-one-year-old pawnbroker they all tease for pursuing girls whose age is the same as his, only reversed.

And Pearl won't spare her. She's been forced to take patrons she doesn't desire, so she's not going to care if the one she finds for Birdie is old, ugly, or even cruel, as long as he can afford to pay.

By the next morning, news of Pearl's crushing disappointment has spread from courtesans to maids to manservants, and everyone is giving her closed door a wide berth. The silence within offers no clue to what her mood might be. Will she get out of bed at all? Will she claim to be sick, refuse to entertain? Will they all have to cover for her, working twice as hard to amuse a disappointed patron?

When they finally hear her stumble to the private bath, everyone relaxes—any sign of life is better than none—and come to a whispered agreement to act as if they've heard nothing when it's time to help her get ready for this afternoon's procession. Maybe if they pretend nothing is wrong, it won't be.

But Birdie should have known better than to indulge in that kind of wishful thinking. Yesterday's delicious sashimi is today's smelly fish, and if yesterday was what Pearl's fortuneteller defines as "lucky," tonight will be as bad as bad can be.

"Oh, it's you, Birdie. Is it that time, already?"

Pearl's voice is a little hoarse, but she's in front of her mirror in her dressing gown, as usual. There are dark stains beneath her eyes, and Birdie wouldn't trust her with any sharp objects, but her face is no longer puffy from weeping. She's more subdued than usual, but at least she's not angry. Not at Birdie, anyway.

Auntie wisely decides not to attend today's robing and makeup session, leaving the courtesans to chatter freely amongst themselves and exchange trivial gossip as they flutter around the silent Pearl. By the time she's painted and robed and ornamented, they've stopped noticing she isn't joining in.

Nobody expects an oiran to look anything but elegant and distant as she makes her regal way down Center Street, and Pearl delivers that attitude flawlessly on their way their way to the Camellia to entertain Takahisa Takeda. It's not until they're drawing to a halt before the familiar covered entrance that Birdie stops to wonder if he's expecting guests tonight. Pearl usually mentions them while they're dressing—their titles, if they have one, their likes and dislikes—but today she hadn't said a word. Perhaps it'll just be Takeda tonight?

As the others banter back and forth and fix Pearl's makeup, she hands the oiran her usual pipe. Pearl takes a puff, then lets it go out, forgotten between her fingers.

"Shall I refill that for you?" Birdie offers.

"What?" Pearl focuses on her with difficulty. "No. Thank you."

That's worrying. She always smokes at least two to sharpen her wits before entertaining. No one expects her to be at her best tonight, but

Birdie figured she had recovered enough to at least make an effort, since refusing to entertain will just dig her deeper into debt. But now she's not so sure. Pearl recovers from disappointment fast, but not this fast. Birdie opens her mouth to ask how she's doing, just as the teahouse mistress arrives to tell them that one of Takeda-san's guests sent word that he has been unavoidably detained and would be an hour late. Can they let him know?

"I will," Birdie volunteers. Because tonight Pearl shouldn't be trusted to do more than paste on a smile and pour sake. Up the stairs and down the long, polished hall, she tells herself not to worry. Pearl has entertained Takeda and his guests so many times she could do it in her sleep. It's not until they step through the door that she understands how cruelly the gods are about to punish them for being unprepared. Takeda's face is already as wooden as a Noh mask, because the guest sitting across the table from him tonight is Masatoki Koga.

Pearl greets them as usual and doesn't seem to notice that the air is crackling between them with something that had been said just before they arrived. As always, Koga's patrician Edo accent makes Takeda sound like a provincial clod, and while both men dress in expensive silks, Koga wears his fine clothing effortlessly, making Takeda look stiff and fussy by comparison.

No surprise, they've been drinking heavily. Takeda always drinks more when he's uncomfortable, just like he always orders the most expensive food when he entertains people he dislikes. Birdie glances at tonight's sashimi glistening on the deck of a model sailing ship, and sure enough, it's the finest selection of fish from Yoshiwara's most expensive sushi shop. Ordinarily, she'd be delighted to see that there's far too much—leftovers are always a welcome bonus—but tonight the sumptuous spread fills her with dread. Over-ordering is a sign of how much is riding on the favor Takeda planned to ask of his guest, and "no" is not the answer he's looking for. It's times like this when he most counts on Pearl to ease tensions, but whether she's aware of what he wants tonight or is in any shape to help him get it, Birdie can't begin to guess.

At the moment, both men look relieved as the oiran takes her usual place between them and dilutes the attention they've been forced to focus on each other. Pearl does remember to smile and whisper to Takeda that the other guest he's expecting will be late, but as the sashimi disappears and more sake is served, her ability to hold herself together flags. Birdie catches her staring into space more than once and manages to nudge her discreetly before anyone else notices, but her comebacks are trite, and her reactions so insincere that even Takeda looks at her askance once or twice.

Birdie catches Jester's eye. He too has noticed that Pearl is just going through the motions. He slips some gratitude from the House of Treasures into the palms of the teahouse's entertainers, so they'll stay to distract Takeda and Koga until the final bowls of rice are served and eaten.

They're just scraping the last bite into their mouths when the teahouse mistress appears in the doorway, escorting Takeda's tardy guest.

It's... Doctor Vandermeer?

What on earth possessed Takeda to invite Vandermeer and Koga on the same evening? The city administrator makes no secret of his disdain for foreigners.

She casts a nervous glance at him, expecting to find Koga flushing with distaste, but he's staring at the newcomer, white as a sheet. Have they met before? If so, Vandermeer gives no sign, just bows politely and apologizes for being late.

But Takeda is watching Koga's discomfiture with the kind of beady interest that borders on delight. Like he expected it. Maybe even counted on it.

What is he playing at? Birdie glances from one face to another, but it's a mystery. If Pearl were herself tonight, she'd have found out beforehand, warned them what to expect. If she'd explained what Takeda wanted out of this evening, Birdie would do everything she could to help him get it, but she has no clue. She'll just have to observe him like her life depends on it and hope she can figure it out before the evening goes up in flames.

"This is Doctor Vandermeer, the shōgun's Dutch Learning expert," Takeda says to Koga, who is reluctantly rising to make a barely respectful bow.

"And this"—Takeda turns to the doctor—"is the Most Honorable City Administrator Koga, with whom I have enjoyed a long and prosperous relationship for... what is it now? Thirteen years? No, it must be fourteen." He beams at Koga with false cheer. "Didn't we start working together right after the Great Meiwa Fire?"

Koga doesn't answer. Birdie nudges Pearl. *Do something!*

"What a great disaster that was," Takeda muses into the deadly silence. "So much of Edo burned, so many lost their lives. Including Doctor Vandermeer's poor brother."

"His... brother?" Koga's face is now a sickly green.

"Yes, I believe he was killed on a street near Kihonbutsu Temple. Isn't that where you live, Koga-san?"

Why is he suggesting the city administrator might know something about what happened to Vandermeer's brother? Birdie knows that's impossible. Because on that night he was—

"Were you there on the night of the fire?" Takeda presses. "Did you see or hear anything that might help Doctor Vandermeer find out what happened?"

Koga's mouth is opening and closing, obviously so outraged by the suggestion that he had anything to do with something as sordid as murder that he's beyond telling them what Birdie knows to be true: he was in Yoshiwara that night, delivering his pregnant mistress to the House of Peonies.

"Takeda-san," Birdie interjects, "I'm sure the Honorable City Administrator would be happy to help if he could, but..."

"Quiet, girl!" Takeda snarls. "If I ask Koga-san a question, I expect an answer from him, not you."

"Forgive me," she stammers. She was just trying to keep the peace. Stinging from the rebuke, she swivels toward Koga and begs, "Won't you rescue this poor apprentice, Most Honored Minister? Doctor Vandermeer just wants to bring his brother's killer to justice. I'm sure you weren't anywhere near that place that night, and no one would fault you if you . . . if you were to tell them where you really were." She shuffles backward and lowers her forehead to the tatami.

But instead of taking her cue and admitting he was in Yoshiwara, Koga leaps to his feet, nearly upsetting the table.

"All right! All right!" he shouts at Takeda. "Your son will get his accursed introductions!"

He turns and stalks through the door without a word of thanks or farewell.

No one moves. Did a government minister just rip the veil of civility right down the middle, at the most elegant teahouse in Yoshiwara? The staff vanishes like rabbits into their burrows, and the other banquet rooms along the hall fall silent as Koga storms past. They hear him call for the mistress and demand she send a servant ahead to secure him a palanquin.

Everyone is too shocked to say anything. Even Jester is at a loss for words.

It's Takeda who finally breaks the silence. In a voice so cold it would shrivel a chrysanthemum, he says, "Thank you for your help, Birdie." Calmly finishes his sake. "I'm glad that someone here understands that there's more than one way a courtesan can earn her keep."

Birdie sways, suddenly dizzy. This is her fault. It's all her fault. She was trying to keep the evening from capsizing, but she just made it worse. If word of her starring role in this disaster gets out, they'll be speaking of her in scandalized whispers all over Yoshiwara before the sun sets tomorrow. She'll never land a patron. And if she can't land a patron, she'll never be an oiran.

Somehow Birdie stumbles home, but she can't sleep.

If only she'd said—
If only she didn't—

But she had, and she did. The damage is done, and only the gods can save her now. She'll go to the shrine first thing tomorrow, pour all her savings into the offering box. Plead with them not to let one night ruin her whole life.

If ever she needed a miracle, it's now.

Birdie wakes before dawn. Unable to fall back asleep, she lies there fretting, first flinging the covers off because she's too hot, then clutching them around her ears because she's too cold.

She'll run to the shrine as soon as it's light outside. Beg the gods to undo the damage. Then she remembers how they tricked her before. She'll have to be careful how she asks for their help. Before she goes to the shrine to make her wish, she'd better learn what the future holds, or she might accidentally beg them to change the wrong thing. As much as she wishes she could go to a fortuneteller who will tell her what she wants to hear, this is a job for Madame Truth.

No seer will be hanging out her curtain for hours, though. She pulls her quilt over her head and feigns sleep as the junior courtesans crawl back to their futons one by one, yawning. She doesn't stir until they're all breathing regularly, then silently dresses herself in an old kimono, inspecting the sleeves for holes before filling them with every coin she's squirreled away in her three secret hiding places.

The few townspeople out and about at this hour glance up at the lowering sky and spare her only the briefest bows as they pass, intent on finishing their errands before the rain arrives. Eyes watering in the stiff breeze, Birdie clutches her head wrap beneath her chin, rounding the corner onto the street that borders the moat. The wind is stronger on the fringes of the pleasure quarter, whipping the moat water into sharp-edged wavelets that slap against the stone walls. She leans into it as it wraps her kimono about her knees and tries to snatch her scarf from her grasp. A distant rumble speeds the steps of those still going about their business.

Her feet grow heavier with each step as she nears Shinjō's shack, dreading what she might learn there. She hesitates before the faded curtain as a rice cake wrapper tumbles past and catches on a corner of the rickety steps before lofting once again down the street. Does she really want to hear what Madame Truth is going to tell her? What if she confirms that last night's debacle at the Camellia is about to make her famous, in the worst possible way? If there's one thing the pleasure quarter loves more than spectacular success, it's spectacular failure.

She almost turns back, then remembers what Auntie told Pearl, the last time she balked at spending the money to get her palm read. Just because you don't know the future doesn't mean it won't happen. Her fate will find her, whether she's prepared for it or not. It's better to know what's coming.

The first plops of rain spot the dust around her, and before she can change her mind, she gathers her robes and climbs the steps. Parting the curtain, she knocks, then slides open the door. Once again, she's enveloped by the fragrance of sandalwood, and just like before, Shinjō is sitting straight-backed behind the low table. As Birdie slides the door closed behind her, the hand counting the rosary beads stills.

"Excuse my humble self for intruding," she murmurs, bowing.

"Your honored self is not intruding. I've been waiting for you."

How could she—Ugh, a fortuneteller *would* say that. The cheap subterfuge annoys her, but she pushes it aside, slipping out of her *geta* and stepping onto the worn mats.

"Please." Shinjō gestures her toward the guest cushion. "What brought you here today, Birdie?"

"I—" She swallows. "I made a mistake last night."

"What kind of mistake?"

Once she begins, it all comes pouring out. Without giving away the identities of the important men involved, she describes Takeda's inexplicable invitation of two men who didn't mix. How he'd goaded one of his guests and she'd tried to avert disaster, but failed.

"I see. And what is your question?"

"Can you tell me if this changed my future? For . . . for the worse?"

Shinjō regards her for a long moment, then instead of fetching her yarrow sticks, she says, "Give me your hand."

Birdie reaches out timidly, then hesitates.

"Give me your hand, Satsu-chan."

She snatches it back. That's what she was called before she became Little Bird.

"How did you—?"

"Give me your hand," Shinjō repeats patiently.

Her hand closes around Birdie's, fingers papery and dry, unexpectedly warm. She clasps firmly, but not too tight. Her eyes close.

What's she doing? Why isn't she examining the lines on her palm or counting the divination sticks? Outside, the wind gusts, buffeting the siding, probing the cracks in the thin walls. Rain begins to patter overhead. Birdie's urge to pull her hand away gathers strength, but the oracle tightens her grip. Then it relaxes, her hand is released. The seer's eyes open.

"No," she says.

"You mean—" A spark of hope flares. "Last night won't change my future?"

"No."

She can't quite believe it.

"Even after what happened," she confirms cautiously, "I'll still find a patron? I'll still have my debut?"

"No."

"*No?*" Now she's confused. "What do you mean, 'no?' I thought you said my future was unchanged! I'll still take Pearl's place as oiran, right?"

The seer says nothing.

"Why . . . why not?" Birdie stammers.

"It's not what you are meant to be."

"But it is!" she insists. "Why did the gods make me her apprentice if I'm not meant to be an oiran? I'm going to be a good one! Everyone says so. Ask Pearl. Or Mistress Moon. Or even Auntie. Are you sure you're not making a mistake? Here." She digs into her sleeve. "I'll pay you double. Can you ask the yarrow sticks or read my palm or something? Just to be sure?"

The seer sits there, makes no move to take the coins.

"All right." Birdie steels herself. "If I'm not going to be an oiran, does that mean I'll be a junior courtesan? Be sent down to the lattice room?"

"No."

She's relieved, until she realizes that could mean something far worse.

"I won't have to leave the House of Treasures, will I?" she squeaks.

The fortuneteller answers only with silence.

This can't be happening. Birdie leaps to her feet. She can't lose the only home she's ever known. How can this so-called seer be so sure? She didn't even read her palm, like a real fortuneteller would. If she were any good, wouldn't she have a fine shop on the main street, instead of this tumbledown shack by the moat?

Birdie glances toward the door, itching to flee the predictions filling the room like a bad smell. But even unlucky fortunes must be paid for, lest even worse luck follow in their wake. Digging deep in her sleeve, she pulls out the first coin that comes to hand, the big one she got from Goldbelly. It's far too much, but the urge to run is so strong she can't bear to be here another second. It clatters onto the table as she flings a parting word over her shoulder and dashes out into the storm.

By the time the rest of her coins are sitting at the bottom of the offering box at the shrine, she's soaked to the skin. Chilled and shivering, her flowing sleeves are twisted and sticking to her sodden kimono as she begs the gods to make Madame Truth's prediction wrong, wrong, wrong. She drags herself back to the Treasure, smoothing back the straggling hair plastered to her cheeks before sliding open the front door.

And is pounced on by Pearl's new pair of child attendants.

Sandpiper and Swallow look so much alike that Birdie still mixes them up, but they're seldom apart, so it seldom matters.

"*Ne, ne*, where have you been, Honored Sister?" one scolds.

"We've been stuck here by the door forever," complains the other. "Auntie is waiting for you upstairs. And Pearl too."

Her stomach fills with dread. The reckoning for last night's disaster has arrived faster than she hoped. Wishing the gods had a little more time to adjust her fate, she refuses to allow the girls to drag her to Auntie's room without re-pinning her hair and changing into dry clothes. But all too soon, she's knocking and excusing herself in a meek voice and sliding open the manager's door. Auntie and Pearl are seated at the low table as expected, but she's surprised to see Jester in the third seat.

Judging by the wreath of tobacco smoke and the empty teacups, they've been here for some time. Any hope that Auntie hasn't heard every detail of what happened last night at the Camellia evaporates. All she can do is throw herself on their mercy.

"*Moshiwake gozaimasen!*" she cries, dropping to the floor and knocking her forehead on the tatami. "My deepest and sincerest—"

"Stop that at once," Auntie snaps, in a voice that would freeze hot coals. "I hear there was quite a scene at the Camellia last night."

Birdie opens her mouth to reply, but Pearl beats her to it.

"Really?" the oiran trills, with a fake musical laugh. "Do you mean when Koga-san left Takeda-san's nice party before it was over?" She lowers her voice. "The poor man. He was so indisposed. I hope he made it home without embarrassing himself. I meant to send a note this morning to make sure he's all right. Have you heard if he's recovered yet?"

What's going on? Pearl is lying through her teeth. And if she can tell, so can Auntie. Why is she letting her get away with it? The manager wasn't there last night, but she has eyes and ears at every teahouse where the House of Treasures' courtesans entertain. Anything Pearl says here can be confirmed. By more than one source, no doubt. Why is she just swallowing this foolery, nodding her approval?

"And what about you?" Auntie turns to Jester. "What do you know about what happened at the Camellia?"

"Well." He gives a knowing guffaw. "It certainly was a scene, wasn't it? We were all quite surprised when Koga-san ran out of the Camellia in the middle of Takeda-san's party. I don't know what you've heard, but the real story is even better. Our new apprentice oiran complimented Koga-san on his monkey *netsuke*, and that reminded me of a funny story about a man who adopted a pet monkey. But just as I was getting to the good part, Koga-san jumped up and ran from the room. We couldn't have been more surprised if the table had stood on its hind legs and started dancing! Believe me when I say that I'd never have told that story if I'd known it was true. Yes, you guessed it—the man with the pet monkey was sitting in that very room. Now, don't be too hard on Koga-san. Would you have behaved any better, if you'd drunk that much sake? What's that? You've never heard the monkey story?" He adopts a confidential tone. "Well, I really ought not to repeat it, now that you know who it's about, but if you promise not to tell—"

"Good. That'll do," says Auntie, knocking her ashes into the cup. Then she rounds on Birdie and barks, "Well, missy? You're just a child, so I expect the truth from you! What happened last night? I hear you were right in the middle of it!"

Birdie is so shocked by this attack, she can't help but yelp, "I don't know! Koga-san was there one moment and gone the next! One minute Pearl was pouring his sake, and the next—" Her throat closes. She hangs her head in shame.

"No, no, not like that," Auntie chides, switching off her outrage as if snuffing a candle. "Chin up, let's see those tears. That's better. And stop that sniffling! It's most unbecoming. Hasn't Mistress Moon taught you that there's a right way and a wrong way to cry in front of customers?"

Birdie is so astonished, her tears stop and her mouth falls open. Auntie scolds her for that too, then finishes her tea. She levers herself up from her cushion, signaling that the meeting is at an end.

"It's time to start getting ready for tonight. May I remind you that one of the most notorious gossips on the kabuki stage has promised to drop by later, so you"—she glares at Pearl—"need to keep in mind what we talked about earlier. And you"—she turns to Birdie—"need to remember what you just heard. If you know what's good for you, the story everyone leaves with tonight won't be the same one they arrived with."

Birdie stands in the hall, stunned. What just happened in there? Is she being given another chance?

She stands there, biting her lip, because if so, she owes Pearl an apology for landing her in the kind of trouble that got her summoned to Auntie's lair. She follows the oiran to her rooms. They shed their slippers and she slides the door closed behind them. Pearl wilts, dropping the façade she'd been maintaining for the others. It's been just two days since she heard the bad news about her debts, and although she's getting better at hiding her despair, it's obvious she hasn't really recovered. She moves the teakettle onto the coals to heat.

"I'm sorry I let you down last night, Honored Elder Sister," Birdie says. She holds her deep bow, waiting for Pearl's forgiveness. When it doesn't come, she cautiously straightens, finds the oiran gazing out the window, lost in thought.

"Honored Elder Sister?"

Pearl sighs. Crosses to her kimono chest to begin choosing what they'll wear tonight. Back still turned, she says, "You'd better get some rest while you can. I sent word to Yasu. As soon as I'm finished with Lord Oda's chamberlain tonight, we'll meet him at the willow."

That's why she's so subdued. Even last night's disaster can't distract her from knowing that sooner or later, Yasu will learn of her debt and tell her four years is too long to wait. She must have decided it will be less painful to break things off now than wait for the inevitable. Birdie's heart goes out to her, but she can't think of anything that will make this easier, so she quietly excuses herself until it's time to get dressed.

Birdie helps Pearl don a kimono, hairpins, and her professional face for the evening, but when the time comes, it's Jester who steps in to correct the already-embellished tale being told about the scene at the Camellia, performing a more polished version than this afternoon's improvisation.

By the end of the evening, the pleasure quarter's most deadly gossip staggers out the door with a version of last night that's far more entertaining and much less damaging to the House of Treasures.

But the hardest part of Pearl's night is still ahead. Tonight's patron doesn't pay enough to be allowed to see her "morning face," so as soon as she has satisfied him and sent him on his way, she and Birdie put on their padded robes and steal out to meet Yasu.

Pearl usually hurries to the shrine, eager to see her lover, but tonight her steps slow as they draw near. Her lips move silently, rehearsing her speech and armoring herself with her oiran training.

Yasu is waiting for them. Pearl flinches when he greets her with his usual ardor, knowing it will be his last moment of blissful ignorance. Even Birdie pities him as he parts the trailing branches of the willow and follows her inside.

Pearl begins her speech bravely but can't quite finish the one she'd practiced. She has spent months imagining the moment she tells him she's free to leave Yoshiwara, and now that she has to deliver the news that she won't be able to escape for years, she chokes on the words. She breaks down, despairing of the debts still chaining her to the House of Treasures.

But Yasu is made of finer stuff than she imagined. He receives the news in silence, but instead of pushing her away, he tells Pearl he loves her. That he'll never love anyone else. He'll go back to Mito, where his family oversees militia training for a more fortunate clan, and work hard. He'll save every *mon* and return with enough money to pay off her debt. It may take years, but they *will* live happily ever after. He promises.

And once he says that, Pearl remembers she'll be earning money too. Ten percent of her fees, she tells him. Together, they might be able to pay off the debt in two years, three at the most. They'll wait for each other. Work hard, think of the future. They *will* be together, they *will*.

But on the walk back to the Treasure, the oiran is uncharacteristically silent. She seems less dejected than before, but Birdie has lived in her shadow long enough to know it's best to keep her mouth shut. Her feelings are still dangerously raw, and until she gets used to the altered shape of her future, it would not be a good idea to remind her that she has not escaped the obligation of her apprentice's debut. Unless she finds a patron to foot the bills instead, the considerable cost will be added to the debt she'll be trying so hard to pay off.

The first frost strips the last leaves from the maples, and everyone wakes to find the gingko trees raising bare branches toward heaven and the ground below paved with gold. The streets of the pleasure quarter empty as one by one, the buskers, fortunetellers, and food stands disappear.

Then Takeda disappears too. He cancels his regular visit once, twice, three times. No explanation. It's far from the first time he has cancelled without explanation, but he doesn't usually do it so many times in a row. Nobody at the Treasure misses him, exactly, but his monthly stipend hasn't arrived either.

The worry makes the chill penetrating the wood-and-paper walls of the House of Treasures worse, and even as its inmates crowd in by the braziers to toast their hands and faces, they feel a cold wind at their backs. Birdie huddles with Peach and Feather by the *hibachi* in the room they all share, watching them play a game of *go* and speculate about Takeda's absence.

Peach places a white stone.

"Do you think he's sick?"

"It could be the influenza. I heard one of the girls at the Wisteria has it."

"Ha!" Feather crows, playing her white stone and gathering up three black ones.

Auntie appears in the doorway.

"Don't frown like that, Peach. You'll get wrinkles. Have you seen Pearl?"

"I think she went to see the massage man," Birdie tells her. "She had a headache when she woke up this morning."

"Too bad she didn't wait," Auntie replies. "Takeda's payment just arrived. That ought to cure what ails her."

"Why was it so late?" Peach asks. "Is he sick?"

"Not him. His wife. Apparently, she's been ill for some time."

As soon as Auntie disappears, Peach mutters, "If I'd been married to Takeda for twenty years, I'd be sick too."

She places a stone in one of the few empty squares remaining, and Feather's face lights up. With a crow of triumph, she scoops up so many of Peach's stones, they spill from her fingers. She'd sacrificed pieces early so she could win big in the end, and her opponent hadn't spotted her trap until it was too late.

1787

Birdie moans with relief as she pulls the ornament from her waxed and pomaded hair, taking care that the charm dangling from it isn't damaged. She carefully detaches the Shinto amulet and lays it aside, even though it was performing no more sacred duty than reminding the men watching Yoshiwara's Second Day parade that shrine maidens are one of their top fantasies.

This year's outfits had been inspired by Pearl's good fortune at evading last year's monkey menace. She'd bought scores of protective amulets blessed at the Yoshiwara Shrine to hand out along the parade route, then dressed her attendants in red and white robes that paid homage to the vestments worn by young women who assist the priests with Shintō rituals. Once again, she's the most talked-about oiran in Edo.

"And," she says, glowing with satisfaction as Birdie helps her undress, "not only were the amulets cheaper than passing out coins, giving the priests the money we'd have spent on frivolous trinkets bought me so much favor, the gods will have to answer my prayers now."

Birdie knows exactly which prayers she means and hopes the gods are in no hurry. Excusing herself to run downstairs and scrape a bowl of rice from the crock before it's all gone, she finds the kitchen buzzing with the news that Takeda's wife has passed away. According to the messenger who stopped to scrounge a snack and exchange gossip before returning, his absence will now stretch into the forty-nine days of mourning.

At first, Birdie is almost as relieved as Pearl. Then the fears that haunt her every time he's absent for more than a week rekindle. What if he doesn't come back at the end of the forty-nine days? He's so fond of saying, "Who needs a mistress if they don't have a wife?" that he might take advantage of this opportunity to cut off his hot-and-cold relationship with Pearl and find himself a more amiable courtesan when he needs one again. That afternoon, she opens the door to Pearl's rooms with caution. Will the oiran be cheerful about her reprieve, or fretting about what might happen at the end of it?

As it turns out, neither.

"Here. Put this on."

Pearl shakes out a long-sleeved kimono Birdie has never seen before. She certainly would have remembered a robe emblazoned with plum blossoms as red as a courtesan's lips, blooming boldly against a background of falling snow. The obi that goes with it is crimson and black brocade, shot through with silver.

"Tonight I'll let you wear these, as a special favor." The oiran unwraps a wooden box containing four long hairpins.

What did she do to deserve this? It's the first time Birdie has been allowed to use the ones carved of pure golden tortoiseshell, without a single brown spot. This set would feed a farmer's family for a year. She's gazing into the mirror, turning this way and that when Pearl grabs the back of her collar and yanks it halfway down to her shoulder blades.

Birdie gasps at the sudden chill on the back of her neck, then her skin prickles as she feels Pearl securing her robe to stay that way. Is she expected to walk around exposed like this? In public?

"You'll get used to it," Pearl says, with a final tug to make sure it won't slip. "Now, pay attention. When you're introduced to Goldbelly's guest tonight, take care to remember his name, because you'll need to use it later. If he does something inappropriate, you must widen your eyes—like this—and say, 'Please don't get me in trouble, Mr. So-and-So! Pearl will be so angry if you make me forget myself.'"

Why does she need to know this? No one has ever tried to violate her person.

"But they will." The oiran laughs at her expression in the mirror. "Because Goldbelly told me that the man he's bringing tonight has expressed an interest in becoming your first patron."

Her first patron? The man who will sponsor her debut? She can't tell if the thrill that's shivering her insides is anticipation or fear. Maybe both.

"When he tries to grab you, cry out, 'Most Exalted Excellency So-and-So!' Address him as if he were a lord. That always confuses them. Then say, 'I'm sure you didn't mean to do that, but I'm glad Pearl wasn't here to see it.'"

"Why won't you be there to see it?" Birdie gapes, alarmed.

"Because sometime during the evening, I'm going to leave you alone with him."

"*What?*"

"Not long enough for him to do any real damage. Just long enough to think he might get away with trespassing where he shouldn't. It will be your job to stop him, but in a way that leaves him wanting more."

How is she supposed to do *that*? She's not ready for this. She's not—

"Close your mouth, you look like a ninny. And your lips look a little pale. Come here." Pearl dabs pomade onto Birdie's mouth. "Just remember, the stories he tells about you later must be of how cleverly you thwarted his efforts, not how much success he enjoyed. It's not enough to be unspoiled at your debut; you must be *known* to be unspoiled." She steps back to survey her handiwork. "That's better. Are you ready?"

The stranger looking back at her from the mirror might be, but Birdie is not.

She's somewhat reassured that it's Goldbelly who will be introducing this prospective patron. At least he might be a nice man, even if he's old or ugly or both. But when she raises her eyes for the first time to bestow the look she and Pearl have practiced so many times in the mirror, she can't hide her surprise.

"Doctor Vandermeer?"

She quickly conceals her dismay. Not because he's a foreigner—Vandermeer is more fastidious about observing the niceties than most men who come to Yoshiwara—but how can a mere translator afford what it will cost to sponsor an oiran debut? And how could she have missed the special feelings he must have been harboring toward her all this time? He's never shown her more than the same cordial respect he offers all Pearl's attendants.

As the evening ripens toward midnight, she still doesn't see it, despite her best efforts to charm him. What's she doing wrong? It's not until Pearl takes a stroll in the garden with Goldbelly, playfully warning Vandermeer to behave himself in their absence, that she finds out.

As soon as the sound of their footsteps fades down the hall, he confesses he's been longing to get her alone. But not for the reason she's expecting.

"I'm sorry to come here under false pretenses, Birdie, but I need to ask you a question, and this was the only way I could think of to make sure no one would stop you from telling me what you know."

Oh. Should she be relieved? Or disappointed?

He lowers his voice. "The night Takeda-san introduced me to City Administrator Koga, why were you so sure he wasn't home on the night of the Great Fire? Something made him jump up and leave the party instead of answering that question, and I can't help but think he knows something."

"I'm sorry to disappoint you," Birdie replies, with an apologetic bow. "The reason I know he wasn't there on the night of the fire is that he was here. In Yoshiwara."

"Masatoki Koga was *here*?" He leaps to his feet. "He *must* know something."

"But how could he?"

"The murderer was in Yoshiwara that night too. Ichiro died in the neighborhood where Koga lives, but his horse was found the next morning—untethered, but still saddled—right outside the Great Gate."

"It was?" That's news to her. "The killer could have gone anywhere from here, though," she points out.

"He could have, but I don't think he did," the doctor argues, pacing back and forth. "If he'd been intent on escaping to a far province, he'd have ridden the horse into the ground before abandoning it. Yoshiwara is the one place in Edo where someone can appear or disappear, no questions asked. Especially if one has the means to buy silence from those who might profit from knowing he was here."

The means to buy silence. She thinks about Koga making payments at the Peonies' back door. Could he be paying them to keep quiet about something far more damning than being her father?

The disturbing possibility that her father might be a murderer becomes an itch that won't go away, and the more Birdie thinks about it, the more it swells into a painful welt that hurts every time she scratches it. She tries her best to come up with perfectly good reasons why Koga had fled the room instead of answering Takeda's question that night, but the more she tries to excuse him, the guiltier he seems. It can't be a coincidence that of all the places in the vast city of Edo where Koga could have been on the night of the fire, he lives where the crime happened and was seen in the place the killer went.

She's brooding about that as she returns to the Treasure pinch-lipped and hunch-shouldered one afternoon, just as Takeda's messenger is leaving. Pearl announces that her biggest patron is back, and he's looking forward to seeing them all at the Camellia on the next Day of the Rooster.

That night, he volunteers nothing about the past few months, so they don't ask. He's a little grayer, a little thinner, and will invite no guests for the time being. He's content to come alone, listen to music, and play *sugoroku* or *go*. Now that he has no wife waiting for him at home, he's less interested in novel entertainments and ribald stories, preferring to speak quietly about ordinary things, relive moments of triumph, regret his disappointments.

"If only my wife had given me more sons," he says one night, pensively turning his sake cup. "The only thing Kiyohisa has ever done right is to marry as he was told." He sighs. "The fool lost another new kimono in a dice game this week."

Half listening, Pearl pours for him and murmurs something sympathetic. Now that Takeda has given up his desire to provoke them all to tears, her tongue has become less barbed, and she's treating him with a little more kindness.

Until she finds out why he's being so civil.

His overseer arrives at the Treasure on the first lucky day of the Fourth Month to meet with Auntie and the Treasures' overseer to discuss the decision Takeda has been mulling over since his bereavement.

He wishes to acquire a new wife to take the place of the old one.

Pearl.

It's every courtesan's dream to be rescued from Yoshiwara, and it's every courtesan's nightmare to be rescued by the wrong man.

"Do you think she'll live in a grand house with lots of servants?" Peach's eyes drift enviously to the misty castle painted on the lattice room wall.

"Would any house be big enough if you had to share it with *him*?" Feather is not at all sure it's a step up.

Pearl scribbles letters to Yasu so frantically that her writing becomes nearly illegible. If he can't scrape together the means to pay off her debts before Takeda concludes his negotiations with Overseer-san, it will be too late.

"Take this." The oiran thrusts her latest missive into Birdie's hand. "Give it to the gatekeeper." She doles out a coin. "He'll know which riders are headed toward Mito."

Birdie dutifully delivers her notes to the Great Gate, and every day she returns emptyhanded. The gatekeepers tell her they're doing their best, but not many travelers go in that direction. She doesn't relay that to Pearl, though. What good will it do to dash what little hope she has?

Takeda continues to appear on his regular evenings, and the fireworks have started again. Pearl's revulsion at the prospect of being stuck with him for life sharpens her tongue and chases away any softness she might have felt toward the widower. But the more she pushes him away, the more he pulls her toward him, like a cat toying with a mouse.

The Fourth Month becomes the Fifth. No word from Yasu. Birdie knows better than to say it, but plenty of men wake up outside the Great Gate and wonder how they could have been so caught up in a dream world. It's all too likely that once Yasu put some distance between himself and Pearl, his passion for her cooled. He hasn't replied to any of her letters, and her barrage of unreasonable pleas to beg, borrow, or steal enough money to set her free may have produced the opposite effect. Repeatedly pulling on the red thread of fate that ties them together may have snapped it instead.

Since the day Takeda's messenger delivered his offer, Auntie has been pressuring Pearl to speed up preparations for Birdie's debut. Once the marriage agreement is announced, Pearl will take her leave of the teahouses where she entertains, bid farewell to her patrons, and no longer be in a position to make the necessary introductions. Pearl isn't dragging her feet on purpose, but she's blindly refusing to believe she'll soon be leaving Yoshiwara as Takeda's wife and can't bear to prepare for the day she does.

Then spring comes to stay and the season of small miracles unfolds. Seeds become shoots, buds become flowers, eggs become birds. And

Birdie returns from the Great Gate one morning bearing three precious words: *It was delivered.* According to a trader just returned from Mito, one of Pearl's letters is now in Yasu's hands, and he has vowed to rescue her.

Birdie dawdles outside the hair ornament shop, imagining what a nice clicking sound those strings of coral beads would make if she were promenading down Center Street under her very own red parasol. Watching the Bamboo's oiran sweep past with her child attendants, she's grateful Pearl never embraced the fashion of shaving one girl's head and dressing her like a boy. A familiar whistle makes her look. Tiger is across the street, prancing along behind the Bamboo's entourage with his nose in the air like the snootiest of oirans.

She ducks into a side alley, smothering her giggles in her sleeve. Her stomach growls. Isn't it about time for that rice cake she promised herself? She rounds the corner onto the street by the moat, heading for her favorite stand. Will one be enough? Maybe she should—

"Birdie? Is that you?"

She spins around. A hand is parting the curtain at the House of Cranes, a familiar face in the gap.

"Why are you dressed so grand today?" Flower asks with a melancholy smile.

Birdie is so stunned at her changed appearance, she can't answer. Flower is much thinner than when she left the Treasure, and it's not just because she's taller. Her eyes are shadowed now, her cheeks hollow. She's still lovely, even though she's wearing the kind of gaudy kimono and fake tortoiseshell hairpins they used to poke fun at behind their fans.

"I was just doing some errands in the neighborhood," Birdie stammers, trying not to let the obvious gap in their stations put distance between them. "Will you come buy rice cakes with me?" She jingles her sleeve. "I have enough for two."

They may not look like twins anymore, but they still understand each other better than anyone in the world. They fall in side by side, ignoring the looks that follow their mismatched outfits down the street.

Birdie chatters brightly about the weather, the new song she's learning from Jester, and arranges her face to hide her galloping dismay at Flower's fall from grace. How can Auntie sleep at night after selling Flower's contract to a place like that?

She buys two buns, then they head toward the Yoshiwara Shrine in unspoken agreement. Together they clap their hands and make their offerings, then skirt the garden to the bench that sits in the shade of the hut where the portable shrine is kept.

Flower unwraps her bun, murmuring a polite word of blessing before taking a bite. She closes her eyes at the pleasure of it, revealing how long it's been since she tasted one.

But Birdie sits with hers in her lap, nervously fingering the wrapper. The moment for asking her questions has arrived, but she can't find the right words.

Finally, she blurts, "What ... what happened to you?"

"Well, I live at the House of Cranes now." Flower studies her rice cake.

"Are you their oiran's apprentice?" Birdie asks with a last desperate stab of hope.

"No," Flower replies, her bleak expression confirming what Birdie already knows. "I have my own cushion in the lattice room now."

"Is it ... awful?" Birdie whispers, even though she dreads the answer.

For a long moment it looks like she's not going to get one, then Flower takes another bite of rice cake and says in a dull voice, "It's a job. It's just a job. You get used to it."

"But ..." Birdie's voice trails off in despair. How could her twin have resigned herself to such a terrible fate?

"When it's your turn," Flower assures her, "you'll get used to it too."

What does she mean, "when it's your turn?"

Then it hits her. After her debut, it *will* be her turn. She's been prancing around Yoshiwara in Pearl's grown-up clothes and looking forward to that event as if it were a particularly splendid monkey show. Until this very moment, it hadn't occurred to her that she would have to *be* the monkey.

"Are you all right?" Flower peers at her face.

"I'm—I'm fine." She's not fine. "I was just—"

She can't let on that she'd hadn't allowed herself to fully understand what becoming an oiran meant until now. Leaping to her feet, the horror chases her through the shrine, her *geta* clattering over the stone path, trying to outrun the truth. Head down, she gasps and sniffles her way to the koi pond, leans over the railing of the bridge, letting her tears fall freely. For Flower, for herself, and for not being able to do anything about any of it.

By the time her tears run dry, her twin is standing beside her.

"It'll be okay," Flower says, in that way of hers.

"No, it won't," Birdie draws a shaky breath. Because she's crying about more than going upstairs with a man. "Because now I'm all alone. You're gone, and so is Dolly." Then she blurts, "I still haven't found my mother, and my father might be a murderer."

Flower is shocked into silence for a moment, then takes her hand to lead her back to the bench.

"Tell me."

Everything Birdie knows and fears spills into her twin's sympathetic ear. What she heard from Vandermeer, what she suspects about Koga, how she'd looked for her mother everywhere, but found no trace.

"Both my parents are alive," she concludes in despair, "but I'll never have a family."

Flower squeezes her hand.

"What about me?" she says. "I'm your family too."

That night Birdie drags herself to bed after a long evening of being uncomfortably aware of the men Pearl is entertaining. Finding Flower was a great comfort, but the facts she'd finally faced are not. The more she tries not to think about it, the more her overactive imagination intrudes, making her frown and blush at peculiar times all night.

The next day, Mistress Moon's lesson is on how to trick a patron into paying for one of her monthly *monbi* "double fee days" instead of the regular day he reserved, but that just reminds Birdie of what she'll have to submit to every night.

"... you should wait to send the note saying you're indisposed for as long as possible, so he's already becoming eager for his visit. Not so late that he's already on his way, though, because that will—" Mistress Moon breaks off. "Why are you making that disagreeable face? It's most unbecoming. You should be grateful I'm teaching you how to handle this situation gracefully, so you don't have to pay for your double-fee days out of your own pocket."

"I just—" Birdie hangs her head. "What if I don't want to do it?"

"Do what? Save money? Or"—she gives a harsh laugh—"satisfy your patron? Make no mistake, missy. However cleverly you tell fortunes and lose at *sugoroku*, if you don't please your patron the way that only a woman can please him, he won't be your patron for long."

"But they have wives!" Birdie cries. "Why don't they satisfy themselves with their wives, instead of coming all the way to Yoshiwara?"

"Because that's not a wife's job. Her job is to give him children, not entertain him in other ways. That's your job, and be glad you have it. When a man is hungry, he eats a bowl of rice. When he's cold, he buys a jacket. When he needs to satisfy his manly urges, he visits a courtesan. Being a courtesan is no different from planting the rice a man eats or weaving his clothes. It's just a job. You'll get used to it."

There it is again. *You'll get used to it.* Easy for her to say, the dried-up old bat. Sitting in her room all day, smoking her stinky pipe, doing Auntie's bidding. She never has to—

"All right." Mistress Moon's face softens a little. "I remember how strange it was, the first few times. Distasteful, even. But trust me, it gets easier. After you've done it a few times, you'll hardly even think about it. Let me tell you a secret. I was afraid too, at first. Do you know what my teacher told me? Pretend you're someone else. Imagine that when you go upstairs you turn into Pearl. It's not you doing these things, it's the grandest oiran in Yoshiwara."

Birdie sniffs. That *might* help. A little. If she pretends to be someone else the same way she turns into a woman who's not embarrassed by compliments when she puts on Pearl's fancy clothes, will that be enough to keep those men from touching the real Birdie?

It will have to be.

The next day, Birdie returns from her errands and slips through the front door, tunelessly humming something she heard at a banquet last week. She stops. It's too quiet. Heading down the hall toward the kitchen, she catches Jester emerging from the debtor room.

"What's going on?" she asks.

He grimaces, beckoning her in.

"Takeda-san's messenger was just here," he says in a low voice. "He's agreed to Overseer-san's price. All that's left is to pick a wedding date."

Uh, oh. If Pearl's oiran days are numbered, her future is in jeopardy again.

"Do you think it'll be . . . soon?"

"Pearl and Auntie are at the fortuneteller now."

That's bad. If they went to one of those astrologers who take weeks to draw up charts based on everything from the dates and times of the bride and groom's births to the number of strokes in their names, Pearl might have time to find her a patron and make the teahouse introductions. But what if they went to Madame Truth? She'll just take Pearl's hand or shuffle her sticks and give them a date right away.

Birdie doesn't want to be here when they get back. If she sets out early for her lessons, stops by the shrine on her way back . . . It will only delay the inevitable, but that might be long enough for Pearl to vent the worst of her despair on someone else.

After her dance lesson, Birdie takes the long way home, stops to admire the new offerings at the fan shop and the comb store, makes a detour to ask the *geta* maker if the new pair he'd promised for next week is ready yet, even though she knows they won't be. The street outside the Treasure is in shadow by the time she returns.

"Auntie wants to see you in her room."

Startled, she spins around. Sandpiper and Swallow are waiting for her again.

"What about?" she asks.

"Something important," one says gravely.

"Is it about Pearl's wedding?" she asks.

They look at each other, then back at her.

"No."

If not that, what? Dreading the answer, she climbs the stairs to the third floor, stopping to straighten her kimono and tidy her hair before facing the dragon in her den.

She knocks.

"Come in," says Auntie. She's frowning over a ledger but looks up as Birdie enters. "It's about time. What did you do, crawl back from your dance lesson?"

"Sorry, Honored Auntie."

"Sit." She gestures to the cushion across from her. Packs a pipe and lights it.

"I assume you've heard," she says, "that Takeda-san has reached an agreement with the Treasure about Pearl's debts. She will become his wife in ten days."

Ten days? Too soon. Much too soon. She tries to hide her dismay, but Auntie takes one look at her face and barks out a laugh.

"I see you're worried about what that means for your debut."

Oh no. They went to Madame Truth. Did she tell them Birdie would never have a patron, never be an oiran?

"I don't know why Pearl insisted on keeping this from you," Auntie says, puffing away, "but the reason you were chosen as the House of Treasures' apprentice oiran is that a patron presented himself over a year ago and offered to fund your debut."

"He . . . he did?" Birdie stammers. "Who?"

"You'll be pleased to hear that after Takeda-san marries Pearl, he will become your sponsor and patron himself."

What? No! Birdie's secret hope that her first patron might be someone as nice as Doctor Vandermeer turns to ash. The first man who will ever take her upstairs will be Takeda? But he's so—

She manages to get herself out of Auntie's room without saying anything that earns her a beating, but as soon as she gets to the common room, she crumples to the floor. Despite her precautions, the gods have once again answered her prayers in the worst possible way.

She *will* become an oiran. She *will* have a patron. But that man will be Takahisa Takeda, and she will take Pearl's place as his captive audience, his sparring partner, his—

She shudders. Can't say the word "lover," even to herself.

The wailing coming from behind Pearl's closed door is met with both sympathy and eye-rolling. Everyone agrees that this level of drama is a bit unseemly. Birdie is the only one who understands that the oiran's despair is only this deep because Yasu raised her hopes so high.

The next morning, Pearl manages to face the world again after a closed-door session in Auntie's room that leaves her mute, but compliant. She takes herself to the private bath, silently eats her bowl of rice, performs the day's duties. Everyone breathes a sigh of relief, hoping the worst is over.

For the first time in weeks, she doesn't send Birdie to the gatekeeper with a message. There's no time for her entreaties to reach Yasu now. If he's not already on his way, he won't make it in time. They make the rounds of every shrine in Yoshiwara, pleading with the gods to spare them both.

The sun rises, the moon takes its place, but their pleas go unanswered. Every morning, the day of Pearl's marriage and Birdie's debut draws nearer.

In only three days, Pearl will leave Yoshiwara, and there's still so much to be done that Birdie can't imagine they'll be ready on time. She steps outside, snaps open her parasol, and heads out to find Tiger, who might know where they can hire a second wagon. Pearl's wedding gifts have been arriving in a steady stream for days, and now they might not fit in just one. On the way back, she'll pick up the—

"Birdie? Is that you?"

A sun-darkened young man who looks like he's dressed for an audience with the shōgun is standing in the shadow of the pickle-seller's stand.

"Yasu-san?" It can't be. "You're... you're back?"

She never expected to see Pearl's lover again. Had he returned to fulfill his promise? To pay off Pearl's debts and marry her?

"I just arrived last night." He stands a little taller. "How do I look?"

Like a doomed warrior from a kabuki drama. His trouser-skirt and jacket are of fine silk, but they're at least a generation out of date.

"You look good," she says. But there's a mended slice in his left sleeve, and why is he holding that arm so oddly?

"Is Pearl at the Treasure now?" he asks. Less eagerly, he adds, "And what about the old guard dog? Auntie?"

"Yes, they were both there when I left." She can't bear to tell him he's too late.

"Well," he says nervously, patting the breast of his jacket where a bulge reveals the string of coins he's carrying. "Wish me luck?"

"Good luck, Yasu-san."

Hoping he didn't hear the note of despair in her voice, she bows her goodbyes without another word. Her foreboding grows as she watches him stride around the corner. How did he get enough money to pay off a debt that ought to have cost him years of honest labor?

She goes about her errands that morning with a heavy heart, dragging them out as long as possible so she won't have to go back to the Treasure before the typhoon that's certain to rage in Yasu's wake has blown itself out.

Even so, she puts her ear up to the crack before walking through the front door. Failing to hear sounds of shouting, weeping, or breaking dishes, she cautiously slides it open. Hears only the everyday twanging of a *koto* being practiced somewhere upstairs and Cook calling for the kitchen maid to fetch another bag of rice.

She tiptoes up the stairs. Still nothing. Had Yasu decided to wait until later? Had someone told him Pearl was as good as married? Maybe he'd gone away without even knocking. But if he did, shouldn't she tell Pearl she saw him? That he'd worked hard and saved his money and come back for her, just like in the romances? If she were Pearl, she'd want to know that someone loved her that much.

She stands outside the oiran's rooms, torn between her years of being Pearl's eyes and ears, and the fear that there's some unwelcome explanation for the calm.

Then it's decided for her. Grabbed by the ear and marched down the hall to Auntie's room, the manager swats the door shut with a smart *thwack*. She's pushed down onto a cushion at the table where Auntie works.

"Not. One. Word." Auntie glowers down at her.

"What do you mean?" she cries, clutching her ear.

"You know very well what I mean. That accursed *rōnin* saw you outside when he arrived."

Yasu had been here. Where are the signs of the knock-down, drag-out fight she expected?

"I sent him packing before he got one foot in the door," says Auntie, puffing furiously on her pipe. "Pearl doesn't know he was here, and that's how it's going to stay."

Poor Yasu. And poor Pearl. This is not how their love story is supposed to end. But what can she do? Auntie is her superior, she can't challenge her. Not directly, anyway.

"Did he not bring the money to pay off Pearl's debts, Honored Auntie?" she ventures. "I mean, isn't Yamada-san's money as good as Takeda-san's?"

The manager scoffs.

"A girl like you can't be expected to know anything about business, but here's your first lesson. His money's not nearly as good as Takeda-san's because it's not nearly as much. Takeda isn't just settling her debt, he's paying the Treasure five times what she cost us."

Of course he is. In Yoshiwara, it's not love that conquers all, it's gold. Eyes stinging with the injustice of it all, Birdie bows her head.

"I understand, Honored Auntie," she mutters.

"I can see by your face that you don't. But if Pearl hears one word about that shiftless ne'er-do-well being back in town, I'll know who to blame. And that will be a beating you won't forget."

Birdie withdraws without another word, but as she lets herself out into the hall, she's already rebelling. She stops in the kitchen to ask when the rice will be ready, then slips down the hall to the debtor room, where she can be alone to think.

The door opens just as she's about to knock.

"Sorry," she says, backing away, "I thought it was empty."

"Actually, I've been waiting for you." Jester beckons her inside. "What did you decide?"

"About what?"

"To tell Pearl or not."

How did he know?

"Who do you think pays the maids to wax Auntie's door?" He flashes his good-natured grin, pats a spot near him on the thin futon. "Sit."

She slowly lowers herself.

"So?" he asks again.

"I promised not to, but it feels so wrong." She picks at the scruffy tatami. "What would you do?"

"Ah. Good question. But a better one might be, what *wouldn't* I do? And the first thing I wouldn't do is burn down the House of Treasures with myself inside."

"What do you mean?"

"Let me ask you something." He leans back against the wall. "How do you think Pearl will feel when you tell her that her lover came back for her?"

"Happy. More than happy. It's what she's hoping for, with all her heart."

"She's hoping he'll return with too little, too late?"

"No, of course not. She's hoping he'll come back and ransom her before she has to marry Takeda-san."

"And do you think she'll have any luck persuading Auntie and Overseer-san to be satisfied with a fraction of what Takeda is offering?"

"Well... no," she admits. And Yasu can't possibly scrape together enough to match what Takeda agreed to pay. Not in two days, anyway.

"And when Auntie and Overseer-san refuse to reconsider," he continues, "do you think Pearl will just quietly marry a man she hates, knowing she came so close to spending the rest of her life with the one she loves?"

"No." If there's one thing she knows about Pearl, it's that she'll fight tooth and nail. But Pearl has tried to refuse their wishes before, without success. That would leave her but one choice. "She'll run."

He waits while she thinks that through. There's only one way out of the pleasure quarter, and it's guarded day and night. If it were easy to escape from Yoshiwara, Pearl and countless other courtesans would be long gone.

"Even if she makes it past the Great Gate," Jester confirms, "runaway courtesans lose their rank, their reputation, and everything that goes with it. Whether she escapes or not, the House of Treasures would no longer have an oiran. Or receive another *mon* from Takeda."

The marriage agreement would fall through. And her debut. Now she understands what Jester meant about lighting her own funeral pyre. Being rescued from Takeda is what she's been praying for, but not like this. Auntie would make sure she suffered for telling Pearl about Yasu and bringing ruin upon them all.

"I... I guess it would be better not to tell her."

"I always knew you were a smart girl." He gives her a lopsided smile as he climbs to his feet. "Not everyone would understand that even when the gods give you the chance to answer someone's prayers, you don't have to say yes."

Birdie helps Pearl get ready for the last night they will ever entertain together, but they exchange no more than a handful of words. There's nothing left to say. Pearl is too despondent to join in as the others excitedly discuss the magnificent new mirror and dressing table that arrived this morning, and the vermilion robes she will wear when she passes through the Great Gate to her new life beyond the moat. Birdie dares not say a word, lest she give away the secret that's smoldering inside her, burning to get out.

As always, the teahouse mistress is there to greet them, but tonight she follows Pearl into the freshening-up room, her face tight. She pulls the oiran aside, murmuring, "Takeda-san has been here for an hour already and is demanding to see you the moment you arrive. He's upstairs with a flask of sake. Alone."

That plows a furrow between the oiran's brows. Weren't Kiyohisa and the shipowner supposed to celebrate with him tonight?

"Take care," the mistress warns. "He's got something on his mind."

To say the least. The moment they step into the room upstairs, he's across it in two strides.

"Who is this Yamada *rōnin*, and why was he pounding on my gate today, demanding to be let in?"

Pearl is confused. Yasu is back? She turns to Birdie, reads the guilt on her face. Her apprentice *knew*, but didn't tell her?

"Speak up, woman!" Takeda grabs her by both arms. Shakes her. "Did you send him?"

"N-no," she stammers. "Why was he at your house?"

"As if you didn't know." Takeda shoves her away. She stumbles. "He demanded that I give you up. Claims you've made promises to each other. Is this true?"

"I—"

He grabs her wrist. "Is it true you agreed to marry him?"

Her eyes slide away.

Takeda pushes her to the floor with contempt. Strides back to the table to throw the rest of his sake down his throat.

"My men sent him packing," he growls, "with a little reminder that it's not a good idea to draw your sword on another samurai's land."

"What did you do?" Pearl gasps. "You didn't hurt him, did you?"

"Not as badly as he hurt my chief retainer. But he'll pay for that as soon as my men find him."

Birdie shakily lets out the breath she's been holding. At least Yasu got away. Unless he leaves Edo altogether, though, it's only a matter of time before Takeda's men hunt him down. Birdie watches Pearl bite back a retort, eyes lowered as she slowly picks herself up from the floor, mastering her feelings as if her lover's life depends on it.

Because it does. The law allows samurai like Takeda to extract whatever justice they see fit, and she has no illusions about what kind of mercy Yasu can expect from a man who tightens his grip on anything he desires, as soon as he sees another man wants it. Pearl and Yasu will both pay for any feeling she shows toward him now.

She pulls herself together and bows deeply.

"I'm sorry that insignificant *rōnin* caused you even the slightest trouble, Takeda-san. I barely know him. He means nothing to me. I tried to discourage him from pursuing me but—"

"*Discourage* him?" Takeda pounces on the admission that they'd been on speaking terms.

She tries to backpedal, but he's having none of it.

His slap sends her staggering.

"I'll teach you not to make promises you can't keep!"

His glare withers the servant just arriving with a plate of sashimi, as he pulls Pearl out the door toward the stairs to their room, intent on punishment tonight, not love.

Someone is shaking her, but it can't be morning yet. It's still dark. Birdie struggles to sit up, then snaps awake as a hand muffles her mouth before she can ask what's happening.

"This way." Pearl drags her out to the hall before hissing, "You *knew*."

The shame floods back. She did know Yasu was back. And she said nothing. Like a thief being led to the flogging ground, she allows herself to be pulled to the far end of the corridor. Pearl turns, and Birdie gasps. Her jaw is swollen, her lip cut, and in the light from the single guttering candle, resentment is drawing lines on her face that make her look older than Auntie.

"You *owe* me."

"I'm sorry, Pearl, I—"

"I will never forgive you. Never. I should never have let Takeda talk me into choosing you as my apprentice. But what's done is done, and there's one last service I need you to perform." She winces in pain as she draws a note from her sleeve. "Yasu paid a servant to bring me this."

Birdie unfolds it. He's begging Pearl to meet him at the willow tonight, at the Hour of the Boar. They must flee Edo and never return. He has a horse waiting outside the gate.

"But I can't meet him tonight. The servants at the Camellia are loyal to Takeda, not me. I won't be able to get away until we're back at the Treasure. I need you to go to Yasu and explain. Take this." She thrusts Takeda's old carp-and-waterfall *inrō* with its octopus *netsuke* into Birdie's hands. "Tell him if I don't meet him at the willow tomorrow night at the usual time, to take this and run. I don't know why it's so valuable, but it must be, or he'd have replaced it years ago. Yasu can sell it and live on the proceeds until I join him. Wear this, so you won't be recognized." She stiffly shrugs the green padded robe from her shoulders.

Birdie slips it over her sleeping robe and stows the *inrō* in one deep sleeve. Without another word, she heads for the stairs while Pearl limps back to the room she shares with the sleeping Takeda.

Stopping briefly to tidy her hair, Birdie shoves in a few hairpins so she won't attract attention by going out half dressed. She tells the manservant at the door that she's fetching some herbs Pearl needs, but he just yawns and waves her through before she's finished. Keeping to the shadows, she hurries toward the willow tree.

But as she approaches the shrine, she hears shouts and commotion ahead. She slows, crouches behind the stone fence, peering through a gap.

Two armed men are struggling with a third, who is lashing out, resisting.

It's Yasu.

Heart hammering, she shrinks back. Peeks out again, but now they're leading him out through the *torii* gate, still struggling.

What's she going to tell Pearl? She retraces her steps with a troubled heart. The man at the door of the Camellia recognizes her, lets her past without a word. She drags herself up the stairs but stops as she reaches the upper floor. Muffled thumps and weeping are coming from one of the rooms. She creeps down the deserted hallway. As she feared, the noise is coming from behind the door where Pearl and Takeda were sleeping.

She ventures closer, hears Pearl insisting, "It wasn't me!"

"Then who was it? And don't try to blame the servants. They know what will happen to them if anything of mine goes missing while I'm here."

"It was—" Pearl is desperate now. "It was—"

"Spit it out, woman!"

"It was Birdie. Birdie took it."

A hard slap, accompanied by a cry.

"That's a lie."

"No, I saw her," Pearl whimpers. "When I woke up, I saw her and wondered why she was in our room, but she disappeared before I could—No!" she cries. Another blow. She sobs, "Check the attendant's room, if you don't believe me."

Birdie freezes. He can't come out and find her here. She's wearing Pearl's robe. His stolen goods are in her sleeve. Hiking up her kimono and grabbing the railing so she doesn't take a tumble in her haste, she hurtles down the stairs and murmurs another lie to the doorkeeper about bringing the wrong herbs.

As soon as the door shuts behind her, she gathers her robes and runs. She doesn't stop until a stitch in her side slows her to a walk. Breath coming in short gasps, she ducks into an alley.

She can't go back to the Treasure. That's the first place Takeda will look. And she can't ask Flower to hide her. She trusts her twin with her life, but no one at the Crane owes her any favors. The first courtesan to spot her would take the opportunity to profit handsomely from that information. But what about Tiger? Yes. Tiger will help her. Tiger always has a plan.

A distant bell tolls as she slinks through the shadows toward the House of Peonies. Now that she's adrift, without a home, familiar landmarks take on new shapes, menacing and alien. An evil smell warns her to choose another shortcut, and she hastily shrinks back around a corner when a scuffle on the street ahead ends with a cry of pain. At this hour, the teahouse and brothel doors have welcomed all those who have two *mon* to rub together, leaving only the dishonest and desperate out in the cold. Anyone who isn't a predator must take care not to become prey.

And it's not just the living she fears. She jumps as something whisks around the next corner, cowering behind a rain barrel until she's sure the cat that might have been a ghostly, two-tailed *bakeneko* is gone.

By the time she finally plods to a halt before the darkened lantern hanging outside the House of Peonies, her *koma-geta* feel like they're made of stone and she's as limp as a rag that's been wrung out and hung on a nail. She gazes stupidly at the barred door. What was she thinking? She can't very well pound on it and ask for Tiger after it's shuttered for the night. Now that he's a fixer's apprentice, he's probably not even here. She'll have to wait until morning, try to catch him coming back at dawn after introducing some foolish man to the delights of the pleasure quarter. Dragging herself around to the back door, she hunkers down in a sheltered spot across the lane to wait for morning.

She drifts off, startling awake as a catfight erupts. Her head nods again, until a night watchman tramps past the end of the alley, clapping the "all's well." The third time he jolts her from sleep, colors are filling in the ink-drawn world. She's grateful she didn't know that lump lying beneath the overhang was a dead pigeon until now. As she watches a maid dressed in blue emerge from the pleasure house down the alley to sprinkle water on the dusty street outside their door, she hears a slightly off-key rendition of "A Stranger in Yoshiwara" approaching. The whistling grows louder as Tiger swings into the alley.

He stops. Comes a few steps closer.

"Birdie? Is that you?" He pulls her to her feet. "What are you doing here?"

He helps her brush the cobwebs and dead leaves from Pearl's padded robe, then takes her arm to lead her away from the Peony into the still-deserted streets. Casting worried glances at her disheveled clothing, he saves his questions until they reach the shrine.

The moment they're seated on the bench by the cleaning buckets, he asks, "What happened?"

She tells him.

"What are you going to do?"

"I don't know."

She shivers, as much from the bleakness of her prospects as the early morning chill. Sometime in the long night, it became clear that there's no way to escape the terrible consequences in store for her. All she can do is choose the lesser of two evils. If she returns to the Treasure, no one will believe her; she'll be stripped of her apprenticeship and punished as a thief. If she tries to hide, she'll be hunted down as a runaway courtesan and sold to another pleasure house to work off her fine.

"You need a place to hide," Tiger says. "At least until we can figure out what to do."

We. Her eyes brim with gratitude. She reaches for his hand, squeezes it, her throat too tight to say the words. They sit hand in hand, as the sky over the *torii* gate pales to gray, then blushes pink. Tiny twittering birds awaken in the gnarled plum tree that has stubbornly survived in this forgotten corner of the grounds.

Tiger sighs, gently gives back her hand.

"I'd sneak you into the Peony if I could, but there's nowhere you could hide without being discovered within a day." And the tale of an apprentice oiran begging for refuge at a rival pleasure house would be all over Yoshiwara by nightfall. "We need to think of somewhere your manager would never look. Some place she thinks you'd avoid."

Some place she'd—

"Dolly," she says.

"Huh?"

"Elder Sister's contract was sold to a geisha house." She smiles at Tiger's astonished face. "She lives at the Nomura."

Hiding at a geisha house is a brilliant idea, he agrees. No one would suspect an apprentice oiran would ever set foot in such a place. They huddle together on the bench for a while longer, as she puts off the moment when she'll have to leave the refuge of their friendship and step into an uncertain future. But as early risers trickle through the shrine gate to ring the bell and awaken the gods, they reluctantly unbend their stiff limbs and climb to their feet. Tiger helps her straighten her hair ornaments and tidy her kimono, advising her to keep her head up and walk as if she's on some ordinary morning errand.

"Sometimes," he advises, "it's best to hide in plain sight."

She looks back once, finds him still standing there, watching her go. He gives her a half-hearted wave, and she pokes out her tongue and crosses her eyes, carrying his laugh with her as she aims for the street where the geisha live.

The geisha house's mistress joins Birdie and Lucky Doll in the receiving room with a fresh pot of tea. She does not look pleased. Without her makeup, and in her current mood, Madame Nomura looks every one of her thirty-seven years. But age has not altered the way she holds herself, and the practiced grace with which she moves. She still commands admiration, even in an everyday kimono. Sinking onto a cushion across the table, she pours. Dolly bows low over the table, thanking her for giving her Little Sister refuge in her time of trouble.

"I haven't given her refuge," Madame corrects her. "And I have no intention of doing so." Turns her icy gaze on Birdie. "But I'll give her one chance to change my mind."

Birdie's tea grows cold as she tells the mistress everything that happened since Takeda decided to marry Pearl. How she'd been used by the oiran to meet her lover, how Yasu had returned too late to ransom Pearl from her debts. How she'd been caught between Auntie and Pearl and said nothing, but paid for it when the oiran blamed her for keeping the secret. That Pearl had stolen Takeda's *inrō* and demanded she deliver it to Yasu, then pointed her patron at her apprentice for the theft.

"Please let me hide here until I can find a way to escape Yoshiwara," she begs, bowing low over the table.

The silence stretches. Hardly daring to breathe, she prays the slight downturn of Madame's lips when she'd mentioned Takeda's name means there's some reason she'd be reluctant to do him any favors. The mistress calls for her tobacco set, packs a pipe, and smokes it, deep in thought. Finally, she knocks out the spent plug and sets it back in the box.

"Let's see this *inrō* that Takeda-san holds so dear."

Birdie fetches it from the sleeve of the padded robe.

The mistress turns it over in her hands, then looks inside each of the four compartments. Pipe. Tobacco. Seven *ryō* in scrip, issued by a respectable rice brokerage. Two slim, ivory signature seals. Madame unwraps the first one and studies the name carved into the end. She frowns.

"I thought you said this *inrō* belonged to Takeda-san."

"It's the one he always wears."

"Then why is Masatoki Koga's signature seal inside it?"

Madame shows her the end of the ivory stick. Birdie's eyes widen in surprise. The characters definitely don't spell Takahisa Takeda.

"I don't know," she says.

"Are they family?"

"No. They're not even friends. Takeda entertains Koga a few times a year, but it always seems like they hate each other."

Madame says nothing. She sets Koga's seal aside and unwraps the other one. This one is Takeda's.

She lines them up on the table side by side and packs another pipe, never taking her eyes from the ivory sticks before her. She smokes for a while, then a smile steals across her face. Rewrapping the seals, she returns them to the top compartment of the *inrō*, then slides the four-tiered box across the table.

"I have an idea," she says. "But first you have a choice, and I want you to understand the consequences before you decide."

Birdie nods.

"As long as the fact you're missing doesn't get out, you can still go back to the House of Treasures. If you return this *inrō* with the contents intact, you can throw yourself on your manager's mercy. I'm sure they've invested considerably in your training, and because customers won't patronize a courtesan who's been accused as a thief, it would be in their best interests to persuade Takeda-san to keep it a secret. You'd probably get a beating, and they might sell your contract to another pleasure house, but at least you'll still be able to work. And who knows? Takeda-san is perverse enough that he might still decide to become your patron. He loves a bargain," she adds in a dry voice, "and could probably negotiate a sizeable discount."

Birdie wilts. The only thing that would be worse than being possessed by him after he's paid a fortune is being possessed by him after he's paid a pittance.

"I see that option doesn't appeal to you. But consider this: if you're discovered hiding here, with that *inrō* in your possession, nobody will believe your word over his. Neither he nor the constables will show you any mercy, and if it's discovered that you have a city administrator's signature seal in your possession as well, your life would be over."

She swallows. "I understand."

"No, you don't. Not yet. Because there are consequences for this geisha house too. If anyone discovers we're hiding a runaway courtesan from one of the leading pleasure houses in Yoshiwara, we'd be ruined. Unless you're prepared to do exactly as I say, you can take that *inrō* and go out the way you came. We won't turn you in, but we won't lie for you if someone comes asking."

Birdie nods, scoots back and places her hands on the floor, lowering her forehead to the rice straw mats.

"Please let me stay," she pleads. "I beg you. I'll do anything you ask."

"Very well." Madame calls for a fresh pot of tea. When they each have a cup steaming before them, she asks, "How long do we have before the news that you're missing gets out?"

Birdie thinks for a moment.

"Pearl is getting married the day after tomorrow. Her grand procession will leave at noon, and I think both Takeda and the Treasure will want the Yoshiwara gossips to be speaking of nothing else. But," she says apologetically, "I'm sure his men are already looking for me."

"I'm sure they are. But if you're right, they won't be doing it openly for a few days." She thinks for a moment. "I'd like to show that *inrō* to someone."

Birdie slides it back across the table.

"This is our new maid. You can call her Birdie," Madame announces, at the beginning of the evening meal.

"Please show this humble person your favor," Birdie says, bowing like the servant she's pretending to be.

The residents of the Nomura return the polite reply, but by the time she straightens, chopsticks are already ferrying rice from bowl to mouth again, conversations resuming.

The next morning, she puts on a plain kimono like the rest of the maids and does her work willingly, if ineptly. Assigned to do inside chores—they can't risk her being recognized outside the geisha house—she sweeps the floors, hauls the futons out for airing, and discovers just how many services had been performed for her every day. The next day, she can barely hoist herself out of bed. How can her body hurt so much, in so many new ways?

As the days go by, it's disheartening to discover Madame was right when she said there was no need to change her name. Without her elaborate hairstyle, glittering ornaments and layers of extravagant silk robes, she's very nearly invisible. Not only does no one suspect she used to be an apprentice oiran, the Yoshiwara gossips have been strangely silent on the subject of Little Bird from the House of Treasures' absence from the festivities. Why?

Relief that nobody is talking about her disappearance turns to pique that nobody has missed her, and then to sadness that nobody seems to care that she's gone. Every night, she crawls between her covers and turns to the wall in silence as the other maids exchange gossip about people she doesn't know, reminding herself to be grateful for the roof over her head and the tasks that give purpose to her days. Because now that's all she's got. No home, no future, not a single possession to call her own. The small wooden rabbit carved by the old man who used to sit outside the shrine, the comb that had been her mother's, and the amulet she'd relied on to keep her safe are still hidden in the upstairs cupboard at the House of Treasures.

But her biggest loss is one she didn't expect. Dolly. Now that they live under the same roof, there's an even bigger gulf between them than before, but now it's in the opposite direction. Geisha only speak to maids to give orders, and they must act as if they don't know each other when anyone else is around.

The next day, the mistress disappears to her lover's villa by the river. The other maids brag that he's one of the richest traders in Edo, as if he were their *danna* too.

Long after the others are asleep, Birdie stares at the ceiling, wondering if Madame took Takeda's *inrō* with her. What had changed her mind about letting her stay? Without knowing why Madame is helping, it's hard to know if she can be trusted. Is she intending to turn the situation to her own advantage, at Birdie's expense? The geisha mistress owes her nothing, and in Yoshiwara, information is as good as gold.

As she goes about her chores, she misses Tiger. Misses Flower. Wonders what they're doing right now. A tear splashes onto the low lacquer table as she bends over her work. She quickly polishes it away, but the grief that swamps her every time she's reminded that every path leads away from those she holds most dear sends more tears plopping onto the shiny black lacquer. Even if she manages to escape Yoshiwara someday, she'll be outside the walls and they'll be inside. They'll never see each other again.

And if she doesn't manage to escape? What then? Must she live out her days as a maid, cowering inside the Nomura until she's too old to be of value to anyone anymore? Or will she be dragged back to the House of Treasures, sold to meaner and meaner pleasure houses, kept under lock and key until she works off her debt?

The days snail by. Madame doesn't return. How could she have been so stupid? Why had she trusted someone she barely knows? Doubts grow and coil inside her like swiftly twining kudzu vines. She should have kept Takeda's *inrō* hidden in her sleeve and taken her chances. Running away had seemed like the only option with Takeda in a rage and Pearl pointing him at her, but maybe she should have stayed and endured her first beating from him instead. Even a future living on painkilling herbs and learning to smile as she followed him upstairs would be better than this endless waiting.

The next day, her stomach is so soured with worry, she can barely eat. She waylays Lucky Doll on her way to the outhouse, begs her to wake her when she returns that night from entertaining.

They steal out to the strip of wasteland behind the kitchen, an unlovely patch crisscrossed with clotheslines and hung with cleaning rags. Birdie seats herself beside Elder Sister on the warped wooden steps.

"What are you so worried about?" Dolly yawns.

"Do you know why Madame is helping me?" Birdie's throat is so tight, she can barely speak. "I've been thinking about it ever since she left, and I can't figure out what's in it for her. What if she tells Auntie? What if she goes to Takeda-san? Do you think I should run, before she gets the chance?"

"Run?" Dolly sounds genuinely puzzled. "Where?"

Birdie twists her sleeves, says nothing. They both know she has nowhere to go.

"Don't worry so much." Dolly takes her hand and squeezes it. "You can trust Madame."

"How do you know?"

"Because she hates Takeda too."

"Why?"

Dolly tips her head back, looks up at the distant stars.

"Madame had a son." She plucks at a stem of grass growing up through a crack in the steps. "His name was Kanzō. But there's no future for a boy at a geisha house, so last year, Madame's *danna* offered him a berth as cabin boy on one of the four new boats the Maedas built for him to sail to the Dutch Auction. When Takeda-san and his partner bribed the sailmakers to delay delivery of their rivals' sails, Madame's *danna* moved the captain Kanzō served onto one of the two boats from his early days that were still seaworthy. They chased Takeda's boats to Nagasaki, and made it in time to outbid him for the choicest lots at the auction. But only one boat made it back to Edo. Empty."

"Why?"

"Armed men attacked them off the coast of Ise." Dolly flings away the stripped stalk. "The so-called pirates fired Kanzō's boat after plundering it, and it went down with all hands."

"And Madame believes they served Takeda?"

"The survivors' wounds could only have been made by a samurai blade, and Takeda was the only one involved in the auction who has such men under his command. But Madame's *danna* had no proof until he spotted the Takeda son at a drinking party in Yoshiwara a few weeks later. Kiyohisa was wearing a kimono made of Dutch cloth from one of the auction lots Takeda lost in the bidding."

Birdie shakes her head in sorrow for Madame, who had suffered every mother's worst nightmare. They sit in pensive silence for a while, then Dolly yawns again and pulls her to her feet. It's past time they were in bed.

But despite Kanzō's tragic story, Birdie gets her first good night's sleep since coming to the Nomura. Now that she knows why Madame has good reason to hate Takeda, she knows she can trust her. Because in Yoshiwara, the enemy of your enemy is nearly as good as a friend.

The next morning, one of the other maids pokes her head into the room Birdie is attempting to clean.

"You're wanted downstairs."

"Is Madame back?" She looks up hopefully from her sweeping.

"No, it's a man."

Her broom stills.

"A man?"

"That's what he told me to say, anyway." The maid giggles. "It's just Tiger."

Birdie dashes down the stairs, finds him leaning on a lacquered parasol dripping a spreading puddle onto the entry stones, his leggings wet to the knees. She reddens at his look of surprise, remembers she looks like a servant now, not an apprentice oiran. She quickly hides her broom behind her.

"I see you're finally learning something useful." He laughs.

She lifts her chin and looks down her nose at him, even though she's shorter.

"If you came here just to make fun of me, you can go now."

That just makes him grin wider.

"Don't you want to hear what they're saying about you?"

Curse him. She does.

"Well?" She scowls. "What are they saying?"

"Nothing."

"*Nothing?*"

"Nothing."

That stings. "Nobody noticed that I wasn't outside the House of Treasures to see Pearl off?"

"Nah, everyone was too busy talking about how unhappy she looked."

Pity replaces her pique. She's still mad at Pearl for turning her into a fugitive, but she can't help but feel a little sorry for anyone who has to spend the rest of her life with Takeda.

"Are his men looking for me yet?"

"I haven't heard anyone asking about you."

Good.

"What are you going to do?" he asks.

"Madame has an idea, but I don't know what it is." She lowers her voice. "Elder Sister told me she took Takeda's *inrō* to show her *danna*."

"That's promising."

"Why?"

"Do you know who he is?"

She shakes her head.

"You probably never met him, since the Treasure is such a hoity-toity pleasure house. He's rich enough to outspend any man in Yoshiwara, but he wears ordinary clothes and prefers geisha to oirans. He's one of the biggest traders in the country. Plenty respectable now, but I've heard from more than one source that he got his start in smuggling or gambling or both."

"And why is that good?"

"He knows everybody. Government ministers, pickpockets, you name it. And most of them owe him, in one way or another. Best of all, he has no love for Takeda."

"Because of Madame's son?"

"Kanzō was his son too."

Ten days after she arrived at the Nomura, Birdie is sweeping the common room when the housekeeper tramps up the stairs to tell her, "The mistress is back. She's asking for you in the receiving room."

Birdie whips off her apron and smooths her hair before going down to find Madame sitting at the table with Takeda's *inrō* before her.

As soon as the maid bows herself out and the door slides shut behind her, Madame pushes a cup of tea across the table.

"I believe I've found a way for you to escape your current situation."

"You have?"

"Can I count on your help?"

"Of course."

"As you may have heard, my *danna* is a merchant. His network of trading partners extends from the farthest north to the deepest south of the lands controlled by the shōgun. But he's not alone in his frustration that the government refuses to let Japanese merchants do business beyond our borders. They still do, of course, but shipments from anywhere besides the Dutch empire enter Japan, in, shall we say, less-regular ways. Ways that are considerably more dangerous. That's why those goods cost up to ten times what the trader paid for them, and the Japanese products that go out in return can be sold overseas for ten times what they bring here."

Birdie nods, impressed. No wonder Madame's lover can afford a villa by the river.

"Imagine how much less dangerous it would be to hide such a shipment amid a cargo of goods being traded legally—timber, for example—all shipped with paperwork signed by the head of a certain respected samurai family."

Does she mean Takeda?

"I see you understand. It just so happens that such a shipment might already be on its way. Were it to come full circle and return with desirable goods sailing under the same name, some people might find themselves considerably richer."

Birdie nods, happy that using Takeda's signature seal will help repay Madame for taking her in. It must give her and her *danna* some satisfaction that they're using his name to smuggle the goods, even if money won't make up for Kanzō's death.

"But why do you need my help?"

"Because the next time a cargo of illegal goods passes through Edo under a certain person's name, it's going to be discovered." Madame's lips curve into a chilly smile. "And when the officials who board the ship inspect the documents, they'll point straight to a smuggler who, everyone agrees, ought to be made an example of."

Birdie laughs out loud. It's brilliant.

"The only issue," Madame continues, "is that my *danna* can't appear to know about the smuggling himself. It would be ideal if the person who tips off the authorities has a relationship to the accused smuggler that would explain how she came by the information. Even better if she's also known to the official who receives the tip." She raises an eyebrow.

"You don't happen to know any Edo city administrators who might wish to receive such information, do you?"

"As a matter of fact—" She grins. "—I do."

And unless she's worse at reading people than she thought, Masatoki Koga will be more than happy to take revenge on Takeda himself.

1788

Birdie eats, sleeps, works, waits. All she sees of the world outside is the view framed by the Nomura's second floor window. Weakening sunlight creeps down the wooden wall of the geisha house across the street, the crows keep watch from the rooftop, and the calico cat sprawls sleepy eyed on the front step as the days shorten into winter.

The second day of the New Year dawns clear and cold, and Birdie hears the festival drummers making their way from teahouse to teahouse the next street over. A tumult of excited feet clatters down the stairs, and the front door slides shut behind the pack of maids racing each other to the main boulevard to watch the Second Day processions. She wishes with all her heart she could join them.

It's one of the shortest days of the year, but it feels like the longest. Rattling around the silent geisha house, she plucks halfheartedly at a *shamisen* then sits down to write her First Official Poem of the new year, but she can't settle. Again and again, she finds her brush poised over blank paper, ink stiffening its tip, wondering what the House of Treasures procession is wearing this year and what Flower and Tiger are doing right now.

When it's finally dark enough to light the candles, she cracks open the upstairs shutter to watch for the gaggle of merry girls returning with cheeks bitten by the cold, the geisha blotting their dripping noses on their sleeves when they think no one is looking.

The maids thunder up the stairs, jostling to be the first to tell.

"The House of Peonies was the best!"

"They were dressed like spring birds!"

"Their oiran's fan was made of feathers and it changed color when she waved it, from green to gold."

They tell her of the Pine's new oiran, the Wisteria's *sugoroku* theme (which was a little hard to guess, at first), and the Bamboo's just-promoted junior courtesans, who look different from the child attendants they used to be. No one mentions the House of Treasures.

"What about the ones who dressed up like shrine maidens last year?" Birdie asks.

The maids look at each other. None of them remember them being in today's parade.

"I don't think they have a new oiran yet," says the one who's the most reliable source of gossip. "Remember when Pearl got married last spring? The girl they were training to be her replacement had to go back to her hometown to take care of her sick father. She's not back yet."

So that's the story the Treasure has been spreading. Are they hoping she'll return? She tips her head, surprised that discovery doesn't kindle a single spark of joy. When she first arrived, she'd have given anything to go back to the only life she's ever known, but now that she's seen oiran life from the outside, she knows what it costs. Not in gold, but in the freedom to decide which parts of herself she's willing to sell. And which she's not.

Winter reluctantly gives up its chill grip, and one afternoon near the end of the Third Month, Birdie throws open the upstairs shutters to take a deep breath of spring, wondering who lost the sandal emerging from a stubborn patch of snow across the street.

"The mistress wants you," a maid calls to her from the doorway. "She said to 'bring your hairpin' when you come."

It's the summons Birdie has been waiting for. Madame told her it would take two months for the second illegal shipment to make it to the Chinese port and back, and she's been counting the days until her freedom from being at Takahisa Takeda's mercy arrives. Dashing to the futon cupboard, she pokes her arm deep between the folded bedding to retrieve the bundle of ornaments she was wearing the morning she arrived at the geisha house.

She brings them to the receiving room, and if the mistress notices that Birdie has forgotten to take off her apron, she doesn't mention it.

"I need one of the long ones with the House of Treasures crest carved into the end," Madame Nomura tells her, lifting her brush from the invitation to Masatoki Koga. It suggests he come to the Nomura tomorrow afternoon if he'd like to hear some information about Takahisa Takeda that may be of great interest. The hairpin will lend credibility, telling Koga this piece of scuttlebutt comes from the pleasure house where Takeda is most likely to have discussed his plans and confided his secrets.

Birdie is happy to play her part in Takeda's banishment, but that isn't all she's hoping to get from Koga. She has given up the dream that he will ever acknowledge her as his daughter, but he might be persuaded to tell her the one thing that only he knows. Her mother's real name. Madame has agreed to ask him.

The mistress reads through her note one more time, polishes the dust from the hairpin, then ties the message around it and calls for a messenger.

Bent in a respectful bow behind the mistress, Birdie recognizes Koga's voice from behind his deep-brimmed hat as he stops to greet Madame Nomura at the door of the receiving room.

"I was surprised to get your message," he says to the mistress. But as Birdie straightens, he stiffens. "Birdie? What are you doing at a geisha house?"

"Please sit." Madame gestures to the guest cushion. "And I'll explain."

As he settles himself at the table, Birdie kneels behind the mistress, eyes lowered.

"Little Bird is here," Madame tells Koga, pouring out two cups of tea, "because White Pearl accused her of a theft that she herself committed. She had nowhere to go, so we took her in. And once she no longer owed the House of Treasures her loyalty, her conscience led her to tell me of Takahisa Takeda's crime."

"Crime?" His tea stops halfway to his lips. "What crime?"

"The kind that I hope you'll find a way to punish."

"Go on."

"In the privacy of the banquet rooms at the Camellia teahouse," Madame continues, "Birdie overheard Takeda-san gloating about his own cleverness at making money in less-than-honorable ways. Some of which have not yet come to fruition."

"I see." He sips his tea, still skeptical. "Are any of these the sort of crimes we might catch him committing?"

"Yes. If your agents were to inspect a certain ship arriving on a day we can make known to you, you just might find proof that Takahisa Takeda is engaged in the unlawful importation of foreign goods."

That gets his attention. Smuggling carries a sentence of banishment. He'd be rid of Takeda and his demands for good.

"Where? And when?" He can't keep the eagerness from his voice. "Tell me that, and my men will be there waiting."

The silence that meets his questions reminds him that nothing in Yoshiwara is free.

"What do you want in return?" he growls. "Because if it's money—"

"No."

"Then what?"

"Birdie would like to know the name of her mother."

"Her *what*?" he yelps. "Why would a girl from a pleasure house think I know the name of her mother?"

"Come now, Koga-san," Madame chides, with a world-weary sigh. "She's not asking that you acknowledge you're her father, but—"

"Her *father*? I'm not her father!"

Birdie's head snaps up, because that's one lie she's not going to let him get away with anymore.

"Don't try to deny it!" she cries. "I saw your ears the night you lost to Pearl at Truth or Dare."

She defiantly tucks her hair behind one ear and turns to show him its pointy tip.

"I know you brought my mother to the House of Peonies on the night of the Great Meiwa Fire," she continues, "and you've been paying them to keep that secret ever since. Why would you hide that from me if I'm not your daughter?"

"Because I care enough about my family's reputation to make sure nobody knows about my sister's little half-breed!"

Sister? Half-breed?

"Don't look so surprised," he sneers. "I can see you've been passing yourself off as Japanese. Or maybe the ladies at the Peony didn't have the heart to tell you of your tainted blood."

Tainted blood? Is he suggesting her father is a *foreigner*? But even as she shoves that thought away, she knows it's true. *Her tallness. Her unfashionably round eyes.*

"You're the spawn of a barbarian scoundrel—" Koga's lip curls in disgust. "—who bamboozled my little sister into believing that getting pregnant with his mongrel would force me to . . ."

Everything Birdie thought she knew about her family is being tossed into the air like a pack of cards. Head spinning, she stumbles to her feet. With the word "mongrel" ringing in her ears, tears spill as she flees the room, ricocheting blindly down the hall. Slapping to a stop in the patch of wasteland outside the back door, she doubles over, sobbing.

It's some time before the storm subsides, but she finally collapses onto the top step, taking ragged breaths. How could her father be a foreigner? Foreigners live far away in Nagasaki. They aren't allowed off

Dejima Island. Except Doctor Vandermeer, who's a special case because he lives in Edo at the invitation of—

The shōgun. The same shōgun who persuaded him to take his brother's place as Dutch Learning Expert. The brother who was half-Japanese and half-Dutch and died on the night of the Great Meiwa Fire.

Oh, no. No, no, no. Her father's not the killer. Was he the victim?

It can't be true. She doesn't want it to be true. But foreigners in Edo are so rare, it would beggar belief if the foreigner who fathered the child inside Koga's little sister and the foreigner who was killed right outside her house that night were not the same man.

Her father was Vandermeer's long-lost brother.

Which means he's dead.

And it was Masatoki Koga who killed him.

The next few days pass in a haze. Birdie struggles to free herself from the troubling truths Koga had dropped on her like a sack of rice.

Tears surprise her the first few times she remembers her father is dead. It's strange to feel such grief for someone she never thought she'd meet, but knowing he's dead makes her feel more like an orphan than ever. And she's no closer to finding her mother, because she let Koga's words drive her from the room before asking her name.

Fortunately, cooler heads were in attendance that night. After learning Koga's sister was Birdie's mother, Madame talked to her *danna* and he asked around.

"Her name was Hatsu-hime," Madame tells her a week later. "And 'First Princess' was also the last princess. Masatoki Koga only had one sister."

Birdie adds it to her meager cache of information. She longs to start looking again, but she can't venture beyond the Nomura until she's free of Takeda.

Yesterday was the earliest that the ship loaded with his "smuggled goods" could have made it back to Edo, assuming the fairest of winds and the greatest of good luck.

Birdie leans out the second-floor window to peer up and down the street again, and...yes! There's Tiger, swaggering up to the door below—who could miss him in that flashy striped kimono?—bringing her the latest news and gossip like he does every Day of the Horse. If the ship has docked, she's about to find out.

She whips off her apron and trips down the stairs. Finds him in the entry, striking a nonchalant pose (as if he wears silk kimonos every day), stroking that thing he calls a goatee.

"Since when can you afford to dress like that?" She aims a scornful eye at the gaudy red and black silk. His career as a pleasure quarter guide must really be taking off. He has a new *netsuke* hanging from his sash, and it might even be ivory. She squints at it.

"What are those supposed to be? Eels?" *Eww.* "Why eels?"

"Eels are the future," he informs her. Stepping out of his *geta* and following her through the kitchen to their favorite perch on the back steps, he boasts, "They may not be much to look at, but eels are going to make me rich."

"Like the one-eyed man who barbeques them over by the moat?" she teases. He's easily the scruffiest vendor in Yoshiwara. "How do you plan to get rich selling eels?"

"I'm not selling eels." Tiger grins. "I'm selling forgiveness."

"*Forgiveness?*"

"Yeah." He plops down next to her on the top step and produces a bag of rice crackers. "It works like this. I pay the kids who live by the moat one *mon* for every ten live eels they catch, then I turn around and resell them for one *mon* apiece to men who wake up in Yoshiwara with a splitting headache and a guilty conscience. The customers run off to release the eels back into the moat and go home believing that saving some innocent eels from death by barbeque balances out whatever sins they committed the night before, and they're safely back on the righteous path to Buddha-hood." He offers the crackers to Birdie, then tosses a handful in his mouth. "It's the perfect business." *Crunch, crunch.* "The eels don't mind, the customer goes home with a clear conscience, and both me and the kids make money."

She laughs, shaking her head, then gets up to fetch them some barley tea to wash down the crackers.

"What else is new?" she asks, hoping to hear of the smuggling raid.

"Well, the House of Treasures still doesn't have a new oiran."

"They haven't given up on me coming back? Surely nobody believes I'm still in the country at the bedside of my poor, sick father?"

"I'm sorry to say that you've been away so long now, it became necessary for him to die." *Crunch, crunch.* "You're now observing the forty-nine days of mourning. Which . . ." He pauses to consider. ". . . has been going on somewhat longer than forty-nine days, if anyone's counting."

"Why do you think they're telling everyone I left with their blessing and plan to return?"

"Well—" He holds out his cup for more tea. "Put yourself in Auntie's place. Would you want everyone in Yoshiwara wondering why someone lucky enough to be an apprentice oiran would run away?"

"All she'd have to do is call me a thief, and no one would blame her," Birdie says, digging in the bag for more crackers. "Takeda would back her up."

"But then everyone would think she does such a poor job of training her courtesans that they don't know the first rule of Yoshiwara—never steal from the hand that feeds you. Plus, customers might worry that where there's one thief, there may be more. That would be even worse for the Treasures' reputation than a runaway apprentice."

"How do you think she persuaded Takeda-san not to accuse me?"

"Dunno. But he hasn't been back to Yoshiwara since you disappeared." Tiger gives her a lopsided smile. "Maybe he turned into the kind of man who doesn't need a mistress because he has a wife."

She shakes her head in disbelief, but as they share the last of his rice crackers and joke about this and that, it's clear that nothing as exciting as a smuggling raid has happened since he last visited.

The next day, however, the news is all over Yoshiwara. Takahisa Takeda is being marched to the waterfront by the shōgun's men-at-arms.

The first drops of rain spot Takeda's jacket and a stiff offshore breeze whips his trouser-skirt against his legs as he strides down the dock, gulls wheeling overhead. He's annoyed to be dragged out here with a storm brewing. Why are they escorting him down a dock that doesn't even belong to his ship-owning partner? Don't they know that the floating rat palaces moored here belong to a rival fleet, the one that usually hauls Maeda goods? When he finds out what idiot is behind this colossal mistake, he'll—Is that *Russian* on the crates peeking out from behind that pile of logs?

He squints, still can't read the writing. Ha! He'd give his right ear to see that smug Maeda bastard's face when these buffoons realize their mistake and march *him* down here to confront him with the proof he's been defying the shōgun's edict against importing foreign goods. Maybe this time they'll even corner the wily old son-of-a-smuggler who owns these boats. He certainly won't shed any tears if that crafty old criminal gets himself banished to a remote island for the rest of his natural life.

They halt before the shōgun's chief investigator, who greets him with a curt bow and hands him a document.

"Do you recognize this?"

It's a bill of lading. Takeda is about to say no, when—Is that his signature stamped at the bottom?

"There must be some mistake." He frowns, handing it back. "This shipment isn't mine."

"The documentation says it is. That *is* your signature stamp, isn't it?"

"My old one," he snaps. "My *inrō* was stolen last year, and the seal that produced this stamp was in it. After the theft, I registered a new one." He digs out its replacement and unwraps it. Thrusts it at the investigator. "See? This isn't the same one used to stamp that bill of lading."

But instead of withdrawing the accusation, the government lackey crosses his arms and says, "Did you report this so-called theft?"

"Well, no," he admits.

"Why not?"

Because he couldn't let the authorities catch that thieving oiran apprentice Birdie before his men did. He doesn't need anyone asking why he was carrying around Masatoki Koga's stolen seal in the same compartment as his own.

"This is a mistake," he blusters. "And I'm a busy man, too busy to deal with bureaucratic mistakes." He thrusts the paper back at the investigator. "Talk to my overseer and he'll straighten this out."

"I'm sorry, but I'm afraid I'm under orders to bring you in. For a matter as serious as this, you must answer to the tribunal." He inclines his head toward the customs building overlooking the docks.

Takeda follows his gaze, and there's Masatoki Koga, his fine kimono whipping in the wind, looking down on the proceedings. With a smile on his face.

Speculation about such a high-profile patron's arrest is the hottest topic in Yoshiwara, and the rumors are flying.

"I heard that that they're investigating Takeda for trying to pass off someone else's poetry as his own," Dolly reports, giggling behind her fan. "The Peonies' poet says it's high time they punished him for that crime."

Tiger, on the other hand, is sure they caught him cheating on his taxes.

"The government never turns a blind eye to that, no matter who you are," he solemnly tells Birdie. "Never, ever, cheat on your taxes."

"Even if your business is less than legal?"

"*Especially* then."

A week later, the real story is out. Crates stuffed with illegal Russian furs were discovered hidden among a load of timber being shipped under Takeda's name. He insisted the timber wasn't his, that he'd never stamped those bills of lading with his seal, but nobody believes him.

Then truth becomes even stranger than rumor, after Takeda accuses the city administrator of falsifying the charges, insisting that Masatoki

Koga is targeting him over an ancient grievance. And not only that, the city administrator is a murderer!

Nobody believes a word of it, of course. In a matter of days, they're calling this "The Fox Scandal" and Koga is the man of the hour for catching him. Honors are conferred, a taller hat bestowed. Invitations to the most exclusive teahouses in Yoshiwara arrive, but are stiffly declined. Pleasure quarter regulars lament their failure to lure Edo's newest celebrity to their banquets, while quietly sending their winter robes to the seamstress to have the fox trim removed until some new peccadillo takes this one's place.

They don't have to wait long. Two weeks later, the minister of protocol is chased down Center Street by manservants from the House of Bamboo. A mock trial conducted by their oiran finds him guilty of cheating on her, but this is his second offense, so the verdict is reached while daylight still lingers in the sky and the pleasure quarter is as busy as it gets. Severed topknot in hand, no cover of darkness spares him from the hoots and jeers as he scurries to the outskirts of Yoshiwara to get it reattached.

And Takeda's name fades from the pleasure quarter like footprints on the shore. The news that he and his household—including his pregnant wife, Pearl—have been exiled to Sado Island creates hardly a ripple on the Yoshiwara pond.

"Birdie?" calls Dolly from the doorway. "What's wrong?"

"Nothing. Just . . . thinking." She's standing at the upstairs window, head tipped against its wooden frame. "Do you ever wish you could light a stick of incense and ask your ancestors what to do now?"

"Yes." Elder Sister joins her at the window. "Strange, isn't it? On the rare occasions when I feel homesick, it's not the living I miss, it's the dead."

Maybe that's where this strange, shapeless melancholy is coming from. Madame and her *danna* have delivered her from ever becoming Takeda's plaything, but Birdie is far from free. She's still under contract to the House of Treasures and owes them years of service. The minute someone spots her setting foot outside the Nomura, they'd be within their rights to haul her back.

"I came up here to tell you Madame is waiting for you in her office," Dolly says. She leads Birdie back downstairs but doesn't follow her in.

"Please sit," the mistress says, putting aside the letter she'd been reading. "I just received some information from the House of Treasures that may be of interest to you."

Oh no. Did they discover where she is and demand her return? Knees trembling, Birdie lowers herself onto the cushion opposite.

"After the successful conclusion of our little operation," Madame says, "I asked a friend of mine to visit them and have a conversation with your old manager."

Birdie swallows.

"About what, Honored Mistress?"

"You."

"Did she tell her I'm here?" she squeaks.

"No. Although she didn't seem especially surprised when my friend said she'd heard you didn't really go back to your village to take care of your aging father. That, in fact, you'd run away with some valuable property that belonged to a House of Treasures patron."

She told her the *truth*? Why?

"Your manager denied it, of course. And my friend agreed it's a pity that people are so willing to repeat scandalous rumors like that, when you aren't around to defend yourself. She then felt obliged to share the sad story of a courtesan who was tarred by just such a tale, and even though it was later proven to be false, the damage was done. The overseer fired the manager for not selling the girl's contract before the story became public. Even after she was cleared, nobody would offer a single *mon*."

"How . . . tragic," Birdie croaks.

"In any case, today your Auntie waylaid my friend coming out of the tobacconist and asked if her 'source' knew where to find you. My friend, of course, claimed to have no idea. Your old manager said that's too bad, because if you were still in Yoshiwara, the overseer of the Treasure might be willing to part with your contract if a suitable offer were made. With Pearl gone, it would be difficult for them to give you the debut such a talented apprentice deserves, but perhaps another pleasure house could profit from your extensive training. For the right price."

Birdie's heart sinks. The Treasure wants her back, but only long enough to sell her contract.

"Apparently, you are far more talented at dancing and composing poetry than cleaning," Madame continues, with a dry laugh, "because Auntie insisted that a girl of your talents couldn't possibly be had for less than a hundred *ryō*. In gold."

Birdie gasps at the ridiculous sum. Who would pay that much for a sixteen-year-old girl who hasn't yet earned a single *mon*?

"My friend was astonished too," Madame agrees. "It's lucky she'd been expecting something of this sort. When she mentioned that one of her courtesans had overheard a certain kabuki actor wondering if there was more to your absence than filial duty, Auntie admitted she might be able to talk the overseer of the Treasure down to seventy-five."

Seventy-five *ryō*. In gold. Birdie doesn't have that kind of money, and neither does anyone else she knows.

But . . . is there some way she could get it? The most obvious options are out. She's only middling good at playing the *koto* and dancing. Her biggest talents are losing games in a way that makes a man feel he's won, writing verses that answer a man's puns with her own, and performing popular *shamisen* tunes on one string. But she's been at the Nomura long enough to know that even though geisha aren't allowed to have patrons in the same way as oirans, the entertainments they offer at the increasingly popular teahouses on Kyōbashi Street go far beyond playing background music. Is there some way she could put her talents to work for the Nomura?

She scrambles to her feet and bows.

"Will you buy my contract and let me stay here?" she begs. "Please? I'll do anything. I know it's a lot of money, but I'll pay you back. Every last *mon*. Please don't let them sell me to another pleasure house."

Madame cocks her head, considering.

"Do you think you're worth seventy-five *ryō*?"

"No. But I will be. I promise."

"Then I suggest you pay it."

"What do you mean, 'pay it?' With what?"

Madame nods at a small, black, lacquered chest sitting unnoticed in the corner.

"Bring that to me."

Oof, it's so heavy, she can barely lift it. Birdie struggles to the table and sets it down with a *thunk*.

Madame opens it. It's filled with gold and silver coins.

"In exchange for the loan of a certain signature seal, those who made a recent trading voyage possible received a percentage of the profits. This is your half. Six hundred forty-five *ryō* and three *bu*."

Birdie's eyes bulge.

"That's . . . mine?" She's never seen so much money in her life.

"Yes. This too." The mistress slides Takeda's signature seal across the table.

Birdie picks it up, confused. Why is she giving back the thing that made such princely profits possible?

"My *danna* got where he is today by being a gambler," Madame explains. "But what makes him a good gambler is that he knows when to quit."

Birdie reads the piece of paper before her again, can't quite believe it's real. Ten days ago, she had counted out seventy-five gold coins for Madame's friend to offer in exchange for her freedom, and here it is. Her contract with the House of Treasures has been paid in full. She could walk out the door right now. She could walk straight through the Great Gate of Yoshiwara, and no one would stop her.

She's been dreaming of the moment she's no longer owned by a pleasure house, but now that it's here, all she can do is scramble to her feet and bow her heartfelt thanks over and over, until the five gold coins weighing down her sleeve remind her that in Yoshiwara, thanks of this magnitude ought to be expressed in more than words.

"Will your friend be offended if I show her how grateful I am for her efforts on my behalf?" she asks, producing the bundle and offering it with both hands.

Madame takes the wrapped coins, weighing them in her hand. Smiles.

"She will be delighted by your generosity."

Good, she'd guessed the right amount.

"And securing the friendship of one of the most respected geisha house managers in Yoshiwara is a smart move," the mistress adds, with a shrewd glance. "What do you plan to do now?"

"I . . . I don't know."

She'd handed over the seventy-five *ryō* to buy her freedom, but she's since realized that true freedom will cost more than gold. She can walk out the Great Gate, but she knows nothing of life on the outside. Yoshiwara is the only world she's ever known. How will she find a place to live? Earn enough money to survive? A single woman's prospects are dangerously limited without family or friends to introduce her. Besides, as long as she still has hope of finding her mother, she can't leave Yoshiwara.

"May I stay here until I have somewhere else to go?" she asks in a small voice.

"Of course. In fact, now that the Treasures' manager has brought your many talents to my attention, it's a shame to waste them on dust cloths and brooms. Our apprentices could use some tutoring in fortunetelling and *go* and the other arts. Until you decide what to do with your future, will you help out by teaching them?"

The next morning, some of Birdie's initial giddiness has worn off, and she discovers just how unprepared she is for her dreams to come true. The only way she can avoid panicking over the vast and empty future now looming before her is by refusing to think about it.

First of all, she has debts to pay. She hasn't forgotten what she owes Flower and Lucky Doll. The next morning, she listens for Dolly's return from the bathhouse, then lugs her treasure chest to the dressing table where Elder Sister is putting on her makeup. Opening the lid, she invites her to take enough coins to buy out her contract at the Nomura. Once they're both free, at least she won't have to face the future alone.

"Thank you for such a generous offer, Little Sister," Dolly replies, smiling at her in the mirror. "But no."

"Why . . . why not?"

"I belong here. I like performing at teahouses."

"But what about when your contract is up?" Birdie cries. Dolly is already elderly—at least twenty-six, maybe even twenty-seven! "What will you do when you're too old to perform? Where will you go?"

"Oh, that's all settled. Mistress and I talked about it months ago. I'm going to run the New Nomura."

"What's the New Nomura?"

"The geisha house Madame is building in one of the new entertainment districts. Her *danna* heard that the shōgun has decided to allow geisha to practice our arts outside of Yoshiwara, so he gave her a piece of land in Kagurazaka. When it's finished, I'll move over there as the ranking geisha. And someday, I'll run it."

"Oh." The word falls from Birdie's mouth like a stone. "I'm . . . I'm happy for you."

But she's not. Why hadn't she considered the possibility that Dolly has plans that don't include her? After all, none of her plans had included Elder Sister until she was on the run and needed a helping hand. Somehow, knowing that Dolly has such a promising future to look forward to makes her own feel all the emptier.

Fortunately, she still owes Flower. In order to pay her debt to her twin, though, she'll have to leave the Nomura and go outside for the first time in months.

"Do you have a moment?" she asks the mistress, bowing from the doorway.

"Of course." Madame closes the ledger and beckons her in.

"I was wondering if you would release me from my promise not to be seen outside on the street."

Madame frowns.

"Why are you in such a hurry? If I were you, I'd wait until word gets around that someone paid seventy-five *ryō* for your contract. Plenty of unscrupulous brokers make a practice of rounding up rogue courtesans to sell in the countryside for a quick profit, and they won't stop to ask if you've got papers or not. You can't be sure they'll leave you alone until potential buyers hear someone paid a ridiculous sum for you and will certainly hunt you down and haul you back."

"How long will that take?"

"It shouldn't take more than a month for word to make it from here to Kyoto."

But Birdie can't bear to wait a month. She explains about Flower. How she can't think about beginning her new life until she has paid her debts in her old one. How every day her twin spends at the House of Cranes is one day too long.

"Why don't I ask my friend to make inquiries on your behalf?" Madame suggests. "How much are you willing to pay for her freedom?"

"Whatever it takes."

"I'm sure my friend can do better than that." Madame laughs.

Birdie thanks her and takes her leave, but drifts to a halt outside the door. Now what?

She returns to the second-floor window, but as she watches the giggling pairs of geisha apprentices passing below, her frustrated longing to be out there with them swells nearly to bursting. Her mother is out there somewhere. She can't bear to wait another day to begin turning over every rock in Yoshiwara until she finds her.

"You're a *foreigner*?" Tiger blurts.

"Shh!" Birdie hisses. "Not so loud." She's not quite ready for everyone and their brother to know that yet.

At first she'd been too upset and confused to tell anyone that her father was a foreigner. Even Lucky Doll. What if she recoiled in horror? Or treated her like a freak, something not quite human? She remembered how she'd had to poke Flower to make her stop gawking at Vandermeer the first time they met.

But after twice being caught staring into space, Madame made her admit what was troubling her. Then she'd laughed at Birdie's fears.

"I certainly don't think of you any differently since I found out," she said, "and unless you keep leaving the entry half swept and the laundry half folded, neither will anyone else."

And she was right. The others may have raised an eyebrow or two behind her back, but as soon as Madame returned from the river villa with a crate of exotic sweets from her *danna*, those were the only foreign topic on everyone's lips. The only reason Birdie hasn't told Tiger about Koga's revelations yet is that he's been too busy prancing around Yoshiwara like some striped peacock.

"Say something in Dutch," he demands.

"I can't speak Dutch!"

"Why not?"

"It doesn't... I don't think it works that way."

"Oh." His face falls, then he brightens. "But nobody else in Yoshiwara speaks Dutch either, so you could say any old nonsense and people would—" He breaks off, seeing the look on her face. "What's the matter?" Then he recalls that's not the only news she just delivered. "Are you sad about your father?"

"A little. But it's not my father I'm thinking about. It's my mother. Now that I know her real name, I'm hoping Madame Truth can tell me more. But I can't step out the front door of the Nomura until everyone knows they're not going to get rich by dragging me back to the Treasure or selling me to the highest bidder. Can you help by spreading the word?"

"I can," he replies with a wicked grin. Being the sole source of new information about the House of Treasures' missing oiran apprentice will make him the hottest banquet guest in town.

He gets to work that very night, and no one is better equipped to set the Yoshiwara rumor mill spinning than the pleasure quarter's most industrious fixer. Tiger spreads the word that someone paid an astronomical sum to the Treasure for their missing apprentice's contract. Every time he tells the story, the number gets a little bigger. They paid a hundred *ryō*! Two hundred! Five hundred! Then he whispers the unbelievable (but highly repeatable) tale that a visiting lord from Morioka delivered her weight in silver to the Treasure and spirited her away to the far north. That one takes on a life of its own, and soon Birdie's name is on everyone's lips.

Until it's replaced by Flower's. Suddenly, men who turned up their noses at the House of Cranes are regretting they missed their chance to spend time with the courtesan who is reportedly so skilled in the womanly arts that an as-yet anonymous bidder is willing to pay fifty *ryō* to buy out her contract.

The House of Cranes' manager counts the last gold coin into her money pouch with a satisfying *clink*, then picks up her seal to stamp her official red signature on Flower's contract. Waving her hand to hasten the drying ink, she can't suppress a smug smile at the unforeseen windfall.

Birdie watches Madame's lips tighten. It galls her to know the House of Crane's manager thinks she just vastly overpaid for the disappointing girl whose contract she just bought, even though the price turned out to be far less than Birdie was willing to spend. Madame's friend had discovered that customers seldom chose Flower more than once. The next time they visited, they chose courtesans far less comely who would at least pretend to desire them.

The manager offers the document to Madame with both hands and a gloating smile, then claps her hands and calls for a maid.

"Find Young Flower and tell her she's wanted in my office. Without delay."

When Flower appears in the doorway, she blinks in confusion at the sight of Birdie and Madame sitting at the manager's table, then remembers to drop to the floor and bow deeply, apologizing for the intrusion and begging politely for the favor of her betters.

Birdie badly wants to rush over, pull her to her feet, and throw her arms around her twin, but protocol must be observed. Flower's eyes saucer as the Cranes' manager informs her that Madame Nomura has purchased her contract. She looks to Madame, then to Birdie, then back at Madame, not daring to believe it's true. But as the manager exhorts

Flower to uphold the honor of the House of Cranes by exceeding her new mistress's every expectation, her face lights up like the girl Birdie used to know.

Madame formally welcomes her to the Nomura, then adds, "If you gather your things now, we'll wait."

But Birdie can't. "May I help her pack?"

They manage to contain their glee until they reach the tiny room where Flower's few belongings are stored, but the moment they're alone, they grab each other's hands and spin around like they hadn't done since they were children. Giddy, they collapse on the floor.

All Flower can gasp is, "How?"

While Flower ties her meager belongings into a faded carrying cloth, Birdie tells her the tale of helping Madame and her *danna* get their revenge on Takeda.

"The only reward I expected was to escape becoming his oiran," Birdie tells her, sitting back on her heels. "But Madame surprised me by giving me a share of the profits. Half of it is rightfully yours."

"What?" Flower tries to refuse. "No!"

But Birdie won't hear of it.

"We're family, remember? I used some of the money to buy your contract, but there's plenty left for both of us to start a new life."

"A new life? What kind of new life?"

"I don't know," Birdie admits. "I was kind of hoping you might have some ideas. I've never lived anywhere else, but I'm not sure there's a place for me in Yoshiwara anymore, and I don't know what's outside the Great Gate."

"Do you want to leave?" Flower bites her lip.

"I don't know. But before I decide anything, I have to find my mother. That's why I'm going back to see Shinjō-san tomorrow."

"Please excuse the intrusion of this humble person." Birdie slides open the door to the fortuneteller's front room.

"Hello, Birdie. It's been a long time." The seer sets her rosary aside with a smile.

"A lot has happened since I was last here." Birdie kneels, setting her bundle on the table before her. With a formal bow, she says, "I came to thank you for being right about everything. I did leave the House of Treasures. I'll never be an oiran. And I'll never, ever have a patron. I wish I'd believed you, instead of trying to escape my fate."

Then she unwraps a small, heavy box and offers it with both hands.

The fortuneteller peeks inside, hesitates a moment, then thanks Birdie for her generosity.

"Is this the only reason you came today?" she asks, studying Birdie's face. "It feels like you brought a question too."

"I did. I'm wondering if the oracle might be able to tell me more about my mother. I found out her real name, and—"

"What?" The seer freezes. "Who told you her name?"

"Madame Nomura. Her *danna* asked around after I learned that the man I thought was my father is really my uncle. Apparently, Masatoki Koga only has one sister."

"Masatoki Koga?" Shinjō pales. "The city administrator?"

"Yes."

"How do you know he's your uncle?"

"He told me."

"You *talked* to him?"

"Yes. But I didn't get a chance to ask if he knows where my mother is now." The memory of that night still burns. "Last time I was here, you told me she's in Yoshiwara, but I've looked high and low and can't find any trace. I thought maybe that now I know her name . . ." She digs into her sleeve to pull out the coins. "Could you ask the yarrow sticks where Hatsu-hime Koga is now?"

Shinjō winces, eyes closing as if in pain, one hand groping blindly for her rosary. But only a few beads slip through her fingers before she flings it aside and rises to fetch the divination sticks. Kneeling, she shuffles them hand to hand, counting under her breath. Birdie waits in silence as the sticks click back and forth, interrupted only by the occasional *tik* of a coin being turned.

The seer flips the last coin and sets the sticks aside. Stares at the hexagram arranged along the table's edge.

"What... does it mean?" Birdie whispers.

Shinjō sits in silence for a long moment, then recites a passage from the *Book of Changes*.

"Despite what has been lost, this is no time to hide yourself away and grieve the past. It's time to decide, make practical preparations and march forth."

Birdie listens, puzzled. What does that have to do with finding her mother?

"It means—" Shinjō takes a deep breath. "—that your mother has been grieving the past for long enough. She's been hiding in plain sight. And now you've found her."

"I've... *what*?"

Shinjō pulls off her kerchief and tucks her hair behind one pointed ear.

"*You're* my mother?"

Birdie feels like a temple bell that's just been struck. She can't believe it. And then she can. But instead of feeling good, it *hurts*.

"Why didn't you tell me?" she cries, as the truth arrows home. "Why did you hide from me all those years? If I'm not an orphan, why did you make me grow up like one?"

"I was afraid this is how you'd feel." Shinjō sighs. "You don't understand."

"You're right." Birdie says, her shock turning to anger. "I don't."

"My brother made me give you up and marry that man in Odawara."

She knows that. It's no excuse. "You could have refused."

"And be cut off without a single *mon*? You think it would have been better for me to live on the street with a newborn baby? Without family, without friends, without a trade? Do you really think you'd have been better off growing up in a prostitute's shack by the moat instead of in the lap of luxury at the House of Peonies?"

"At least I'd have had a mother," she says stubbornly.

"Until I died of the influenza," Shinjō retorts. "Or something worse."

She... has a point.

"Go on."

"The manager of the Peony told me that if I went through with the match, they'd take care of you and raise you as their own. And she promised my brother they'd keep your parentage a secret. All he had to do was pay."

"Well, at least she kept one of those promises." The one Koga paid for, to save his own reputation. "But I guess you know that, since you did come back to Yoshiwara," Birdie adds bitterly, "even if you didn't come back for me."

"I couldn't! Believe me, I wanted to return to you with all my heart, but the House of Peonies was the first place my brother would look, and as long as I was married, he had every right to drag me back to my husband in Odawara. I learned of a temple in Kamakura where a woman can legally divorce her husband if she stays behind its walls for three years, so that's where I went. I spent the next three years raking leaves and scrubbing floors and dreaming of the moment I would walk out the gate a free woman, how I would come straight back to Yoshiwara and scoop you up and never let you go."

"But you didn't."

"I did! Three years and twenty-four days after they dragged you from my arms, I walked back through the Great Gate and headed straight for the House of Peonies. But while I was cutting through the shrine garden, I... I saw you." Her voice falters. "You were playing with a pair of child attendants, who were chasing you around the pond and pretending you were too fast to catch." Her face softens with the memory. "You were shrieking with delight. Then you turned back to see if they were gaining on you and ran straight into me. You looked up and I held out my arms and..."—her face crumples—"you burst into tears. The girls ran up and apologized and took your hand. They were too young to have been there when you were born, so they didn't know I was your mother. As they led you away, you... you never looked back." She hangs her head. "I'd been so busy picturing our joyous reunion, I forgot you were just a baby when I left. I never imagined you wouldn't know me. Or that you... wouldn't *want* to know me."

"Really?" Birdie can't believe her ears. "That's why you hid from me? Because a toddler who didn't know any better hurt your feelings?"

Shinjō flinches. "You don't understand. I was so devastated, I couldn't possibly knock on the Peony's door and demand they give you back. All I could do was run to the fortuneteller who gave me advice while I was waiting for you to be born. She told me the answers I sought were beyond what she could provide. Only the oracle itself could tell me if I deserved to be your mother again. She took me in and taught me how to read the yarrow sticks."

"Oh, I see." Birdie's mouth twists bitterly. "Now it's the sticks that are to blame for deciding I should be an orphan?"

"No. But they spoke to me far more powerfully than we expected, and I learned I had a gift for recognizing the truth. Strangely enough, that's the main thing that kept me away from you. The happiness you had with Lucky Doll was real, and it would have been wrong to take that away. What could I possibly offer in return?"

"A real mother, perhaps?" Birdie is unmoved.

"Or an unwelcome stranger who abandoned you at birth," Shinjō counters. "What I feared most of all was that I'd tell you I was your mother and you'd burst into tears again. It... it would have killed me."

It would have killed *her*? Birdie leaps to her feet, choking on the words, "You should have at least tried. You should have—"

Her throat closes, confused tears spilling, unprepared for the sorrow and anger mixed up with the joy she expected to feel when she finally found her mother. She stands there, face tight as a fist, tears leaking out in spite of her efforts to keep them in.

She hears Shinjō rise, draw near, hesitate. Then arms encircle her. As she's pulled into her mother's embrace, Birdie stiffens, but her resentment is no match for the one thing she's longed for all her life. She gives in to the belonging, and they rock with a shared heartbeat, letting go of all the loss and loneliness they've both been carrying for so long.

As the opening bells begin to chime at pleasure houses all over Yoshiwara, they pull apart, giving each other quavery smiles.

"I should go back," Birdie says, swiping at her tearstained cheeks. "Madame Nomura will be worried. But before I leave, can you tell me something about my father? Is he really . . . gone?"

A profound sadness fills Shinjō's eyes. She nods.

"Was he really a foreigner?"

"Yes. He was the shōgun's translator."

"What happened to him?"

"He tried to save me."

"From the fire?"

"From my brother." She takes a ragged breath. "When Masatoki learned I was pregnant with Ichiro's child, he was furious. I thought if I hid my condition until it was too late for there to be any choice but to marry the father, he'd let me spend my life with the man I loved, instead of the one he chose for me." She shakes her head. "What a fool I was. I knew he had no love for foreigners, but somehow, I imagined *my* foreigner would be different. That once he got to know Ichiro, he would—" A tear escapes. "When I finally told him about the baby, he locked me in my room and swore the servants to secrecy. Not because word might get out that *my* honor was besmirched. He was worried about *his*. When he found out I'd managed to get a message to Ichiro saying I was locked in my room and begging him to come save me, he ordered a watchman to stand guard, day and night. When Ichiro arrived, he couldn't get past the front gate. A few days later, the fire came." She shakes her head. "Ichiro should have ridden in the opposite direction, but he was afraid that if the servants fled in panic, I'd be trapped behind a locked door. And by the time he got to the house, he'd realized the gods might be giving us this one chance to escape. He told me that with the fire throwing everything into chaos, two more refugees wouldn't be noticed or questioned. We could ride to Nagasaki, far beyond my brother's circle of influence, where his family would welcome us with open arms. But Masatoki arrived just as Ichiro was helping me onto his horse. He saw us together, outside, in public. Wouldn't listen to reason. Accused Ichiro of abducting me. I tried to stop him, but . . ." Overcome by an upwelling of grief, she can say no more.

But Birdie can guess the rest. As the Great Meiwa Fire roared toward them, consuming everything in its path, Masatoki Koga drew his sword and killed Ichiro Vandermeer.

"Why didn't you report it?"

"How could I?" Shinjō shakes her head helplessly. "He's my brother."

"But he killed my *father*! If you won't go to the authorities, I will."

"No! You can't. This isn't your secret to tell."

"It's not yours to keep! Not anymore. What are you so afraid of?"

"If I tell what I saw, it would destroy his life."

Birdie opens her mouth to retort that it's no less than he deserves, then understands what her mother is really saying. She's the only person still alive who can bring Koga's life crashing down around his ears. Hadn't Doctor Vandermeer said that without new evidence, his brother's killer would never be caught? Shinjō is the eyewitness he's been looking for. If Koga finds her first, he'll make sure she never tells.

"But don't you see," Birdie pleads. "If you go to the authorities and swear to what you saw, they'll arrest him. He'll be in jail. You'll be safe."

"I can't risk it."

"Why not? I could bring the investigator here. No one needs to know you're the new witness until after he's arrested. You'll be perfectly safe."

But her mother is still shaking her head.

"It's not me I'm worried about. Don't you see? If they arrest him, I'm not the one who will be in danger. It's you."

"Why me?"

"Because it won't take my brother long to figure out who's giving new evidence against him, and even behind bars, he can threaten to hurt you unless I change my mind and refuse to testify before the magistrate."

Birdie's shoulders slump at the truth in her words. Koga killed once to get what he wanted, and it wouldn't take much to persuade him that ridding the world of a half-foreign mongrel would be a service, not a sin. Even if she is his niece. Or maybe *because* she's his niece.

"But if you don't come forward," she says in despair, "neither of us will ever be free of him. You're the only one who can testify to what happened that night."

"No, I'm just the only one who would."

"What do you mean?"

"There was a man who stepped out of the alley as we rode away."

"Who?"

"I didn't recognize him."

"But he must have been there for a reason," Birdie contends. "Or had a connection to someone who lived nearby. If we ask around, maybe we can find out."

"Believe me, I thought of that. But even if we tracked him down, he'd deny he was there."

"Why?"

"Because he was a thief. Halfway to Yoshiwara, my brother realized he'd dropped his *inrō* and *netsuke* during the fight with Ichiro, and when we rode back to get it, it was gone."

But doesn't that mean the man walked away with proof he was there? And not just any proof. If the dropped *netsuke* was as distinctive as the monkey Koga wears now...

"The things he stole—" Birdie's pulse quickens. "Do you remember what they looked like?" If anyone can identify a man by his *netsuke*, it's her.

"How could I forget?" Shinjō's face hardens. "They were a gift from Father on Masatoki's coming-of-age day. The *inrō* was a traditional carp-and-waterfall design, but the *netsuke* rather uncannily predicted what kind of creature my brother would grow up to be. A man whose power extends in every direction and controls everyone around him. Like an octopus."

Birdie steps out onto the ramshackle steps, heart racing. She knows exactly whose *netsuke* that is. If Takahisa Takeda tells a magistrate what he saw that night, Koga could be tried and convicted without endangering her or her mother.

But that will take some doing. She'll need Doctor Vandermeer's help, and before she tells him why, she has to be sure he can protect the witnesses who deliver his brother's killer. That's something she dares not explain in a written message, because if it falls into Koga's hands, he'd make sure that none of them are in any position to deprive him of his freedom.

It takes her two days to find the right words to invite Vandermeer to meet her at a teahouse on Kyōbashi Street without giving away who sent the message or what she intends to tell him. By the time Tiger knocks on the Nomura's door on the next Day of the Horse, the note is hidden in her sleeve, ready to hand over if he agrees to deliver it.

They sit on the back steps, unwrapping pink Girls' Day rice cakes and drinking the first barley tea of spring while Tiger tells her the latest version of her ransoming. Apparently, it has already joined the can-you-top-this classics of pleasure quarter extravagance that are traded over late-night sake.

"You're now worth your weight in gold," he boasts, "and get extra craftiness points for gorging yourself on rice cakes before stepping on the scale."

Birdie laughs, clapping her hands in delight.

He rewards himself with a bite of sticky rice cake and asks, "*Mumff* new at the Nomura since I was last here?"

"Well . . . I found my mother."

"You *what*?" He stops chewing to stare. "Where?"

He's gratifyingly amazed as she tells how her mother became Madame Truth, then offers his condolences after she describes the night of her father's murder and her dismay that it's her uncle who killed him.

"That's terrible. What are you going to do about it?"

"Make sure he finally gets punished. But I need your help. Can you take a message to someone at Edo Castle for me?"

"Of course. Who?"

"The one man who wants justice for my father as much as I do."

Birdie checks her hair ornament. Straightens her fan. For the third time, she sits a little straighter as footsteps approach the teahouse room in the corridor outside, then wilts as they pass by without stopping.

Doctor Vandermeer is late. What if he doesn't come? This will be the first time Birdie has seen him since she discovered he's her uncle, and he still doesn't know of their connection. Part of her longs to see his face when she tells him she's his elder brother's daughter, but Tiger pointed out that once he finds out she's family, she'll owe him more obedience than she's prepared to give. Until she secures his help ensnaring Masatoki Koga while keeping her mother's identity a secret, she dares not say a word.

"Birdie?" Vandermeer squints at her over the shoulder of the teahouse hostess bowing him into the room. He clearly didn't expect her to be the mysterious source awaiting him with information about his brother's murder. "What are you doing here? I heard that you left Yoshiwara. Aren't you supposed to be somewhere in the . . . the countryside?" he stammers, confused. Looks down at the note in his hand as if he's not sure how it got there. "Are you really the one who—"

"Yes," she says, holding a finger to her lips to silence him until the waitress has fetched their tea and she can ask they not be interrupted.

When they both have steaming cups before them and the curtain has been discreetly drawn across the doorway, she explains why she asked him to come.

His mouth thins to a grim line as she tells him exactly what happened the night his brother died. That Ichiro had ridden to his beloved's side with the fire roaring through Edo, intending to free her and flee to Nagasaki. But the gods were not smiling on them that night, because just as they were departing, Masatoki Koga arrived.

"So, he *was* there!" Vandermeer cries. "How did you manage to find evidence I missed? Who told you he was involved?"

"He was more than just 'involved.' He's the elder brother of the woman Ichiro intended to marry. When Ichiro wouldn't hand her over, Koga killed him."

Vandermeer shoots to his feet, eyes blazing.

"How do you know this?"

"She told me."

"Ichiro's woman?"

"Yes."

"She's alive? Here? In Edo?"

"Yes."

"And she'll testify?"

"No."

"But—! Why not? His killer must be punished!"

"I know. But Koga is a powerful man. She's afraid."

"Nonsense. I'll escort her to Edo Castle myself. Justice must be served," he announces briskly. "Take me to her. I'll remind her it's her duty to tell a magistrate what she saw."

"Can you guarantee a judge will believe her word over a city administrator's?"

Vandermeer opens his mouth to reply, then frowns. He knows how easy it would be for a high-ranking *hatamoto* to cast doubt on accusations being levied by a woman. And—even though he sits at the right hand of the shōgun—a foreigner.

"Fortunately," Birdie says, "that won't be necessary."

"I'm afraid it is," he tells her apologetically, returning to the table. "Evidence won't be accepted by the court unless the witness testifies before a magistrate."

"A witness *will* testify before a magistrate."

"I thought you said she refused?"

"She did. But she's not the only one who saw what happened that night. As they rode away on your brother's horse, she looked back and caught a glimpse of a man stepping out of a nearby alley."

"Who?"

"Takahisa Takeda."

"What?" He rears back in disbelief at the uncanny coincidence. "The same Takahisa Takeda who introduced me to Koga?"

"It's how they met," Birdie explains. "Takeda blackmailed him for years with the proof he walked away with that night."

"What kind of proof?"

"This."

She sets a carrying cloth on the table and unties the knot. As she peels back the corners to reveal the carp-and-waterfall *inrō* and the ivory octopus, Vandermeer gives a start of recognition.

"That's the one he was wearing when I met him. But how does it prove he was there that night?"

"Because this *inrō* and *netsuke* were given to Masatoki Koga by his father on his coming-of-age day. It was pulled from his sash during his fight with Ichiro on the night of the Great Meiwa Fire. Takeda found it lying in the road and took it."

"How can we convince a magistrate it's the same one?"

"Look inside the top compartment."

She pushes the lacquered container across the table. Vandermeer wiggles the top section apart and plucks out the seal. His brows shoot up as he reads the characters "Masatoki Koga" carved into the end.

"But if Takeda-san was there, why didn't he come forward? He's from an old and respected samurai family! He had a duty to report the crime. Why didn't he?"

"Because if he had, he wouldn't be where he is today. Every time Takeda invited Koga to Yoshiwara, he blackmailed him into doing him another favor. I know, because I was there. My question is, if Takeda were to tell a judge what he saw that night, would that be enough to convict Koga without anyone else appearing before the magistrate?"

"I'll have to check with a colleague to make sure, but—" Vandermeer pauses to think it through. "If someone who knew Koga as a young man confirms the *inrō* and octopus were given to him on his coming-of-age day, and someone who knows Takeda tells the judge that he's been wearing them since the Great Meiwa Fire, I believe I can persuade the shōgun to let me visit Takeda on Sado Island and talk him into providing the evidence we need. Even in disgrace, he's still the head of a respectable samurai family, and if he testifies that he was there when Koga killed my brother, the magistrate will have to convict. And then"—a grim smile spreads across his face—"I'll finally be able to go back to Nagasaki and tell my father that Ichiro's killer will pay for what he did."

"Takeda-san?"

Irritation at the interruption flares before Takahisa Takeda remembers he's supposed to be meditating. His wife insisted his stomach trouble would only get worse unless he calms his fiery nature by embracing the teachings of Nichiren, the monk whose own firebrand behavior was tamed by his exile to Sado Island. He has to admit, he does feel better after contemplating the garden. He can sometimes do it for as much as a quarter of an hour before he finds himself seething impotently at his brother, who is taking full advantage of his enforced absence from the family seat to usurp his position as head of the family in every way but name.

"Takeda-san?" His chamberlain knocks again. This time he adds, "A man calling himself Doctor Vandermeer is here to see you."

Vandermeer? He scrambles to his feet. Are the powers-that-be finally admitting it was pure trickery that got him banished from Edo? In two strides, he's across the room.

"Show him into—" Where? He no longer has an audience chamber. "Take him to the teahouse in the garden. And be sure you seat him in the most honorable spot, with his back to the hanging scroll. Ask my wife to see to his comfort while I change into more suitable attire."

By the end of his second month of being in command of no one but the few loyal retainers who'd followed him into exile, he'd begun to feel a little foolish in the formal trappings of a samurai who might be called into the shōgun's presence at any time. But he can't greet this important guest dressed like a country bumpkin. By the time his inexperienced manservant has hindered more than helped him into the finery he hasn't worn since he was last in Yoshiwara, the cup of tea in his guest's hand has stopped steaming and Vandermeer is standing at the teahouse window, gazing out at the small garden beyond.

"Welcome to Sado Island," Takeda says, greeting his guest from the doorway with the kind of bow a man who is starved for hope gives to the man who might deliver it. "I apologize for the meager hospitality of this poor hovel."

"It's more than a visitor who arrives without advance warning deserves," Vandermeer replies graciously, returning the bow.

Takeda signals to the awkwardly hovering manservant for the tea to be refreshed, inviting Vandermeer to take the honorable seat as he lowers himself onto the cushion opposite.

"I trust you had a pleasant crossing?" Takeda says, hoping it wasn't too awful. Sado makes an excellent place of banishment because few wish to make the choppy sail from the mainland twice.

But Vandermeer must have been ashore long enough for his seasickness to subside, because he assures him that his current mission was worth the discomfort.

"What mission?" Takeda asks, pouring fresh tea.

"The chance to right a very old wrong."

Takeda's hopes deflate. The treachery that got him exiled three months ago can hardly be called old.

"I came here at the shōgun's behest," Vandermeer explains, "to hear your account of what happened on the night of the Great Meiwa Fire. And ask you to testify before a magistrate about who killed my brother."

Takeda's teacup freezes midsip.

"What makes you think I know anything about that?" he asks, setting it down carefully.

"New evidence has come to light."

"What evidence?"

"An eyewitness."

The missing woman? How did he manage to find her?

"But," Vandermeer adds, "she's too afraid of the man she accused to come forward officially."

As she should be. He's living proof of how dangerous it is to threaten Koga's charmed life.

"Why should I be any less afraid of retribution?" Takeda grunts

"Because Masatoki Koga has already hurt you as much as he can," Vandermeer replies with brutal honesty. "And making him pay for his crime would give you the one thing I'm sure you crave."

Revenge.

"Excuse me, Honorable Master," his chamberlain interrupts from the doorway. He bends down to whisper, "Madame Takeda commanded me to fetch you before you say another word."

Takeda frowns, but he can't afford to ignore his wife's counsel. Becoming a mother has revealed hidden steel beneath Pearl's glossy veneer, and he'd be a fool to dismiss her advice just because she's a woman. She's the one who persuaded him that exile was an opportunity to regroup and fight another day instead of taking the rash and foolishly "honorable" way out.

"Excuse me for a moment," he apologizes to Vandermeer. "There's a small emergency I must attend to."

Pearl is waiting for him outside, their son in her arms.

"I thought it might be prudent to listen in," she murmurs, drawing him away. "And I hope you agree we'd be fools to give him what he wants, merely for the sake of revenge."

"But—!"

"Don't worry, you'll get your satisfaction. But I've known Doctor Vandermeer for longer than you, and the thing he desires most in the world is to tell his father that his brother's killer has been found and punished. Right now, you hold the key to that man's happiness. A man, I remind you, who has the shōgun's ear. Which means," she says, hitching Atsuhisa higher on her hip, "that he should be willing to give you your greatest desire in exchange for helping him get his."

"Do you really think he can get me a pardon?"

"No." She frowns. "The verdict is still too fresh to be reversed without the shōgun losing face. But I do believe it's possible for Vandermeer to persuade His Excellency that you could better serve him from your home province of Kai."

Smart woman. Clever of her to think of something that would improve their situation significantly, and wouldn't be impossible for Vandermeer to deliver.

"But," he says apologetically, aware that his wife has ambitions of her own, "I'm afraid that the society in the mountains of Kai will be no more stimulating than it is here."

"I know," she says. "But at least Atsuhisa will get the kind of respect the son of the head of the Takeda clan deserves. And you can put a stop to your younger brothers' schemes to move their own sons ahead of him in the line of succession."

On the day Birdie looks out the upstairs window to find the nest in the Nomura's cherry tree empty, Doctor Vandermeer knocks on the door of the geisha house.

"It's done," he tells Birdie and Madame, with a formal bow. "Takahisa Takeda's evidence persuaded the magistrate that Masatoki Koga is guilty of killing my brother. He was given a choice between honorably ending his life here and now, or as an old man in exile. He and his household are on their way to Sado Island, and Takahisa Takeda has returned to his family stronghold in Kai, with his wife and son."

Birdie's heart soars. They did it!

"Is your father satisfied with this punishment," Madame Nomura asks, "even though his son's killer lives?"

"Yes." Vandermeer gives her a grim smile. "He would prefer the man dead, but he does appreciate the exquisite punishment of being confined to an island for the rest of one's natural life. And knowing what happened that night—especially that Ichiro died honorably—is giving us all a measure of peace we never thought we'd have." He hesitates, then sets his teacup in its saucer and turns to Birdie with a quizzical look. "There's just one question my father asked that I can't answer. How did you manage to discover who killed my brother when everyone else failed?"

"Well—" She takes a deep breath. "I expect it's because of the baby."

"Baby? What baby?"

"It's the reason Masatoki Koga fled to Yoshiwara after killing your brother. He took his sister to the House of Peonies and left her there until she had her baby."

"She was pregnant?" His eyebrows leap. "Was it Ichiro's child?"

"Yes. She gave birth to his daughter five months later."

"Ichiro has a daughter?" he cries. "Is she alive? Where is she? Can you take me to her?"

Birdie smiles. Then she rises to her feet and gives him a deep bow.

"I'm already here."

Birdie steps through the door, then stops, astonished at her mother's transformation. As Shinjō rises from her seat behind the low table, she doesn't look like a shopkeeper. Or a nun.

"You look like a lady," Birdie gasps.

"The last time I wore this, I was one," her mother says with a shy smile, smoothing the hand-painted silk robe. Then she looks past Birdie to the man behind her.

Birdie steps in to catch her as she topples to the tatami, but it's Doctor Vandermeer who kneels to administer smelling salts.

"Are you all right?" he asks, peering down at her with concern as her eyes flutter open.

"You . . . you even sound like him," she replies weakly. "When I saw you standing there, I—"

"You wouldn't be the first," he says with a sad smile. "I'm Jiro. His younger brother. Sorry to startle you, but I thought it only right that I come in person to tell you the news. Masatoki Koga has been banished from Edo. For life. He'll spend the rest of his days on Sado Island as punishment for killing Ichiro."

Birdie tosses her coin, rings the bell, folds her hands. The past hour had been filled with her mother and uncle trading stories about her father, but it was cut short by the arrival of a customer in urgent need of the yarrow sticks' advice, so they'd said farewell, promising to return tomorrow. Birdie walks as far as the Great Gate with Vandermeer, but that's as far as she'll go.

Before they part, he says, "The shōgun has granted me leave to go to Nagasaki so I can tell my father that Ichiro's murderer has been tried and sentenced. Will you come with me? My family would very much like to meet you, and if you like it there, they'd welcome you to stay."

Unprepared for the unexpected invitation, she thanks him, says she'll think about it. She watches him disappear through the gate, but even though she's now free to do the same, she has lost her desire to leave. If she hadn't just found her mother, she'd have been tempted to seize his offer, but now, all the family she needs is in Yoshiwara.

If she can find somewhere she belongs. Now that she has thanked everyone who needs thanking and reunited everyone who needs reuniting, she can no longer avoid the question of her own future. And her surprisingly burdensome fortune. There's still a large sum sitting in the black lacquer chest, but gold is too heavy to carry around and too easily stolen. She must either ask Madame to keep it for her in the Nomura's treasure house or turn it into something besides gold.

But what?

She used to long for more rice cakes, prettier hair ornaments, her own room, the kind of comforts only a successful oiran can afford. But now that she's got more money than she knows what to do with, what she really wants is something money can't buy. A place to call home.

She'll always have Lucky Doll, but Dolly has chosen the Nomura as her family, and the geisha house doesn't feel like home to Birdie the same way the House of Treasures did. Auntie and Pearl chose her, trained her, needed her. She belonged there. She's surprised to discover how much she misses the sisterly teasing of the junior courtesans and stopping by the debtor room to ask Jester for advice. She'd be asking him for some right now if—

She halts halfway down the shrine steps. Just because he doesn't live right down the hall doesn't mean she can't find him. She squints up at the sun, now beginning its slide toward evening. She's spotted him more than once emerging from the illicit dice game that floats around the street by the moat.

She's sitting on the stone wall across from the gambling den, swallowing the last bite of her second rice cake, when he emerges with a satisfied smile. Pausing to drop a heavy string of coins into the nearest monk's begging bowl, he turns to saunter back toward the House of Treasures.

She hurries across the street.

"Jester!" she calls.

"Birdie?" He turns, a big smile creasing his face. "It *is* you! Why is the apprentice who's worth her weight in gold hanging around the sleaziest street in the pleasure quarter?" He's obviously heard some version of Tiger's story. Maybe even helped spread it.

"I'm looking for you," she says. "I need some advice."

"About what?"

"What would you do if you had more money than you could possibly spend?"

He throws his head back and laughs. But he asks no more questions until they're seated on the weathered bench near the shrine's cleaning buckets.

She pours the true story of how she came by her troublesome riches into his sympathetic ear.

"...but the thing is—" How can she say this without seeming ungrateful for having more money and freedom than she knows what to do with? "When I belonged to the Treasure, I had nothing and I wanted everything. But now that I have enough money to buy anything I want, the only thing I want has no price. If you were me, what would you do?"

"Well," he says with a wry grin, "I doubt I'd be asking for advice from a man who's a prisoner of a pleasure house because he can't pay his debts."

"I'm not." She casts him a side-eye. "Because you're not really a man who can't pay his debts, are you?"

"Shh!" He glances around furtively. "Don't say that so loud."

"Were you really penniless that night you came to the Treasure for the first time?"

"Actually, I was. But," he admits, "It was hard work to get that way."

"What do you mean?"

"Well..." He tips his head back to regard the clouds floating overhead. "I've always been blessed—or cursed, depending on how you look at it—with money. My father had a talent for making it, and I inherited it, both his money and his gift. When I was a young man, I ran around taking big risks, but everything I bet on just made me richer. I was welcomed everywhere, moved in the highest circles. And"—he shakes his head with regret—"the lowest. No matter how much I spent, it just attracted more. More invitations, more introductions, more money. But the more friends I made, the more I wondered if they were really my friends. The more I belonged everywhere, the more I belonged nowhere."

"How did you end up at the Treasure?"

"I tried the Peony first, but they threw me out the next day."

She giggles and says, "Dressed in a maid's uniform." If what Tiger said is true.

"Don't forget barefoot," he confirms. "But that's where I learned that belonging is a two-way street. I chose the Treasure because the Treasure chose me. I know it's where I belong because the women of the Treasure need me as much as I need them."

"I wish it were that easy for me." She sighs. "But living in a pleasure house isn't the same for a woman as it is for a man. In Yoshiwara, women are allowed to be rich or free but not both. Where am I going to find a House where someone like me belongs?"

"Simple." His eyes crinkle at the corners. "If you can't find a place like that, why don't you make one?"

1798

TEN YEARS LATER
Kagurazaka Geisha Quarter
Edo, Japan

Birdie sits before the tall mirror and positions her final hair ornament. Pushes it—*ow*—in. She shakes her head and smiles, enjoying the swishy sensation of the dangling silver strips. Now that she's the ranking geisha at the New Nomura, no one dares scold her. She rises to allow her dresser to wrap her in her favorite purple sash.

Tonight, she's wearing the kimono that Jester—or Jester-san, as he's now respectfully known—had brushed with one of his epigrams when they were entertaining together last week. The green willow-patterned silk is positively drab compared to the riot of colors she used to wear as Pearl's apprentice, but in the years since Madame Nomura accepted her offer to invest her half of the smuggling money in the geisha house's new branch in Kagurazaka, a fashion for understated elegance has been steadily replacing oiran excess.

Lucky Doll has her hands full just being the mistress now, and when Birdie became the top entertainer two years ago, she moved into the ranking geisha's spacious room. Last month she decided to divide it in half, though, so when Madame retires at New Year's and hands over the running of the cramped Yoshiwara branch to her assistant manager, she'll have a place to call her own when she's not at her *danna's* villa.

"Arms up, please." The dresser ties her *obi* in back, then knots a golden cord around it to keep it in place.

She swivels to inspect his handiwork in the mirror.

"Perfect, as always." She leans into the glass to inspect her teeth. "Do you think these need a touch-up before I go?"

"They could be blacker," he murmurs.

Always tactful; that's why she likes him. She kneels before her dressing table with her pot of tooth stain. Tiger told her he's bringing a surprise guest tonight, so she'd better err on the side of perfection, in case he's a man of rank. Sorting through her fans, she tucks the one with a poem about children catching fireflies into her *obi*, adjusts the angle in the mirror.

As she makes her way down the hall, a *shamisen* tune drifts from the apprentices' room. She slides open the door to compliment whoever has mastered the demi-quavers of "Teardrops on My Sleeve" but swallows her words as soon as she sees it's not one of the sixteen-year-old apprentices who's plucking it.

Mina's tongue is poking from the corner of her mouth, and Birdie suddenly understands why Jester found it so disturbing when he heard her innocent twelve-year-old self play that love song so skillfully.

Mina breaks off and looks up.

"Are you going out now, Honored Auntie?"

"In a moment."

Mina scrambles to her feet to bow her goodnights. She looks more and more like Flower every day, but fortunately shows no sign she inherited the unnerving gift of second sight that makes Flower far better at telling fortunes than entertaining men.

When Birdie returned from her journey to Nagasaki with Vandermeer, she was dismayed to find Flower had been left with a lasting memento of her time at the House of Cranes. She was six months pregnant. She'd advised her twin to visit her mother and ask Madame

Truth for advice, but that fateful meeting sent Flower in a direction none of them expected. She and Shinjō recognized their connection at once. The yarrow sticks confirmed that her future lay in becoming Madame Truth's apprentice, and they both politely declined Birdie's offer to make a place for them at the New Nomura. But as Mina grew into a little girl as lovely as her mother once was, the divination sticks agreed that a seer's shack in the pleasure quarter is no place to raise a daughter.

"Have you practiced your calligraphy today?" Birdie asks.

Gets a wrinkled nose in reply.

"Put that *shamisen* away and do it now." Honestly, the girl shirks her handwriting practice as much as her mother did.

Birdie's senior apprentice is waiting for her by the front door, and Lucky Doll emerges from her office to follow them out with the flint, sparking a shower of gold across their shoulders for luck.

Stars flow overhead in a bright river between the roofs of wooden teahouses, strung with welcoming red lanterns. It had been a balmy evening just like this—feasts just getting underway, the punchlines of stories drifting from open windows—when she'd skipped back to the Nightingale to tell Pearl about Kiyohisa Takeda for the very first time.

She's heard that Pearl returned to Edo after her husband succumbed to cholera in the last outbreak. Now a respectable samurai widow, she's raising her boy in the sprawling Takeda compound near the castle.

Takeda's other son had surprised everyone by stepping up to the challenge of running their side of the business after his father's death. The other dissolute young men Kiyohisa had wasted his time and money with in his youth are finally coming into their own, and once his brother-in-law took his own father's place as shipowner, the two ex-rakes are not only keeping the empire afloat, they're expanding it. It was Tiger, of course, who told Birdie that the former Takeda ne'er-do-well had just become the Treasures' newest patron.

"I wouldn't have recognized him if I hadn't heard his name first," he'd admitted. It isn't just that Kiyohisa no longer wears flamboyant purple kimonos or plucks his eyebrows. Much to Tiger's chagrin, he's also given up gambling.

"He wouldn't even take me up on a friendly wager over which junior courtesan could play 'A Stranger in Yoshiwara' fastest," Tiger complained. "And the tight-fisted so-and-so barely even drinks now. How am I supposed to make decent coin off a guy who's never too drunk to calculate how little he can spend and still keep up appearances?"

Birdie looks up to find the mistress of Kagurazaka's most elegant teahouse waiting for them by the door, casting a long shadow in the glow of the lantern. She welcomes them and leads the way to the private room that Tiger reserved for tonight.

Through the door, Birdie hears him regaling his guest with an oft-told Yoshiwara tale.

"... but it wasn't keeping the prisoner inside the pleasure house that turned out to be the problem, it was persuading him to leave! Jester-san did such a good job entertaining the customers while they waited for their courtesans that the courtesans soon had to wait for them. Sometimes for an hour or more. This was terrible for business, and the pleasure house was leaking money faster than a broken bucket. In desperation, their overseer finally offered to forgive his debt, telling him he was free to go. But Jester said he couldn't possibly leave. That he owed money all over Yoshiwara and if his other debtors spotted him on the street, they'd send him to prison. The only way he'd agree to venture beyond the safety of the Treasure was if the overseer gave him enough money to pay them all off. No one knows how much he forked over, but you can bet it was a tidy sum!"

The customer guffaws in appreciation and Birdie lets out a small cry of surprise. She recognizes that laugh.

Sure enough, when she slides open the door she finds Tiger sharing a table with Goldbelly. The silk merchant disappeared from Yoshiwara shortly after introducing Vandermeer to Takeda, and she hasn't seen him in years. He's a little grayer and more prosperously plump than before, but his beaming smile and delight at seeing her are unchanged.

"Are you here to win back your *sugoroku* title?" she asks, displaying her dimple. "The last time we played, I believe I won."

"Why, so you did. Are you offering a rematch?"

He wins this one with a few deliberately unwise moves on Birdie's part, and is soon bobbing his head in time to the catchy tune her apprentice is performing.

She watches him enjoy himself, wondering how she could have been so wrong about this gentle man, assuming that the gold coin he'd pressed into a little girl's hand was something dirty and improper. It wasn't until she left Yoshiwara that she learned not all kindness is tainted by desire. She'd been taught to use others' love, never feel it herself. To armor herself against it, never embrace it. She'd worked so hard at being who Auntie and Pearl and the Treasures' customers wanted her to be, she hadn't known real love until Mina was born.

Birdie has never been drawn to the men who professed their undying love for her over the years. She'll never be a wife, the same way Tiger will never be a husband, but they've become the best of partners. Even though they're both adept at becoming what others want them to be, they never stopped being their true selves with each other.

By the time the evening draws to a close, Goldbelly is begging her to help him and Tiger entertain some merchants who will be in town next week, and Tiger is reminding her that the patron who has engaged his services tomorrow night is new to Kagurazaka, and she'd be doing him a favor if she can cure him of laughing at his own jokes.

She walks back down the hill with her apprentice in companionable silence, bidding the girl and the drowsy maid good night as their sandals are stowed.

She yawns, but there's one last thing she must do before she retires. Lighting a candle from the one burning in the entry, she tiptoes between the servants sleeping in the front rooms to the parlor at the back.

Kneeling before the Buddhist altar, she lights a stick of incense before the goddess of compassion, then rings the bell softly and folds her hands, repeating the words of gratitude she murmurs every night. If Pearl's lie hadn't forced her to flee the Treasure and become an outcast, she wouldn't be the free woman she is today. If her mother hadn't fled the secure life of an Odawara *hatamoto's* wife, she'd never have known her daughter. And if Flower hadn't been made to endure life at the House of Cranes, Mina would never have been born.

"From the mud, the lotus," she whispers, as the smoke curls toward heaven.

GLOSSARY OF JAPANESE WORDS AND PHRASES

Japanese money in the Edo period: 1 *ryō* = 4 *bu* = 16 *shū* = 4000 *mon*. The amount of rice a man ate in a year (about 150 kg/330 lbs) cost one *ryō*; an average laborer was paid 65 *mon* per day.

dai kichi 大吉—"greatest good luck," the best fortune you can receive in Japanese fortunetelling

daimyō—a powerful hereditary warlord who governs a province under the *shōgun* and is required to live in Edo every other year

danna—lover who formally agrees to support his mistress's living expenses

fundoshi—a long strip of cloth wrapped and tied about the loins as underwear

geisha—a woman who provides music and dance entertainment for patrons while they wait for courtesans to arrive

geta—wooden sandals held onto the foot with thongs that go between the first two toes

hatamoto—a samurai of the highest rank in the ruling class, who has been granted the privilege of speaking directly to the *shōgun*

inrō—a multi-tiered case made of lacquered wood, about the size and shape of a hip flask; used by kimono-wearing men to carry around pipes, tobacco, medicine, money, or other small objects
    koma-geta—the tall platform sandals worn by oirans and oiran apprentices in the Edo Period
    koto—a thirteen-stringed, zither-like instrument used to play Japanese classical music

monbi—the several "double fee days" each month on which patrons had to pay twice as much to be entertained by courtesans. These were set by pleasure house managers, and regular patrons often agreed to cover one or more when negotiating their contracts. If a courtesan couldn't persuade a customer to cover all her *monbi*, she had to pay for them herself.

"Moshiwake gozaimasen"—the most humble and formal words of apology

ne, ne—the polite verbal equivalent of tugging on someone's shirtsleeve to get their attention

netsuke—a large bead anchoring the cord of a man's tobacco pouch, or *inrō*, to keep it from sliding through his sash; often an animal or figure carved from precious materials

obi—a wide sash, often made of stiff brocade, which is wrapped around a kimono and tied in an extravagant knot in front or back, its style denoting the wearer's social status

oiran—a first-rank courtesan in Yoshiwara (Edo's pleasure quarter)

"Ohayō"—"Good morning"

rōnin—a samurai who serves no master, stripped of his stipend and place in society, but still allowed to carry two swords

-san—added to a person's name as the equivalent of Mr./Mrs./Ms.

-sensei—added to a person's name if they are a doctor, lawyer, or master teacher

GLOSSARY

Shintō—the indigenous Japanese religion practiced at shrines that honor the eight million gods who reside in natural features such as waterfalls, rocks, trees, etc.

shamisen—a three-stringed Japanese instrument that looks like a banjo with a square soundbox and is used to accompany traditional Japanese dance, songs, puppet shows, and kabuki plays

shōgun—the man holding the title of hereditary military dictator of Japan in the Edo Period, between 1604 and 1868

sugoroku—a popular board game played with dice

Tanabata wish—on the festival celebrated on the seventh day of the seventh month, people write wishes on strips of paper and hang them from bamboo branches

tatami—rigid rice straw mats that are roughly 6 ft. × 3 ft. (190 cm × 90 cm) and pieced together as flooring in traditional Japanese rooms

tokonoma—a floor to ceiling alcove with a low platform at the bottom for displaying an art object (often a vase filled with seasonal flowers) and a seasonal scroll or painting hanging on the wall above

torii gate—the pi-shaped gate at the entrance to a Shintō shrine, usually made of stone or red lacquered wood

umeboshi—intensely sour and salty plum pickles, a staple of the Japanese diet that symbolizes the rising sun when placed at the center of a serving of white rice

AUTHOR'S HISTORICAL NOTE

What's real and what's not in The Samurai's Octopus

One of the best reasons to read historical fiction is that it takes us to times and places we can't visit any other way. Experiencing the characters' world through their eyes, we get a first-hand look at what it was like to live in a bygone era, and a good book leaves behind something that feels more like a personal memory than a collection of dry facts. But that can only happen if the tale stands on a foundation of righteous research.

So, what's real in *The Samurai's Octopus* and what's not?

THE WORLD OF YOSHIWARA

Not only was the walled pleasure quarter of Edo a real place, you can still walk its streets in modern-day Tokyo! Search for "Yoshiwara Tokyo" in your map app, and due north of Sensō-ji Temple you'll see the Yoshiwara Shrine on a corner of Nakanocho-dori (Center Street). Oiran processions made their stately way down this street to long-ago patrons awaiting them at the elite teahouses on Ageya-dori. The square of streets surrounding Center Street is unchanged since the 1790s, but the nine-foot-deep moat that surrounded Yoshiwara's walls is now buried under busy boulevards, and the elegant teahouses and brothels that lined its five streets and avenues have been replaced by grimy "clubs" and apartment blocks that sadly fail to echo its past glory. If you look hard, though, there are a pair of historical markers on Center Street at Yoshiwara's old northeastern boundary, where the Great Gate once stood.

You may be surprised to learn that the more outlandish details of oiran life in Yoshiwara—like oiran "tribunals" and topknot-lopping, the giving away of pipes, tobacco, and other treasures during the New Year's fashion parade, the extravagant ransoming of courtesans by paying their weight in silver—were no figment of authorly imagination. Many accounts of crazy Yoshiwara stunts survive in the historical record and the literature of the day. Practices like planting cherry trees in full bloom along the boulevards, then ripping them out again as soon as the blossoms fell were well-documented in famous woodblock prints.

Ukiyo-e prints by artists such as Utamaro and Hokusai now hang in elite museums, but they were originally ads designed to drum up business for stars of the "floating world." Yoshiwara beauties modeling the latest fashions and engaging in the latest trends were the most popular subject, but actors starring in the season's kabuki plays, leading sumo wrestlers, and scenes of pleasure quarter decadence also sold like hotcakes. To this day, everyone who works in Japan's entertainment industry belongs to the *mizu shōbai* world. Actors, sports stars, musicians, and other celebrities merely occupy the more respectable end of the spectrum that includes bar hostesses, host club touts, and prostitutes.

ELABORATE HAIRDOS, WEIRD EYEBROWS, AND BLACK TEETH

An oiran sauntering down a Tokyo street today would still turn heads, but only because her chalk white face, black teeth, and eyebrows painted like tiny feathers halfway up her forehead would make passersby elbow each other with curiosity, not desire. How could such a bizarre makeup style ever have been considered alluring?

The truth is, Pearl's hairstyle and extravagant layers of robes would have looked nearly as strange to ordinary citizens on the streets of eighteenth-century Edo as they do today. But inside the Great Gate, Yoshiwara's unique fashion aesthetic ruled. If you've ever made the mistake of buying a sunset-hued muumuu in Hawaii, then get home and wonder "what was I thinking?" you begin to understand how landing in a place that's profoundly different from home can shift your idea of what's fashionable and what's not.

Becoming an oiran's patron was the ultimate status symbol, so being seen with a woman whose appearance proclaimed her rank was key. By the time Pearl and Birdie appear on the scene, oiran fashions had been evolving within Yoshiwara's walled confines for nearly two hundred years, and the only way courtesans could stand out in this hotbed of competition was to look more and more extreme. By 1790, an oiran's hairdo required augmenting her natural knee-length tresses with pads of additional pomaded hair, sculpting them into front poufs and side wings and stretching them over a foot-tall disk that rose from the back of her head like the full moon. This elaborate confection displayed her status, showcasing the many enviable hair accessories bestowed by her admirers: hand-carved combs, ornaments studded with gemstones, and no fewer than eight rare tortoiseshell hairpins that fanned around her face like rays of the sun.

Pale skin was prized as a sign a woman didn't have to work outdoors to survive, and once a courtesan attained first-rank status (an official designation that was strictly controlled), she could paint her face with an exclusive chalk-white, lead-based foundation and enter into legal contracts with her patrons in a three-sips-of-sake rite that mimicked the marriage ceremony. She was then allowed to blacken her teeth like a samurai wife, staining them with an iron filing and vinegar mixture. This beauty convention had been practiced by Japanese women of status for hundreds of years, because even giving one's face a little whitening boost with rice powder makes anyone's teeth look unpleasantly yellow by comparison. It was also considered uncouth to show one's teeth in polite society. A successful courtesan reddened her mouth with a costly balm made from safflower petals that shimmered with a greenish iridescence, so when she bestowed a rare smile or engaged in witty banter, a man focused on her lips rather than the darkened chompers beyond.

The odd fashion of plucking out a courtesan's natural eyebrows and redrawing them halfway up her forehead was also a tool of misdirection. Oirans maintained their power over the men who supported them through manipulation and negotiation, which often required them to hide their true feelings. Mobile eyebrows are the hardest-to-control giveaway to a woman's reactions, so redrawing them on a less-expressive part of the forehead enabled her to project a vaguely interested "poker face" instead of the natural expressions that might give away what she was really thinking.

GROWING UP IN YOSHIWARA

Did Japan really allow girls as young as six to be indentured in the pleasure quarter? The short answer is yes, but let's remember that a trip back in time is very much like traveling to a foreign country. One of the reasons we make the journey is to experience different customs, beliefs, and ways of life, and as guests in that place and time, let's resist the urge to judge late-1700s Japan by modern standards and take a step back to understand the bigger picture.

In those days, "childhood" wasn't the period of carefree schooling and play that children enjoy today. Child labor wasn't regulated anywhere in the world until the nineteenth century and in feudal Japan, the survival of the family was more important than the survival (or happiness) of individual members. Children were expected to contribute their labor to the family unit as soon as they were able, and it was the head of the family's right to hire them out to wealthier families or

AUTHOR'S HISTORICAL NOTE

apprentice them to artisans. Women were also considered legal possessions, and their bodies and labor could be used to secure loans or even traded to pay debts. It wasn't uncommon for brokers to roam the countryside, scouting girls (like Flower) between the ages of six and fifteen, and paying their legal guardians ten years' advance wages in exchange for their service in Yoshiwara. Certain poor provinces were renowned as a source of pretty girls, and it was a common joke that their most valuable "crop" was producing more daughters than a family could afford to raise.

And although prostitution is seldom any woman's first choice of career no matter where or when she lived, in eighteenth-century Japan it wasn't viewed with the same kind of moral shame as it is in Western cultures. In Edo Period Japan, it was believed that a man must regularly indulge his manly urges in order to remain healthy and strong, and going to a prostitute was no more sinful than going to the gym. Conversely, selling those services was no more shameful than selling a thirsty man a drink of water. The shocking part of the transaction was that the courtesans of the pleasure quarter sold emotional intimacy and the illusion of love, not that they allowed men to use their bodies. It was the deception and delusions encouraged by Yoshiwara and the wasting of money that would otherwise be used to support a samurai's family that was condemned by the moral authorities, not the promiscuity.

In fact, being indentured to work as a prostitute in Yoshiwara was viewed as an act of Confucian filial piety when a daughter contributed income that her family desperately needed. Once her contract ended, many women left Yoshiwara to marry and raise families, without stigma. There was even a *sugoroku* game board that charted a woman's path through life, and players could land on a square labeled "work as a courtesan," followed by getting married and having children.

And most indentured girls didn't start out working on their backs. They went through a period of training—years, if they were little girls of six to twelve (like Flower) who first served an oiran as child attendants. The age at which a woman could legally work as a prostitute was eighteen, but since the girls' legal guardians were usually in far-off villages, there was little to stop a greedy brothel owner from trying to recoup his investment as soon as possible. There are records of high-ranking courtesans debuting as young as twelve, but those are the rare exceptions, not the rule. Records dating from 1720 show that fewer than five percent of sex workers were under the age of sixteen.

The historical record also suggests that the youngest girls (like Birdie and Flower) were relatively well taken care of. Parading around with a pair of child attendants was a status symbol in Yoshiwara, and it reflected badly on their oiran and pleasure house if they were ill-treated or underfed. Accounts dating from the Edo Period suggest that the children working in Yoshiwara sneaked as much stolen playtime as children outside of Yoshiwara and enjoyed similar pastimes. Indentured girls in Yoshiwara also enjoyed a higher standard of living than if they'd stayed in the poor villages where they were born. They didn't suffer in the all-too-frequent famines like those in the countryside, were given decent clothing and shelter, and didn't have to do back-breaking agricultural labor from an early age.

And oddly enough, becoming a successful courtesan in Yoshiwara was one of the few opportunities for upward mobility in feudal Japan. After a Yoshiwara pleasure house trained a woman in the dialect, manners, and arts of the ruling class, it wasn't uncommon for her to enchant a wealthy samurai patron so thoroughly he made her his wife.

WHY WAS THE PLEASURE QUARTER WALLED OFF FROM THE REST OF THE CITY?

The places men go to indulge their vices typically spawn all kinds of trouble, and it's much easier for the government to police and regulate those crimes if they're corralled in one place. Yoshiwara's Great Gate kept weapons out and women indentured by their male relatives (or serving sentences for prostitution-related crimes) in.

Edo's biggest problem in the 1700s was that its population was overwhelmingly male. The shōgun's "alternate year residence" edict required regional warlords to live in the capital city every other year so he could keep an eye on them, and that meant thousands of samurai and their retainers were separated from their own women for twelve months at a time. Men outnumbered women more than two to one. Without a licensed pleasure quarter to service those vast armies of men, the city's constabulary would have been swamped with fighting, rapes, and other crimes that spring up around too many men contending over too few women.

The government was also threatened by the 240,000 masterless samurai who had been deprived of their homes, social standing, and incomes when the ninety families they served were stripped of their lands and titles for fighting against the victorious Tokugawas in 1603. Outcasts whose only privilege was bearing a sword had few options for earning a living, so a number of them worked in the pleasure quarter as brothel or teahouse security. Naturally, some of these *rōnin* continued to carry a grudge and plot against the government, so the pleasure quarter's governors employed many spies to report rumors of unrest to Edo Castle. In exchange, the Yoshiwara powers-that-be were given the freedom to administer the pleasure district as they pleased.

And last but not least, Yoshiwara was walled and gated so prostitution could be taxed. By enclosing the world's oldest profession in a single district, the government could keep track of how much money flowed through it and deftly dip its share from the stream.

ARE ANY OF THE CHARACTERS BASED ON REAL PEOPLE?

The world of Yoshiwara in *The Samurai's Octopus* is as close to historical reality as I could make it, but the characters and their stories are fiction. The one exception is Jester, who wasn't a living historical figure, but is the main character in a famous *rakugo* story called "*Inokori Saheiji*" or "A Prisoner in the Pleasure House." This traditional tale is still popular today—performed by a single actor kneeling on stage, playing all the parts with only a fan and a hand towel as props—and audiences still line up to hear the tale of the clever ne'er-do-well who schemes to get himself imprisoned in a pleasure house. If you search online, you can even find it performed in English!

If you'd like to delve into the books that provided so many excellent details about Birdie's world...

BOOKS ABOUT DAILY LIFE IN THE SAMURAI ERA

A Stranger in the Shogun's City: A Japanese Woman and her World by Amy Stanley
Everyday Life in Traditional Japan by Charles J. Dunn
Tokyo Before Tokyo: Power and Magic in the Shogun's City of Edo by Timon Screech

ALL ABOUT YOSHIWARA

The Nightless City: Geisha and Courtesan Life in Old Tokyo by J.E. de Becker
Yoshiwara by Cecelia Segawa Seigle
Seduction: Japan's Floating World 2015 exhibition at the Asian Art Museum of San Francisco; catalog text by Laura W. Allen with essays by Julia Meech, Eric C. Rath, and Melinda Takeuchi
Selling Women: Prostitution, Markets, and the Household in Early Modern Japan by Amy Stanley
吉原という「別世」*(Yoshiwara: A Different World)* 2024 exhibition at the Geidai University Art Museum; catalog text by Yuko Tanaka, Ryo Furuta, Keiko Tanaka, Megumi Soda, Masako Tanabe, Tomoko Matsuo, Miho Someya, and Hiroko Honda.

AUTHOR'S HISTORICAL NOTE

YOSHIWARA FASHION, MAKEUP, HAIRSTYLES, AND ENTERTAINMENT

Fashion and Make-up of Edo Beauties Seen in Ukiyo-e Prints produced by the POLA Research Institute of Beauty & Culture

Japanese Popular Prints: From Votive Slips to Playing Cards by Rebecca Salter

Symbols of Japan: Thematic Motifs in Art and Design by Merrily Baird

The Complete Woodblock Prints of Kitagawa Utamaro: A Descriptive Catalogue by Gina Collia-Suzuki

Utamaro and the Spectacle of Beauty by Julie Nelson Davis

日本髪大全 *(The Complete Collection of Traditional Japanese Hairstyles)* by Keiko Tanaka

江戸衣裳地図鑑 *(Encyclopedia of Edo Era Clothing)* by Hitomi Kikuchi

着物と日本の色 *(Kimonos and the Colors of Japan)* by Katsumi Yumioka

GEISHA LIFE, FASHION, AND HISTORY

Geisha by Liza Dalby

Geisha, A Life by Mineko Iwasaki (translated by Rande Brown)

ACKNOWLEDGMENTS

Before this story made its way to your bedside table, all sorts of confusing character names, brow-furrowing coincidences, and carp that didn't acquire ornamental colors until a century after Birdie tossed pebbles at them were weeded out by friends and colleagues who selflessly waded through less-than-perfect versions of this story so you don't have to.

Please join me in giving heartfelt thanks to Craig Tanisawa (Bringer of Truth), Marcia Pillon (Our Lady of Character Insights), Lisa Hirsch (Queen of Constructive Critique), Emily Sellers (Empress of Essential Feedback), Deborah Dasovich (Honorable Reader Extraordinaire), Chris Nolan (Critical Eye of Epic Proportions), Makarim Salman (Lord High Commissioner of Koi, Historical Factoids, and Deep Japan Knowledge), Paula Span (Grand Maven of Style), Vaani Tiwari (St. Freshness of Viewpoint), Susan McCarthy (who bade me drink of the Chalice of Improvement wrapped in the Glove of Kindness), and Judith Gorog (Patron Saint of Salt, Pepper, and Spice, without which nether life nor books would be worth the price).

ACKNOWLEDGMENTS

Special thanks go out to Liza Dalby, whose garment hem I'm not worthy to kiss and who honored an early version of this book with feedback on all things geisha and Edo Period, as well as loaning me rare academic sources from her library. Fellow authors Susan Spann and Katheryn Catmull have a permanent parking place in my heart for reading pieces of this manuscript and pulling me from the slough of despond by assuring me Birdie's story would someday be worth reading. And finally, big thanks to Hiroyuki Otomo, the *rakugo* artist who introduced me to Saheiji, the prisoner in the pleasure house.

This book could never have been written without the visa that gives me access to everything that's impossible to research if you don't live in Japan, so major thanks also go out to Kyohei Niitsu-*sensei* for using his impressive lawyering skills to make it possible for me to live in Tokyo instead of in a state of constant jetlag.

I'm so lucky to have had April Eberhardt of April Eberhardt Literary as my friend and agent for so many years, and will never stop being grateful that she made my writerly dreams come true.

And to Rene Sears, there has never been an editor who inspired, encouraged, and improved a book more than you. I am so grateful for every correction, word of appreciation, and your extraordinarily skillful help launching this book into the wide world. You're the best! Deep gratitude also flows to Master Book Launcher Ashley Calvano, Production Manager and Copyeditor Extraordinaire Meghan Kilduff, and Inspired Cover Designer Jennifer Stimson for turning my sea of words into a thing of beauty and making *The Samurai's Octopus* into a book we can all be proud of.

And finally, to my ever-expanding family (you know who you are!) my love and gratitude for never complaining about how much time I spend down weird rabbit holes in Japan and for not rolling your eyes when I tell you about them in excruciating detail when I get back. This book wouldn't exist without your love and support. Thank you, from the bottom of my heart.

ABOUT THE AUTHOR

Dear Friend,

Thank you for choosing *The Samurai's Octopus*—I know how hard it is to find time in your busy life to escape into a book, and I'm honored you chose to spend a few hours with me and Birdie. If you know someone who might enjoy *The Samurai's Octopus,* I will love you forever if you pass it on or give it as a gift. I've always thought that a recommendation from a friend is the best way to discover new books, and sharing a good read is one of life's great pleasures.

With warmest regards,
Jonelle

JONELLE PATRICK is the author of six novels set in Japan, and has been writing about Japanese culture and travel since she first moved to Tokyo in 2003. She writes and produces the monthly e-magazine *Japanagram*, runs the travel site *The Tokyo Guide I Wish I'd Had,* and blogs at *Only in Japan*. She teaches at writing workshops, appears as a panelist at Thrillerfest, and has been awarded a cultural visa by the Japanese government for writing about Japan.

A graduate of Stanford University and the Sendagaya Japanese Language Institute, she's also a member of the Mystery Writers of America, International Thriller Writers, Sisters in Crime, and the Historical Novel Society. She divides her time between Tokyo and San Francisco.